NEW WORLD BURNING

a novel

Daniel Watkins

Two Mountains Publishing
San Francisco

For ordering information, please contact Bookmasters, Inc.
(800) 247-6553
email: order@bookmasters.com

www.newworldburning.com

Library of Congress Cataloging in Publication Data

Watkins, Daniel.
NEW WORLD BURNING: a novel / Daniel Watkins

ISBN 0-9768065-0-9
1. Nathaniel Bacon   2. Bacon's Rebellion
3. Early Jamestown   4. Governor Berkeley
5. 1676 Virginia
I. Title
2001012345

for Sheri

NEW WORLD BURNING

Nathaniel Bacon's War

Virginia 1676

Part One
1650

here are those in number that saw the fiery · night storms tearing above the blackened earth as if to cauterize a heavenly wound. And those too, whose daylight sky was darkened with a million and more birds, the weight of all dissecting the limbs from the thickest trees. The surviving trees only then to be eaten by a crackling swarm of insects, the single member of each smaller than a slivered fingernail. And no one spoke of anything but vengeance. The New World was ours now, or what so many with nothing safe to call their own had come to claim. After all, we had witnessed the English breed a full-grown generation of Virginians, and now each of them was whispering, "Tha bloody savages. Wot tha bloody savages've wrought."

But I, having been touched by the savages' own natural God saw a living wisdom to these things. From savages I learned that only human beings will do *proud* works, and that the dog will imitate kings. That everything built from the hand of man is the unfathomable will of nature, and done to suffer change. Like the fancy English books that make out our course to that of the Egyptian Nile, and whose banks full of monuments are ground into sand. But in making this account, let it be clear that I have seen terror in the faces of men, terror struck by my own hands. The same hands that have made much of what is called quite beautiful. And such beautiful things were more than I can number, until such a time I knew a man called Bacon.

At present we are starving; Mr. Lawrence and I. Our munitions are all wasted, and eight days gone since we ate the last of our meager horse. Now we stagger through the frosted wilderness like a couple of lost sheep, shorn and exposed at the ribs. Exposed too, to natural implements that just a year ago, my nimble mind could have put to use. The wolves are getting braver, and what refuge our feeble fire affords is tormented by the irony that even as the wisps of smoke will keep them back, we'd welcome them on for a scent of roasting rabbit. And even yet, as though my thoughts become more reckless as they encroach upon my death, the only thing I can fix upon is a poison bush that grew wild about my family's privy.

The damage this plant had done to my fair skinned wife, and our oldest daughter was a concern of great shame for me. But I was so taken by the beauty of its flower, so plentiful in deep purple that my girls were gasping with fever before I gathered the sense to cut it down. It took my good friend Tacatomac, a quiet Pawmunkey man, who stopped his July fishing to come and name the toxin. In those years my Indian friends often stayed at our house, but now in the silence of this freezing night, it is our defenselessness to just such savages that I fear. We lie exposed to any and all, Mr. Lawrence and I, for the Pawmunkeys are but one in a list of peoples we have slaughtered.

His cough is uncontrollable, and he stands a better peace not to awaken at all, if sleep can be called what he's having. For myself, gazing indirectly at the mounds of moonlit snow, my mind makes shapes and images until all manner of memories are formed. I see a one-time friend and neighbor, Thomas Grent appear before me where I found him in a wood-break three weeks ride from here. He was planted to the chin in ground he had just cleared from the southern tip of his farm. But by the time I spied him through the cover of a blackberry bush, his corn, his barn and farmhouse too, were all in a smoldering pile. A small group of Susquehanna were building a fire a few inches from his face and admiring his unwillingness to scream. They had stripped off his scalp before it could singe, and the bloody smoke stood ready to split his blistered head. But by a merciful God, I managed to strike it with a musket ball first.

Then another hallucination, just as steeped in cold and hunger, is brought on by nothing more than the wind tossing up its fairylike tufts of snow. It puts me back at the Portsmouth docks, in South Hampton, England, the year of 1650. The lime dust from the oyster factory lifts across the air and settles in plumes across a pamphlet that I hold dearly in my hands. It is an advertisement for the New World called Virginia.

My numb fingers tremble not from the cold, but from the excitement I feel at such a spectacle. A majestic Indian sits calmly astride a creature half turtle and half cat, a thing more than twice the man's size. The background is filled with a phenomenon of foliage, with mysterious creatures, unknown and unnamed, teeming wild upon the page. It was a common publicity piece, but it held me in its mesmerizing spell, making a simpleton mock of my future. For Virginia held land, and somewhere within its glorious domain laid a plot I knew I would someday call my own. I knew this with all the power this fantastic picture had upon me. I was fifteen years of age, innocent of the realities to indenture, and burning to see the Port of James City.

Life, and much of the time that it consumes travels unknown to us in awkward circles, but there's a certain way that I've seen that it takes to its playing with ridicule. The years of my youth were spent in an England torn apart by ceaseless war, where every peace brokered merely shuffled former allies into enemies anew. There were Cavaliers and Anglicans, Catholics and Protestants, Scotch Presbyterians, and fire breathing Puritans, not to mention the backstabbing Royals in Parliament, too. And though the fearless Cromwellians prevailed over all, it was never quite clear whose cannon ruled the day. The shipyards where I lived at Portsmouth were a particularly popular place for this sport but the last straw, (at least for my poor struggling father) came when our town was hit with the typhus.

Having sensed my strongest wish, a wish that coincided with the growing dangers, unbeknownst to me he quietly arranged for my passage on the *Tidal Flower.* (Though he never championed King Charles, his tolerance for royal indulgence was more than for that of the Roundheads.) And his greatest fear by far was that his only son would go missing, having been pressed into Cromwell's service. In due time, ridicule would raise its sleeping head, (in this case to nod at my father's caring regard) for these were the days that Governor Berkeley in Virginia had proclaimed his plantations finally safe. The protracted Indian wars that he had fought and had treated for so long had at last been successfully ended.

While I, in spite of my untamed excitement, was to experience an altogether separate kind of dread. The morning that I delighted to see my ship set anchor, I stood in witness to the cargo that it bore. The *Tide* and the *Flower* that my vessel was bringing to Virginia was a record-breaking load of felons and indentured of the lowest class. Up at sunrise, I watched with morbid fascination, as rows of people, some seeming permanently bent, being roughly shoved aside by the desperately poor. The registrar, who barely looked up to notice, placed a mark upon each eager, jutting forehead saying, "No matter how sick, no matter how starving, a chance here to work in the New World." Which he made sound like a funeral dirge.

But God shone upon me when I learned that my hammock was strung into an upper-deck, to be alternately shared with Shep, the first mate. This unbelievable fortune, I also learned, was God's gracious hand on the heart of my good Master Salt. Henry Salt was the sole proprietor of *Henry Salt & Fitters,* and I was just four years apprenticed, when he generously answered my father's concerns. Together they managed me a head-right passage, (a promise to the Charter that I would stay five years, *as if there were any doubt,*) and in exchange for my indenture was fifty full acres of river front land.

Imagine a youth whose high-toned ambitions were suddenly made possible by his father's wondrous sacrifice. (Not that the notion was new to such a man. Being the only son among four sisters, and with a second wife's death in the birth of the last, he still had provided me the chance to learn reading.) And imagine this glory in a country where the right to all land was taken long ago. Each and every parcel titled out by noble decree. I could not wait to stand on my own soil, the soil to repay the good Henry Salt's loan. (The settling of which I calculated in the tobacco I'd harvest in my third year.)

It was the 2nd of March when we finally embarked, and my impatience at our delay (the difficulty in obtaining wartime provisions) fretted me to failure ere I'd begun. But all at once in a tear-stung farewell to my father, my sisters, and the good Henry Salt, I was on a ship in full sail for the first time in my life. And where, if hastened by a favorable wind, we were to meet with *The Dawn* and the *New Gastow Faire*. It was a small fleet as the ships went in that year, but any companions, (as any true seaworthy mate would know) made the trip that much safer.

But then, as sure as the foretelling of a troubled passage, we never made our rendezvous. The prevailing current at the time of the year, being unusually changeable, had forced the companies we intended to keep far away to the south. At the same time these very same tides were showing us little in the way of mercy. They rolled our overloaded and off-balanced weight fully to one side, and then dropped out empty right beneath our hold. It was a motion that cruelly punished those miserably quartered below. Each pull and fall was answered with a host of wretched gasping, from spaces hardly big enough to breathe. Being so confined, the immigrants held on and heaved together, sometimes bile and sometimes dry, but the awful sound truly never ceased. One lot would finally give it a rest, while a new one then started in, until a circle of days was gone through like this, with the washing out of hogsheads the only work done.

The captain, a slyly sad man named Jarvis, finally called for my carpentry skills by having me cut the deck with more vents, and though I was happy for the job, it seemed little more than futile. For I, no sailor by any turn could see that when we hit the open sea, the shadeless sun and heated bodies would make the hull into a furnace. Still, I was determined to do my best, for among those faces, full pale and queer with terror, there was no question but for Henry Salt, I might just as well be looking at myself. It was also apparent that the rotted tarps provided for covering the new grates would do nothing against the water, and sure enough, when the great sea struck, the murky pools began to swell up. Suffice it to say, that conditions below deteriorated rapidly, but Captain Jarvis seemed more or less resigned. His policy, however much unstated, let it fall to the passengers to keep themselves alive. Until it was all I could do to focus on the good days, (meaning, the constant work of my chute rope and bucket, I could make the hold where they lay into a wallow.)

But when all that can go bad is finally listed out, it is the sight of a deck, entirely slipped beneath the surface that sends a landsman into panic. It was on just such occasion when I met the cold comforting stare of Captain Jarvis standing like a specter above me. I was clinging to the main for life, wrapping it tight as I could with my arms and with my knees, while he leaned into the wind, and calmly watched the sea engulf us. Try as I might I couldn't keep my head from being smacked into the timber by the gale. I had just been crying to the Almighty for deliverance to a firmer land than was on the ocean bottom, when I opened my eyes to see him looking curiously at me. (Jarvis that is, and not the Almighty, although at the time it felt the same difference.)

"Ya'll be alright," he said simply. "Sea-legs come at twenty."

I managed to stand; too embarrassed to ask what he meant, and away he was gone. If it was my age he was speaking of, then he might have saved his breath, for I was certain that I'd never set sail again, but the way he leaned his ear in sharp, listening to the wails below me, he made clear his concern was not for me, as much for his human cargo.

I later learned that if you didn't die of dry heaving by the time we reached the parallel of twenty then you'd crossed the point where you might survive. Only then, I was told, did Jarvis start to count his profit. And as I made my way back to my bunk to be violently sick that night, I heard a baby, of all things, bawling enough to wrench its tiny heart. I heard it stop and start again between my bouts with the shivers, all while wondering if Jarvis had put me in the column that he marked his 'losses.' I wondered too, what column he'd provided for a newborn.

When the storm had passed and the cleanup was done, the days began a dull melt. Like the running of any ship I suppose, and its necessary routines at open sea. Those of us boarded to work kept to a regular pace, making sails, mending rope, and scrubbing the deck most any day of the week. As part of a regular crew we were assigned the normal details, those quite apart from the guards who brought up the immigrants. And there was never telling when these airings would be. Sometimes a group would take their twenty minutes of sun at the half-hour past breakfast, and then be back again that very afternoon. While another group might have to lie in their holes for half a week. "Stretch outcher' rot, an'leave me no limbs," the steward always sang by way of announcing their presence.

There was a gentleman named Staunt aboard that wanted a closet for his books above his door. I jumped at this chance to have a break from my workaday chores, and even made bold the opportunity by asking what sense Jarvis had for his exercise of felons. To my surprise, Staunt squarely admitted that the rotation of the scum, (his very words) was a system that he himself had devised. He went on to say that he was something of an expert in the codes of human behavior, and had found that in randomly shifting outward expressions of favor, one created an instability in the oppressed that made the prospect of wholesale riot untenable. He used quite a few fancy words that I have long since forgotten, but I remember the phrase 'oppressed' sliding so easily off his tongue that it gave me a case of the chicken skin shivers. I avoided him thereafter, and began thinking that I'd best keep to my own counsel and suppress my offhand prying questions. Having already had my fill of distress, I resolved to spend what time was mine by finding things to cherish. Points of radiance I came to call them, and rejoiced when I chanced to discover one anew. The salt spray of sea that I caught by dropping my face over starboard, which brought me alive and awake before the rising sun. Naming the colors in between a rainbow, like gello right before green. The richest blues a sky could offer, so endlessly open and reachable, enough to make you want to try a step. The top deck nooks that sheltered the pages of my journal, and gave me sudden rest from the unforgiving sun. I made these efforts to fill my ready mind from dwelling on the miseries below, and the inner light returned to me was its own reward. It called to me at sunrise and pulled me through my days, like a magnet I became toward the sunset, pulling our ship ever west.

There was one night however, that brought me in close to the darkened life beneath. A night of knocking, soft and insistent at my narrow bunk door, which snared me from a dream so sweet, that it took me a moment to think. I cautiously looked into the hatchway, and in the shadows I discerned an immigrant couple, most strongly identified by their stifling stench, with their faces all covered by oilskins. I was too groggy to be bothered with their purpose, and thoughtlessly shoved closed the door. But one of them caught it with a step, or so I sleepily thought, and quickly jammed the doorway stuck. My mind raced, assuming something fearful, and I grabbed up my nearby carpenter's plane. While I struggled to force close the door, I heard a frantic whisper, "Naught!" and in a jumble of opposite efforts, looked down to see a tiny babe jammed on the floorboards between us. In the straining back and forth, I had squeezed off one of its feet. I jumped back in horror, and the door was gingerly tapped free. The closest one, still hidden in his canvas wrap, picked up the dead infant, and gently swayed it towards my tiny porthole. The ship, lifting and falling with the roll of the waves, allowed the blinking moonlight to reveal the black body of the infant terribly scarred with pox. "If you please, sir," he said, giving the window his deliberate attention. I finally understood that he only wanted access to throw the baby off, and I nodded my head, resigned. Out of respect I turned myself away, (but feeling more repulsed) and when the deed was done he simply said, "Bless, and g'night." Then twisting his whimpering bride around, together they slinked down the hole where they came.

When I overcame my initial horror, I realized that his primary motive was in hiding the fact of a possible plague. If word had gotten out, it would have meant panic and violence, followed just as surely by a cleansing purge. Any suspect passengers would be forced over the side at the mere rumor of spots. And then I am most shamed to admit that I did not return to bed that night. My fear of the babe's infecting my bunk was only equaled by the fear of sharing such news with the mate. On his return I even ended by letting his hard-earned sleep serve like he was my guinea pig. The mate meanwhile, being free of my tossing bad conscience slept in the bed like a stone. But there is an even deeper fret attached to this event, that I confess however irrational goads upon me still. As tiny a thing as it may sound, it is this sad sequence that marked the first occasion when anyone had ever called me, "Sir."

These, and a mixture of torn feelings however were given no time to be nursed. By mid-latitudes dysentery was rampant, just when we hit a new off-season storm. Half the way over, half a hundred drowned and were dumped overboard without ceremony. "Shark food," my cold-minded bunkmate said with a wink, "God's little vicious cleaner-uppers." And some that we sent over were not yet fully dead. Each of the victims was tied together with their torn and tainted clothes, and then slid off the side on a specially fitted ramp. Wave after human wave of bodies we sank, their black faces looking back at us as if in contempt at those with the nerve to survive.

And too, ashamed as I am to admit it, the upward end of this culling was a ship that ran swift as a lark. "We're making time now," Captain Jarvis happily reported, steering us past a threatening squall. The truth be told, the number of dead had by then so benumbed me that I saw the kill-off as a blessing. I was only fifteen, not yet set foot in the land of my dreams, and was already made hard by what we'd overcome. After these, my first and only months at sea, I felt that I was living in a liquid world with a body I hardly knew. I gained a new respect for the strangest of fellows, like Jack in the larder and his deceitful rations trade, or my bunkmate Shep, who always saw money in another person's grief.

Adding to my confusion was the night that turned to

jitters when I took a turn at watch. I was awake but dreaming, propped against a barrel top, and occupied with the moon made stark inside a black ink cloud. A disembodied hand suddenly stuck out the grate behind me, followed by the arms, and then the torso of the dead infant's father. He paused long enough to quickly gather up his length of pilfered rope, and without making a sound, he offered me an object that he took from inside of his coat. He was abjectly pathetic, but certainly just as innocent of the contagion he had been blamed for the few days or so before. The vicious threats placed upon their lives had even made the girl he was with (they were not, as I'd naively believed become true man and wife) to fling herself overboard. But despite this loss, not to mention that of his baby, he wanted to show me some appreciation by the gift of a chicken leg. I looked at the bug-infested piece, obviously ripped from the captain's livestock, and I crushed it like a mealy sponge. I smeared the pasty stuff back into his hand and sensed his fear of me was every bit equal to the fear that I'd felt of myself. "As you please, sir," he mumbled before turning to slip away.

Only later did I understand that the bony claw was only his attempt at a sacrifice. But right then, smelling his breath upon my neck, breath that reeked of his confinement and used up air, I wanted no part of his festering superstitions. To him I was a being that was blessed, and made all the more appealing for being within his reach. Unhinged as he was, he made me the key to his survival. But as cold as I'd then become, I rejected his petition. I pulled him round by his filthy shoulder, and said, "you are never again to call me, sir."

In the next days, in view of the young woman's suicide, Captain Jarvis placed a curfew on the lower decks. Their sunlight was to be restricted to an hour a week. And for those who reacted to the rule with violence, their time up would then be used for public whippings. As a form of punishment anyway, being lashed was nothing new. He had always beaten the thieves. And God knows by then our rations were scant enough to warrant it, still, it was a duty that he clearly didn't enjoy. Our steady captain was now helplessly facing a drain off of his profits, further injury to sickly men weighed heavily on his mind.

On the other hand no one is quicker than a convict to spot a weakness, and take advantage of a turn in events. They began to snatch at anything that they could somehow fit in their mouths, and Jarvis countered by having me build a set of foot locks to serve as a painful example for thieves. These, I installed inside a contraption he called 'the soulless,' which was a pitch black hole where one was dragged in the water backwards to the point where he couldn't breathe. It effectively brought the stealing to a cease.

The last days however, everyone was hungry. Always. This included the captain, the bonded, and all other passengers and crew. Everyone that is, save the privileged Mr. Staunt. But one thing I can say for Jarvis is that he took his dose of treacle just like all the rest, and I never once heard him complain.

It was I guess, the twelfth week out when I got my final indication of just how desperate *The Tidal Flower* had become. On a windless night I entered the tiny quarter of my bunk, and found a wretched girl about ten years of age. Her face was flat against the floor under a shelf, and she was knotted by rope to a cleat. "Where do you belong?" I asked, but she refused to give me an answer. She was bound up (or down I should say) in such a way it was impossible to see her face so I didn't know if she understood me, but her wisp of a frame shook constantly with fright. We passed an oppressive hour like this with her whimpering steady and low, until at last I couldn't stand it, and loosened the grip of her cords. She immediately bolted, and I quickly jumped to block her, but the next thing I saw was my bunkmate grabbing her first.

"What do you think?" he yelled at me, "'that maybe she belongs to you?" In my confusion, I could find no answer then he struck her down once, before tying her up again. I squatted back as best I could to accommodate our cramped condition, considering the curious question that he put to me.

"Let me advise you of something," he said, holding out a small piece of turnip that the girl snapped up in her teeth. "This is my property here, and if I see it's come to harm, then you'll be the one to pay."

I spent a grievous night in anger at the plight of the poor girl, and so rattled by her whining that I couldn't even think. It turned out that the mate had bought the child from her parents for a three-day dole of oats. "She might fetch me ten to twelve pounds onshore in Virginia," he reported the next day. "Nothing hard between us, but a man has to make his own way." He seemed immediately cheered at our having reached some understanding, and then quickly followed on. "It's just a little business. When I'm too old for all of this, I plan to have stakes in a ship."

I went on to find out that the parents had bargained the daughter in order to rescue their son. They'd come to a starving decision, and gave him the better chance to live. When I figured out who they were, I purposely made an approach, but they never so much as looked at me once. As fearful and as weak as they'd become I could not coax out a sound. I finally gave up, but staring at the hopeful way they made of their little son, I had the sudden realization that surviving this harsh voyage was but a rehearsing for what waited on the James.

* * * * *

I can see now through the thin smoke of our fire that Mr. Lawrence has awakened. There's a fairly cold dawn, and I must now go see to his shivering. But make no mistake;

I've surrendered myself to futility. What ministrations I make will not matter. It is God's will alone that is alive in these woods. Something I've come to believe that has no need of our salvation.

"Pile it on!" Mr. Lawrence screams, "Don't be shy men! Pile it! Pile it high!" and his eyes, staring wildly into my own, are alive with flame. He does not see me as I attempt to calm this delirium, but I understand well what he does see. He is watching his very own hands fueling the fire that burns his very own house. But the heat within his mind is what rekindles his fever in very real ways. His body kicks out in alarm. Alarmed at himself I think, and the uncharted territory toward which his rebellion had made. Destinations, he knew even then, from which there would be no return. "Pile it men!" he shouts once more. "More grass from the barn! Throw on a mattress from the upstairs!"

I know the burning is what he sees, for I was among those carrying a torch. In fact I set fire to the very same structures that I had built up in my innocent youth; the innocent years of my indentured service. And as I marched filled with shame of the drunken mob down towards the Jamestown Church, my eyes remained on Bacon, our self-destructive general, as he embodied our self-destructive quest.

"C'mon, my good men!" Mr. Lawrence looks me straight in the eye. But he does not see me any more than he sees the naked limb above him, or the slab gray slate of winter sky. Then, as if counter to my will, he sparks a thrill by his enacting. Like the whip in the air the night the world came all unhinged, the night that General Bacon decided to burn Jamestown.

Even here and now, in the presence of our impossible survival, I am touched by the way intention plays fool to concluded events. Just hearing Mr. Lawrence rally forth his mental riot forces me to smile. For Mr. Lawrence was never what you'd call 'a man among men.' In truth he was uncomfortable with the frontier peasant; nor did he support the war against the Indians, but bitterly regretted its diversion from his new Virginia plan. This is a certain and surprising fact, but in this time of our escaping, I have listened to him well enough for me to understand.

The flaw that hounded us into disaster was Nathaniel Bacon himself, and his need for the slaughter of any savage, whether sleeping or awake. A passion, by the way, that fit the frontier planters like a glove. But irony sings forth again in the eloquent form of Richard Lawrence, who babbles here before me, and who needed men like Bacon to make his ideal real.

"I'll not stand by and have her made your plaything!" Mr. Lawrence shouts.

His tortured meditations have shifted focus once again. I try forcing a piece of sassafras to his lips, but he angrily spits it out. I have been listening to his internal dialogue for twelve long days now, and have begun to think that there is some demon putting it to use. I have no other way to explain his survival. But what kind of demon, I wonder, would waste his time to entertain a single wretch like me?

"Stand off! Stand off!" he yells, and stretched upon the ground he pantomimes a shadow box with foes rising out of his mind. "Stand off, you pigs! Pigs and swine! No more men among you!" He pounds his head back in the ground and twists it in the frost until it clings onto his beard. Then I realize where he's visiting now, and with what sort of men.

In the summer of 1675, Captain Davies Thrick had captured more than thirty Doeg Indians that he planned to gain more profit from than by making them examples for a mass execution. And Mr. Lawrence had unlawful contact with the Dutch, so a transfer of the prisoners was arranged. The receipts from the sale were supposed to be distributed among the New Kent farms as a form of restitution, but the night before the ship arrived, Mr. Lawrence made an unexpected call upon their secret cell. His purpose was to approve the final sum placed on the Indians by their sex and age, but he found no guards, or any of our militia at their outward posts. What he did come upon was the first of many scenes that tore his heart from his noble idea of rebellion. It was a frontier form of slaving of which I'd heard, but could hardly bring myself to believe, where a man who shoots the greatest amount of seed in the course of an hour lays claim to whichever squaw it was that satisfied him last. I have even been told of gamblers that will wager on the outcome, prying at the female to facilitate the men.

"You! You!" Mr. Lawrence shouts, "for I will not call you a man!" and he strikes out his hand at the frozen stump behind him. "What soldiers here! What Godless form of animals?!" And then, exhausted, he lays back down, rolling aimlessly atop his patch of snow.

"Corstair!" he suddenly whispers, and now I am astonished. I move in close hoping that he's ended the nightmare. It is the first time in two weeks that he has known enough to call my name. "Corstair!" he whispers again, and reaches up to bring my head down level with his own. "There! Just there! There it is again!" and his hands turn my head to the place where he points.

We are soaked to the skin and covered with mud, but through a gap in our embankment we see a savage child peering at our spectacle, curious and timid. It's a little girl, I am quite sure but the snow-covered dwarfs of pine where she hides make me think that it's a dream. Catching us catching her, just now, she moves, and darting to another limb, I distinctly hear her laugh. The sound of her jingle voice is at once so startling comprehensible that I'm convinced this shared delusion will have us dead by afternoon. My eyes jump about wildly from tree to empty tree searching for the hostile party, and I cringe like a tortoise, expecting arrows and a severing jab. I can scarcely draw a breath, but the weakened Mr. Lawrence leaps from his bed and chases after the child. She runs throughout the undergrowth. I see him smacked down by a sturdy branch, then recover his stride, and stumble forward again. I picture his mind gone so amuck, that his goal is to kill her and then eat her perhaps. But the girl is still laughing and runs unafraid, as if it's a game she's only just invented. There's nothing for me to do but run after, and it's difficult going, stopping and starting and wheezing; holding myself up only to find that I'm falling again. The cold in the air freezes my sweat and the phlegm that I cough stays thick in my mouth. I think that I will drown, while Mr. Lawrence gasps just ahead, unnatural in strength, like someone possessed. He shows no sign of stopping, but when we can go no longer he grabs me in close and silently marks a spot to our right. The woods are so dense here that I think that I will lose him, and so I place his hand in the back of my belt. We move together like this in a cautious slow motion until all of a sudden we are tumbling down a hidden ravine. Without a thought, like animals reacting, we are on our hands and knees, striking up the middle, only to be caught in a sinking swamp of debris. And just as quickly as it started, the game is over, the girl and the laughter are gone, nowhere to be seen. She has left us completely exhausted. She has left us here for dead. Mr. Lawrence looks without speaking upon this pitiful grave as I try to push my arms back up and forward, and then weakly at our sides. I must free the air that's trapped inside this tomb of fallen trees. Doing so I reckon a particle of sun reflecting a dozen feet above us as if it is resting on the surface of the snow. Using me like a ladder Mr. Lawrence pushes up and together, grimly silent, we gain our footholds by a relay. Slowly, and then quite suddenly, we are out and breathe again. The sky has pushed away its gray, and a startling blue opens up our spirits. And then in the same impossible once, a chorus of laughing children surrounds us, giggling nervously, as in soft derision. They laugh and slide on snow covered limbs, which to us, were like a dangerous vault. I shake my head as if I'm being wakened. For now I see that the pit, which held us in its freezing grip is but a shallow embankment. It is a gift from my deprived perception. Unbelieving, I shake my head again at the little hands and arms that welcome our delivery; surely the most unlooked for turn, this happy, gay reception. The children pull us up by our shoulders and tattered clothing, as if saying, all is well now, come on out, come out, you're well, you see, come out, come out and breathe for awhile. I see Mr. Lawrence being led to the side of an iced over pond that is punched out for fishing, the baskets nearby hold a catch very large. A little one, the original girl I'm sure, offers him something hot to drink. He does not take the bowl, but falls down, gently placing his tear-streaking face down on her feet. And all the while his body shakes, he sobs and heaves in such sweet agony that I'm afraid for his weakened heart. The little girl tries her best at holding Mr. Lawrence's mud caked hand onto the cup, but she is confused and perhaps a little embarrassed. Caught between her laughing friends, some who are busy throwing snow, and the shaking stranger's sobs, she smiles bravely back into the forest. And there within the tree line stand the adults. There are mothers holding bewildered babes that stare out at their breasts, and men, both young and old, speaking low and urgent, trying to make the hard choices. There are grandparents sitting in chairs of fur, wrapped all alone with their thoughts, as others move back toward the trees. One of these elders leaves from the rest, and taking the bowl of steaming broth from out the girl's hand, he touches it to Mr.

Lawrence's forehead. "O'misi, o'te, kitasamitin," he says, and makes a gesture with the cup, turning to a path that runs up the hill behind him. Mr. Lawrence leans forward, half in a crouch, and follows the old man like a dog. The children have now all stopped to watch, while adults along the bank avert their eyes. And though I understand some part of the language, there is nothing for me to do but humbly trail behind.

he cave that Mr. Lawrence and I have been shown is our new home, and whether it is a hospital or a prison or both, it does not matter. For it could not be more appreciated than if it were a palace of a king. It has a natural hearth where we keep a well-vented fire, or rather where the fire is kept for us, for we have been under the constant attention of a woman appointed as our warden-nurse. Speaking for myself, as well as Mr. Lawrence, we couldn't have imagined anything better.

Her name is Seycondeh and we converse in a broken Algonkin tongue that I inevitably infuse with English. She has been a vigilant caretaker, but Mr. Lawrence has not been able to lose his hacking cough and I am so nervous of his expiring that he will startle me from much-needed sleep. His wild imagination sometimes grips him still, but with each day we successfully pass, I believe that he slowly recovers. When he is visited by these spells Seycondeh applies a compress to his chest consisting of some sour smelling herb, which she has tried to explain, but of which I am unfamiliar. It does however, have the remarkable power to soothe his fevered mind, and the day following often stirs him to a state of a profound lucidity. This happy circumstance is one that I exploit, for I am determined to call his account of this tumultuous past year. In as far as Seycondeh can keep him alive.

God knows he's already survived much more than was his due. For among the numerous Virginia gentry that ended their lives on a hangman's rope, Mr. Richard Lawrence held

Daniel Watkins

a position of particular privilege. He sat on the governor's council after all, and all while plotting the governor's demise.

But while he sleeps here beside me, if I'm so allowed, I'll continue my tale where it started with myself as a youthful apprentice to the colony at Jamestown.

* * * * *

Over three months at sea, and two weeks past the month of May in the year of 1650 my ship the *Tidal Flower* was grounded by a sand bar moving toward the mouth of the James. The ship listed badly, but with Captain Jarvis' speed and skill, we were able to conduct a transfer of the immigrants onto the flatboats and other Jamestown ferries. Our saviors surrounded our ship in such a quick flock they looked like a swarm of alligators I'd seen pictured in the Florida swamps. But believe me when I say, that for those of us alive on board, there could have been no happier sight. For we, still healthy enough to see it after all, were finally in the hands of those who'd spent a night on dry land.

For the immigrants trapped below however, the joy they had gained in smelling the shore was dampened by endless delay. The *Tidal Flower* was as full of disease as any boat could be, and the sea-rotted souls within its dank hold were so sick that they could not stand. The vast majority, each one a coin in Jarvis' purse was forced to remain on board until they had passed his inspection. Then they were given a cursory wash with a shave, and a fresh looking smock of cheap linen. "There's no going back on a good first impression," Jarvis said, manhandling the bodies in line.

But for me, the glory of green that shone from the trees and the smell of the soil was a tonic. Even the cynical hearts in our group took the moment to praise the earth that they beheld, each one offering prayers of new thanks, and beginnings. And when we rounded the spit that harbored James City, though shocked by its puny size, I was filled with an excitement I could not hide. I actually cried out in strange sounds that erupted quite involuntarily. The dock was no more than a simple ramp of clay, but was filled to the brim with heady smells, the strongest of which was tobacco and fur. Men sat casually balanced on twisted piles of logs, taking in the day, or talking to a fellow who looked like he'd only just invented his clothes. There was a great deal of feather, bone and leather; and altogether wild looking sorts swapping tales with fancy men. My dim sighted eyes came boldly alive with so much that was new, and so suddenly thrust before them. One character in the crowd, who looked like a down and out pirate was shouting curses at a half-naked Indian that sat perfectly upright asleep.

Hypnotized by such a novelty of sounds and scents, it took a moment for me to notice one strange assembly, appearing to have as much interest in me as I had in them. But I was so carried off by my enthusiasm that I leapt from the boat before it was fully secured. Then, no sooner had my feet hit solid land than the scene began to swim. I fell like a stone to the ground, and was immediately brought up again in the grip of a strong pair of hands. There were slaps upon my back and I heard a warbled roar of laughter. "One and a half seconds." A man from the group declared, raking in a collection of coins that sat on the top of a barrel. "Got to get something on this boy's bones I'd soon better wager," he stood me up and winked, and then slipped a shilling in my pocket. The others continued to laugh, as one of them picked out a new mark to make of a sea weary soul, who'd be quite unaware of the falling-down gamblers.

"Sycamore Stevens," the man said to me, "are you the young Corstair?"

"Yes sir," I replied. "And a little unsure of my bearings."

Daniel Watkins

"Have a seat then," he replied. "Before we give you a proper walk around."

I found a level rock apparently put there for this purpose and looked at the man who seemed to know me. His age was difficult to discern. At first he did not appear that old, but some other quality, harder to figure, gave him a demeanor that was well past his prime. It wasn't that his coat was frayed, a condition no worse than any of the others, but there was a certain weariness behind his eyes, an emptiness lurked in his smile that was menacing and deeper. From the moment that I sat to catch my breath, I saw him fix on each arrival as with a predatory hunger, an impression that stuck with me for being so ill fitting. That we, the most haggard of beings, just stepped off a ship of the starving, could be the objects of such drooling attention was somehow simply wrong. But then, before my light head could fully comprehend it, I was gawking at a naked Indian.

"You'll see a great deal more of them," the man sighed, "than you will no doubt want. But we're at peace for now, they say."

"Forgive me, sir," I responded. "But how do you know me?"

"I do some clerking work in Requisitioned Labor. That's me. Boring old Clarence in Requisitioned Labor," he replied with a feigned resignation. "But my friends all call me Sycamore."

"Philip Corstair," I replied, offering my hand.

"I know, I know, a Mr. Henry Salt got me your papers on the *Beacon's Reach,* arrived a month ago. Your Mr. Salt's a prudent man to send your papers by way of a separate ship." Then he looked at me strangely. "You don't have to tell me how your passage was, I can see that well enough. Can you stand? If your stomach's settled we'll see if Madam Porter's got her turtle soup."

I stood, and slowly managed my opening steps towards the outer walls of Jamestown. The first thing that I noticed with my apprentice craftsman's eyes was that the timbers along the palisade were rotting and neglected. Then, passing through the city gate, the same was just as true for every other structure. I walked the drab rows past mud-daubed huts with mottle-thatched roofs barely six feet high, and a wave of concern traveled through me. Scraggly chickens and pigs roamed freely about, picking at the manure in the mud, or taking up residence inside these bleak hovels if they found one to their liking. But the keenest point by far was how utterly abandoned Jamestown looked. I did not encounter another single soul walking the rut-strewn streets, and every squat quarter stood dark and alone. I concentrated on avoiding the sinkholes, some a full yard deep, and fought the good fight of keeping spirits up. But to speak the truth, my new and green elation had all but ebbed away. Shabby coops for the tenants that I'd seen in the worst parts of Portsmouth were better off than this. With each dreadful step, I slipped further into squalor and doubt. Doubt about the land, doubt about the living, even doubts about my precious dream of owning a plantation. The ease with which I'd formed my grandiose thoughts was suddenly surpassed by the enormity of the work, and as Mr. Stevens went on about his comments, I found that I was barely listening. Then he led me round a turn, and a well-constructed church appeared like a light at city center. It was stoutly hewn in whitewashed wood and polished brick, and stood in front of several homes built of equal quality. I was quick to see that each was still mysteriously empty, but they did provide renewal of my hope.

"Jamestown's only a stopping off place," Sycamore said when he saw that I was puzzling. "A place for transients, really. Outside of shipping days and the labor auctions, life in Virginia surrounds the plantations."

Suddenly I thought of Jarvis and the torment he was

Daniel Watkins

stirring up in the cleaning of his shipload treasure.

"But now that the Indian wars are over, the governor has plans to build and restore. That's his place there." He pointed up the lane to a clapboard house, two stories high with casement windows painted in a bright limestone wash. Miraculously, it was mud-free, and all things considered, absolutely elegant. "'Course you won't find him there now. He'll only use it when he's here to run the government. He's off seeing to his twenty thousand, and the brick work on his estate at Green Spring. Like all the rest, he's a planter and has little use for town..."

"Excuse me, Mr. Stevens..."

"Sycamore, if you please."

"Mr. Sycamore. What is the twenty thousand?"

"Acres, my son. Acres of land."

He paused for a second, as if in observance of the swimming in my head.

"Although I'll let you in on a little kept secret. Berkeley has grants that control ten times as much. Being a sometime government employee, I've spied the rights to them myself."

And so the weakness returned to my new walking legs, and Sycamore Stevens had to catch me up again. I had survived an angry sea to stand in a street more dung than earth, with more mud than in all of England, but the only way for me to comprehend the extravagance of Virginia's wealth was by fainting.

"C'mon then," Sycamore said. "Madam Porter's place is by. Then we'll see you rest in your room."

We ducked beneath a darkened doorway and into a hut with split log flooring. The mud seeped through every uneven tree trunk, but I somehow reached an upright cedar stool without my having tripped.

"Now then," Sycamore said into the dark, "a bowl of soup for my seaworthy friend, who's only just come to the aid and repair of our fair city."

From out of the dim light, a thin-framed woman with a hitched-up skirt popped up and bobbed so unexpectedly that she gave me a sudden fright. But then she warmed me with her smile, and I welcomed the smell of what was hot and home cooked that she was carrying in her hands.

"Well, he's just a boy," she said, setting down two bowls on the splintered surface. "But, welcome you are, young sir. Now, if you happen to wake with a touch of the ague don't be fooling around. You make sure you come see me right away. You don't want to wait 'til it's gained a full bloom. Ah, he's just a boy." She said placing a hand upon my cheek. "Did that thieving Jarvis bring me my taffeta?" she abruptly broke off to ask, and changed her expression to scorn.

"Madam Porter's determined to have a fancy dress shop," Sycamore explained. "Everyone's a schemer here, you see?"

I could not claim to have her answer, but I thanked her for her kindness and ate three bowls of her delicious turtle soup. The turtle, like so much else was a first for me, and I amazed myself with a starving abandon. Then, as the meal settled in, it refurbished my enthusiasm, and I overflowed with questions. Wild life, plant life, farm life and anything that Sycamore could tell me about the Indians. He indulged me with his patience as we sat in the half dark, and only once, when I asked about the rules to the head rights for my land, did I sense again his hungry luster. But his attentive manner mostly calmed me, familiar, as he must have been, with a youth that had just escaped the stifling bounds of England. Within the deep-set of his tired eyes he seemed happy to sit and simply be with me, as I gorged myself on Virginia's remarkable food.

"Where are all the people?" I asked between mouthfuls.

"Tending their farms, clearing new land. Planting," he

said. "Some of our more singular sort have slipped off to the woods in search of the beaver pelt trade. There's always more work here than any can do. The idler, the gambler and the drunk are the only ones that live in Jamestown throughout the year." He paused as if to prepare an allowance for himself and then he continued quickly. "But we'll have our more distinguished visitors now that new labor's arrived."

"What visitors?"

"Men in the market to buy men," he replied. "Those who can afford to have the first look, before Jarvis takes his inferior wares on up the river. And believe me," he added leaning in, "the pick of the crop will go to the type gents who aren't that impressed with the governor's twenty thousand."

Again, I had to catch my breath. "Is it possible?"

"More than possible. The rich in Virginia, they say, can only get richer. Unless they're outright fools. The labor that they buy today will clear new land, and increase their harvests. But it's through their banking and loaning that they gobble up the farms unable to compete. And those acquired lands, my friend, are invaluable. Already cleared and labored over, developed and now desperate, going for pennies to the pound."

"But, but what of… men… like me?" I stopped before I said the word, unaccustomed as I was to conferring myself with maturity. "The one's that have done their service and paid off their passage?" I quickly asked. I was also still struggling with the concept of so much single ownership. Here, I vaguely thought, there must be many kings.

"Most will be dead before that day arrives. If the seasoning doesn't get them, I've even seen some who were worked to death. And by that turn you're lucky to be working for the city young Corstair. An unscrupulous owner can work you day and night. And more than a few of them do it. *If*, and a very large *if* it is, by the time a servant can start out on his own, he's usually fixed with so much debt he'll sell his rights and take the next ship home."

"But *this* is their home," I said, surprising him with my sudden authority. "Surely some make it through, and stay. I mean, there is so much here for… all."

"On the frontier, lad. The frontier. And that's a place for making up your own laws."

"And there? Men have built their farms?"

"Yes," Sycamore hedged as if my questions had become a distraction. "And by the grace of God they'll raise a family and survive the angry savages," he said sharply. "But that's away from your cares for now. The first thing is joining you to the Jamestown crew. The governor wants a certain vitality put in this town. To show his defiance of Parliament. His testament to the Crown, you see."

My head was already brimming and anxious, but just the mention of the troubles I was sure I'd left behind, brought on a sudden exhaustion. Quite unexpectedly, it was all I could do to keep my head out of my empty bowl of soup.

"C'mon then," Sycamore said, placing a hand on my shoulder, "time to find you a place to rest. You'll be up at first light chopping trees."

I reached in my pocket to find the shilling that he'd slipped there, and offered it to pay for my meal.

"It's taken care of," he said. "Keep that as the good luck piece for which it was intended. I have a feeling about you."

Against my fondest wish I was not shown one of Madam Porter's rooms, but a retracing of my steps back through the city gate. And in the time that I'd been occupied by Sycamore and his tour, a worn out platform was erected attracting a lively crowd between a front wall and the river. A small group of militia leaned casually around one corner far more engaged in sharing a joke than in looking to offer protection. But then, the whole weight of my fatigue was swept and cleared as my eyes took in the sight of such colorful confusion. Everything was bustling in upon the primitive port. From out of nowhere it seemed that half a dozen sailing vessels, nearly the size of our ship, had moored in mid-stream up the river, and at least a dozen new dingys were docked upon the bank. Looking up and out across the water I beheld a bewildering fleet of sloops, rafts and scows, being poled and rowed in to us from assuredly exotic destinations. In the afternoon haze, they appeared to fairly sprout on the face of the wilderness, as if they'd just emerged from some fantastic painting, a landscape so strange and lush that I had to blink twice, unconvinced it was a dream.

"Most of the owners gave up on the *Tidal Flower* and had already headed home," Sycamore said, as he watched the proceedings take place. "But that crafty Ned Reed got his sail turned round on the water and brought 'em all back in. He'll drive the auction, and come away winning, you watch."

The growing assembly included a variety of homespun shirts, still damp with sweat as if they'd only left off from their plowing. Others sported fine Spanish boots, and smelled of perfume and powder. But of everything new, and all that appeared, most joyous was my seeing how easy they mingled. The fancy men were trading rude jokes, and loud sharp complaints along with those that looked merely common. The effect that it created in me was one of losing my old sense of balance. Once I had to stop I was so completely transfixed by a man in frock sleeves pounding the back of a field hand. Bits of food were readily freed from the laborer's beard, but by then they were both bent over laughing. In all, I was triumphantly returned to my New World rapture.

Until, that is the first of *Tidal Flower's* servants were pushed on the front of the stage. I sought to recognize some of the faces, but the gauntness with which I was familiar had been altered by a scratched on type of rouge and plastered down hairpieces that made them look frighteningly hideous. It was obvious that Jarvis was starting the auction with his prime and his most healthy, but their far away looks and painted on lips gave an impression of horror. The effort to pretty up his merchandise only had them looking like a group of depraved dandies recently retrieved from their coffins. The Sargeant at Arms, who also served as the muscular auctioneer, gave Jarvis a baleful look before he even got started, but then on calling the first man in line, he quickly got down to his business. The poor man for sale however seemed to struggle with confusion, and when not showing teeth promptly enough the Sargent pried them open. Strapped to the Sargeant's practiced hands were a bludgeon and a whip.

"One Samuel Acton," he yelled, pulling at the grimacing Acton. "A hundred weight ten, at two meals a day, and knows a little about cooping." The last bit of fact, he got from a list from which he was referring. "Who'll start us off at twenty?"

"Twenty?!"

Before another word, or any sort of offer, a robust older man had leapt from the crowd and put himself up onstage. He then locked Acton's arms behind his back with a smothering embrace while giving the startled man a sound shaking. "He's got no strength to build on!" the elder man exclaimed. "Won't make it past his first winter." He finished off by lifting Acton up at the elbows and sweeping him about in a circle. "Nothing to him!" he yelled, "nothing at all!"

The Sargeant became cautious but made no move to intercept the old man. In fact, he was even retreating. Then having regained himself on his feet, Acton took a quick step back and smashed his fist to the old man's head. The old man sprawled full out on the floor. "Strap him, strap the bastard!" the crowd began shouting at once, to which the Sargeant at Arms, as if waiting on the crowd's authority, obligingly responded.

Captain Jarvis, now upon the scene, quickly jumped behind to stay the Sargeant's hand.

"Off my property!" Jarvis shouted, "I'll see that he pays."

"Throw him in the stocks without water!" yelled one in the crowd. "He'll learn what he is in the heat of two days!"

"Well, enough," the Sargeant replied, catching his breath. And then presumed to calm things a bit by pointing at the crowd with his whip, "But there's more for my commission on any more disorder!"

Then just as the Sargeant and Jarvis were poised for a serious row the old gent was back on his feet, pushing himself between the quarrel. He tore at the cuff of Acton's frayed blouse, revealing the brand of a convict. "A mere felon to boot!" cried the old man. "What are you thinking Mr. Jarvis? Twenty pounds for a half-starved miscreant that you've only brought over to steal?! Or is it *murder* on yer mind!?"

"Flog him!" Someone shouted with glee. "Perform your subject duty!"

Just as suddenly, as if stricken by a change of heart, the old man then took a turn at soliciting the audience. He called for anyone willing to take the troubled man. No one showed any interest, but there were a number of loud titters to show his performance was clearly enjoyed. "He's got spunk though," the old man admitted as he pinched and prodded poor Acton about his legs. For his part Acton showed only his hostile restraint, but the fact that Jarvis had roped his arms about his waist greatly influenced the matter. The old man grabbed at Acton's backside and said, "I'll give you twelve with no more comment."

"Done," replied Jarvis with a tone of regret. He seemed anxious to move past the incident lest it sully what he expected to glean from the rest of the afternoon. "But if I get a hint of collusion here," he said eyeing the Sargeant, "I will have my price."

"Second!" The Sargeant at Arms cried without pause, and pulled the next man from the line. "Here is one Steven Friar," he called from his list. "Let me present a simple man proven to work without favor."

He then gave a warning glance at the irritated Jarvis, as the guards escorted Acton off the stage. The crowd apparently satisfied that a fair transaction had been treated, settled back to see how the pricing would run, or what further entertainments that the auction held in store.

"That old dog, Reed is the fox of all counties," Sycamore laughed. "He just got himself a forty pound man, and just that easy."

I could not say that I completely understood, or if I could that it would matter, for what I'd seen on this my first half-day upon the soil of Virginia could only make sense to one of *them*, which as yet, I was clearly not. "My room?" I braved the question. "I think that I should like to lie down."

"Of course," Sycamore smiled, "of course."

Further on behind the platform I passed the greater mass of new immigrants sequestered in a holding pen. Jarvis had set his crew and a few of the militia to the work of further cleaning, while he managed the rotation of wigs. I took a minute to watch as he gingerly transferred one ragged hairpiece from a man that had just been bought onto a prospect about to be bargained for. Then in the midst of this sadly powdered herd, I spied the girl my bunkmate had taken as a hostage. I felt drawn to her, astonished in the naked glare by the starkness of her frame. The hours I had stolen, teaching her some letters suddenly came back to me as reckless, and even cruel. She looked back at me in silence, her eyes vacantly dim, covering her terror, and I all I could think to do was place Sycamore's shilling into her dirty fist.

"She'll be alright," Sycamore said bluntly, turning me

round by my elbow, "All a girl needs is wits enough to get married. If she survives the next year, the womanly sacrifice can even bring her wealth. The colony is greedy for white females, no matter what their station. As a matter of fact, in respect to white females," he added as if becoming more peeved, "you will find us very indulgent."

As unsure I was of his meaning, I was simply too tired to give it much thought. He then led me around the outer walls and into a small encampment at the border of the woods. "This is what you will call home," he said when we reached the second tent. "In a short time I am sure that a young man of your ambition will procure a proper room. But for now your duty is to the colony, which houses you at its own expense."

I looked at my molding quarters too dazed to make comment. I had the feeling though, that my giving away the gift of his coin had brought on this chill to his regard. I pointed to a shallow trench filled with tar stained wood that was lined all around the tent.

"What is this for?" I ventured.

"You'll want to make sure to keep your supply of coated wood well stocked," he said, looking out at the dusky sky. "For the summer months, be doubly sure. As a matter of fact, you would do well to set your fires just now, as you see we're coming on twilight. So," he added quickly, and nervously started to pace. And all while watching out behind me at the air. "You'll have a foreman, named Jakes who'll be round first thing in the morning. He's hard, but he's fair. He breakfasts at four, and you wouldn't want to keep him waiting. Again, my welcome and good luck to you, young Philip Corstair."

Then he walked away, brisker than a stranger, with his sudden formality compounding the fact that I was the only one occupying the camp. I was not however afforded the luxury of working my loneliness into despair, for a flying army of insects suddenly arose so thick about my face that I could hardly breathe. No sooner had Sycamore gone than they covered my arms and neck in a high buzzing shrill that seemed designed to drive one mad. They were miniscule in size and in seconds had entered my eyes, nose and ears. I rolled over and over, slapping at my face and the air, and soon became crazed enough to start digging myself in the ground. I then crawled into the tent looking to wrap it around me like a blanket, but a hundred more were stuck beneath my clothes and to my skin. Relentlessly they pierced, needling, and torturing, taking delight in my private most places. Then I spotted a tinderbox of flints left out on the tarpen floor, and in a near panic I connected it to the ditch of treated wood. I jumped for the trench and set a shaky fire, my hands swelling beyond recognition, trying hard to make my fingers work. Spreading the flames around me, I laid low to the ground for as long as I could manage, gasping at the level of the smoke. The horde that attacked me soon held back a distance, though kept their high-pitched presence for several hours more. The greatest insight in to this torment was learning that the oily ash could relieve my constant itch.

Sheer exhaustion then came on me, as though fighting to control my body through a sleep full of fits and starts. The jumping up to check the fire, the questioning of where I was, the staring out blank and lost. I was as frightened as I had ever been. The wood filled up with an ongoing chorus, from creatures shrill and harsh. The biting chirps, the hoots and shrieks, the deceptive, lurking sighs. A coo that turned into a caterwaul.

"What sort of place," I finally asked aloud to God, or whatever was there to hear my call. "Could be so alive and wild? And how could anyone be other than a stranger?"

It was well before sunrise when I ran to meet Mr. Jakes. I'd spent an endless night marking minutes into hours and seconds into minutes, until finally, I could no longer wait for day. Fortunately, the blue-black dawn cloaked the embarrassment in my face, when without a word of introduction, the first thing that Jakes did was to point toward my very own tool bag. In the flurry surrounding our landing, I had quite forgotten about it, but with thanks to some unknown stranger it now sat before me stowed in the shed.

"Number one is this," Jakes scolded. "You lose something in here, and you'll be making its replacement on the sweet little time that you can call your own. Providing of course, the smithy lets you in his shop."

He was a barrel-chested man with a large head and pug nose that looked both stern and jolly. It was not a face that initiated fear, but I could see that he was not to be trifled with either.

"Yes sir," I replied, but admittedly I only saw the man that stood behind him. I remembered him from a night on the ship shortly after we'd gotten underway. He was caught above deck lying as peaceful as you please in one of the rowboats, doing nothing but staring at the sky full of stars. He was punished quite severely, as an early example of what could be expected for those who broke the rules, but after receiving his beating he looked right at me and whispered, "It was worth it." Then he winked, and was hoisted back down the hold inside of a taut net. He was smiling at me now, and as the lamplight struck his open face, I felt a surge of human comfort, a touch of which I'd hungered, and yet not even known. We fell in together behind Jakes, who then made a dutiful tour of every utensil that he kept like a mother hen unto its own.

"You can shelve your things along here," he said holding a candle up to a partition on the wall. "They'll be yours to redeem once your duty is served. The man working with you here's called Bill Forsythe," he said to me while turning to my old, new friend. "In case you noticed, by his lack of totin' tools, that he's just a common convict. My name's Jakes, and take heed, I'll miss the loss of one stolen nail."

This he stated without emphasis, and took a quick breath before laying into the rest of his speech.

"I can go along with anyone that's willing to better himself. Ask anyone. And I've always had an interest to help a man that's new. You can ask anyone about that too. Our strength is the support of our community. Something no less, an' no more than the way it is. It's the way you have to be out here. Ask anyone, an' you'll see that you're both being treated fairly. And once your service is done, if you've proved that you've been honest, you'll always be free to borrow what you need."

The first morning light came seeping through a crack in the wall, and he lifted his eyebrow as he caught me scratching my armpits. He straightway craned me forward at the neck, checked my welted skin, and the ravage done by my night with the bugs. "Here, take this," he said, lifting a jar of foul smelling ointment from a closet above his head. The odor was so strong that I could not imagine its use.

"What is it?" I asked.

"Bear fat," he replied. "The place you work today is hell for the little mites. Smear it on your skin just like the Indians. You'll stink like a heathen savage, but you'll be thanking them for it by the end of the day."

The putrid paste was so revolting that it took my breath away. I forcefully held back my stomach, gasped in a quick spurt of air, then shoved the jar shut in my pants. Then, in the early grayish light, we strapped on the hatchets and handsaws, shouldered the two-man team whip, and the three of us walked through the woods in stone silence. When we reached a thick stand of beech, and fir several miles in the peninsula, Jakes left me with Bill Forsythe, a packet of smoked eels in a rolled loaf of oats, and two canteens of water.

After letting us know that he expected the thickest trees in a four-acre square to be ready for use in a month, Jakes hiked back out for the settlement. Feeling a little overwhelmed and more than a little lost, what followed next struck me as even more peculiar.

Bill Forsythe appeared to be amiable enough, but he was still very much a stranger. And when a full ten minutes passed with no more sound between us than the drone of waking bees, I started to make nervous noises. He was sitting very calm on a tuft of brown needles, arms folded and eyes closed, evidently refusing to speak, refusing it seemed, to move a single muscle. Confused, I spoke aloud, calling out my intentions, and picked out a hatchet with the best fitting handle. I was thinking that he was about some kind of protest, a mutiny to which I wanted no part, and so I gave him a respectful nod and started clearing out the bottom of a healthy twenty-footer. No sooner had I delivered the first lick, than I felt a strong tug upon my shirt. I turned to see Forsythe with his knees dug in the turf, holding to his lips an upright finger. With his other hand, he pointed to a narrow hole beneath a nearby birch. I stared in this direction, growing more uneasy with his silence, and honestly trying to make out if he was daft. Finally, convinced there was nothing to see I, turned back to my work only to have him twist me round again. Then a mother red fox, of a size I'd have never believed, scurried from the hole beneath the tree. She had a pair of newborn cubs caught gently in her teeth.

"Let's give 'em the proper time to relocate," whispered Forsythe. "After all, it is *their* home."

Thus, was I truly introduced to Bill Forsythe.

He was a full ten years my senior, yet smaller in stature than my evolving growth, and yet he had five times the strength that I could ever muster. And too, as I was quick to learn, his diminutive proportions entirely disguised what he held in his heart. In that often strange and timeless harsh wood, he partnered and carried me dawn to dusk days that without him would surely have broken my back. But Bill put rhythm to our step, the slide of a saw, and the swing of an ax so they seemed to come light and alive. As days and weeks passed, when my body turned hard and my hands into leather, I sometimes stopped to catch my breath, and Forsythe would still be about his singing. He went through every hymn and bawdy tune he knew, and when he finished up with those, he made them up on the spot. And in that season while we were together, Jakes never had to threaten us with discipline, not a single once, nor was he forced to toil with us, in order to keep his quota.

More remarkable still was the fact that Bill would take out twenty minutes for something wondrous that he'd spied. I quickly learned that if he took a turn at fascination, smack in the midst of work of any type, then it was I who must quit and go to join him. He'd fix my eyes on a phosphorescent butterfly that floated aloft a warm breeze holding a tree snake mesmerized. Or have me listen to a calling dove that was hidden under brush, with a sound so deep in its throat that it was heard only by pinning my ear to the earth. He was of course, the first to paint his skin with the rancid salve, just as a festering swarm of black flies threatened to make us their dinner. "And you'd better come on too," he said, stuffing his nose with a piece of bark. "That way we'll both have the stink, and none will be the wiser." The best and worst of it being that it worked.

And throughout the whole of those hard days, Bill taught me more than survival. He opened up worlds, both outside and in, that revealed what was ancient and new. Forcing me, through the magic of his words, to examine what I always overlooked. He handed me gifts that were right before my eyes, but only that he could pluck from hiding.

Our camaraderie did not escape the notice of Foreman Jakes, who counted, at the very least on its production. So early on, in a joking nod to New World justice, he quietly arranged that the felon Forsythe, be remanded to my supervision. Thus, within the first weeks of that remarkable summer, Bill was released from his pit in the jail, and I was made ward to my very own master.

Later on, I'm proud to say, I got so used to falling asleep under nights filled with stars that I felt more at home in a tent than under roofs where we worked to make some notable's house a bit more comfortable. Still, green that I was, I was not made to be foolish. I knew that later in the fall with its serious drop in the temperature, I'd have to find me a properly heated room. Until then though, the long yellow days of summer shone brightly all around us, and actually *living* in the city that we were shoring up, was without attraction. Throughout those warm months Bill taught me the stars, and a dead to rights song of the bullfrog, and more natural philosophy than was in all of the books in Cambridge. He taught me how to hunt, the patience required for stalking a deer and how to avoid a boar pack approaching. Many a night was taken up in learning to give a voice to my thoughts, and in listening to his parable ways of speaking. To be sure, I was often perplexed at how a man so learned and right, had come to this wild land as a prisoner, but the mystery of Bill Forsythe, Bill Forsythe, the felon, was a part of him that I never questioned.

Then, "So, what did you do?" slipped out one day, as I pointed thoughtlessly at his brand.

It was mid July, and we had just re-dug our run-off trench under the threat of distant thunder. The night was rolling out a blanket of thick clouds, unusual in an air so cool and the wick from our lamp just happened to highlight Bill's scarring. Outside of this, it was so dark that I could barely see my shovel. Then, the sky above us, blacker than a cave in the ocean exploded like an electrical terror. Deafening cracks followed all round 'til they were coming right for us, and lighting their advance in brilliant flashes. I had been shocked by such a storm once before, on a return from collecting stray sheep, but then I felt protected by the forest. Even so, my only response at the time was to shake to my knees, and offer up prayers in a flurry. But Bill had kept looking out above the trees as if he wanted to greet the fearful rumble. "Six miles off," he said very calm. "No need to worry less she changes her direction. The wind's heading strong to the west."

"I love the rain," he said to me now, once we'd got inside the tent. "No bugs." And then he smiled. "Murder."

His quiet confession, so at one and at odds with the full gathered storm, took the question away from me without force.

"I was tutoring a young man in Kent when I fell in love with my patron's wife. He caught us in the act of fornication, naked as the day of my birth, I was forced to defend my life."

I felt a great discomfort and immediately regretted my prying, but Bill was unperturbed. In fact, he related his crime of the ultimate passion with a scholarly resolve. I'd seen him more animated describing the traffic of ants.

"My lover was able to save my life by the gift of three hundred pounds payable to a certain magistrate's in-law. As well as a percentage against any future I procured in

Virginia."

I diverted my nerves by attempting to secure the door flap, and then reached to siphon water that was welling in the trench.

"It's just as well," he said lightly, "their son was a terrible student."

"I cannot believe it…" I blubbered awkwardly, unable to return his look. "You…?" I felt like a complete fool, but Bill was suddenly serious.

"Ask questions Philip Corstair, never be afraid to ask questions! This is the New World that you've entered, and you must never stop learning. Promise me that. A man that does not share what little knowledge he has, is a man that is not worth knowing. Excluding the knowledge of his wife, I mean."

Cutting the mood with his lyrical laugh, he commenced with a rowdy crude song. Then, a strong gust of wind rushed up at us broadside, and fully collapsed the tent. We laughed ourselves silly trying to gather the rippling canvas up under the powerful storm. It took us a thorough soaking before we could get it restored, and then just like that the night just miraculously cleared. Not even on the ocean had I seen a sky so dense with stars.

"But look at this," Bill sighed after awhile. We had retrieved a dry towel, and he was carefully wiping down his musket. "A confirmed killer who's been given a gun to go on a hunt for the government. There are times, young Corstair when a man cannot make up his fate."

Plainly spoke I loved Bill Forsythe, and God knows the amount of labor we provided this new country was enough for a team three times our size. In a considerable short time, the number of improvements we accomplished included the construction of a stable, (horses were a coming thing) and the widening of the barrel roads. We refitted the old tower at the top of Jamestown church, and with no cooperation built an office for the taxman under hostile frontier glares.

The volume of the work, and fulfilling the quotas, left us little room for leisure, but there's happiness to be found in something you've built up that turns out sound and useful. There's happiness in breathing forest air. And the spearing of fish in whitewater streams, and fresh oysters opened on carpets of green. There is happiness too, in listening to the free howling wolves under a full white moon.

But as the autumn of that year slowly turned its way to winter and the ground grew hard beneath our tent, I developed a spreading fever that started as a trifling in my chest. We combined any number of prescriptions, but Bill could neither sweat it out nor steam it free. He became obsessed with homemade recipes, of cherry root, hot sumac, and hemp. He laid into learning what he could of native plants and therapeutics, while fiercely objecting to "the bleeding European cure." Not that he was inept at the technique used by barbers, but because he condemned the "whole bloody thing."

"There is no such jumbo as a body with its humors," he said with defensive authority. "We are of a whole or not at all. Taking a man's blood will only further weaken him. You don't have to stab a man to death to figure that."

But when the world outside would no longer stop its downward spinning, I knew I'd have to ask Madame Porter for her help. If I could sleep for awhile in the extra space she used for a new ship's stock, I'd promise her my handiwork and keep from the sight of her guests. And so I spent four tormented days, wrestling with the secret scheme of abandoning our winter camp; while knowing I was abandoning my one true friend. But on each of these nights the weather dropped a little colder, so that all I could think of was Madame Porter's oven in the end.

The week that I got sick, Bill and I had just completed the expansion of her upstairs lodging by the addition of two rooms, private and well lit, to meet with the requirements of her new client list. But I also counted on her gratitude for her new tavern floor, which was a job I'd done on my own.

"That's about as fine a deal in renovation as one can expect from our fair minded Labor Commission," Bill winked at me when the floor was done. The joke between us was how much we improved the lot of individual citizens without our claiming one copper cent. But I sensed something vague in his demeanor that masked something more in what he meant. And what hit harder than the hacking cough tearing at my chest was the suffering of having to let him down, after giving me so much. Simply stated if I was to survive then I must find heat and rest, but I also knew that no such space was given to convicted felons, and further, by law could not even exist. The fact was that Bill Forsythe would die in jail before permitted to share a roof with a gentleman. The idea of his having a room to winter in beyond the confines of his prison would require nothing less than a miracle of grace. When the time came and Bill was no longer consigned to my 'official' custody, he would be returned to languish for the winter inside his frozen pit.

Then, on the last afternoon I could speak about these things, Bill did not return. Foreman Jakes appeared at the tent, and reading from a legal script, stated that the felon Bill Forsythe had already been removed. Without a further word on the subject, he helped me pack up my belongings, and thus I spent my first disconsolate night, sipping Madame Porter's broth inside her heated kitchen.

Early the next morning, renewed in strength but conflicted by guilt, I was surprised to see Bill at the work site. He looked woefully deprived of sleep, but he greeted me with patent cheer, and no outward sign of resentment. Nor was it an indifference that I felt, at least not directed at me, but there was *something*. A fleeting bite in his voice perhaps, or a distance in his manner, all which he quickly covered once we'd set to our assignment. Soon enough though, I began to feel a play-acting chasm had risen up. It was surrounded by awkward silence and I hadn't a clue as to how it might be broached. "Directly," Bill would have barked, and I would have, I suppose, had I a guilt free conscience.

We were just outside of town, past the broad and commons, closing a latrine that the early winter rains had been overflowing. I happened to glance above the thawing muck, and there was Sycamore Stevens standing beside the gentleman Staunt. It was the first time that I had seen him in more than a month, which was a notable occurrence in the tiny circumference of Jamestown. I'd heard from Madame Porter that he'd taken up with speculating, and together with Mr. Staunt were scavenging the marginal farms.

I nodded to be civil, but the more I learned of Sycamore Stevens, the more he provoked my feelings of distrust. Certain phrases that he dropped, such as "No doubt about a father in a station like yours ever coming abroad." Or, "Not much dowry in his daughters I suppose." Or, "There's a lot that you'll be needing to get settled on your own."

All said in a tone that left me with distinct unease. At the last comment he even rubbed his fingers in a mimic of counting money. Early on, when I mentioned that I might receive a small reserve from my father, he gave me a paper to sign, saying that all outside investment required a registry. I couldn't for the life of me understand what he was getting at, but Bill suggested that my father or Henry Salt might have even sent me funds already. Money, he quickly added, that Sycamore Stevens held back undisclosed. But unwilling to make accusations with no proof, I kept my suspicions to myself, and then, as the summer season bloomed, was glad to forget about Sycamore Stevens.

"Well, look what comes from keeping shit for company," Sycamore said in a light joking voice. He pinched Mr. Staunt, who was in turn pinching a perfumed handkerchief to his nose. It was obvious that he was only fooling, his tone was so harmless and self-effacing that he could have been talking about himself, but a complete and sudden rage took hold of Bill Forsythe. He leapt from the hole where we were standing, and flung a shovel full of waste into their faces. Before I even realized what was happening, he buckled their knees with a powerful blow and threw them together beside me in the pit. He then struck the backs of their heads, and dropped them dazed or unconscious, with their mouths hanging open like muted nesting birds. Quickly rifling through their purses, he extracted a handful of gold coins and a box full of snuff. "Hardly worth the Indian trade," he laughed, "a Spaniard maybe, but who knows?" He laughed again, a strange and shallow sound that never got out of his throat.

"Holy Jesus Bill," was all that I could offer, suddenly perturbed at the men coming over in the first place. Then, as a reflex to self-preservation, I shifted about, to look for any witnesses. I had no idea what Bill was up to, but I did not want to be seen as a partner to his crime. In the time it took for me to turn full back around, Sycamore and Staunt were stirring in the filth beside me, and Bill Forsythe was gone. I hoisted the two men up over the edge, and strained my eyes at the opposite line of trees. There was not a swaying branch, or a flash of woolen coat. Bill Forsythe had disappeared into the bush.

When they regained their wits, Sycamore made a grab for my arms, while Staunt surveyed the shit that was slapped upon his clothes. "Wipe it off!" he screamed at me, cuffing my face with his sleeve. But even if I'd chosen to, with Sycamore holding my arms tight behind me, I could do nothing for the moment at least. He then slapped me full on the cheek and rubbed the residue from his hands into my nose. He removed the contents of my pockets, consisting of a fishhook I had quite forgotten, an extra workman's glove and a bent pewter spoon. Sycamore behaved like the hook was a weapon and tightened his grip to a clinch. Mr. Staunt kept digging, frustrating himself with my pockets, and being only happy when he'd torn them all apart. He then turned his head back towards the woods, moving it slowly in half circles as if to picture Bill's route of escape. But the pungent ground before him held nothing but cold sludge, and his smeared and perfumed handkerchief surrendered to the mud.

"I understand that the felon Bill Forsythe was under your supervision," he stated, suddenly, and unnaturally calm.

"That is not true, sir," I replied. I was determined to keep my head. "Our camp was broke apart on yesterday evening. And Bill Forsythe was returned to his cell."

"Which is where you'll be staying," Sycamore snapped, "until we have your knowledge of his whereabouts. I expect no small amount of justice for your complicity in what's happened here."

By then it was clear that Sycamore the clerk, and not the gentleman Staunt, was pressing the need to make a change of clothes. For Staunt slowly studied the surrounding wood for another long time, as if he were taking this common felon's measure against his own.

"If you please, Mr. Staunt…" Sycamore sputtered.

"Shut up!" Staunt screamed back. "You and your devices! Have you any more facility than a worm!? Not another word!" And then he held back, almost forcing himself to hold his breath.

As the minutes became frozen, Sycamore slowly loosened his grip, and we stood clumsily together watching Mr. Staunt walk twice to the edge of the woods and back, as if Bill was only hiding out like some small child. Then, after stretching these moments out in torture he led us back through the Jamestown streets like a marshal at the head of a parade.

I saw a few idlers step out from the tavern to offer us whimsical stares, but more curious was our finding that the jailhouse was empty and the sheriff's office abandoned. The lack of authority to officiate an arrest however did not prevent Mr. Staunt from locking me beneath the bolted hatch in the floor. I could see at once why Bill had chosen to run. The hole had only room to crouch and was colder than a tomb. Even after many minutes, my eyes hardly sensed any light, and I had to use my ears to keep away from the scuttling of rats, hissing over their crumbs. Slowly then, by using my hands, I began to take an inventory of what Bill had left behind. A chamber pot, a cracked clay cup, and a wooden bowl. Things that could prove very useful to a man in the woods on the lamb, and other items too, like the mystery of why he'd left a fine boned comb. Then in a corner, pungent with dry piss, I dug up a page he had torn from his diary. It was bound with a flint and a candle nub, and tied to a heavy bolt key.

"My dear Corstair," I read. "Forgive me for inflicting this inconvenience, but I am afraid it is the best that I can do. I have borrowed a musket, a pair of hunting knives and a supply of powder from the magazine outside the sheriff's office. And you'll have to make do for the short term of your stay without the prison blanket. You should return the key to Sheriff Wyland with my regards, and proffer this note as a testament to your innocence. I am sorry to have involved you with this pair of local thieves, but the time will come when they and others like them will have their reckoning. Virginia is a land that has set upon a course of collision, and make sure that you count your friends carefully when that day comes. Forgive me most for my having brought us to this end. You are a good man. An honor to know. And God willing we will meet again, if only at my gallows tree. Keep your faith in yourself full alive. Bill."

Stunned and terribly sad, I squatted, running the comb

through my hair, as if to make a connection through the memento he had left behind. A gift he'd purposely forsaken, as a symbol I suppose, of his becoming wild. Then, just before I came to grief, Sheriff Wyland threw open the hatch, and called me to face the offended parties. I had to wince in the sudden light, while Staunt and Sycamore, freshly washed and refurbished, stood apart, ready to extract full justice. But Foreman Jakes had also been summoned, precipitately on Sheriff Wyland's part, and I received no small amount of comfort in the way that he was planted between the accusers and myself.

"The boy had no part in the actions of the convict," he stated before anyone spoke.

Sheriff Wyland was an older man, said to have come to Virginia by making his own kind of escape. As a constable in Bristol he had lost control of his township over Puritan hysteria that had turned neighbors into vengeful mobs. Reportedly, when he'd had his fill of sniffing out witches, and conducting phantom gossip trials, he found a home in Berkeley's no nonsense Virginia. The governor, as everyone knew was unashamedly pro Charles. His down to earth nature let me feel somewhat assured that he would not weigh my guilt with association, but I was plenty wary about how the law favored a man like John Staunt.

Jakes started vouching for me in a surprising disregard of Staunt, so that he fairly took control of the floor. Sheriff Wyland simply nodded and waited to hear my own account, clearly more concerned with the whereabouts of the fugitive than of anything else. I showed him Bill's note, which he carefully read aloud, but when I produced the key to his armory, his jowls drew back tight in a rage.

"Right then," he fumed, wheeling everyone about. "Mr. Jakes post your reward, and help me gather the militia. We'll be leaving right away."

"What about this!" Sycamore argued tearing the note

right out from Wyland's hand. "He's accusing me of thievery! Our purses in his grubby hands, and yet he states it plain!"

Mr. Staunt then took the paper to give it his careful view, while Jakes took the chance to push me towards the door.

"Well!?" Sycamore screamed. He started stomping on the floor.

"An interesting prophecy," Staunt said, when he had read enough. "S-s-o cryptic." This, he hissed to himself, and then at me. "Now tell me, what does it mean?"

"I do not know," I replied. Which was perfectly true.

"Don't lie to me, boy!" He tried slapping me again, but Jakes caught hold of his hand. I'd never known a face could turn so purple-red.

"I suppose we'll have to catch him first before there's more to say on that, Mr. Staunt," Sheriff Wyland had lost his patience. The two men for my part had formed an unwitting alliance, but still they were standing Staunt down. "Now, do you wish to aid in that effort or not?"

"Oh, I'll find him, sheriff," Staunt replied, suddenly going softly strange. "With or without the help of your militia."

"What about this?!" Sycamore insisted, grabbing for the paper again. "My reputation at stake!"

And all then pushed past him out the door.

* * * * *

I can now say beyond any doubt that the arrogant Staunt never caught up with my good friend, the dear Bill Forsythe. Nor did Foreman Jakes, nor Sheriff Wyland, nor any of the town's militia. Bill Forsythe disappeared into that forbidding country as if it were his home. He could have drifted into death from harsh exposure, or else been murdered by someone that he'd come to trust. He could just as well have found a tribe of his own to lead and become a great Indian chief.

Many years later I would find myself smiling, half-sad and hopeful, whenever I heard tales of the 'White wild man of the woods.' In the forest he roamed, madder than a frothy toad, given to unspeakable horror. He was even said to like the taste of human flesh. But I only spoke of the real Bill Forsythe. Fond and with wistful respect. The others I tried only when I was too tired, when little ones of my own wandered too far, or refused to take their rest.

"Kitasimin? Kitasimin a'hkosi kitasimin,"
says the man who occasionally comes
for a visit. After politely announcing
himself thus, he bows and sits in the lip of our cave. He has
the body of an eighty-year old, and yet his face and manner
are very childlike. His name is Tintipon, and he is completely
blind. When I asked Seycondeh about him she told me he was
an important medicine man many years ago, but that he'd
lost his powers to a younger man who was rich enough to
freely give out gifts. Tintipon was then reduced to traversing
the distances between various clans in order to beg for food.
Evidently whenever one grew weary of his company, he simply
moved on to the next.

But I am forced to wonder just how much of his power
that he's truly lost by accomplishing these feats. Navigating
this rough terrain is no small task for anyone, and yet the old
man carries it off while being stone blind. Not that I fully
understand Seycondeh's answer. She tried to explain that he
found his way about by listening to the owls, I think. Or maybe
it is clouds. But however confusing the matter is to me, it is
enough to serve him quite well.

I will say that I've grown rather fond of his company,
and the songs that he sings have a comforting effect upon Mr.
Lawrence. They even sing together, finishing up on a single
note, straining to find a kind of harmony, and then sit in the
silent manner of two old men lamenting their disappointments.
And foolish as it may be, I have grown to feel protected in

Tintipon's presence. In the place of any real information regarding Mr. Lawrence's and my future, Tintipon has become our adopted guardian spirit. As long as he is allowed to visit, we can at least lay a stake upon seeing another day.

I hint and hope that Seycondeh will bring us news about our fate, but she ignores my queries claiming that it is of no concern to her. *I* am concerned however, and grow more so every day. The beaver is still plentiful here, and I have spotted men in the valley below hauling travois sleds overflowing with carcass. When I pointed this out to her, trying to learn if they were trading with the English or the French, I was treated to a forty-five minute tirade on the subject of her cousin's husband.

"Wi'kima'kan wi'kim, ne no'tin, ni'ki tahw ata' wa'kan! Mihce't amiskwak mihko! Mihce't, mihce't amiskwak mihko!" she ranted. "Iskwe'wiw, ni'ki iskwe..."

Her complaint is about her cousin, a soft-spoken woman who is regularly beaten for not providing her husband with his meals. But her negligence is the direct result of all her time being taken up in the preparation of his pelts. The bright new pot that the white traders gave her, Seycondeh says, was only to be used in the cleaning of his furs. Besides which, her house is nothing but a stinking bloody mess. And if the beaver guts invite the dogs and vermin, her husband only beats her again.

"Ne ni'ki iskwe," Seycondeh grumbled, ladling out our broth.

I've been forming the impression that Seycondeh, who has the rare status of an unattached woman, has no use for men. Why she should devote herself to a couple of weak members of the breed, and what's more, who are white, representing at least one cause for her people's strife, is a mystery that I cannot fathom. But I am most troubled by her cousin's cooking pot. Whether it is English made or French, it means that her village has its European ties.

Mr. Lawrence looks up from one of his black robe blessings and happily sips his soup. (For reasons that I'm also not aware of, he's been reciting Latin for the past few days.) In return I offer him an encouraging smile. At the time of our escape, the governor was restoring the peace that we had broken with a very free hand on the hangman's rope. And now, watching Mr. Lawrence with his childlike eagerness to please, I think about what he is incapable of reckoning. That any tribal chief wishing to secure the governor's favor could negotiate a pretty good price for the delivery of our heads. It is in this grim spirit then that I must hasten on with my tale.

* * * * *

When I finished my indenture to the colony, I was granted a fifty-acre plot south of the James in Henricus. It had no access to the river from which to launch my harvests, but with a Herculean effort I scratched a rough passage in the form of a sunken log road. Entering the books as Philip Corstair; landowner, was a heady experience for a nineteen-year old, all alone in this teeming wild world, let me tell you. But an attentive apprenticeship taught me much about the lay of this new land, and my service as a lowly Jamestown bondsman was not without advantage. Watching one of the duty officers receive an African girl in the form of a bribe for instance, or learning that a certain wealthy planter had returned from abroad with a case of French pox, was not the kind of knowledge that I gleaned from Bill Forsythe, but it was useful information in an ordinary way. In fact there was no telling what one could witness while replacing the eaves on a piece of thatch roof, or framing up the door to an outhouse. But I made a point of keeping whatever I witnessed most discreet, so when my years were finally done I had a head full of clutter, some of it of value, and all of it unique.

A year later I felt nothing less than awe at the gathering of a crop from my very own ground. Ground from which I inexpertly teased out a portion of Henry Salt's tobacco and an acre each of corn and squash and beans. Admittedly, my first go at farming did not amount to much, unless you count potatoes that flourish just as well on their own, but I must have passed an hour simply staring at those bushels. With swelling eyes I looked upon my future, flowing with exhaustion at the goodness of the land. Then, on the day that I finished laying out the floorboards to a cabin by the pond, I shocked myself by muttering out loud that I needed to find a wife. It was an Indian summer of 1655, and I was entering the prime of my New World life.

Helen McGrath was three years my younger, and as strong in reading numbers as she was in common sense. By this means she escaped the lot of an early forced marriage, and landed a job copying records in the Office of Credit and Trade. The timing of her appointment coincided with the fact that Donald Hartly, who'd held the post quite firmly, was old and had taken ill. The position was supposed to be filled by a man of course, but necessity conspired, as was often the case in colonial affairs, and there was simply no one else to take the post.

Still, what Helen accorded as her marvelous good fortune, was a target of ridicule from the proper Jamestown wives. I saw it so myself, in fact. And the very men with whom she worked inside the office declined to recognize her on the streets out in the light. But Helen had that boldness of spirit, and resourcefulness of temper that could bend the most contrary of minds to get her way. And I can frankly say that she commanded all of my notice at a half-hour before noon on June the 4th 1654, when she stepped from the skiff of the *Clarisse Kissed*. The name of the ship, which I took to be an omen had brought me the unknowing lass that I knew must be my wife.

A month into her employment I was able to convince the head clerk that he could do with a new trunk for his filing, and I drew out the time of installation for just as long as I could. As I fretted on how to make Helen aware of my attentions, catching her rich auburn hair spill down on one of her ledgers could send me into an aching shock. Not to mention her scent amongst the inks and precious papers carried out to me from clear across the room. After a spell of a week of this or so, I got the nerve to ask her where she learned her numbers. She smiled at me, a knowing smile that easily saw what I wanted, saying, "It isn't such a difficult game to play. I shifted my own age on papers to get a place aboard ship." And she had me completely ensnared.

At the time I was preparing for the end of my service with my head being spun by a dozen new turns. I had to sort out the necessities, those that I could purchase from those that I could borrow, against nothing less than a lien upon my deed. So in all it was an inopportune moment to pitch woo. But nature had called, and I was pressed to answer, and Helen had me feeling like I was a gentleman guest.

The position that I took when I talked it over with myself was that we were New World orphans, Helen and myself, and therefore free of parents who'd be quibbling over assets. A fact, which carried the obvious fault of my having little more than debt to contest, but I discounted this detail by my newly gained status as freedman. Anyway, and in spite of my deficiencies, she allowed me her company at several social events. There were two services, standing and kneeling together at church, an exciting afternoon of horse racing (on the governor's plantation no less) and a picnic by the river, with just the two of us alone. I remember this momentous day, as being nearly crippled by my awkwardness, but of somehow stumbling through. We mainly spoke of individual hopes, the determination to make this land our home, and agreeing that what we'd left in England could not compare to our future lights. She surprised me with her candor, and startled me with the tales of corruption that she, with her own eyes had already seen. "Oh, the impossible greed of it," she said, referring to men like Sycamore and Staunt, and their expanding array of land grabbing schemes.

"Those two cadgers have managed to issue notes on titles set aside for rights not even assigned," Helen stated disgustedly. "The slimy eels have set up a company that protects their holding on a parce until it's 'sufficiently' populated. Then they bid up the price 'til some poor slacker's selling just to pay his debt. And the governor's no better," she went on, astounding me with her blasphemy. "He turns his eye because he wants to offer all the land he can get to the fleeing Loyalists. He calls these overweight immigrants "Stewards to the Yahds of our God given King," she said, imitating his pomp. Then she would laugh, sprinkling out the sound like a breeze through a set of hanging crystal.

I immediately thought of that fateful day in the ditch with Bill Forsythe, and of Staunt and his obsession with his pointless search parties. I realized then that these manhunts were more a pretext for his gathering information on the condition of land, than any presumption of justice. He was on the lookout to prey upon the marginal planters, with offers to finance their lots by acting the part of lending them a hand.

But on that sunny day, with Helen and the gently rolling river, our blooming romance forced old anger aside. I suddenly found myself speaking very forward. I spoke of her bravery, and the respect I had for the grace with which she endured. Then I told her she was pretty, and if I had my fondest wish, it would be to pay off her indenture.

I was just as surely under the effect of the wildflowers,

with their rich colored cloaks and their summer perfume. Not to mention the owning of land, an unparalleled thrill, in a class beyond all known. But Helen responded light as the air, barely seeming to glance at my audacity, while staring beyond much as not, at the boy trying to hold her in love. She laughed, and let me know that though the thought was kind, it was just as equally absurd. Then demanding I lie quiet, until the pounding in my chest became quite still, my heart seemed to rise like the dragonfly that hovered before it suddenly and simply disappeared. Then, as if responding to this exquisite awful yearning, Helen leaned upon me with a kiss.

The human heart, I later recalled my youthful voice professing, was made along the order of pronounced and helpless shock. For by the end of that very summer, Helen McGrath had upped and married her a very proper man.

Jacob Morehouse was a middling goods importer with a reputable business in a one-room office on Front Street. He was a man with whom I had no dealings, but appeared withdrawn and calculating in his manner. This was a quality worth noting for being entirely absent in the merchants of that day, and went far in pointing out the clever way he valued such a match. Helen had her security and Morehouse, a wife who could work on his books. And though separate in temperament as any two men could be; Mr. Morehouse and I were now forever bonded.

Oh, how I steeped in covetous thoughts! What glory in a bargain had the dry dealer struck! A woman to keep straight his columns, while keeping him straight up in bed! For weeks on end I brooded, ever so slowly on the bitterness of Helen's rejection, which only left me numb with loss and anguish at my experience with love. Finally though, on some nights at least, I forced myself to grapple with an understanding, of Helen herself, and where she had begun. What, after all did I have to offer her, but a barrel full of hopes and a stretch of untamed land?

But still. From that point on I did what I could in avoiding Helen Morehouse, and the debate in my head could provoke me to a rage. Many an hour I spent outside the precious hold of sleep, grasping at a woman's place inside of English law.

I am however, thankful that the events, which came to surround me, demanded all the attention I could give. With the arrival of three new recruits, Foreman Jakes gave me his blessing and formally ended my stay. I had as much seed as I could cultivate, an ax and a saw, and a credit bought harness and plow. I had a cart of provisions from soap to lamb jerky, with a strong net to fish, and a musket with powder and shot. (Borrowed on a lease account as well.) A barrel of wheat, a small stone for milling, a rusty old scythe, and two pair of fine breeding hogs.

Now add to this list, a morning of dazzling luster. A morning no mosquito dared sully with his annoying and impish whine. I pushed off from Jamestown's shore in Kenyon Giles' flatboat, poling my way up towards my fifty, just near the point of the river's curl. We were off to the side and out of the steady flow, in the funny current that shifts in an opposite stream, and I was moving at last toward the dearest plot in Virginia. That special fifty that had been waiting for just the swing of my ax, and the singing soil cut of my till. Giles had one hand dragging a small line out for bass and a keg full of rum in the other, the teeming woods were all about us, ceaselessly whispering their wilderness words, and there was me, feeling so full I was bursting, sitting on top of the world.

All that I required of Giles was that he help me past the dead wood snares, a most sober caution due to the fact that of everything I carried, more precious than my cargo, was my beautiful magnificent ox. Tethered in the middle of the boat, I talked to him in an ongoing patter to soothe away his anxiousness, (having witnessed no doubt the loss of his cousins, drowned in this very same stream.) And though Giles was laughing at my jibbering innocence, I could see clearly that the huge black eyes were giving me back their thanks. The soft gloss focused when he admitted that he knew my fate entirely rested on him, and he pledged me every minute of his strength, if I'd see him get safely to shore.

When we landed, I surveyed the first plots that I'd use for planting, before even building my tent.

Despite the stern advice offered, I spent the whole of my first winter in the woods by myself. Jakes and Madame Porter went over and again giving me this counsel in concern for mental health. They had, after all, seen first hand what isolation and the wilderness could do. But I had a need to sit out on the land, to speak to it of my steadfast protection. My time in so doing was for myself as well, to face the hard changes, to learn how to bend and survive. I needed to feel how the earth breathed in the cold, and to hear what it said about the coming spring. To be sure, most days were spent in chopping firewood, procuring enough store for the ox and myself, but there's much to be known about the qualities of fuel that cannot be taught in fair weather. Then too, were the strategies applied to ice, and its effect upon the quartz and granite. The learning when to work around, or burrow through to hidden water. There was finding and bringing in edible grass, and the primitive barn to be built. A mosaic of changeable labor, when to move quickly, when to be rhythmic, and when to be perfectly still. In all, my Jamestown friends had no need to worry; I was too overwhelmed to have had enough time to form any questions or doubts.

I shot and ate more duck that year than anyone has a right to tell. I had skillet duck for breakfast with minced duck in strawberry pies. I had wild onion duck, and duck in every stew. I had duck in bowls of beer that made new limits to what you'd call home brew. I had duck twice a day for more months than any logic of migration, and even still they came on. On and on and on. Both in early mornings and again in the afternoon. Astonishing in numbers, in numbers that darkened the sun. Until finally, I gave up shooting, having grown tired of the constant re-smelting, and tediously picking out lead. Those late autumn days were so rich that I even gained a touch of arrogance. And it pains me now to admit that I once laughed like a fool at fear. Until that is, a marauding bear, a late winter sleeper, set me back to thinking right. She could've swiped my head right from where it rested, but passed me by for (what else) a pail of duck fat.

Then, when the sharp angles left in the early cold light began their northern-most thrust, the ox, as if listening to ancient voices took up its full time residence inside the barn. I watched him settle comfortably between the woodpiles and the hay, until his huge dark eyes slipped back into themselves to await the arrival of spring.

Time enough, I thought, as it was coming on Christmas, "I think I'll go into town." Hearing the sound of my own voice was something I'd got used to, but lately had become an empty echo in need of human cheer. And so I walked the cold woods without a hint or inkling as to how this heartening pleasure was about to change my life.

Madame Porter welcomed me warmly, and recruited me in hanging some festive fir on the spot. She herself was lost in celebration as witnessed by the shameless count of candles she had placed about. But my good tide was crushed to the floor, when she let slip that Helen "the poor child" was very near death's door. "If the Lord hasn't taken her yet," she paused, releasing a woman's sigh.

"The infant never lived, of course. Way too early, so I hear," said Foreman Jakes, awkward at his best in expressing sympathy. "But I've taken no new orders for a grave site as yet." Adding, "What's your morbid interest, son? On the birthday of our baby Jesus. How goes the work on your farm?"

He would have been the last one to know about my feelings for Helen, or anything I imagine, remotely akin to lost love. But I hardly minded. I was suddenly stuck deaf to his conversation, and attacked by a headache that came on like a scream. "Morehouse has committed murder," my thoughts began to rage. Then I calmed enough to think of Helen, and how if she lived, she'd likely be under a surgeon's blade. Then I stood, and flung myself out in the street to find the Morehouse's place. "See here, young Corstair," Jakes called out behind me. "Well, a happy good Christmas to you."

The wintry gray streets were shadowed by the rows of houses, lifeless and shut tight. I drove myself through the cold lanes, mumbling senselessly, hopeless with fear. It wasn't hard to reach. It was a full time in town home that he had built for noticing. It even had an entire upstairs level added on top. It set back a few yards from a white wrought iron fence, and had the uncommon feature of a stair run outside to an entrance at the back. I stood for a moment without a fixed plan, and spying no one about, slipped over a rail and skirted the edge of yard. There were two chimneys, another sign of his pretentious wealth, that both gave off smoke in a steady stream. Helen's bed would be upstairs, I thought, with her lying in the room that caught the heat. Silently, I moved up the stairs and freed the latch inside a shutter to step into a narrow darkened hall. There was no sound, no one stirred; only a gentle snoring and the burning fizz of a charcoal heater the next room beyond. I turned into a small anteroom lit by a single candle, and saw the barber asleep in a high-backed chair. He was propped up by the doorway, breathing in little gasps and snorts from the back of his open mouth. I held tightly to my own breath and moved right beside him, quiet as a cat.

Daniel Watkins

Helen was as pale as a spirit. Her eyelids so thin that if she'd had the desire to do it, she could have seen straight through them to me. The bloody bowls and knives of the doctor's trade were in evidence, but she was still breathing at least. Emboldened and reckless I placed my hand upon her breast; I felt its faint erratic rhythms, when she astonished me by opening her eyes. She was lost of all comprehension, as if peering from a distance, beyond all human cares, but then her brow slightly crinkled, puzzling, perhaps wondering if she might be dead. It was opening enough, and into it I concentrated all my prayers.

"Allow no more bleeding," I whispered, and she closed her eyes again.

Then I took up her hand, and acting the part of a conjurer, strove to convey through strength of memory what was true of my brave summer girl. That she, having faced the ocean and a wilderness of furies, could not sacrifice her life for the death of another man's child. I stopped just short I think, of making a deal with the Almighty if He'd allow me to keep this living soul. Then I dropped every blade I saw into a sack at my waist. Atop an open Bible on the stand beside her head, I placed an apple from a wild tree grove that grew to the side of my hut. I knelt down, and instead of kissing her, fixed her vacant features in my mind. I felt a bold presence, yet one that was also full of dread. The reaper hovered in her room; I knew it just as surely as I was there myself. And how easy and how fragile, I thought, for a life to be taken by the lips of a lost love's kiss. I lifted up and with every ounce of grace that I possibly possessed, recalled her living.

I slipped back out past the sleeping surgeon and headed for the docks. The outside air was silent, the night of Christmas Eve. I decided to find a drunken boatsman who would want to share a turkey I could shoot for him tomorrow afternoon. Then, I'd be back the next day, and the next day after that. And if my silent watching kept her living, I'd stand a frigid vigil, for each new granted day.

On my way down to the river I passed the *Office of Jacob Morehouse Trader,* one dim glow behind a window shuttered up. "He's given her up for dead," I said out loud, and the words nearly froze in my throat. "Now he's in his counting house, counting up his losses. Merry Christmas, Mr. Morehouse! Me-r-r-y Christmas!"

My voice echoed out in the nighttime forest. The trees creaked back, indifferent. Evergreen.

The whole of that winter was one of anguished devotion. I maintained my silent watch on an opposite corner beneath Helen's window, placing myself, when I dared, clearly in her view. January and February were months that brought but a trickle of immigrants so Madame Porter provided my old mat in her pantry in return for some work on her new dress shop. She avoided mentioning any other business besides being pleased to have the use of my handiwork. I was learning that such a response was common to the manner of a seasoned colonist, since surviving the specter of disease was largely done by superstition. It was not naming malevolent spirits that diminished their powers upon us.

I watched Jacob Morehouse come and go in the steady way that he conducted his trade, while I tried to discern his true sympathies. His face, always turned down, revealed very little, and he kept his appointments like clockwork. I was relieved however, with the prompt dismissal of the surgeon, as it informed me that Helen had staked claim for her life, but then there was no other change. Each morning I watched him leave the house at seven, to return at eight each night. Day after day, he made the same purposeful stride, staring down and never stopping, even working Sundays, which was a blatant offence to the law. By the third week he had hired a boarding servant to sleep in a room that adjoined his sickly wife's.

I always carried a bundle of wood, or wore my tools and apron, but the women that I passed on the street still gave me a knowing nod. I certainly did not reveal my longings, or extend anyone my trust, and so I spent a month this way observing Helen's progress from afar. I never approached the girl that did the nursing, although I saw her often enough, carrying her basket to market or hanging up sheets that froze in the cold winter sun. Then, on a day like any other, when I knew she was out with her shopping, I risked another visit to Helen's upstair's room. I silently slipped through the second story door and found her sitting by the window looking down at the spot where I'd stood.

"I've been waiting, and wondering when you would come in," she said turning around. Her voice was without the brightness I remembered, but neither was it wholly frail. "Come over by the fire and warm yourself at last."

I moved toward a stool by the heater, anxious about speaking false words.

"No," she stopped me. "Please. Help me with this chair. I want to sit down next to you."

She was as jumpy in my presence as I was in hers, a sign that I took as a renewal of her strength, as she moved with the furniture to the warmest part of the floor. An electric tension flashed between us, full of questions and things best left unsaid, and awkwardly self-conscious, I concentrated on avoiding her touch.

"If it's alright," she said simply, as if reading my mind, "I would like to take hold of your hand. It would... help to calm me, I think." When I clumsily bumped her elbow, I reacted as if I'd been burned. "I promise," she tried a smile, "that I won't break."

She then held her hand out in the narrow space between us, and closed it onto my own. Surprisingly warm, her fingers curled round mine, delicate as an exotic flower I'd discovered once in full bloom at nighttime. I sat stiffly up, too nervous to respond, afraid of even answering her affection. I felt as if suddenly blinded, and experienced a moment where nothing held together or made the least sense. Then just as quickly I returned to a well of regret, and an abundance of gratitude that she'd staved off her death. I thought that I would likely swoon. I looked away and saw her smile reflect up from the water bowl, beside her well-worn Bible.

"If I could only know," I stuttered, "how to bring you some comfort…" I finally felt brave enough to peer into her eyes, and saw a bolt of fear break her facade. In the next second her face was so harrowed and empty that I took her at once in my arms. I felt her give way, and then shudder, as if trying to cast a dark weight. My thoughts grabbed for anything I might say to re-assure her, but I only had pity and helpless remorse. It was as if some stranger were trying to make use of my weakened arms and legs.

"The midwife tells me I'm so scarred and perforated that another child is… impossible." She was looking at me now, her youthful beauty gone, a vessel wrung weary through with tears. "But… I'm alive… after all…"

I clasped her to my chest, willing my heart to beat for us both, and return her the life that she'd wakened in me. But her body collapsed, heaving with sobs, keening to a dark beyond my reach. I was powerless in the face of such despair. I stared dumbly at the script of *Solomon's Song*, the page and its verses struck by the light, when a cloud shifted, passing the sun.

"I don't think it necessary to publicize our problems so obviously my dear."

We turned, and there was Jacob Morehouse, watching us from the doorway with a bottle of brandy and two glasses in his hands. Helen and I stood immediately apart, my heart jumping out of my throat.

"No, no, be at ease, by all means, be at ease. I have no wish to alarm, will you have a seat?" he prattled. "A glass of brandy?"

"Jacob," Helen responded over quietly, her attempt to appear recomposed. "I wish you to leave my room at once."

"I see no cause for any *further* inconvenience," he insinuated. "In that all of the interested parties are finally here."

Before I could comprehend this pronouncement, he handed me one of the small glasses, which he then carefully filled. "You of course, are the young Corstair," he said smiling. I am Jacob Morehouse. Please, sit down."

"Jacob, how…"

"My dear Helen," he said sharply. "Please arrange yourself comfortably back in your bed. May I bolster your pillows? Perhaps, Mr. Corstair can assist."

"See here, Morehouse," I interjected, "I'm not sure what game…"

"Game?" he shot back. "If I were a man of games I would probably have you arrested. But, that," he indicated the chair in which I was to sit, "is not efficient to our business."

To my further astonishment I watched Helen pause, as if in mid-thought, and dutifully climb in her bed. She then surrounded herself in blankets and sheets, as if her new defense were silks. I, on the other hand, felt entirely naked. I looked at the snifter of brandy strangely planted in my hand, and shifted my gaze between Helen and her husband. She appeared calm, but her expression was searching, as for something her mind might produce to escape. Morehouse stood by, patiently waiting for me to sit. I had not considered my impulsive risk in being here to have taken things this far. There was no way for me to handle such a turn. Then, something inside me collapsed. My will to fight or even retreat, was touching something more with Helen, and I simply gave him sway. I felt the hope and pain in her embrace flow through me in a paradox of strength. I set the whiskey on the table and took a seat.

"I assume that you are in love with my wife," Morehouse

said right away.

"I do not have to tolerate such treatment, Jacob," Helen replied, although she sounded dull and remote.

"The law, my dear, requires that you do. But the law is not so inflexible as to refuse good common sense. Especially, when it can so clearly benefit mutual concerns."

"Speak your point sir," I said. "Exactly what is your concern for me?" Watching him pretend to sip his brandy suddenly made me mad.

"Why Helen, of course," he stated, tossing out her name, as if to make her presence discounted. "Under the law you see, Helen is my wife by consent of legal contract. I am therefore obliged to protect and provide for her. And in so much as I fulfill this requirement she is for said purposes, my property. Whereas for you she is but an object for your *love*. Do you understand?"

I was so startled by the tone of this outrageous conversation, made all the more absurd by its setting, that I quite forgot that this was my first encounter with Jacob Morehouse, *Trader*. Helen on the other hand was even more difficult to decipher. She seemed neither shocked nor humiliated, but merely to be holding still. This, I assumed was the price of her survival, and this sudden shift of awareness, gave rise to a pity that surfaced in my chest.

"I understand much more of life and love than your merchant sensibilities can admit," I blustered. "I also know what it means to stand by one's wife, most especially when she's threatened by death."

"Good, excellent, good," he said. "I won't ask how you've arrived at such knowledge in the span of your short years..."

His condescension galled me, but now that I had him in close range I could see he was much older than I'd thought. His long moustache had a dyed black sheen set off by a wrinkled face over-powdered. Just how, my mind scoffed, had Helen... my Helen, managed this? Then, like a mighty shame I remembered how I'd shared my wish to buy off her indenture for our marriage.

"... we merely need to drive our different positions together," Morehouse went on. "The key responsibility for the wife you see, no matter what the circumstance, is to bear her husband's children. Preferably sons."

And with this he actually smiled. Smiled at me and then at Helen, who had finally turned away. It must have been her brush with death that was giving her its counsel, a grip that held the two of us in tact.

"I, for instance, would cherish the thought of a son. A boy to become as fine a man as you one day, my dear Corstair."

"See here, Mr. Morehouse," I said, standing up, "neither Helen nor myself have need of your humiliations. I will say, because she obviously will not, that your wife is possessed of more strength and honesty than what you deserve. Either you speak your mind without insult and clear purpose, or I will bid you good day. I only ask your permission that I may look in, until such occasion as her health is fully restored."

"Just so, just so," he feebly applauded. "I'm counting on it in fact. What I want is for you to take her off my hands."

I moved to strike him, but he caught hold of my hand with a surprising agility. He then twisted me round with a wrenching hold that betrayed his pretentious genteel. Once again I found myself painfully seated in the opposite chair.

"Please remain where as you were," he continued, "until you hear me out. No matter the cause of our individual wishes, divorce, as you well know is no easy matter. But be secure in the fact that this is something that I will use all my influence to obtain. It may be that in the quiet persuasion of time such a document will exist. In the meantime, I am willing to offer you two hundred and thirty-three pounds for taking Helen on as a conditional compensation for our separation."

"I will have no such money!" I started up, prepared to strike him again. But Helen shot me through with such a look, that I held onto the arm of the chair.

"The state of adultery coupled with the state of barrenness will go far towards bending the favor of the law," Morehouse went on, completely undeterred. "Might you consider, Mr. Corstair that the woman you love is now indenture free? What terms did you bring here to offer? What more could it be that you need?"

I took a moment to contain myself with the shock of his proposal, and I studied his deep-set eyes for a trap. I could not even look upon Helen.

"If I follow the full suit of your insults, Mr. Morehouse," I replied, feeling just as much unlike myself, "what of *our* legitimacy? If I'm to take you at face value, what is the law on *our* married state?" From the corner of my eye I saw Helen slightly raising her head.

"The only element that I mean to guarantee is the legitimacy of *my* heirs," he answered me. "As far as Helen is concerned, you may draw comfort in the fact that this is an issue which she will not bring to question." He indicated her presence at last, more with a nod than a look. "Admittedly, there are parts of the arrangement that only time can bring to a close. But without any prospect for children of your own, there are no additional impediments. After all, we are still new at making this New World, Mr. Corstair, are we not?" He then produced the thinnest of smiles. "I put my trust in that practicality, in fact. The law can be made to see that it is my concerns that have been most inconvenienced. Shorted, really by the surprising turn in Helen's health..."

And then I did strike him. I stood, fully in command of my body, and landed a solid blow to the side of his face. It

Daniel Watkins

broke the glass that he swirled about his lips and produced a bloody gash down the middle of his chin. It also tore the skin from my knuckles, exposing the underneath flesh.

"Enough!" Helen shouted visibly alarmed. She leapt from her bed pulling out a length of linen, and held it to his chin. Then, ripping the cloth down the middle, she wrapped another part around my throbbing fist. "Philip, I must demand that you leave," she said, gently pressing the wound in her fingers.

I turned away but Morehouse grabbed me from his chair once again. His speech beneath his bloody bandage was passionate and clear. "Perhaps I spoke too soon regarding those qualities of yours in regards for my sons," he said, throwing off Helen's arm to attend him. "Now *you* can be assured, Corstair. These sons of mine, which I am bound to have, will have everything to do with the future of this land. And if your misplaced pride should now refuse me, it is because you are too simple to value what service you have."

I was in a crisis of confusion. I could not imagine what Helen must have felt. She stepped back a ways as if only suddenly aware that she was the key. An unheard of means to give this scheme a meaning. Or perhaps she was just torn by repulsion, unable to digest such raw ambition. I crossed the floor, disgusted as well; caught up in a maze of my own humiliation. And then her voice came colder than ice, so much that it cut out the heart of any pretended thought. She also sounded strange, as if she were speaking from a void, without breath.

"I will accept your offer, Jacob," she said. "On the condition that I do not spend another night in this house."

Her husband grew small right before my eyes. He shifted the bed sheet up to his brow like the split in his chin had reached up his head.

"Providing that Mr. Corstair will still have me, of

course."

Of course I would still have her! I almost shouted aloud, but immediately I spun into circles of doubt. Foremost was the fact that I had no ready place for her to stay. I had barely started hewing the lumber for a new log cabin; surely she didn't mean us to live in the barn with the hogs and the goat and the ox. Then I allowed the pleasing picture of the disgrace that this would bring to Morehouse and his precious estate. Suddenly I laughed at the twist Helen had just dealt her husband's grandiosity. Morehouse too, gave out a shocked snort, but quickly moved to cover it by dabbing the cut on his chin. Doubtless, he expected to conduct their separation under the cloak of her continued convalescence, needing her compliance to make a quiet move. If only just on paper, the mission for her health might have sent her back to England for instance, giving him the proper time to reclaim his precious name. But standing there between her two bleeding rivals, clad only in her nightgown, she looked sure of her intention to leave him right now.

"Without my cooperation," she stated calmly, "I could become a very loud annoyance. Virginia is not New England, you know. But I'm prepared to make this sacrifice for your *blessed* generations, Jacob. For you to erase the Morehouse shame at its *source*."

"Well of course, my dear, as you wish," he coughed fitfully into his bandage, "if you think you're well enough."

So Jacob Morehouse, with his arrangements hardly accomplished, could but sit for his weakened wife's defiance, that was proving entirely too strong.

Helen accepted the Morehouse proposal of a 'reverse dowry', and took immediate residence in a cabin upriver called *The Greenbriar.* This was part of an estate run by a widow named Beatrice Albright, who made a discreet business of boarding "former unfortunates & prospective wives," along with other 'promised girls', from places that were simply known of as "abroad." Widow Albright was the model of an original entrepreneur, who had herself refused the pressures to remarry, which was no small feat in a land run by men. She had, as was said in those days, gone pure country. She lived in the tiny community of Henricus, far enough upriver to provide refuge from the 'prying ninnies out of Jamestown,' to a place where, "talk of the past is piddle, this is Virginia now." It was an attitude that gave us quiet welcome, and shelter enough to complete Helen's care.

All of our time was now spent working the plantation, and attending to our separate chores. While I would struggle to free us from another stand of trees, Helen hoed the yard for summer vegetables. She made lanterns and rope from the plentiful hemp, and built up a garden of herbal medicines. There was also the attention that she gave to our growing stock of animals, and defending their feed from the streams of invading mice. She always kept a kettle on that simmered something useful, and her vitality was quickly restored in the blessed open air. (As particularly evidenced in my returning home one night, and falling in the new fence holes that she'd dug.) The days ran on, seeming to intersect, and settled into welcome routines, (if such a thing is allowed to be said of living in a wilderness.) One day however, that clearly stands out from the rest, was the afternoon that our design of winches and pulleys was put to its final test. Unbelievably, within just a couple of hours, the two of us had done the unheard of; we'd raised a timber frame up for a house. We then slaughtered a pig, and made love in the wee morning moonlight. The rest of the world may have had its way of thinking, but Helen McGrath was none other than my wife.

We marked the bulk of the Morehouse money for a track that would bring us to the river, but then we discovered that this lot had already been secured. We were standing over a survey map on a rare return to Jamestown, with Helen giving me that look of hers that said she'd expected as much. "Under the governor's patent," she repeated the clerk his words, while he stood facing her, more than perturbed. "Imagine that."

The little runt then regarded her like she was made of stone, which meant of course, that her presence in his office was the unforgivable annoyance. Undeterred by his patronizing, Helen demanded the charts for the interior, which the clerk then made an exaggerated effort of handing out to me. But when we'd left his office we had rights to two hundred consecutive acres, (a cause for celebration, even for having to file them with *Sycamore and Staunt, Registrars of Estates*, for yet another fee.)

"Imagine that," Helen said to *their* clerk. Her sarcasm that day was getting plenty of work. Then back out on the street, she even surprised me with the extent to which she was furious.

Fortunately we did not meet up with either of the scoundrels, but she was in such a fit over their "grubby little hands and legal extortion," that she started testing out what we'd called 'the Morehouse stigma' on every other person that we passed. She cut a path straight towards unsuspecting couples, be they strangers or people that knew her well, and ask about the state of their dear families, or make a comment on their good health. Most reacted with humor, or like she was touched in the head, but some were so offended they simply turned and ran away. A very, very few, meaning only the Bedford-Trents, (an elderly couple with their own box at church,) displayed rancor at our unwedded bliss. But the unspoken truth about Jamestown society was that it only counted offspring. And this was a value not exclusively male. *Any* white child that survived its vulnerable years was regarded as a marvel full of worth. The real sin lay in a couple having none.

"I think," I said, when she'd finished her charade, "that the office gents grow cold about a woman doing business, *in general*. Not because of our circumstance."

She acted like she did not hear me, but then I perceived a little smile. And on our way back upriver, we were towing another pair of oxen, a nanny goat for milking, and the pieces to a fine and sturdy cherry wood loom. We then made a special stop over at Cryer's kiln, where I saw the naturally frugal Helen order brick for a fireplace with space enough for a walk.

Make no mistake; Morehouse was like a cross she bore, burning deep upon her shoulders. And every Jamestown slight she received picked at the wound like pepper. But there was never a fundamental question to resolve. Whenever she looked back and saw that frigid, fateful morning, she transformed into a living grateful force.

We were young, and hopeful and happy, (in spite of our losing that valuable riverfront land.) But back then no one knew that the whole of Virginia would have to pay for the governor's inside patents, (unless it was that wizard Bill Forsythe.) Had we guessed, Helen and I would have pulled up stakes and headed further west even then. No one, whether he dressed in fancy boots or had to scrape the mud from his well-worn pants, could have known that precious river holding would one day come to destroy us.

"**A**nd the first night that I sleep inside the walls of our finished home," Helen said in a hushed voice, "sanctioned by the church or not, I insist that we be married."

It was near dawn, and I had just slipped from her cabin window with my head propped up, attentive on the sill of rough pine. I regularly performed this silly maneuver out of respect for Beatrice Albright, who insisted that her boarders were not whores. Then too, Beatrice was quick to account for what she called "the special circumstances." The plain truth was that a come of age female in the colony was far too precious a commodity for anyone to reject out of hand, no matter what you might say behind your closed doors. And in the case of Helen McGrath (legally Morehouse,) Bea had a more special circumstance than most. In any case, Helen meant to have a wedding as her proper send off from the Albright place.

Within the first week of her residence at *Greenbriar* she'd made the acquaintance of a Chickahominy shaman named Tah-ye-naw, and taken the opportunity to learn much about natural cures. But in those days, as with now, in the village of Henricus, an unmarried white woman frequenting the company of an old Indian chief could stiffen a person's jaw. Added to this the fact that the old chief spent much of his time drinking rum at the backdoor of the Henricus tavern, made Helen a likely subject for shunning, or at least some severe counseling from the church. But Helen, who seemed to grow stronger by flaunting her eccentricity, was bold enough to challenge gossipers right inside their tracks. Beyond the stretch of any common decency, she announced that the goodhearted Tah-ye-naw was going to perform our wedding.

The day of our nuptials attracted, I guess you could say, a less than delicate lot. They showed their hearts by readying for the occasion, by hanging on the taps of free ale. As I poled my way up to Henricus, I beheld them scuffling along the shore near an arc of wild roses that Helen had placed in the bow of our scow. I had scrubbed myself clean by an hour-long bath, and wore my first store-bought suit that made me itch and sweat, but I'd given her my solemn word that I would keep it white.

The day was still and sultry and waiting nervously for Helen I must have had a little whisky, because I think that I passed out. Strangely though, when I came to on my feet no one seemed to care. I turned and saw Helen, facing just above me at the end of the rickety quay. I gasped aloud and felt a set of hands behind me, guiding me in my steps. Helen wore a rainbow of beads and shining tiny shells that she'd woven through her hair. Her hands were wrapped in a delicate bouquet of white and yellow buttercups. The sun beamed from off her shoulder, and as she stepped towards me, the world simply slipped away. Even the rowdies, the ones only there to make fun, grew calm. I distinctly remember the rustling of her silks, and a powerful misting of tears, and a feeling that I'd been bewitched. It was a miracle that faced me now, glowing in her one time ghostly face.

We must have been paddled to midstream, for I recall Tah-ye-naw struggling to his feet in a boat and then taking hold of our hands. He swayed our arms unsteadily to the east, then back to a point in the west, as if gathering in a blessing.

"En oht, Eskaw s'am, Ehtaw naw, Esw ki's, E'yiht. E," he said, balancing his free hand along the horizon. Then he fell like a slab of stone into the water. Helen and I were then toppled in, and our finery fully soaked in our struggle to fish him out. Needless to say, the unholy hooting was relentless from the shore.

"So, baptized too," Tah-ye-naw sputtered when he was finally back on board. "Two ceremony for the price of one."

We laughed with him, and thus began our life as Mr. and Mrs. Corstair.

But as everyone knows, the careless joy shared in a wedding day's frolic has nothing to do with staking one's life to a boundless frontier. The truth was that through our first few years, the two of us scarcely subsisted. In three years time I had managed to plant but a tenth of the land, and most of that was in mounds I had to build between the rows of tree stumps. What is more, even this middling feat could not have been accomplished without the hiring of strangers. When nature decided to turn against us, by say a late frost, or roots dug too deep for me to budge, I'd have to hoof it over to Rutlow Crossroads.

The mill, as it was called, was a collection of freed men who had buried all their rights to land in a mountain full of debt, and more often than not, in a taste for home fired whisky. But I was able to get an honest day's work out of those that weren't down with 'the stomach,' or in a drunken rage from being swindled. And the hard truth is that in order to tame a plot of wild land one must live in such bone weariness that it grinds out the life in a man's dream to farm. It sits upon you every waking hour like a chain that you are forging, and does not stop with sleep. When you look up from where you're digging, you're always seeing something that needs to be done. So that after an especially brutish spell, you question if it was an hour or a week that passed since hoeing the row that you're on. It's the kind of tired that makes your heart beat like a machine; one that is constantly broke.

Daniel Watkins

There's the endless fighting back of weeds, and the chopping and tree dragging. There is the building up of planting mounds, and the sinkholes to be drained, and the sudden rush of harvest before the tobacco gets too dry. And while it's true that the leaves produced their promised riches, they soaked up your labor at a sacrificial price. At different times throughout the year, the jealous attention required by tobacco threatened the rest of your crops. Even the ones that we counted for our food. I lost bushels of corn to a flock of sneaky blackbirds, while I was picking the worms from tobacco leaves. And there is nothing to describe the pit in your stomach as you watch a rainless summer turn the green shoots into dust. In the end it thoroughly wore me out to harvest a mere four acres, the quality of which brought a sub-standard price.

Helen and I were disinclined to invest in an indenture. For one, we could ill afford it, since we knew well that to keep a growing full time worker took much more than most owners allowed. So, by the winter of our third year we realized that without the helping hands of sons, there was no hope of us standing up to the immensity of the wild. The worst part of course, was that Helen was infertile, that much we understood. Then, midway through that dormant December, the children of Ethan and Mary Treadnell came to our home like an unspoken prayer.

Helen and I were finished with our evening meal, and had rekindled the debate over taking on a boarder, when the dogs set off to barking at the front of the house. We opened the door and there the children stood, half-frozen, and staring at the ground. The youngest was the only one that was not afraid to look at us, with his head beneath the palm of Jeremy Bliss, where the ferryman had placed his open hand.

Let me add here that in spite of fate's appearance; its knocking at our doorstep so to speak, the means by which it came was not particularly profound. Helen and I stifled our surprise, and immediately set a table, as this was a common plight in the community of struggling planters. One was expected to do for others, and there was never an accounting of who had turned up needy or dejected at the wheel of helping hands. There wasn't a farm or a squatter that I knew of that wouldn't cut his final carrot into halves. It was a fellowship beneath all else that we understood, and the only earthly way to cope in climates that turned hostile. And so by this bold occurrence, and in spite of Helen's and my desponding, we were made into an instant family.

The youngest was Stuart, age five, the middle child, Sarah was a healthy seven, and Zachary, their quiet protector, was coming up on age nine. Neither Helen nor I knew the Treadnells, but through Jeremy Bliss, we learned that they had remote holdings some seventy miles west of the falls. The month before, father Ethan received a kick from a young buck elk that he shot, and it tore a gash deep in his head. With winter coming on before he'd finished preparations, he did not have the chance to give his wound the proper time to heal. In the next week, when he was hauling in a wagonload of firewood, he simply keeled over in a faint. "Father slept for a couple of days, but he never woke up." Sarah, who was becoming sociable, recounted the events. She went on to say that then her mother started acting strange, "Afraid to go out, and she would not eat, but shut herself up, only singing." A week after they managed to bury Ethan, the mother wandered off in the middle of the night and completely disappeared.

Helen and I listened, careful not to push or prod, and holding back the urge to take them up in our arms. Especially that cub of a boy named Stuart, who was oblivious, asleep in his seat. Zachary finally offered that they could have made it through the winter, but this he added only after clearly gaining the advantage of our fire. Jeremy Bliss then made much over each of the children's bravery. He later told us that Zachary wanted to stay, fending for himself alone, and was most stubborn to give up the search for their mother. But when the day came that Sarah walked off with little Stuart on her back, he came to his senses and followed.

We made a prayer that night for Mary Treadnell. And for all the lost souls made mad by the wilderness. Then we built a makeshift mattress, and placed the sleeping children together at the foot of our bed.

The season for gathering, the season to disperse, and the seasons for building up and tearing down; these are the rhythms, carved in stone from ancient tongues, as timeless as the Bible. And so, by like reflection present how these small strangers came to form a family, and slowly turned away from immeasurable loss. And what that painful turning gave to each of us was a foundation forged by trust. In this life I have only gained the values I know by walking in a steady march behind the till. No small thing when you're weighted, at times, with so much fear that you cannot even recognize yourself. But Helen and I were still young and inexperienced enough to steer each of these terrified lives through their unspeakable passage. A path made clear by trial and error. God knows we made enough mistakes, but so it was with the wisdoms we found, done by our not knowing. The dangerous, (children wandering off alone) and often messy, (leech stings soothed by urine) made bonds grow deep, whether the worst was overcome. The greatest part of usefulness was, to be sure, was learned in the doing of plain hard work. And by the end of that first winter, Zachary and I, with a hand from little Stu had burned and cleaned a fifty-acre plot inside the forest. The following August saw it yield a ton of prime top-leaf.

Sarah soon turned eight, and was a more ingenious child than anyone could find. Especially in regards to her handling of animals. Our first March thaw brought us a major infestation of mice. She designed and built a large, clever trap that she set inside the open space beneath our granary vats. She then introduced it as a home for several civets tamed to her control within a fortnight. Later our apple orchard, that set a ways off into the woods, was beset by a longer legged variety of thieves. Sarah simply marked the place, (unnoticed by us,) with the scent from our ever-eager dogs. The deer began to take their raiding elsewhere.

The next few years saw our plantation grow stronger, taking in the best of our labors and our leisure, growing with it too, the fond respect we held for each other. The winter could bring fevers to scrape you down to your last nerve, and summer, the inevitable snakebite. But we gave solace when the country turned its harshest, and embraced its many joys. In the larger view, I suppose we were nothing special, as difficult a thing as that is to say; we made our lives a part of these elements the same as anyone else. We accomplished hard work. And like any other farm staked out beyond the river, surviving was celebration enough.

Then, in the autumn of '61, the Corstairs became two more. Our new arrivals were those that lived in 'the territories parallel.' A place understood by those with whom we shared the land, but who also walked an entirely different world. It was a world that we English more often dismissed, and most often paid the price, and was peopled by a breed that seemed to emerge directly from the earth. Her name was Pankepo, her brother was Mekatah, and together they were welcomed as daughter, sister, brother and son into the Corstair clan. I distinctly remember being made haughty by these additions, for representing as they did, what I fancied was the spirit of the truth in New World life. I believed that we were the model, not just for the English and the troubled Appomatocs, but for other tribes as well. A show of our success could light the bridge between us, and bring about a thorough peace.

Now of course, I regret this deluded condescension, and continue to do so every breathing day.

Laura was the name that our new daughter eventually decided on, I think because she was attracted to the exotic sounding '*r*' that was strange to her Appomatoc tongue. Anyway, it was the *type* of name that she and her brother Mekatah insisted that they have. Her real name, Pankepo, roughly translates to Furthest Leaves. She was nine years old, and her brother Tomas, as he Christianized himself, had recently become eleven.

Helen and I knew their parents well, having traded with their tribe from the first days of our settling. Their father, Kotaka, had even helped survey the extension of our holdings, whenever he wanted to indulge his 'English folly', or so he said. He also gave me incalculable insight and stores of practical advice. He taught me the type of soils to look for from which spring the deepest wells, and a peculiar mud that forms in pond flats and dries into a salt. Helen and the children's mother had also shared knowledge of crafts. A certain watertight stitch that was made from knitting, and a novel idea for planting, that she called rotating the crops. This particular technique proved to be of significant worth given the rich amounts of shelf that tobacco leaves consume.

Their deaths came at the hands of a skin peeling pox that drew itself out like a cruelty, but by the end, both had agreed that their children should learn the English ways. And though it was never spoken, I always felt that their trust in us was due to the uniqueness of our family, our unorthodox marriage and our living in the face of the 'strict white rule.' Kotaka had died miserably, his tongue and lips grown black from 'the European disease,' but his last breath was spent convincing his son to learn what he could about the English. "The paper learning," he whispered, "and the skill with tools."

Helen and I were greatly indebted to the Appomatoc. They proved to be a generous people, (at least they were with us) and without their help our lives would have been more difficult, perhaps insurmountable as such. So when the children, with great pain, were presented to us, we were honored to take them in.

Then, like a self appointed anvil sent to straighten out the devil of the woods, several months after this adjustment to our family, an Anglican missionary called Cornelius Stamp put a primitive shelter up. It was ten miles to the south, by way of violating the treaty by the way, which he'd named his Hill for Heathen Hope. After several more months and not a single Indian visitor, he decided it would be easier to work on savages that already lived among the whites. Naturally enough, the Corstair family was the first upon his list. I was surprised to find him soft spoken, and a very sincere sounding man, and the morning he came out, he told us that if Tomas and Laura would come to his church every week on Fridays, he would teach them how to read. This was a good deal, what with Helen and I up to our knees in planting and the two of them so eager to learn. But after the second session Tomas returned to tell me that he and his sister would not be visiting his Appomatoc village anymore.

"Why would you want to do that?" I asked him in his native dialect.

"Please! English only. Please!" he responded.

"I will still visit with your people," I quickly told him. "And I will welcome them here at the house."

He grew silent, and for a moment looked confused.

"Do you really wish to grow apart from your cousins? Your uncle, your aunts?" I prodded, shifting back into his native tongue.

"Such things," he answered strangely, "cannot be discussed in such chaotic and devilish language."

I watched this earnest youth on the brink of becoming a man being torn before my very eyes. He actually strained under the force of the powerful foreigner's words. And he had not a clue what he was saying. I then retrieved our newly purchased riding horse from out the back yard pasture, and rode straight out for the chapel in the woods. Tomas' mother had argued from her deathbed that her own family not be allowed to take possession of her son. This was not a thing she considered lightly. She had dismayed over breaking with her spirit connections, with her very own ancestors perhaps. She had to have believed beyond all natural inclination that what she was doing was best for her son.

"Strange way of converting the Indians," I said, as I rode up. "By isolating the children from their natural home. I'd have thought you wanted shining examples of your work to be sent back to their relatives. Attracting more moths to the flame and such."

"It is imperative that they be purified first. When they are clean in spirit they can start anew." Reverend Stamp was tying a bushel of thatch over an open spot in his roof. None too soon, from the looks of it, for it had just begun to rain. The structure itself was entirely open-sided, and his oversized Bible was flapping its pages like a broken winged crow in the wind.

"The children will not be coming here anymore," I said. "Helen and I will attend to their education." I turned away, suddenly just wanting to be done with him and gone. I certainly didn't want to be stranded in a storm with him beneath his ragged roof.

"Saving souls, Mr. Corstair, is the *only* education."

There was a sudden glint in his crystal blue gaze that I felt he had often rehearsed. I was tired and irritated, and in no mood to get wet. I'd been up very early that morning hoeing out a stubborn patch of clay, and yet I did not threaten, or give him a cutting retort. In fact, seeing him standing in what would soon become a mud hole, he only struck me as inane. I looked at him, fascinated by how he'd fooled me when he first visited our farm. But now, with his face drawn tight against the coming storm, I saw there was madness in his eyes.

"Do you wish to see *everyone* in your family burn as hopeless sinners?!" he cried. There was a violent stirring of tree limbs.

His voice sounded out so piercing that it felt like it hit me in the back. It nearly goaded me into turning around, and hand him a what-say about my family and my wife. But just as quickly I judged the effort to be wasted, and kept moving ahead through the growing dark. About a mile down the path I was sitting out the storm under a bow of thick pine, and I started in on brooding about the man. I was struck by how close in age we were, but could see how the woods had already worked upon him, like a large black snake taking its time to get rabbit down whole. His oversized head with its greasy jet hair was more matted than a rat's bed since the first time that I'd seen him. His rail-thin frame bulging hungry veins. It was not a figure that roamed about unnoticed; I'd seen it before, but in men that were much older. They lived their lives tormented by their bodies, and seemed to wallow in pain as if to pay some kind of debt. But it was this early stage of the sacrifice that was setting Stamp apart. I looked above at the heavy green eaves, nearly black in the dripping dank air. This wilderness will take all of the fire a man has to give, I thought, and purge him like a useless demon.

A short time after this, Cornelius Stamp published a formal decree. He announced that any English planters who were harboring Indians, (his exact word, *harboring*) without proper indoctrination from the Church were under threat of immortal peril. And what is worse, a few of my poorer neighbors, the non-*harborers*, I suppose, took him at his word.

Daniel Watkins

But the short of it was that anyone truly doing any *harboring* was *harboring* for the purposes of slavery, and reading the Bible to savages was not a likely way they'd spend their time. When tested into comment, these, my fellow countrymen would reject the notion that an Indian had a soul to begin with, before the sticky business of saving it could even begin. In any case, a so-called saved Indian fetched no better price than any other, "Come now," they said, "the troubles with the savages are over, aren't we all getting along?"

Reverend Stamp's edicts were given about as much attention by our Appomatoc friends. Whenever the children's Auntie Shee-sa came to call, she would wrinkle up her face in a voice of deep concern and ask me, "How are you feeling today, Mr. Philip? How is your immortal peril?"

I'd typically respond by launching into a critique about the misuse of the Anglican Church, and Cornelius Stamp in general, while Aunt Shee-sa sat knitting and nodding her head. Then, after appearing to consider the lengthy case I'd just stated, she'd conclude that I was certainly as fine a preacher as the Reverend Stamp. A month might pass before I'd realize she was having me on.

On the other hand, a white family that openly embraced the Indians invited suspicion, if nothing else. Then, when the price of tobacco fell into a bottom, conditions were created to set the fires of prejudice alight. My neighbors all complained, and cursed their luck like a bleating herd of sheep, but kept right on with their planting. They labored as if the force of their blind will would miraculously carry them straight through the obvious; the market for tobacco had ended. Then, as if the glut we'd created weren't enough, the king made it known that he hated the stuff. He declared the smoke unpleasant and unhealthy, and wanted an end of production outright. But there, for all to see, in the middle of this stubborn standoff, the Corstair plantation still thrived.

I had never hidden the fact that I lay great store in Indian advice, especially in the realm of cultivation. And so doing, several seasons before the fall of tobacco, I built a business out of fertilizer by using a native formula that did wonders for spent soil. And I started producing it in volume after Cabot's fishery gave me its offal by the load. Needless to say it was a right smelly business, especially in the summer months, so we limited our production to winter and early spring. Soon enough we had more demand than we had of product, and while no one noticed, we'd pulled completely free of tobacco's debt-filled hole. In the beginning it was only idiot talk, stoked by jealousy and ignorance, but later on, when market days turned truly grim, the serious gossip arose. Just how did the Corstairs sit so well in the midst of our worthless weed?

Word got round that we only planted at night, under new moons, and in ground that got drenched in hot goat blood. That our fields were protected by a demon, which the savages could only conjure up. This demon brought us just the proper amount of rain, and ate every kind of root sucking bug.

Rumors such as these gained more currency the more ridiculous they became, especially with the planters that took the hardest hit. These were a new wave of immigrants, ill equipped and inexperienced, that faced the harshest conditions entirely alone. On the far off shores of England, they'd been promised a result that amounted to gold, but when finally done with working off their passage, they were strapped with land full of stones. And whatever they managed to clear in the scrub was barely a grade above barren. Some had even packed it in and were living in the swamps like animals.

But for the Corstairs, the most powerful lie that circled round behind us was the one that had us getting tax relief directly from the "gov'ner. " It seems that this was part of a deal he struck for the taking in of his heathen 'treaty children.' The upshot of it meant that we didn't have to pay what the government required for protecting the planter's frontier. As a device to sow the seeds of sedition, it was effectively clever. For as this lie was bandied and then expanded it turned into a rebellion of its own. The churned out result was an unparalleled push into tribal reserves, by abandoning one's bankrupt holdings to the governor and his debt hounds.

But let me here admit that these are years in which I must have slept. For rebellion seemed to have come upon us all at once, arriving featureless as the night. An angry sun was suddenly awakened though, and it struck at the land with spiteful light. It shed upon the hidden, and the creeping underneath. And it was splitting the young country fully in half. Like the richness of England from which we had fled, there were those that had all, who were willfully driving those that had naught.

Part Two

1675

The angriest man that you have ever met will eventually grow cold given enough failure. But what keeps him alive, on his day to day bent rigid numb sick scrap of earth is a quality that simmers. Especially as it accrues, year after year in the witness of such plenty. This was the breed of hard working hopefuls and land grabbing adventurers that streamed endlessly to us from Virginia's beckoning shores. By 1675 the governor's Indian treaties were decades old, and his long held borders were frayed to the middle. Illegal hunting and trapping on tribal land had become so commonplace that it was no longer considered a crime. Everywhere you looked fields and farms were squatted now.

I was in our smithing shop firing the shape into a new barrel when I got a view of Tomas quickly changing mounts from Old Ben, our thick-footed plow horse, to Nell, the horse we used for carriage rides. By the time that I stood and looked out the door he was off down the western road at a pace. The late afternoon light had grown diffuse but I still made out the hurt and anger in his face. I could not leave my work, nor was it my practice to approach him direct, but I hoped to learn of his troubles when he returned to me in his time. Then, on a day shortly after, he hit me like a hammer when he told me that he'd learned his true father had one time killed a white.

"That is a disgusting lie," I replied as calmly as I could. "Where did you come on such a fabrication?"

"I dreamed it," he said sarcastically, displaying yet

another trait that I'd never seen. "Since becoming white," he pressed on, "I have learned to brood. Just like a little spoiled English girl."

It was Zachary who later told me that Tomas was thrown off our neighbor Bacon's place by a group of men he'd never seen before. He had traveled there with a parcel of Helen's herbs to see if Nathaniel's wife, Elizabeth, had recovered from a bout with the grippe. But he saw neither Elizabeth nor Bacon to make the delivery. What he saw was the boss of two drunken burleys who told him that he'd best clear off before they scalped his savage head and fed it to the dogs.

Thus, began my one-way journey into hell.

I had Zachary saddle two horses, and we immediately set out for Bacon's place to see what was the matter. But even as we drove them, I could well imagine what it was. Stories had been gathering over the span of those past few months of isolated farmers being struck down while walking through their fields. Of thieving raids and property burned on plantations that had edged on Indian lands. Some said that war was already upon us, in the north and to the west, while the governor's response was to sit on his hands, unwilling to upset his precious fur-trade. Zachary and I were not halfway down the narrow road when we ran into Carlton Baird riding directly for us.

"I'm going to Cider Creek," he shouted, in the way of a greeting. "There's a big rendezvous of all tha frontier farmers. Got to push the Indian's back. Say that roving bands been taking the women an' children, up in Rappahannock."

I did not know Baird well, nor how much truth there was in the story, but neither I, or any member of my family was about to go off looking for an Indian war. What I was going to do was investigate a bully's threat that was put to one of my sons. "I have business at the Bacon place," I told him, "and no wish to answer these reports."

Baird cocked his head and looked at me slyly. "Well, if it's Bacon you're for, n'en you best come along with me. He's tha main event of the party."

"What's that?"

"Neighbor Bacon's over at Cider Creek right now. Organizing our revenge."

I rose up in the seat unable to disguise my astonishment. Nathaniel Bacon? This was news for which I had no response. True, Bacon was one of the newcomers, but Nathaniel Bacon was *rich*. He even had a seat upon the governor's privileged council. My mind began to reel with a sense of heightened fear and apprehension. How did things get this far without my knowing? Feeling like a sudden fool, I came up blank staring into surrounding brush. While sitting like this for some odd awkward moments, I heard the squawk of distant fighting buzzards, and all I could think of was how Nathaniel Bacon was never cut out to be a farmer.

"Why'nt ride with me then, Corstair? Zach, you should come on, too." Baird said. He brought his musket up across the horse's nap. "It's near fifty mile piece to Cider Creek, an' our three shots together are a far sight better'n one."

I continued to feel crippled by the denial of such violence reaching my life and so quickly closing in. I had to see Bacon and learn of his plans, to search out his reasoning face to face, *and* I had to secure my large and extended family.

Naturally Tomas and Laura were first on my mind. Over many years we'd become used to religious threats and jealous grievance, but this was clearly a shift much darker, and with a deadly purpose. By 1675 the Corstairs had expanded our farm into a system that reflected our growth in accordance with our large family's needs. Tomas and Laura still remained with us, but Tomas, looking to venture into transport, was spending a lot of time on the river trying to start a river to bay barge. Zach, Stu, and Sarah were married and had their own families, but they lived just a country throw apart. Most mornings we returned from our sunrise chores to share a common breakfast in the 'big house.'

"What do you want to do, Pa?" Zachary asked.

I was always respectful of how he deferred to my judgement, even if he made most of the decisions these days.

"Gather everyone together at the main house," I told him. "I'll take a musket, and see what's going on. When I return we'll decide how we'll proceed."

And so the oldest of my adopted children, Zachary Treadnell-Corstair turned his mount around and headed back towards home. His quiet way of setting about things would go far towards calming the worry of my absence. He waved before he disappeared through the trees, leaving me as always, with the astonishment at being a thirty-nine year old grandpa to six. I watched Carlton Baird tip a flask to his white grizzled maw, and suddenly I fretted about the whereabouts of Laura. At twenty-three, and still unmarried, she had recently taken up with a man named Feather-Smith, a half-breed Siouan trader.

"Well, come on then," Baird said. "We'll still be moving come nighttime." He offered me a taste, but I was already in the grip of a woozy feeling quickly taking hold. I silently fell in behind him, seizing up with dread, and followed Baird into the thickest part of the trees. All other thoughts turned to Nathaniel Bacon.

He had entered the colony just two years before, with the type of a reception done up for the exalted. But he caused his first stir right away, when he was given a seat on the Governor's Grand Council, and he left it entirely alone. Stories quickly circulated of the scandals that he'd left and his escaping English justice, but a land in its growing pains, which was to say, ours, often embraced a man turned out by old-world vice. In any case, as Nathan himself once told me, "My earnest wish is to forsake society's double-dealings and become an honest planter."

And I can say on strong authority just how much of an honest effort he made. Once when I collected Zachary and Stuart to give him a hand with his clearing, we found him on a burned out plot cursing up the trunk of a hickory tree. And whether it was mixing his manure, or learning how to drive a plow, he always proved an eager student, immediately wanting to try the thing himself. Finally, of course, he had to hire a man named Cyrus Watford that he put in charge of the work.

I took pleasure in Bacon's company, and his letting us have access to the river, shortened our harvests to market by much. Helen developed a quick and deepening bond with his wife, I think by and large, because of the Bacon's rebellious love match. Elizabeth was beautiful, and devoted to Nathan with a passion as true as it was blind. It was a known fact that her father, a well-connected nobleman, had disowned her the very hour of her marriage, but it was their utter disregard for the protocols of gentlemen that mostly enhanced the Bacon's popular appeal. To every common that strove upon his rustic corner of Virginia, the Bacon's were the ideal of intrigue, a picture book rendition of the troubled ruling class. But the news of his heading up a war against the Indians stung into me like acid. I instantly became more apprehensive about the threats being made on Tomas, and the place where this happened, being Bacon's land.

Baird and I spent the rest of that day walking our horses through the low-slung limbs and bracken that pass for one of our trails. Branches rising dense enough in places so there was nothing to do but dismount and pull the horses behind. Fifty miles of this, I thought, doubting the wisdom of having brought along them along at all. But the moon was bright enough for us to keep going throughout the whole night, and by early the next morning we could smell the fires of the outer-most camps.

When we reached what I judged to be near center I stood in the saddle amazed. They had gathered in the seeming hundreds; woodsmen, trappers, traders, and farmers, hunters and miners, owned and rented men. And most of them were howling drunk. Here and there I noticed a familiar face, but by far in the majority were those I'd never seen before. "Where had all these strangers ever come from?" I said aloud beneath my breath.

The scene had all the elements of a seasonal Frontier Rendezvous. The early morning smoke hanging in a haze over simmering stews, rabbit and deer parts drying out over racks to the side of a fire. There was music and bawdy dancing with burly bearded men jumping around in blankets like a dress. There were countless camps of barter, and a yipping constant jabber trying to up the rate of exchange. There were tales being spun that were wild enough already, and in the animated voices, still expanded on. But the sight that alarmed, sending my pulse into my ears, was the total lack of Indians.

I would have thought it impossible. A congregation this wild and large, spread from open field into the woodland? But there was not a servant, nor a squaw, nor even a conniving slave. Not a single Indian, not a one. I blinked in disbelief, finding myself staring at a pike that someone had planted in the distance. Mounted to its top, above the craggy smoke, was a Wiccomican infant's head. I turned away in disgust, and refocused my intent to face Nathaniel Bacon.

The actual Cider Creek Post and Trade was little more than an oversized lean-to with its beech bark roof nearly all slid off. The entire structure, if you could call it that, was slumped beneath the weight of a fallen spruce that no one had taken the trouble to remove. I saw Bacon standing on top of a stump at the head of a sober group of planters, and listened for what he had to say. Baird moved our horses to a trough, as I slipped into the crowd trying to pick among the taut faces one that shared my doubts about a war. Bacon was his animated self; his hands and head jerking in perpetual motion, in the annoying way he had of distracting from and drawing emphasis to the point he was making at the same time. The one thing clear was the effort he'd put into not appearing like an aristocrat. But his frontier smock was still too clean, and I judged that it was made for this occasion. The mud that was caked to his boots and leggings however, added a little something rugged to the touch. Sweat stuck his long locks to the base of his neck whenever he would pause or throw his head in an obvious pose, but there was no doubt he had found himself a rapt reception. The eyes and ears of everyone there had fully encased his performance.

"We are here, having the duty and privilege of being God fearing Christians, are we not?" he asked without considering that anyone would answer. "And what great duty is this? What indeed of any greater moment than being called from half way round the world to turn these savage heathens from their dark and hopeless ways?"

I became immediately incredulous. This was a hawking catch-of-the-wind philosophy if I'd ever heard one. Over the past two years, I'd spent more than a few leisure hours in gentlemanly debate with him and his strong ideas about atheism. He once even told me that, "The idea of a paternal deity does not conform to modern thought," and more, " That this creaky concept will fall away of its own weight, like a rusty shackle." But more important was this: My own son Tomas, and dear Laura? Are they but savage heathen now?

"Where is the governor's militia?" someone yelled. "Where is his protection for all our tax?"

"He's consorting with the bloody enemy right now," another replied. "Collecting all he can in pelts and tributes.

The governor's protectin' *them.*"

"It's a well known fact," Bacon shouted back, "that Berkeley is using his Indian friends to drive us off our lands. He won't be content until every one of the middling farms is sacrificed in his land grabbing schemes. Every portion of the border that we have fought to gain is under the greedy claws of one of the governor's favorites."

I felt another surge of protest. As a full-fledged commoner and middling farmer myself, I was completely shut out by the class that Bacon was a part of. It was in fact, his own cousin, and one of the governor's 'favorites' that secured him his rich riverfront land. The exact plot that Helen and I had first staked all our hopes on. But I restrained myself, determined to press him on the more immediate issues.

"Who here has had an Indian fight?" I asked. "Who here carries proof of these attacks?"

Bacon looked out, seeing me for the first time, and gave a slight bow of his head. It was a standard sign of recognition, but I knew something better. There was an involuntary shame within his eyes. Shame because he alone amongst this hostile audience held the knowledge of our shared experience. Knowledge of the days that Tomas and I spent working in his fields, helping him haul his large stones off. Knowledge of the afternoon that Laura coaxed a family of skunks from out the inside of his root cellar.

"Welcome neighbor Philip Corstair." Bacon said, adjusting his composure. No one responded to my question, but there was clearly aggressive regard. Strangely, it was only in that moment that I realized just how badly my relations to other planters had declined. It no longer mattered that I was a respected landowner and had worked a successful farm for twenty years. The unforgiving point was that I had two full-blooded Indian children living under my roof and sharing my own name.

"Here's your proof, Corstair!" someone coming in from the fringe was shouting. The men around me parted, and George Gathers, a planter that lived quite a ways upriver was unrolling a leather tarp onto the ground. It opened up displaying a collection of charred and crumbled bones. Most of the pieces could have been from any number of animals, but the blackened, broken skulls were human, that was plain.

"The Flint family," Bacon said, as he approached from behind. "The parents were hacked to pieces in their beds. The children were then taken out one at a time and burned alive. Locked inside of the outlying sheds." He grabbed hold of my shoulder as if he were offering me his strength and comfort, and then hoisted himself back up on his stump. "All planting men bear witness!" he shouted staring down at me. And suddenly his eyes were different, darker, and cold. "Those refusing to take a side in the fight for freedman's land are dishonest to our hopes! The hopes of those who come after us, and a betrayal of good Englishmen, of every kind!"

Still watching me he took a moment to regroup, as if he hadn't expected the excited applause. Then, satisfied that everyone knew I was the one who dared to speak out, he lifted his gaze back over them. I received more harsh looks, particularly from George Gathers, as he tied his bones back in a sack like pieces of a broken pot. I turned out to the opposite field and saw in the distance a few of the camps standing off alone. These were a scattering of tents put up by fiercely independent men. Men that traversed freely, with the ability to trade with any tribe. Men that could live off the woods, entirely on their own. They knew that any Indian would be shunned for life for defiling, as George Gathers did, the sacred remains of their dead. But amongst rational Christians, heathens were full of such superstitions, and lived with many childish fears. I did not know the Flints, but what had been laid before me could not be justified. I bristled over someone's bones being used as tools to provoke me. Then I noticed Carlton Baird had disappeared, doubtless to keep himself removed from the stain of my obvious cowardice. I tightened my resolve at getting hold of Bacon, but outside of his hooting circle that he was molding into a mob.

I needed assurances for Tomas and Laura's security. I needed to see him in close. I was counting on my simple presence to remind him of who he was. And the other mix of issues, nearly as threatening as well. This apparent hatred of the governor for one, a man that by my sights had only offered Bacon a helpful hand. There was some inner clash of character working here, and I was determined to have it out with him before he pulled me in.

But now finding myself neglected, I could merely watch him from afar. I studied the angry whisky faces, seeing how he fed upon, and then directed their rage. His stride among the crowd was like a preacher politician's, somehow treating every grief and tribulation as the governor's personal sin. "And isn't it peculiar?" I could hear the rhetorical lift in his voice. "How the price for our commodities falls further and further still?"

I was stunned and perplexed at his call for a wholesale border war. Indeed, in many parts, the boundaries were so bent and thin that the actual lines would be drawn against themselves. But while mingling in the midst of this reckless group, and being so busily ignored, I took the time to try and weigh out what Bacon truly was that I didn't want to see before. Given the troubles that he seemed to have brought with him, and the miscreant schemes of his past, could the simple prospect of *failing* account for this dangerous man? There were his looked for riches in tobacco, which of course came to nothing but a loss, but this was a consequence that he suffered right alongside of everyone else. So what additional need, what startled desperation could account for usurping authority here? My God, he wasn't even truly a seasoned Virginian. He'd only been with us for barely two years. And in the end, all that I could see before me was an ambitious young man's panic to make a legitimate name for himself. But why go so far as to treasonously charge the governor? What I considered, with an ever-building distress, was that when this high class rite of passage was over, just how deadly would it get?

I tried counting the number of bullheaded planters, some that I'd lent my advice, but I only grew disgusted. Drowning in debt of their own making, and convinced it could be paid in Indian blood.

"I'm Rupert Johnson!" A man announced earnestly above the excited din. "And I'm here to report half a crop of stolen corn!"

I turned to the woods and saw a gang of vagrants hacking blindly away at anything that might pass for firewood. Nothing but runaways and felons, up and down, throughout. A community, on the whole, where stealing a man's corn would be considered a very small crime.

"Are the Indians," asked Bacon, this time spitting the word out. "In league with Governor Berkeley? Protected by his greed? And must we lose our honest livelihood riddled to pieces with his tax?" Another batch behind him roared in defiance.

A spasm of pain tore across my back beneath my shoulders, and I suddenly felt like an old man, getting older. These were my neighbors. Together we made up a fraternity that was forged by hard living. To live out here one had to be willing to accept responsibility for things beyond what could be called your due. And so aghast, I took in the scene playing out before me. Callused hands embedded with dirt, being pound to together, intimidating applause. The light streaming from Bacon's shirt that shone like the sun from his stump. I could only shake my head. The men that I once knew did not give sway to such screeching fashion, the only craving they had was to provide so their families survived.

"Who is willing?" Bacon was suddenly brandishing a scroll. "To sign this oath vowing to end all aggression from the savages? With or without a militia from the governor!"

Off to one side another cheer erupted around a man who had made a bearded manikin to tear an Indian puppet to shreds. And the pace of the day finally swelled and converged until it was enough. The men began an enlistment, the march of the simpleminded. There were promises of more fertile soil, soil that would no doubt be put to more tobacco, tied like a package, into Bacon's bold decree. I was witnessing the birth of a renegade aristocrat, shouting half crazed in a wild breeding forest, a part of the woods where no proper Englishman had ever been seen.

But then. As if some brave voice was reading my mind, behind me came a sound of dissension. Peasant frontiersmen were already forward, putting marks on his list, when I heard someone clearly mutter, "treason."

"Watch yourself, Mr. Bacon." Cecil Rhodes finally spoke up.

I must say that he looked very pale. He was I think, the only man there that was older than myself.

"That piece of paper in your hands is a hang-able offence."

"Very well," Bacon countered, covering the moment with a smile. "Then we'll have a march unto the governor and have him sign us a commission."

"I do not believe that he will," Rhodes replied.

"Oh, he'll sign it clear enough," Bacon continued.

He was either seriously convinced, or refusing to give up his bluff. But one thing that did always strike me about Bacon, he had more in confidence than a mountain billy goat.

"Else he'll find how little beaver he has to sell."

This last he phrased obscurely enough to keep himself out of prison; I only wished he were as cautious about sparking off conflicts with no foreseeable end. War with the Indians would seed distrust and hostility for generations yet unborn. Bacon had set a path to destroy all that Berkeley had built for so long, treaties with territories still in the making. The Mannock, the Appomatoc, and the enduring Pawmunkey peace. Indeed, before this threatened war was over, the whole Algonkin nation would be enjoined.

"Whyn't taker yon savige head'n' stuff 'it fir 'at pepper."

"What's that?" Bacon leaned his ear in to one of his toothless scribbling flock.

It felt like I was entering a nightmare made suddenly horribly real. The anointing of Nathaniel Bacon, privileged of England, being made our frontier king.

"Hi'siya 'at dirrInjun head." Another man explained.

Of late with his filthy subjects, learning him how to converse.

After a day and a half of waiting, shunned and frustrated I left Cider Creek without having had my audience with Bacon. He on the other hand, had successfully mounted his full course campaign. Clearly, he relished the nonstop attention and busied himself, at least partly, in avoiding me. Surrounded by an entourage, he marched through the fields conducting interviews with ready participants to gauge the extent of dealings with the Indians. He showed a definite knack for stringing unrelated incidents together, and form a wider, more sinister conspiracy than what was actually said. Hostile speculations included reasons why a tribe had recently moved, and forming it to a pattern of aggression. His efforts were aided by reports about the Pequots in New England, who were already waging a terrible war. Where a dozen Massachusetts settlements were said to have been destroyed. "The long feared Indian confederation is upon us!" Bacon proclaimed. "God will not protect the foolish farmer who has delayed in his defense!"

"The safety that I seek is not from marauding Indians," I said. It was the only time I could grab for a chance to speak. "But from the private men in arms that are being hired to protect us."

But my voice was drowned by a hundred other throats, each one drunker than the next, and gathering up a new thirst for what I called; pre-emptive revenge. By the time that Carlton Baird and I departed, it was clear that land for blood was the going price, and any nonwhite blood would do. People I had once called friends regarded my family as prejudiced, unwilling to see what was truly going on. I was reminded in very strong language of the way that the savages had deceived us in a massacre some fifty years before. A time, by the way, when no one present at this particular rally was even born. But there is no question of the horror that this countrywide slaughter had caused, and this from the most trusted Indian family friends. Then too, this was a time when we English were nowhere near the numbers we'd become.

Baird and I shared very few words as we trudged our way back to our homes. We crossed through great swathes of tribal lands that were fully slashed and burned through, dotted out with settler's shacks. These tacked together slip-shod places actually seemed to seep. But these were my kindred English, who just like me, come for the dream of owning their land. They were here after crossing a vast gateway, after running down the giant waves before the wind. Now they were strewn across the wilderness like a slum.

* * * * *

"Where is the woman today?" Mr. Lawrence asks me. He is anxiously peering out at the gray sky that seems to coat the entrance to our cave. I am fully aware of his concern. Astonishing a fact as it is, in the midst of our desolation the old man has established routines. It is already past noon and our Indian nurse Seycondeh has yet to make an appearance. The alteration of her schedule is distressing him.

"She'll be along," I answer him. I have no knowledge of course, as to where she is. I am distracted, reliving the massacre that lay facing me, turning its burning bits over and again in my mind. Walking through the cinders of the house. The severed torsos on smoking mounds, Sarah's newborn split in two. I stared upon it, dumbly, as if it had a function of which I did not know. No. But of course, that would be me. To move about as if it counted, to find that someone might be missing, as if they could have survived. And all the while knowing that every living member of my family was dead.

* * * * *

I looked upon the smoldering landscape, mindlessly counting body parts, eliminating and seeking hope. I performed like this. Stoned and cold, a machine to make a human assay. There was a level beneath it though, that was holding out a chance that someone had been taken for a hostage. Zach's little boy for sure. And being bold enough to think it, perhaps my dearest Helen had somehow bartered for her life. But as I faced the choking grimness, the bile rose up from my guts. There was Tomas with his eyes removed, rammed the whole length of him upon a pole. His mutilated body bearing blind witness to his betrayal of tribal ways. The charred remains of our barn animals were ripped inside and out, and stuffed with indecipherable human pieces. There was Sarah's husband Gordon with his mouth sewn onto the scrotum of a hog. Sarah herself stripped and sliced with such surgical strokes that my mind locked numb to see the murdering purpose. I found Helen and Laura at the spring house bound and draped with their heads beneath the water. Entangled in their nakedness, the violations plain.

"God, oh my God have mercy, my God…" Carlton Baird was making whispery sucking noises beside me. The gathering at Cider Creek had taken me away for more than four days, and the horror in my absence was now laid out before me, or at least the part of me that understood. My conscience lay well beyond anything so clear. I should have stayed home. And having done, I could have been happily dead. And these and a thousand other demon forms that came howling through my head.

As it was I fell upon the ground, and took to grinding bits of stone into my hand.

"My God Corstair, you must come with us now." Carlton Baird said at last. I looked up at him but I did not know what he was.

It took us two days to lay the mangled bodies in a crude attempt at rest, but I do not have the sense to recall how this was done. I do remember Baird taking off his shirt with which he covered and buried Helen. I can also hear his distant voice assuring me that the separate families would be buried altogether, although I watched him put all the children side by side in one large gaping pit. And I remember that the air was wet with drizzle, and that before he filled the muddy hole I wiped the soot from off of Laura's lips. I remember too, my loss of feeling. How I could not command the motion in my arms or legs, and a bewitching wonder that so much emptiness could fill a man all up. I do not remember leaving, or with what departing words. I do not remember even if any were said.

The only clear picture that I have of this time is of Tekanepet, a Susquehanna warrior and old acquaintance, who was suddenly walking towards us on the path. Until then I had been following Baird, silent as a drone, but with the sight of Tekanepet I was suddenly impressed by how far north we'd come. Baird immediately raised his musket, and Tekanepet disappeared.

"It's alright," I whispered. I remember that in spite of the misty weather my throat was very dry. "I know him."

Baird tilted his gun to the ground and after a minute Tekanepet emerged from the thicket beside us. He was not painted for battle, but judging his pack he appeared to be carrying a long distance load.

"I am peace, Corstair. You see me," he said, and approached. His open empty hands extended from his sides. "I want only to talk peace." Years before, Tekanepet and I had taken fishing trips together, and I had always appreciated his interest in practicing the English tongue. "You follow me? To the clearing by the lake."

"It's alright," I assured Baird. We were both more surprised than fearful. "We will follow," I nodded to Tekanepet. I had decided that he was going to tell me who killed my family. And why.

We followed a creek to our right at a distance behind him until we arrived at the small pond that it fed. Tekanepet let his sack rattle as he walked. He was trying to alleviate any fears we had of ambush, but Baird kept looking in the bush like there was a signal being relayed. When we reached a pine needle clearing Tekanepet removed a blanket from his satchel and made a gesture for us to smoke. We sat down, and in a strained and awkward silence, he prepared his tobacco, which he then struck with an English flint.

"There was a raid by the Doegs more north," he said when we each had taken our turn. "They killed a white man called Robert Hen."

"Did they also kill my family?" I asked. I looked at him evenly, allowing him time to read the death that I knew was in my eyes.

He betrayed both panic and shock, indicating how little he actually knew. Carlton Baird got up and took his musket to the edge of the circling trees. A crow screamed from a branch high above, and Tekanepet silently stared after its path. The shaved half of his head was growing out into different lengths making him look something like a madman, but I also knew that he meant it as a sign of peace. It was his face that surprised me. Beneath his blank expression was compassion, I was sure of it, compassion with a healthy mix of fear. And though I had no idea about the purpose of his journey, he wanted to let me know that he understood what the future now would bring.

"You are my friend, Philip Corstair. You ate my food,

and you know I do not pray to Jesus."

I simply looked at him. He had nothing to say of any value so I let my mind go blank again.

"I have given you a bed in winter, I have offered you my wives."

Behind him I could see Baird pacing and peering into the woods, leaning forward, and listening for anything foreign in wood filled sounds.

"What do you want?" I asked, wanting to conclude this meeting. I did not care what he wanted.

He pulled back his sack and emptied out a variety of finely honed knives. The longer ones, some well over a foot, were sheathed in a thick coat of fox elaborately embroidered with tassels of real gold. Each one represented a job that I knew took many painstaking days. I vaguely wondered where he'd come upon such work.

"Guns," he answered. "You and I know what has come. Right now the English Colonels Mason and Brent have many men. I have many sorrows for you, Philip Corstair. I wish to make you know that I will fight at your side. You are white. And you can get me guns."

Just behind Tekanepet's left side Baird slipped his hand over the fine bone handle of a mid-sized blade. I'm not sure if Tekanepet even knew he was there. I watched in a peculiar kind of stillness while Baird slit open Tekanepet's throat as clean and as easy as a slice of cornbread. The blood poured downward from a circular fountain in a smooth and steady flow. It was a very fine knife that Tekanepet was hawking, with very little effort it had cut his neck completely through. The crow that had been screaming suddenly returned to its branch, shaking down a small cluster of leaves.

"Time to find Brent and Mason," Baird said, wiping the blade on the dead man's jacket. He then packed all the knives back into Tekanepet's satchel and stretched it across his back. "Nice set of knives, " he said.

* * * * *

"I never wanted this for these people," Mr. Lawrence suddenly announces.

Seeing his silhouette against the mouth of our cave reminds me of how frail he is. Despite Seycondeh's attentions, or today's apparent lack of, I am forced to admit that I do not think he has much longer to last. Nonetheless, I am thankful for his company while it's still mine to claim. He has succeeded in bringing me back from the dreadful details of scenes I've traveled hard to forget. Back into our healing cave that wraps its walls around us like a protective womb. Back from places that I've witnessed whose violence can only be measured in dreams. My particular brand of violence, for instance, was of every formidable stripe. Passionate and indifferent, wanton and calculated, and each one applied with the same purpose. The losing oneself in forgetting.

I gaze upon the pictures of medicinal procedures that are etched into the ceiling above me. They offer miraculous accounts of animal spirits returning, and death like a disheartened actor pretending to skulk away. But, I am no longer innocent, and know what sort of life this hole of earth will finally give birth to, if it still has the power to give me any life at all.

"The war was for a government, Corstair. *Our* government."

He is getting agitated. Maybe he thinks that Seycondeh will not come back. Maybe he thinks that I drove her away. Why else bare his conscience to me now? Over killing ill planned, or killing ill timed, or killing off kilter? Is there such a one?

"I needed Nathaniel. Nathaniel had the love of the men,

and the men, well…" He is giving me one of his hopeless looks. The way he used to stare at nothing during those months when we successfully unseated the governor, and all the men wanted, was to kill some more Indians. The 'men' included myself.

"Goddam Berkeley's tax!"

He is definitely agitated. If Seycondeh does not come back and take him for his walk this tedious task will fall to me. Mr. Lawrence's legs are as brittle as a pair of dried worms, and he cannot move without assistance.

"First he steals our lands, then taxes the blood out of everything we own!" he shouts.

I can see that he is well on his way to his familiar rant about Berkeley, but in view of his fragile health, I appreciate his pluck. He is using his usual terms of course. Acting like he has some exclusive hold upon justice. Here, he often substitutes, *our* and *we*, for instance, like being a spokesman for the better social cause, when he really means, *my* and *I*. Denial is a potent common denominator. But I mean him no disrespect. Clearly, Mr. Lawrence is a scholarly, intelligent man. But even so, I sometimes do not listen to him hard. It is times like these, when he speaks for the benefit of some *general* public, that he'll skip a significant detail. I think he thinks that he's providing the *broader* truth, the proper space for *principles* to be involved. It has taken me awhile to catch on to this trick, but this is how we've come to get along. Half like a wife and the other like an Oxford don, who will forget that he was eating soup. Even now we can get caught up in denying what life has brought us to. Is not happiness after all, something abstract? You see? I'm getting to sound more like him all the time.

But I will share one *general* rule that the scholar Richard Lawrence has taught me. And that is that every shred of history important enough to record is entirely personal.

Several years ago, before this whole thing started, Governor Berkeley removed Mr. Lawrence's name from one his estates. In complicity with his own London agents. Lawrence had the title; sealed and drawn by a tight and tidy transferred sum. It may be nothing more than an insignificant secret, but I know it was at least one cause for *his* declaring war.

"Seycondeh!" he suddenly shouts, and I stand up, growing more impressed by the strength in her healing herbals. "The savages were not the war, Corstair," he says loudly, "and you know it!"

"Here, let me help you," I say, offering my hand. "Time to get up."

"Where is she off to? Plotting our death?" He rattles a sigh, and tries to keep his grip upon my arm. Then winces back in pain. "You didn't scare her off, did you?"

Now I get his all-knowing stare. The one he gives to reveal what you most want to hide. And though he knows my reputation plenty, even Mr. Lawrence will sacrifice half a smile at my *pronouncing* it. That is, in his removed and *general* style: Philip Corstair; the man that accounted for the single most Indians killed, before even joining Bacon's army.

aird and I caught up with Colonels Brent and Mason as they were preparing to cross the Potomac into Maryland. Brent was in the process of loading up the horse ferries, but Baird had decided that the water was a little too choppy to risk ours. I simply followed his lead and we ended up with a loosely formed unit of farmer soldiers under the command of George Mason. The night was uncommonly warm, but it did not discourage anyone from adding to the bonfires that were strung out all along the bank. If anything, the men took delight in signaling their hostilities, and if the Doegs thought the death of Thomas Hen was without consequence, they had only to look across the river to see what they had wrought. As for the slaughter of my family, I could not bring myself to think on it. It lay somewhere deep, into a void that was smothered by unreachable sorrow and shame. I knew that I'd have to give an official accounting to someone soon enough, but I could not do it up 'til now. It hung behind me, like an unspoken horror between Baird and myself, and I trusted him enough to keep it that way.

I sat dazed by the fireworks, watching twenty-foot trees turn into flames, to the purpose I suppose of bolstering resolve. But if anyone along that river had any doubts about these actions, you wouldn't have heard it told. We were chasing Indians into territory beyond our jurisdiction, eagerly anticipating the largest armed assault in the last thirty years. A time that was so far back that my fellow combatants were not even born. Regrets were for those who had managed to miss out.

Not that I considered the matter that much. My mind was wholly incapable of holding that long onto any thought, and I found myself in a role best described as Carlton Baird's companion; the mute. I had observed him shield me from the more excitable festivities, 'til I was finally off sitting by myself in a patch of dirty sand. There, a man approached that I recognized from the rented day labor that straggled Rut Road.

"There's been some hinting 'bout yer heavy loss, Mr. Corstair," the man said. He looked as though he'd survived to his late twenties, but age was a hard thing to gauge among the class at Rut Road. "I'd be right proud to walk 'long side you."

I'm not sure what he read in my blank expression but he must've seen enough to think I'd tolerate his company. I guess it was too much to ask for Baird to leave the unspeakable unsaid.

"Name's Ned Fanning," the man began again, and extended his hand. I looked at him calmly, avoiding his touch. "You know, I twern't all the time ragged labor," he added, and decided to wipe his hand on his dirty pants. "I was man a property, jus' like yer. N'en tha damn gov'ner came an' forcet me off my own lan' with all his damn Nav'gation Law."

I looked away, and then I determined just to sit it out, staring out ahead into the dark. He leaned forward to peer at me, jutting his head in an odd angle. His tongue rolled out and the firelight glistened over toothless gums. He was, I expect, measuring the effect of his bold and treasonable speech on a man who had just lost everything. "I'd been tradin' my 'bacco to the Dutchmen for awhile back there," he continued, "'fore Berkeley's Brits done caught me. Ne'n, jus' payin' the penalty, cost me my farm. But there weren't no other way, Mr. Corstair, no other way to it."

"Here, too."

Another man approached what I began to notice was a growing perimeter, and behind him came three more. Still another, clearly older than the rest, held back in the shadows to one side. The dank ground where I'd chosen to be alone was suddenly attracting outcasts left and right. I resented the intrusion, but strangely comforted to see another person of my years.

"I finished my seven year hard labor three year ago," one in the group then offered. "An' all tha lands I get to choose from is inna bottom so wet it fills back up ever time it's drained. An' you know there's a hundred thousand empty acres 'at come right up to my wasteland. Untold hundreds, an' thousands. Prime acreage that ain't been touched. Cain't be touched, by gover'ment decree."

"All tha freedmen they send out just scrapin' by now. Hunnert mile to markets, an' the filthy savages come an' steal you blind when you gotta be in town."

"Fifty pounds tobacco tax is what the governor charges! Fifty pounds for our so called protection!" a red-faced man spit out. "And his protection ain't nothing but a string of worthless forts the old man put up to protect his precious beaver!"

"Protect his precious young quim, you mean."

This last comment provoked a burst of swig-slapping laughter, a reference to our seventy-year old governor's recent bride. The new Lady Berkeley could well have been Berkeley's own daughter in terms of years.

"Show some respect here!" The old man suddenly bellowed.

The rest of the men snapped around with a start, as though looking for anything to fight. But only someone very foolish would come to the defense of the governor on this riverbank.

"This man here has just received the greatest and most grievous blow," he explained, and placed one of his hands on my shoulder. It surprised me with its heft, but he must have sensed my disapproval for just as quickly, he took it off.

"You needn't mar the sanctity of a man and his memories with mention of our governor's scandals and decadence."

I looked at him then, somewhat taken aback. How had he linked his inflaming reproach of the governor to speaking on my behalf?

"My name is Isaac Trebble, Mr. Corstair. And I am acquainted with the knowledge of your family and your incomprehensible loss."

I studied what seemed to be his two faces merging, coming in and out of shadow, as the breeze played shimmer with the firelight. He had a white head of shoulder length hair and a long white beard to match. All of which would brighten for a second, before going back to black. I tried to think where we had met.

"I make it my business to know many things," he continued mysteriously. "Hear me speak. I know firsthand of the war in New England, where the bloody heathen has already killed hundreds and burned more than twenty settlements. I have ventured in from Virginia's shores, where I saw a Christian family, Mr. Corstair, with adopted Indians just like yours; and all of them perished. Swallowed without notice by a great ocean storm. And before it was done, the raging water, took the lives of dozens more. Vanished, as if they'd never even existed. I have walked a hundred miles through rows of fallen trees, covered with a million squawking pigeons. A squawking as powerful as a thunderous roar."

Isaac Trebble toned on, gradually spreading his woeful gaze away from me, and across the breadth of the crowd. I glanced about, feeling suddenly reduced to the discomfort that a church pew would present to some small child. His spell had bound the men around me however, who leaned in awkward positions, gathering his every word.

"I have just passed a night with other righteous men," he continued, his voice was fully rolled out now, wrapping them in like a blanket. "Men just like yourselves, struck still and gawking at a fireball spreading its demon sparks throughout the western sky. Everyone that's seen these things *knows;* my friends. We are at the opening of Hell's door! Nothing of this ilk has happened since the treachery of the savages back in '44."

He then gave way to a dramatic pause letting responses like, "God save us," and "Amen," fill the gap in mumbles.

"Just as we surely know that only the blood of Jesus Christ can cleanse us! It is our calling; it is the truth and our divine right! We must wash the heathen from this country and forever close this gate to Hell! Only God-fearing Christians can sanctify this land! Cast out serpent worship! And witchcraft's demon spells!"

There was much that these men complained about. Their promised dreams, gone in the corrosion of a selfish government. But what, when done with their bottle brave impotent rage, were they possibly prepared to do about it? Well, Isaac Trebble spooked them into a breakaway gallop. Howling like a pack of wolves, they grabbed up their guns and blindly ran to the pitch-black river. And what with the tidal surge, and the splashing mass confusion, it was a miracle that some poor fool, forgetting he couldn't even swim, hadn't drowned himself. But just as Trebble finished his sermon the providence he was calling for arrived in the form of Colonel Brent's flat boats. I was just glad for the chance to linger behind, searching the old man through in my mind to make some prior connection. Then, as was apt to happen in those hours where I roamed inside this massive shell of displaced grief, the importance of it suddenly lost appeal.

Such was the slipstream quality of my present at that time. I had a sense that things were moving around me, and that I engaged in a series of motions, but the actual activity never registered very much. Nothing took the form of having meaning, so to speak. In this instance I was thinking I should seek out Isaac Trebble to question him on his prophecy, and I looked for him right enough, until I wandered under a midnight sky standing alone in the water. I think I was trying to break a code. There was one star that blinked on for three, and off again for five long seconds. This coincided with the loading of the boats that swirled the wake above my knees, and then there was the Book of Revelations.

"Jus' 'tween you an' me, Corstair," the man named Ned Fanning appeared before me again. His tone was low and into my face, fairly reeking of liquor. "I kilt dem Doegs what started all 'iss. Me an' Kyle James. Tha man you used to hire bye an' bye."

I looked at him, suddenly suspicious of his reasons for sharing this information.

"'Em damn Doegs made tha mistake ah killin' my friend, Robert Hen just 'cause me an' Kyle took some a ther damn hogs. So's me an' Kyle jus' turn 'roun' an' kilt' some of 'em back." Ned Fanning stepped toward the nearest boat floating in from the shadows. "Bushwhacked a couple, two or three, while they wer fast asleep. Annat's all ther is ta that," he said.

It was almost magical how effortlessly he was swung out onto the water, and how quickly in the darkness he disappeared. I stepped into the very next boat that came and took its place.

When we landed on the Maryland side, it was still well before first light. The tree line was thick with an ominous mist that shut the loudest braggarts into a watchful silence. Peering in the predawn woods, I, along with Virginia's very bravest was sobered by caution. We met in small whispery groups at the edge of the wood and then marched up a narrow path single file. Muskets were draped across tightened forearms with powder and pans placed ready and open. All eyes were fastened on the thickets, and all ears were attuned to the slightest dark motion. And all while slipping in the fresh manure piled by the horses of Colonel Brent's men. Four miles passed like this, tense, but without incident when we came upon a fork where Brent had left a mark that he made a turn to the left. Colonel Mason motioned us forward to the right.

A little after sunrise, and a quarter mile into this wood we came upon a shelter at the corner of a clearing that looked to be a hunting camp. As the morning fog started to burn off, we saw a silhouetted movement inside the hut, of perhaps a dozen men. We quietly halted and fanned out in half a circle, picking the best positions in the surrounding trees and brush. I remember being impressed by the silence and the tact with which the men accorded themselves, one could have almost assumed us professional soldiers. All of a sudden there came an explosion of guns some half a mile distant to our rear. Fresh reports and echoes resounded through the forest but then we had little time to think. The terrifying explosions of so much gunpowder going off at once, was evidently driving the Indians in the cabin into hysterics. The dozen or so braves poured out, jamming up the doorway, in a panic that stood beyond what men will do with fright. I saw right away that they were Susquehanna, and saw too, what little difference it made. All the men about me bolted upright, firing their weapons, until there was no space left that wasn't filled with the sound of screaming lead and screaming Indians. Amazingly, they held no weapons, but waved their hands high above their heads, when everything became so frenzied that what orders Mason signaled were lost. A second wave of warriors then came up behind the first, holding forth a half dozen gourds as if trying to offer us the contents. In the noise and confusion, the gourds appeared like war clubs, and the men responded with a heavy barrage of shot. The Indians then seemed to go mad. They doused themselves and each other with water from the gourds, while running backwards in delirium, covering ground in widening arcs and circles. Falling down, kneeling, crossing themselves, and shouting all at once, "Wee baptizeed! Wee Christian! Wee baptizeed!" Another line of musket fire exploded into the bodies that lay before them. A final rush of braves came on, and seeing the others so riddled and torn ran for the shelter of the woods. They were immediately cut down from the back, but most remarkably, in the middle of this free-for-all yelling, the fire and the smoke, the running and reloading, and the laughing all insane, the tallest brave turned round and calmly strode right up to Colonel Mason. He pulled at Colonel Mason's arm, hoisting it up and down, shouting, "Susquehanna ne-touw! Susquehanna friends!" Then in the thick of the smoke, he turned away and simply disappeared. Colonel Mason immediately dropped his musket and ran throughout the scattered remnants of our line screaming, "Halt Fire! Halt Fire Men! Halt! For Lord's sake shoot no more! These are our friends the Susquehanna!"

When the last barrage had finally stopped, what Susquehanna that survived had fled, and fourteen of their braves had been left in contorted postures along the forest floor. The clearing smoke revealed the darkened pooling blood, the brains and entrails, the slow burning leaves covered in a greasy film. I counted out three that I killed myself, but that was Baird's work for keeping me in guns. And what struck me the most was the sudden and profound amount of silence. I have since become quite keen to this mysterious presence. The way it penetrates, descending, and unsettling, always there observing what is thought.

If Colonel Mason was angry, he kept it to himself. But everyone noticed he was standing off alone. His immediate response was to distance himself from the slaughter, but then he turned and just squatted, all the way down to the leafy floor. Perhaps he'd assumed he could invoke some military discipline, and now he was despairing this mistake. But there he sat, looking stunned and distracted, even past reproaching men rooting for mementos. It was the approach of Colonel Brent's horsemen that put an end to that. One man rode up and kicked Ned Fanning in the head as he pulled off an ear from a fallen warrior's face.

"Alright men! Form a line!" Mason yelled, finally coming to his senses. Colonel Brent then appeared, dragging an Indian boy behind him that was tethered to his saddle.

"Ten Doeg warriors encountered, and all dispatched," Brent reported. "What has happened here?" The expression in his face was impossible to read. Impossible to say if he was happy with our results.

"It is my duty to assume responsibility for a most unfortunate mistake, Colonel. These men were not a party to the guilty Doegs," Mason said. He stood directly in front of Brent's horse. He began as if he wanted to accept all possible charges, but then was distracted by the Indian boy, who was refusing to stand up.

"Misfortune acknowledged, Colonel." Brent said. "We'll leave it as a signal to any others that would risk being renegades. A regrettable mistake, nonetheless. I'll ride ahead and draw up the necessary report. If you'll do me the service of taking possession of the prisoner?" He looked back at the youth he had dragging behind him. The boy was pressing his face into the ground with all the force he could muster. Colonel Brent handed Mason his end of the rope. "His father was the Doeg King, and a lying murderer."

This, Brent stated with such officious sincerity that someone to the right of me made a slight guffaw. Colonel Mason immediately stared daggers at the man, but he was hardly alone in being amused. That Colonel Brent would grant the Doeg King an interview before killing him was richly appreciated in the light of what we'd done.

"Perhaps you'll find more royal qualities in the lad than he has exposed to me. Hee-up!" he cried, and wheeled his horse around. Almost as quick, the column he led was back on the trail to the river.

Colonel Mason did not look well. He dangled the end of Brent's rope in his hand as if it were a rattlesnake not entirely dead. He looked back once more at the final carnage, his face a mix of disgust and fear. Suddenly, I thought of the white haired Isaac Trebble, and searched through the powder streaked murky young grins. I don't know why, but I wanted him to be there.

"Hup, march!" Mason shouted.

There was no question that something had gone out of him. The Doeg Indian boy dug into him as well. He worked on Mason's gut, just as surely as the ruts that he was tearing up, while being dragged upon the ground. Finally there was nothing to be done but stop and build a makeshift litter. Then tie the little prisoner up inside. Mason wanted out of those woods like he knew its evil spirits were rising up to stop him, but he would not stand to let the boy get beat. We each had a turn at carrying him, like the prince that he reportedly was, all the way down to the river. It was either that, or pry him free from every bush and shrub.

*A*fter crossing back into Virginia the men that had farms to tend decided they'd pretty much performed their civic duty, and so departed all in a group. As for myself, with nothing but the haunt and smell of ashes to return to, I settled in with the drifters and vagrants on the western side of Mason's property. Shortly on though, I was called to give my account at a hearing of the Corstair massacre. The meeting was set up to be a formal inquiry, but since I was supposedly suffering from the after effects of such an intense shock Colonel Brent approached me and the subject with careful delicacy. I must say that considering the fact that I was squatting on his property, I was well treated from the moment I entered Mason's well appointed home.

"Mr. Corstair, it is a powerful honor to have you here with us," Brent said after asking me to sit. "May I say that I am proud to be in the company of so brave and fierce a soldier."

I nodded. "Alright."

Brent and Mason looked aside at one another, and then offered a Bible for me to swear upon.

"Please allow me to extend our deepest sympathies for your horrifying loss," he continued.

"Yes sir."

"And I want you to know that this atrocity will be set to rights. Restitution of your property, such as it can, will be done."

"Yes sir."

"Now. If you please, Mr. Corstair, can you tell us, prior to the mass… incident, your experience with the savage threat?"

I looked at him unsure of what he meant.

"From the, uh, … adjoining tribes?"

"None, sir."

"Across the territories? To and from the meeting at Cider Creek?"

My stare remained blank, and I turned to Carlton Baird for help. I wasn't so ready to describe our encounter with Tekanepet, but Brent spared me the trouble by nervously changing tact and suddenly asking about my acreage. The annual yield and average rainfall, information in all, that he seemed happy to have Baird fill in. They surprised me in fact, with how much they already knew. And as the session wore on with my memory producing more lapses, they ended up doing the talking. I listened as far as I could, but I never escaped the feeling that they were speaking of someone else. Anyway, by the time the testimony finished, they were far more interested in my Indian kills than in anything else.

"…A motivated Indian killer… can use a man like this one." I heard someone behind me say.

Then the meeting was adjourned, and my answers to their questions sealed with other papers in support of their Maryland invasion, and taken by courier to the governor in Jamestown. I will say that Baird and I got an awfully good lunch. And it felt good, I suppose, to be so included with the men at the top. Then as the light trailed off into late afternoon, Baird emptied his last mug of Mason's homemade punch, and bade us all good-bye.

He headed back to his neglected plantation, while men like me, with nowhere left to go, made the most of appropriating Colonel Mason's woods. I found myself embraced in the company of these down and out sorts, and was whisked on a tour of the various campsites. Words about my courage seemed to presage every stop. I just tagged along with this committee of sorts that spread the news about, and tried to make sure that everyone had something to eat. They also recruited volunteers to patrol along the river. Everywhere we went there was talk of some new action, and where to expect the savage's revenge.

Before the week was done though, Colonel Brent made an official call to address our outdoor habitat, (quickly turning rooted) and reported that our foray into Maryland had so enraged the governor he was calling for an inquiry with the power to indict. "Further malicious incursion shall be treated as a capital offence," he read, and then ordered that we immediately disperse. But the surrounding woods were filling up with ramblers and the dispossessed, bringing rumors of yet new attacks, arriving every day. Brent listened with considerable suspicion, but the truth be told, I think he was intimidated by so much poverty sitting in one place. And then, most of the gathering was harmless. Men wanting little more than fellowship, and a respite from what living they scratched from hard bent days. In the end Brent simply returned to Mason's house, more or less to wash his hands of us I think. We chopped firewood, shared a secret or two for snaring game, distilled and drank a pot boiled awful tasting whiskey. But for all that, our presence amounted to little more than a general nuisance.

The most curious thing during this time concerned the little Doeg Indian boy who was staying in Mason's house. He was said to have fallen into a kind of deep sleeping trance, and would not wake to eat or drink, nor have any food forced upon him. More astonishing was the fact that no one was entirely sure if he still even drew a breath.

With my well-known relationship with the natives, I was brought in to see what I could help, but the boy's bizarre behavior was beyond anything I'd seen. It was Colonel Brent, strangely enough, that had taken his condition most to heart, and developed a morbid fascination in the youth's apparent trick at staying alive while seeming to be dead. In any case a few days of this passed without any change, when Brent, (who was a die-hard papist) suddenly declared that the boy was bewitched and ordered him to be baptized. The problem then became the lack of priests or ministers at any convenient distance, which presented some confusion about how this should proceed. Brent asserted that as a military man, and quite unsure of his Latin, he could not possibly conduct the service, and so after much debate, it was decided that Colonel Mason's clerk should perform the rite. A basin of water was fetched from the spring then all in the room joined hands and prayed on it twice. Water was then dripped upon the lad's forehead, while the clerk read aloud from the Bible. But the child's face remained deeply indifferent, as if into a sound sleep. Brent then suggested that the clerk should speak much louder, and the clerk, a Mr. Mayberry, already feeling much abused, fairly shouted out the Holy names. Then he wet the boy's brow with the sign of the cross, and a few stepped forward while another few stepped back as if making room for some explosive miracle.

Nothing happened. On closer inspection, I might say that the boy's dark complexion seemed to have grown paler, but nothing occurred that was vaguely counted on. One by one the witnesses departed, attracted to the outside shade of Mason's trees and to drink some more of his punch.

Then, we had hardly finished the first round when Mrs. Mason ran from the house in a fit of excitement. She was altogether beside herself, declaring that the boy had just come round. We immediately followed her to his room where we stood amazed at the child sitting up and gaping back at us, acting as if he were equally perplexed. Mrs. Mason started cooing at him, gently spooning him a cordial in a broth, which he readily accepted although he was still unwilling to speak. For Mason, and most especially Brent, the miracle served as evidence to a destiny, the promise that would be fulfilled by our righteous cause. Everyone else started praying, almost in a frenzy, and professing their greater understanding of God. I stood by and closely studied the child. There was nothing false that I saw in his eyes. They only grew wide and astonished, at the burst of excited English talk.

A short time later I returned, not entirely sober, to my grass-stuffed bed on the western edge of camp. Just after being pulled under the gasp of my snores, I was awakened by a series of shouts that circled over my head. Reluctantly, I brought myself up on an elbow, and grabbed the attention of a youth that trotted by my tent. He told me that a thousand men had been mustering back in Maryland to hunt down and kill a murdering tribe of Susquehanna. With my head still a muddle, I watched the scurrying about to collect God knows what of belongings. The men were, it seemed, bound to go join the Maryland fight. As I reflect on the look of this chaos, the determination of it, now, (since this was something that I missed at the time) I can see that I was being given a moment of clarity, in the form of the kid that I had stopped beside my tent. (Had I been more aware, I should even say that he'd been sent.)

"Look here, Mr. Corstair," he said. He was smiling at me, and seemed not at all anxious to get away. "I ain' come all iss wild way without knowin' I got ta take my chances."

He must have been about my age when Helen and I first started out.

"An' tha way things are right now, if I ain't allowed ta do no mor'n be some kinda hero, so be it. I'll kill an Indian or two if that's what it take for me ta get along."

His name was Christopher Longley, and seemed an enterprising, dare I say, genuinely happy young man. He had that rare ease of manner in those that see what's laid before them, merely as an adventure, or at least an interesting interlude. It was not so much in what he said, but something that he carried. Like someone standing in the midst of a massive collision, saying; "Well, what else can I do?"

In this case he should have been running with the others, grabbing to be the first in line, but here he was back with me, and as grateful as being anywhere else. We strapped together some clothes inside of a blanket, and the longer that he lingered the more attracted I was by his daring that seemed so detached. Christopher Longley had what was called 'ground knowledge,' a necessary ingredient for accepting what was true.

"The settlers up in Maryland are pretty much torn down middle. Half see us reckless Virginians as causin' all the trouble, an' lay it at the feet of Brent and Mason."

The landscape itself seemed to move about me, with everybody running past my swimming head. But before I knew it, I was aboard my saddle, listening hard to what Christopher Longley said.

"The other half's up at arms, an' itchin' ta strike back." He poked my leg, and I looked down into his face. "An' ne'n, there's another lot of people, but they don't seem to count at all. Those be tha ones that don't believe no Indian attacks has even taken place."

His natural remove and winsome eyes grinned up at me at once.

"You might as well come on along, Mr. Corstair, an' see what's ta see outa this. Colonel John Washington's takin' men across tha Potomac, right now. No matter what tha ole gov'nor has to say."

And then he must have decided that I was the fool to keep dawdling, for he whacked the flank of my horse, so that he quickly fell behind. When I'd gotten her back under a canter, whither or no, I was being whisked along with our militia. The men moved in excitement, full of big news about Colonel

Washington, and when I turned back to look for Longley, he was gone.

"As Gawd my witness, but didn't she wrestle ta git at that trunk full a' nuthin' but her frilly dress?"

An indenture turned backwoodsman, who called himself Smokey Ray Joe, was recounting his experience as a porter on the Jamestown docks. We had by now settled into a steady rhythmic march that took up the whole afternoon. And while I wished only to bask in the slow passing softness of the early autumn colors, the surrounding men conveyed themselves in nothing but nonstop blather. The leaves filtered a scattering of light that turned green to orange-yellow, making the forest into a startling stained glass cathedral at different times of the day. I enjoyed the pace, leaning back in my seat to squint up into the ceiling, but I had never heard so much complaining.

"No'n, when she saw what a mess been made ah them dresses on tha passage over, she knocked a full barrel a' tobacco right out my hands, and into the bleedin' James. 'Ats how bad she was tryin' to git at that ship's captain." Smokey Ray chuckled in spite of himself. "She might be a wee little thing, but she got herself a build-up kind of pow'r."

This observation, among a list of such insults, was about Lady Berkeley, the governor's new wife.

"Now, who't you think gone an' paid fer all 'at? Got myself lockt up in tha hoosegow fer ninety-aut days, onna counta I wern't able but to half salvage that load a' weed."

But gripe as they may, our spirits were made lighter by the simple act of moving again. Moving was enough for now, even if the purpose remained illegal or unknown. The monotonous conversation boiled down to the necessity for vengeance, how it applied to the white man's duty, with no limits being placed on cursing the idiot governor.

When we finally broke free of the forest, we stood in a field beside the river, where the sight of so many men and much materiel was spectacle like. At every bend, the shores teemed with activity, with the jagged tree line itself being hacked and lumbered. I climbed a small bank overlooking a virtual armada, where the boats were all linked into a floating bridge. There were vessels of every size and cut of sail, some moored to stones still taking on supplies, while others were so loaded down they floundered in midstream. Still others, having just delivered one load of men on the Maryland side, were returning to be filled again. I heard Smokey Ray release a low whistle as he squatted down beside me on the bank. Whatever was happening in Maryland was now part of a massive movement. Skirmishing had past the point of frontier justice; this was full out war, and carefully organized.

We attached ourselves to a camp on an outer fringe, but when word spread of our arrival, we were sent for by the colonel at once. "Does Washington have his orders from the governor?" I suddenly thought to ask the man that headed the escort detail. I had gotten nervous, for all I knew we might have been getting arrested.

"Hell if I know," he replied. "But I hear you're a hell of a group fer killin' Indians."

As we approached, Colonel Washington was bent under a loaded wagon, shoving it onto a barge, but when he spied us, he greeted us warmly, and straightened to his full height.

"You're Colonel Mason's men, are you not? Welcome. Welcome. Look here men," he shouted to the others. One by one they dropped their loads and stared. "Look and learn! This here's a veteran fighting corps. Top notch."

I felt my face go flush, but he commenced to pounding

me on the back, like we were suddenly old friends with a great many things to talk about. Nonetheless I was instantly taken in. He projected a relaxed confidence, embracing you in trust, which was a quality not easily accomplished with calloused planters like our lot. I could not help but like him.

"Are you Corstair?

"Yes, sir."

"Well then, welcome again. There's three hundred Maryland horseman waiting for us to join them over there," he said, tossing his thumb back over his shoulder, "And I'm taking you over so they can meet a real Virginian fighting man."

I knew right away that he was being facetious, but I still felt mystified. Suddenly, a corridor was formed, and I was taken to the front of the quay. Space was cleared around an empty boat where a cushioned seat awaited me, the only one that was not fit out with an oar. Halfway across the strong current I got up the nerve to look at the backbench of rowers, beaming as they heaved, up to the front at me. I imagined what it must be like for someone who impersonated royalty. But at that very hour, (unbeknownst to me) I was the focus of multiple rumors expanding on what was now being called "Colonel Mason's Mishap," which was in itself, an insincere name. I was Corstair, the man with a dozen kills. And then, as if the value of a lie could grow by my appearance, when we landed on the Maryland side, I was made lead to a unit of horseman. I must add here, lest false pride completely overtake these senseless acts, that a Maryland Colonel named Truman then pulled me aside and said, "*I* am the commander. *I* am the one who leads." Leaving one matter, for me at least, in no uncertain terms.

I was then quick to learn that mine was not an assignment to be cherished, for Colonel Truman turned out be quite an intolerable man. He was superior to the point of being spiteful, and flaunted himself about like a cousin to the king. But Washington encouraged me by sharing that he needed a liaison with the Marylanders, "Someone to hold their respect, and keep the clodhoppers in line." So, after a bit of going back and forth, I was given charge of a motley brigade, where each man rode his own workhorse. Indeed, most of these fellows treated the occasion like they'd only just joined for a good sporting hunt, but for some other unknown reason I was given the most beautiful animal I'd ever held.

"Wake up, men!" Truman began to bark. "There's ambush waiting! Ambush more deadly than a coiled rattlesnake! Waiting! Waiting for you in there!"

He was pointing to a clearing behind him, wide as any boulevard, which looked like a well traveled logging road. You'd have to be deaf, dumb and blind to be surprised 'in there', I thought, and wondered if he had actually planned on finding any Indians. But the shrill in his voice snapped the men into order and turned them quite somber as we formed our patrol.

The next thing I noticed was Truman's way of abusing his horse. He took joy in wheeling him about, a hairs length from a straggling column, or driving him up hard onto a dangerous perch. It was something that a workingman would naturally see as careless, risking damage to an animal of such worth, but I saw that his display was not so much for the horse, as it was for the men. Colonel Truman was sending a message to any who might question his command; any sign of disrespect would be answered back with force. All in all it was a strenuous, and unnecessary act for a group of stumbling volunteers, any one of whom was free to go home at any minute. My response was defiantly passive, and I let my unit slowly lag behind until he grew tired of racing back and forth. Indeed, the enthusiastic colonel finally gave up on us, and left us on our own. "Some one's gotta be a hero," Smokey Ray said, as we watched the man vanish up the grade.

We kept our pace up the road until it became no more than a wild pig trail, where the trampled underbrush suddenly shot down a sharp ravine. Truman was gone, but the signs he left pared off down a course so steep that I thought about it twice before I followed. But we dug into our stirrups, as we slipped and slid unhappy horses for the whole descent. I had started to think that he'd purposely tried to lose us, when we bottomed out beneath boughs so thick that they blocked out all the light. Then, just like that, the eastern sky broke out upon an open field, with Truman standing in his saddle pointing to the prize. Our scattered horse militia stumbled from the forest, and before us was the hilltop fort of the Piscataway Susquehanna.

Truman was much too proud to acknowledge that we'd managed this difficult trek, but nonetheless I could see he was impressed. As for me, I'd had a brimful of his natural arrogance, but had to admit that he knew his way around. When the last of our group was drawn up and assembled, I sent a few men back for Colonel Washington to show them the way with all speed.

I studied the strategic height on which the village stood and saw at once that there was no chance for a direct assault. Not without the aid of a non-existent cannon. My craftsman's eye gave an appreciative gaze upon structure's design. The walls were built of sturdy hardwood trees spiked deep into the earth, rising to a consistent thirty feet. The prongs along the top were twisted outward and so densely intertwined that the thought of anyone scaling them was beyond all expectation. The trunks themselves were spaced close enough apart as to prevent the passage of a small child, but still provided excellent sight lines for their weapons. Finally, the only visible entrance was through a tight maze of briarwood that no one could safely pass without permission.

I could only make out the interior of the village by

Daniel Watkins

climbing a towering pine. There were several dozen huts and hovels surrounding a central common, where the smoke from the long house signaled that our presence was being fully observed. At that very moment, a council was being conducted, doubtlessly working out the Susquehanna's response. I calculated a total population of no more than a hundred, since many of the hunters would be out for winter meat. Or raiding, I quickly thought, somewhere in the country behind us, and doing more damage than we could do here. Truman directed us to walk our horses along a wide perimeter, and then we simply sat.

"I think we can take the place," he said at length. "Get this done with while surprise is in our favor."

It tried to ignore him, but he stood above me, prodding for a reply. "I'm waiting for Washington," I finally said, turning my back.

The light was fading; blending the differing shapes out of focus, while the two of us exchanged awkward glances forward to fort, and back to the trees behind. Then I saw a giant wave of moving brush, of clinging leaves on woolen trousers, and clusters of fern sprouting from shoulders and heads. Slowly, I could make out an emerging line of protruding muskets and then a row of boots and swords. But all of it came forth in a slow and dreamlike motion as if a wall of bark came alive from the trees. Then, equally as eerie when I turned back to Colonel Truman, I met with an opposing surprise. The entrance to the fort was opened, and out strode six Susquehanna warriors, just as fine as you may please. I watched as they proceeded abreast, along an unhurried path. Three of them carried torchlight.

"What the hell?" Colonel Washington said, riding up, and dismounting.

"They want to parley," I told him. "Negotiate a peace."

"Well, goddamn it," Truman replied. "I just want 'em

dead."

"Hold on a minute!" A man named Grivsley suddenly spoke up. He was one of Truman's officers paying men to follow him right out of his own pocket. I'd heard him on the trail before, talking about eye for eye justice, claiming several of his kin had recently been killed. "I *seen* two of them warriors," he whispered hoarsely. Like the rest of us, he was straining in the dark to mark the Indian's approach. "I swear them two in front were the ones that got away from us after they attacked my cousin's place, down from Chestman Hill."

"Be quiet!" Colonel Washington snapped. "Stand by Corstair. I might need you to do some translatin.' Wait for my signal. I'll let you know when I have something to say."

As the warriors drew closer I could see that they carried no weapons. All of them were chiefs, most likely from the outer clans, each presenting an imposing figure pressed against the blackening sky. In their eyes there was concern, but they showed no fear of the muskets being massed at their sides.

"Amiskowiyiniw," the eldest began. He gestured to the fort with a skinning type motion of his hands.

"He means to scalp us all!" Grivsley suddenly charged, and before I could make any sense of it, he lopped through the speaking chief's head with a single stroke of his sword. The next warrior in line grabbed at Grivsley's arm, and just as Grivsley jammed a dagger in his chest. Then it was all screaming chaos. A dozen men fell out from our ranks and laid into the chiefs, cursing and clubbing them down with their gunstocks.

"Captain Grivsley! Hold fast!" Truman shouted, but the damage was well past done.

"He killed my brother 'n law!" Grivsley yelled back. Somehow he was still in the middle of the scruff. He grabbed at the neck of a terrified brave with hands that were covered in blood. "Sure as he's the Devil!" He then snatched up one of the torches and shoved it towards the faces of the remaining chiefs.

"Enough!" Colonel Washington yelled, firing off a shot from his pistol. "Reform your lines!" But the men were confused, and moved to one side in a disorderly file. "Colonel Truman! Seize that man!" Washington ordered, shaking an angry fist at Grivsley. "And secure the prisoners." He then jumped on his horse and rode to the front of the lines. Everyone expected an all-out attack from the fort at any moment.

But with darkness fully fallen, I doubted that the Indians would retaliate so quickly, figuring that we had at least until predawn. I then relit one of the torches that was smudged into the ground and tried to appraise the situation. The Indians were crushed into a bunch, badly bruised and bleeding, as leather binds were being knotted from their wrists across each face.

"Captain Grivsley," Truman called out peevishly. "Return to your men."

Grivsley casually walked over to a squad of Virginians, making a tittering noise in the cover of the shadows. His own men were busy tying up the four remaining chiefs, and stripping the dead, who were mucked upon the ground.

"Corstair." Colonel Washington said, suddenly appearing beside me. "Were you able to get what that man was trying to say?" He nodded towards the oldest chief, now dead and naked in the dirt. "Why was he making that scalping signal?"

"He was trying to explain that they were a beaver tribe," I said. "Skinning pelts for the white traders, I expect. I didn't have time to get it all."

Washington's eyes moved slowly from the Virginians who were crowding their hero Grivsley, to the Susquehanna being stretched out on the ground. "Well." He finally sighed, futile and resigned.

Then he steered me from the mix of jeers and gawking. "Take my pistol," he said. "Assemble a squad from your group and take the prisoners some place out of the way. There you will gather your intelligence, and report back to me." He suddenly spun about. "You men form a position at the rear and make camp! Be prepared for a call to action."

As I accepted Washington's gun I saw one of the tightly bound braves giving me a smirk. He made as if to spit, but the choking cord from his wrist to his neck was holding him back. I wondered if he understood English, and if he somehow knew what Washington had ordered me to do. For all of Washington's contempt for Grivsley, or for that, the popularity Grivsley was enjoying from his men, Washington wanted this mess done away with, and the evidence of it removed just as fast. I picked out a group of volunteers, and directed them to make a moving shield around the surviving chiefs. "Any molesting of the prisoners will be severely dealt with," I said. I wanted this execution to be orderly at least. But knowing too, that the only intelligence I would gain was by keeping the smirking chief alive.

"You men there," Washington addressed the Maryland group behind me. "Now that you've picked them clean, you can bury the dead. Colonel Truman, I'll have a word with you and Captain Grivsley in half an hour. I'll expect you at my tent."

I moved through broken clusters of men that pressed in around us, staring in at us from out of the pitch. Their haggardness briefly lit with hatred as they passed beneath our torch. These were a different breed from my boatful of beaming rowers. These were empty men. Empty from sheer exhaustion, it was built into their faces like the sweat that stained their homespun clothes. They gaped from sets of deeply pitted eyes; broken by the hopeless farms they'd staked their lives upon.

Unlike Captain Grivsley they were beyond any joy gained by inflicted hurt. They were more like ghosts, clinging to the earth, but devoid of any purpose. I kept my focus as straight as I could 'til we were safely released from their gaze.

"Who's doing the raiding south of the James?" I demanded. The warrior with the cynic's glare was staring at me now as if he were willing to talk. I found a place to stop, and sent a couple of men forward to scout a spot to dump the dead.

"Seneca men," he said. "I... know nothing of... raids..."

He seemed to have trouble breathing, as if speaking was suddenly grabbing at his strength. I was surprised that he even bothered to answer, even if it was just a lie.

"How many of your people are inside the fort?" I asked.

"Few that... are left," he wheezed, "... was sent to warn... before you attack..."

"This is good as anywhere," interrupted one of the men returning, "pretty rocky up ahead."

He gestured toward the blackness with his musket, and I used the distraction to shoot the second brave in line. The rest of the men then quickly followed, firing freely into the bunch, casting tell tale explosions throughout the night air. The speaking one watched without wincing, and raised himself up in a rasping death song.

"Silence!" yelled the nearest guard.

The sound of the chief's singing was getting him so rattled that I stepped in between the aim of his gun.

"Warn me?!" I demanded, yanking up his shirt with such force that I tore it apart. Then everything went dark all at once. The guard let go of a torch just beside me, jumping clear in back of me behind a rock. I grabbed it up, and held it out above the chief, lying prone upon the ground. The skin beneath his tunic was covered in green-black boils. They splayed out across his chest from the cluster in his armpit.

"I come from the coastland," he said. "Where we believed our village was protected from the losing-arm disease."

The men had begun to slip off, but I got a quick shot and grabbed a fresh musket. "No one is to know of this until I've had word with Colonel Washington!" I said, with the best bluffing force that I could. Keeping such news from the camp was going to be impossible. I suddenly saw the mass of our army scattered to the winds, swimming back across the river, in a panic to escape the plague.

"Extinguish the torches!" I yelled. A couple of the flames were shoved in the dirt, but there was one man that hesitated. "Do it!" I yelled again, raising my gun. "You men fall in two lines and clear the way ahead. And bear in mind what a fearful shot I am. I will march behind with the prisoner. If any of you dares to break formation, he'll do so with a ball through his back."

Without a thought I grabbed the warrior to his feet. The men were angry and confused, but they held together in a frightened pack. "Do you have guns?" I asked the chief.

"Guns, yes." he replied. "But no strength to lift them." He stumbled as I forced a walk, stopping several times to restore his breathing. "What will you do, English?" the chief asked without looking at me. We had not accomplished half my immediate goal; I had no idea what to do with this information.

"I will return you inside," I told him. "To die with your people in dignity."

"If you'll be excusin' me, your lordship," one of the men started, "but we'd be more of a liking to kill him ourselves." I shot his hat off into the bush.

"Is there anyone else that does not want the chief to

infect more of his own people?"

The chief gave me a look, disbelieving, and fascinated at this surprising turn of events. Then, struggling on into the shadows, we swung a quiet loop wide of Washington's lines. I let the chief guide us as he would, and carefully studied his every painful move. Finally we reached a small hatchway at the rear of the fort. When at last we crouched together at the buried door, the only Susquehanna chief to survive our brand of justice slipped back under the walls with the death stamp on his skin.

I moved past outposts, where men made such a busy noise of constructing their tents that the threat of attack was apparently forgotten. I headed straight for Washington's camp that was spreading out already with drinking begun in earnest. When he came out, the first thing that I did was return his pistol, which he weighed in his hand as if to measure its deeds by its warmth. I stood by, deliberating the quandary of making my report in the company of others, but when I saw the men in my patrol surrounded by excitement, there was no hesitation in my voice.

"There's plague inside the fort." I blurted. "Or, at least the appearance of such." The words hit the air like a shock of explosive. Everyone came to anxious attention. Washington, on the other hand, seemed not overly concerned by the devastating news. He did take a step back however, and then looked straight up, as if he were expecting divine appointed words. His arms, he stretched apart, to make of himself a wide and willing crucible.

"God wills us," he smiled, "to sanctify this ground."

I was confused. I could not tell if he truly believed what he was saying, or used his invocation as a means to control, and keep the calm. But the effect certainly worked upon the men. The morbid fear struck to the right and just behind me, dissolved as though Washington had purged it to the air.

"Our side is God's side!" Came the first of cheers that followed. (Rum being also reverentially raised.)

I took another chance to step in close. "If I may Colonel," I said speaking low, "given our proximity to the disease, God may not confine the deaths to the Susquehannas alone."

"God certainly can if He so chooses." he replied. "What would you have us do?"

"I hope," Truman butted in, "that you are not entertaining the thought of calling off this mission. I, for one do not believe it. I never heard of any savages attacked by black plague."

"I hear tell they got it from some Spanish below tha Caroline coast," another officer offered. "An' it did a sight more killin' than what tha Spaniard cannon done."

"Nothing but gold teeth rumors," Truman replied, "to serve the oily Spanish and take our English land. See here Colonel Washington, I've got half a dozen planters killed these past months, and I will not abandon this operation while I have the swarthy pagans in their hold."

Colonel Washington looked at Truman with unconcealed contempt. The turn in Truman's face conveyed he'd already received at least one reprimand. And Captain Grivsley, I noticed, had apparently been dismissed from his own paid command. "I will not chance a contagion upon the men," Washington stated calmly. "All will be fine for us. We'll keep the Susquehanna locked up with their filth. 'Til the time that they're eaten with splot, or else simply starve. Either course, they'll be dead." He released another smile. "Find me a fiddler boys, and help yourselves to a drink. Mr. Corstair and I will join with you directly."

As usual, his easy-going fashion went far among the men. It wasn't so hard to be with a man who enjoys life's give and take. But once we were inside his tent he turned to me most serious. "I want you and Major Allerton to go back and examine those bodies," he said to me at once. "If there's any trace of the disease, burn them at once. We are the only ones to know of it."

ithin the hour, and with Major Allerton, I was back in the field inspecting the executed Indians. A task that was not made any simpler by him switching the torch between hands in order for him to breathe and keep a kerchief to his face.

"Why did Washington send me?" he asked, as if I had the privilege to know. "Doesn't trust the Marylanders, I expect," he answered himself.

I pulled off one of the warrior's robes while Allerton took a stick and lifted a medallion made of silver. *Friendship enduring as the sun,* it read, in English. (No tribe that I knew of had ever written down a language.) It was embossed with the sun's shining rays that now were covered in blood.

"The fools," Allerton said. This was after *I* had concluded a search of the bodies. "Treacherous double tongues," he added, "every damn one." I didn't know if he was talking about the inscription, or the fact that we found no disease.

It was daybreak when we walked back into camp with no more actual knowledge of the conditions inside the fort than we had on starting out. But if the Indians were only playing an elaborate game in order to scare us off, it was unsettling enough for Washington to forestall further action. In the days that followed, the ground that we claimed, from its cultivated fields to a mile in the surrounding woods, took on the appearance of a regular town camp. Gambling, dancing and all night drinking became as notorious as they did routine. There was no end to the contests invented. Joshua

Place won a long legged mule for standing atop a sawed off poplar for more than thirty hours. Cecil Bradley received a fine bucksaw for smoking a pipe through his ass. But it was young Will Stackhouse that garnered the highest acclaim. He successfully wrestled an aging bear we'd trapped at the bottom of a smoldering turf pit. (Actually not a feat as grand as it sounds since the bear kept rolling itself over to look at its smoky behind.)

But this is not to say that these diversions kept us from the business of trying to kill Indians. About every other week or so, a self appointed captain formed a restless drunk patrol to sneak up on the outer most walls and fire off a few blind rounds. The Susquehanna had little trouble in forcing them back. One of the firsts of these forays was conducted by a man named Walter Samples, who crept up to the gate and got his whiskers set ablaze by a blast from an Indian musket. "Well, Corstair," he sputtered at me when he was laid back inside his tent. His face was charred to peeling layers and the best that we could do was to try and keep him still. "I don't know about disease, but they sure got them guns." His bandages covered his eyes down to his neck, but I got the feeling that he smiled.

Despite my initial encounter with the pocked and goitered chief, everyone assumed, including myself, that the crafty devils were only out to trick us. Still, there was nothing we could do to penetrate the fortress walls. Then after a month or so, the Indians surprised us again, when they started to mount the skulls of their dead atop of the twisted spires. This was a striking development. For whether it was effected by the plague or the beginnings of starvation, that they'd risk so offending these new departed spirits was a mark of clear desperation. The eerie display was meant, I suppose, to scare us off, but the simple matter was, the outcome they'd intended turned the opposite. A band of roving rowdies, calling themselves, "the benevolent buzzards," gathered whenever a skull was presented, and cheered each addition with an irreverent dirge.

Here's to the brave, and back-stabbing knave,
That carried away all of my grain.
His squaw lit a fire, and my pot she admired,
While her thatch was the jovial cave.

Then, after raising a mug to the best of these wits, they made bets on who'd be first to blow the skull apart.

But it wasn't all fun and games. The humdrum of a siege with only mild and sporadic resistance could dull the senses before things suddenly turned deadly. One night a group of braves slipped out from the village, slit the throats of twenty of our men, and never left a footprint. The dead fools were passed out drunk and never knew what hit them. A handful of others were killed as a result of our own brawls, (usually someone caught cheating at a cockfight or some other gambling abuse) and then, we lost two more, as the result of a long standing feud. Another man was found strung up to a sycamore tree accused of doing buggery. Colonel Washington dispensed his backwoods justice as equitably as could be expected, but the week in, week out strain of having so many idol men itching for a battle was wearing at his command.

For me however, the most interesting aspect of this adventure was in the official response it incurred. Which is to say, nil. There was not a single command or order that I got wind of coming from Governor Berkeley. It was as though we were being purposely ignored. On the other hand, we were hardly making a secret of this war. We Virginians had made a lot of noise crossing into, and establishing a military base in Maryland, which was something many of its residents saw as an invading force. And still we heard nothing from the governor. There was instead, plenty of interest in his apparent disinterest, and it sparked more fireside debate than speculating on what went on inside the Indian fort. Then there was Colonel Washington, who was at least as perplexing with every passing day. He was well aware of the hatred being brewed and directed towards the government. It stood right before him with powder kegs of military force.

I tried keeping myself to the job at hand, which was starving the Susquehanna out from the impending failure of their fort, but my ears meanwhile heard nothing but a government being cursed at by the angry poor. Cursing more than anything else the lack of productive work. Being so filled up with static hours, and surrounded by such men, I began to form a picture of the future, such as where the country was headed, or if Berkeley were merely hoping that we'd settle our misery *here*. As though while sitting back in Jamestown or on his plantation at Green Spring, he thought that perhaps we'd simply go away, or become the *Maryland* poor. But certainly the more time that there was for us to spend drunk in the woods, the more time there was to make bold threats of sedition.

There were the standard complaints about the trade monopoly, crippling every try at commerce, but mostly about the way that it wrecked tobacco. There was the runaway rate to borrow money, (which you had to invest in order to survive) and the vanishing opportunity for a man to work his own farm.

Then. There was the poisonous hatred for those that the governor had deemed his favorites. Those royally connected newcomers, arriving with political advantage, and given the richest reserves of land. And last but far from least, came Berkeley's appetite for tax. He taxed the head of every male, whether he owned a hundred thousand acres, or was merely a servant on that land, and exactly in the same amount. (The tax he'd applied most recently was for the construction of his useless forts.)

"'Bout as good for hunting down a thieving Indian as a

gopher is for climbing trees," was typically said.

"It were tha fresh quim that softened him in the head," someone would respond.

This was the feeble attempt to break from the doom and gloom seriousness that took hold. It was a well-worn digression that seemed to follow sessions becoming too heated up to do anybody any good.

"This ain't a lie," someone would pick up. "Nothin' melts a man's brain faster'n fledgelin' poon-tang. Hell, th'ancien' Egyptians knew 'at."

The crudities would then be embellished, with a slight competition to sound the most ridiculous. In this particular case it was a well-known fact that Lady Berkeley was a widower, fully in her thirties, but the butt of the joke was directed at our governor, a man that was seventy years old. His aging long-wigged head, sitting on top of his spindly frame was often creatively described, especially when bobbing atop the fiery First Lady.

"What differnce do it make what he uses fer a cock?" A farmer new to the group interjected. "Sir William has a reg'lar parley with each of tha chiefs in the Algonkin nations. We can take care ah these Susquehanna here. Kill a few more of them, or sit it out 'til all frozen hell, but we still goin' back to tha same damn conditions."

"You right there," another man assented.

The laughter subsided. The cold sober words having cut through the evening like a knife. Men were suddenly avoiding each other's looks, turning their eyes out toward nothing, staring at the trees in silhouette. There was a certain conscience, an unspoken guilt about being so unattached. Perceived as being part of a gypsy army that lived no way better than the savages up on the hill. And the other half of this truth was just as difficult to face. But the plain fact was, that this well armed adventure was making these young men happy. They were living a life of freedom for the first time in their lives. They had created a haven, a secret kind of pact, outside the world of responsibilities, or the expectation that they make something of themselves. Their most honest worry was how long the Indians could keep this going by continuing to hold out.

"What do you think Colonel Washington's gonna do with us?" A voice finally asked. "Think he'll stand up to Berkeley?"

"Don't count on it," someone answered. "He plays it too close to the vest."

"Bacon would." The new man said, prompting the camp into instant agitation.

"Damn right he will! Where is he?"

"Where the hell is that cussed rich man?"

"He knows enough to stay away. He knows this here's Washington's show."

"Hear tell he's got some Appomattocs he took prisoner back on his plantation. Says he caught 'em stealing his corn."

This was news to me. I had almost forgotten about my firebrand neighbor, and his fancy hold upon these men.

"Say he's got Berkeley so mad that the old man took away his council seat."

I had decided to go to sleep by now, but this caused me a drowsy laugh. Nathan had never taken the council seat seriously enough to sit on it, but it was an indication of just how rattled the governor had become.

I jerked myself awake, hearing a barrage of more accusations, but everything blended in a cloud. The atmosphere grew thicker, smelling rank of clothes, and grease and fire. Of sour breath, and weeks of living, near a mass of sewage building up nearby. The voices were speaking about what's coming, and the taking back what's rightfully yours. Groups of younger men talking to their elders like this, and the older men simply nodding. I saw jaws being clenched, and tightening of fists. And the words being spoken, even in anger, becoming one. I drifted in and out, the sound fading, more indecipherable, but for the simple name of "Bacon." "Bacon," someone said again, and then, "Bacon," I heard it again. Like a chant, it was buzzing above me, challenging a much-needed rest. "Bacon," I was thinking. "That bold mistake of a breeding. Nathaniel Bacon." I dreamed.

"It was a rousing good time, I'll tell you. In spite a' what else. All told I had me a rousing good time." I picked this up in passing from one of our frontier soldiers at the end of our seven weeks stay. I was at the head of a line making its way back to Virginia after we'd burned the Susquehanna village to the ground.

Clearly beyond the capacity of anyone's ability to believe it, the previous night, the entire Indian settlement, a hundred men, women and children, had walked straight past our disheveled camp. When we blearily arose and stood at the edge of our wasted field, we stared, uncomprehending, at the empty fort walls. The Indians had turned Washington's siege into a mockery, and there was nothing he could do to keep himself in check. When he addressed his aides he spit like a bobcat wrapped up in a rabbit trap.

"Major Allerton! Form a unit and go find the murderers," he said. We were standing at a pile of bodies made up of ten of our guards. Each one of their heads was smashed, and their weapons gone. "You! And You!' Washington barked, "Bury these men. The rest of you come with me."

I was selected along with fifty-odd others to probe the outer barricades for signs of an ambush. But once we were safely passed the gates all that we found was a slow rolling fog. The mist sat upon the abandoned huts turning them cold and tomblike. It sifted through the skulls still mounted to the outer walls, making the skittish jump sideways. Most unsettling, and forcing me to blink my eyes, was an ancient couple at the far end of the courtyard sitting upon the steps to the long house. A young girl sat between them, twisting her attention from the woman to the man, acting playful, but turning slowly back and forth. All three of them were naked, and apparently oblivious to us. The little girl held out a row of sticks, which she carefully palmed in one of her hands, from which the old man studied, and then picked.

Colonel Washington and I took cautious steps skirting the outside of the center. The men behind us spread out their lines. Each one of us held a ready gun, pointed at the vapor.

"Can you greet them without scaring them off?" Washington asked. We had just reached the point where we had to walk out in the open.

"Kiwa pamina nimosom! Kiwa pawi!" I shouted.

It had a very small effect. The little girl gave a slight pause, as if curious to greet us, but then she went back to her game. I sensed Washington's rage turn into fear, as we watched this queer family pay us no mind. For several moments the fog billowed through the yard thick enough to hide them from view.

"Well, let's go then," he finally whispered.

While we strode into the clouded ground everything seemed to go still. I heard the little girl laugh and our boots upon the gravel.

"Where are the others?!" Washington loudly demanded loudly, when we stood before the steps.

This, he directed at the old man, but the game of short sticks was all the old man cared to notice. His eyes were engulfed by a milky film, but seemed fixed upon the little girl's hands, giving them his rapt attention. The woman then moved by carefully folding the girl in her arms, as if she needed to keep her from running off. They were old beyond any telling, and I suddenly felt embarrassed at being made to look on so much wrinkled skin. The little girl, I finally realized was dim. She readily accepted the old woman's embrace and they each became perfectly still. I was still myself, amazed by their total lack of fear.

"Where?!" Washington shouted, striking the sticks from the little girl's hand. She did not look at him, but whimpered a bit, digging herself at the withered woman's breast.

"E wa paiyahk," the old man began to sing.

"E wa paiyahk," the woman repeated, rocking back and forth, and stroking the girl's thick black hair.

"Silence!" Washington shouted.

And the girl whimpered louder, using her hands to cover her eyes. Washington was humiliated. The bizarre encounter was throwing everyone off their nerves.

"What are they singing?" he asked.

"They are old and the girl is weak," I lied. "They have no where to go but heaven." I did not feel like telling him that the song to me was gibberish.

"Ask him if they had plague here," he commanded.

"Mih-cet otahkosiw, mih-cet sek otah?" I asked. Surprisingly, the old man stopped singing to reply.

"Wapiski-wiya peyak akhosi," he said, looking at me for the first time. He held me in a white marble gaze, and began his singing once again. The woman then joined in, and the girl commenced to yip like a little dog.

"He says that the only plague he knows is white men."

Washington turned away disgusted with himself as much as the strange behavior of the three. He glanced briefly at his sergeant, heading up the line, and wheeled back out across the fog. As soon as we had gained the exit, three percussive echoes rang out from inside the fort. A small flock of migrating ducks scattered from a pond turned into a latrine, and above it

a beam of sun turned rainbow in the mist.
  "Let's get off this hell hill," he said.

ajor Allerton never got close to those slippery Susquehanna. He was so bewitched by their audacity that he tiptoed back to Virginia expecting to be ambushed at every turn in the creek. But while he was unable to find the vanished savages, the savages had no problem finding us. Before winter was done nearly forty souls along the frontier were lost on their southern swing of terror. Vicious assaults, made all the more brazen for having warned us of the attacks well beforehand. One mangled survivor out at the Pendleton place lived long enough to relate the way the Indians calculated their revenge: ten whites for each one of their chiefs we had killed back up in Maryland. A number from out the hat of justice, as good as any I suppose, to provide an end to primitive retribution. We later learned, from a credible Pawmunkey man, that this was their non-negotiable terms for peace. Plus the compensation for their property.

And soon it was painfully apparent that the rigors to which they took their savage claims stayed pretty much on course. After one such attack, (we were always chasing *after* an attack it seemed) we came upon the Sadler family in an isolated region called Sandusky. Twelve bodies, aged from newborn to past fifty were strewn upon the limbs of a basswood tree. Their dismembered parts dangled above a pack of wild dogs. We worked all morning at bringing down the pieces, and covering the graves with heavy stones. The dogs stayed just beyond the range of muskets, waiting 'til we were gone.

This was along about the time that men began collecting around me as if I were their leader. Curious to see just what they thought it was they followed, I busied myself with making up and breaking up our camps. Apparently they did not know, or perhaps they knew and did not care, that I had no more plan or purpose than a strand of straw, tattered by the breeze. Meanwhile, as if he'd finally taken stock of these manifest horrors, came a belated response from Sir William himself, our once and again outraged governor. The gist that I got out of it was that Mason and Brent's strike into Maryland was vaguely illegal, and our Piscataway siege, (now that it had unsuccessfully ended) was an indictable offence. It was enough to leave you wondering, what if anything anyone had bothered to tell him. Or was he still pretending that this mad dog was out at a full run. The cycles of attack and revenge were busily at work engulfing the lives of whole families.

But everyone that I had ever known regarded Berkeley the aristocrat, as an enigma. Personally, I had no doubt that bands of vigilantes tearing apart the peace he'd spent his lifetime to build was more than his ancient nerves could bear, but then, he was also fully vested in the fur trade. This was a conflict interest, more raw and transparent than any that a frontier farmer could forgive. Then, when reports were confirmed that Massachusetts Pequots had burned scores of English settlers, panic seized complete control of reason, in both the rich and poor. Now, what every Virginian feared (or wanted) was an all out colonial war. Berkeley rallied, and consolidated his efforts into one force, and under the threat of prison without a trial, he ordered our patrols to disband, and charged his good friend Henry Chicheley the job of dealing with the Indians. He gave Sir Henry a proper commission, but then strapped him with the most absurd conditions that we had ever heard. There was to be no engagement with an enemy without Berkeley's prior and written consent.

"Not even a sporting shot?" joked one of my men.

"I'd be in bolt of shock if Chicheley ever gets downwind

of an outlaw Indian."

"He'll find savages. Just soon as he does his paperwork."

"At last," one of the older settlers sighed. "Berkeley's got the right man to do his bidding. Delivering up the wilderness civilized style."

But Sir Henry simply ended by folding up his tents. Before his troops were even assembled, he decided it best to decline the governor's call. Chichcley was a pompous fool, but sometimes even a fool can see a useless errand. In this case foolishness was taking an army through an endless backwater, expecting the peaceful surrender of hostile ghosts. My motley crew on the other hand, took the governor at his word. We turned away from the forbidding forest, unwilling to further taunt arrest, and looked to shelter up at Bacon's place.

When we reached his property's southern line, I was met by an armed and nervous field hand, who informed me that his master "won't home." "Mr. Bacon's got some grisly biz'ness," he reported, "up at his second plantation north of the Curles."

I quietly nodded, accustomed by now to expecting the worst, and finally found Bacon on a raised plot of clearing that looked out over his hogshead road. He was laying down his overseer, honest Cyrus Watford, into a carefully carved out gravc. The stealthy red skins must have come up quick and surprised him. For right beneath his scalp ripped clean, there was a look of shock frozen on his face. Nathan kept trying to say something like a prayer, but then stopping short, and turning away. I stood off a ways in the nearest shade, uncomfortable to intrude, while breathing in spurts to avoid the putrid air. Not to mention the fact that I was witnessing a part of him completely unfamiliar. Exposed beneath the wall of Bacon's sure exterior was a man that was beside himself with grief.

"Walk with me a ways, Corstair," he motioned to me

after a time. And the two of us paced a distance staring at our boots. "Berkeley has revoked all trading rights with the Indians with the exception of himself and two of his top favorites. He's pretending it's to stop more guns from crossing into savage hands but we know that he only means to monopolize the pah...pah...peh..lts..."

He could no longer bring himself to speak, but broke instead to his genuine condition. Perhaps it was in concert with my own severe loss, or to Cyrus Watt, with his mauled and blackened body so near, but Nathan and I suddenly had ahold of one another like a pair of anxious women. We remained like this for a number of minutes, or at least until we'd both stopped shaking. I remember at length in our embracing, the approach of a curious fox. At first sniffing in a sideways motion, then rising up on two feet, with its forelegs stretched outright.

"I cannot... y-your... fa-family..." Bacon said.

He almost seemed naked, stripped of his famous knack for words, appearing boyish even, beneath the wet veil of his face. For a moment he let his tears distill our communion, and flow from a young man so far above my station, down to me.

"The governor's advice for all the outer planters is to gather ten to a house. For the duration," I finally tried restoring matters at hand.

This produced such a bursting guffaw that I became afraid that he'd gone silly and unhinged.

"Tell you what," he finally said, "I'll have Elizabeth send out hoe down invitations. We'll roast a hog for each of the burning farms that our government protects."

I was happy, at least, to see that Berkeley's quaint ideas for our welfare had given him release from so much tension and death.

"The men are sending *you* the invitation," I replied. "They're expecting you to lead them, Nathan. To find a way out of this."

Watching his face turn more cunning, I could see that he had thought things through this far. He stared significantly for a moment, at an anonymous point on the forest floor.

"I am meeting tonight with Henry Creighton and William Byrd," he said. "They are both powerful Berkeley men, but have lately become disaffected. Gather what freedmen you can, and join us at the Curles. Together we will make our own policy."

Attracting men with nothing to do and nothing on their minds but vengeance, took but little time or distance. As word traveled out, thirty more met with the twenty that rode with me, and we were joined by forty more before we reached Charles City. As our procession moved on, back and forth to the Curles the chant of "Bacon! Bacon!" was heard ringing through the trees and the surrounding fields. Small bands seemed to emerge from every cove and inlet, or appear like magic straight up from the ground.

Bacon was waiting for us, and gave us a hearty greeting as we approached his northern gate. He instantly strode into our midst, I mean right among men of the meanest rank, and I began to sense something very real in him had changed. He'd acquired an interest in others, genuinely spoke, a striving, I'd not seen before that was not merely designed to manipulate. He listened earnestly, trying to understand what kind of folks these were, how they lived, and what sort of places they called home. He then announced that he was providing his best land for hunting, along with open fishing rights, and by the end of his reception he had the hardest of doubters on his side. Later on, when all the hoop-la had settled down, I took a bath in cranny of the river and dressed in my only other shirt. I tried looking at myself in the glass that cased the entrance to his porch, and for the first time in, I honestly couldn't remember, I entered a house with a door.

Elizabeth began by offering her condolences, going so far as to say that she would surely have gone right back to England if it hadn't been for Helen, my wife. I then recalled that she often spoke like that, with an intended good will that could just as well open darker thoughts. I nodded without speaking, unsure of what I felt. Feeling if Helen's coming to this land herself, can be viewed as an idea of success. Unless of course horror were the criteria; the ideal outcome of the Corstair quest. (You can see how much the devil by now was fiddling with my thinking.) But in a simpler vein, I had always felt that Elizabeth never spoke her truest feelings. She was a person that only after a considerable amount of time was spent in careful watching, could one determine what she meant. In this case she was actually trying to express her loyalty to Nathan, which truer to say was that she would never abandon him.

She went on for a bit, about how inadequate she was to the sympathy she felt, but the greatest impression she made on me was in naming each of my children with a fond and an equal respect. She drew no distinction between her admiration of Tomas and Stu, or Laura or Sarah, and Zach. She completely omitted the slight stony eye that usually accompanied addressing "the family of the Corstair English, and their savages." (Hannah Baldwin actually said this to me one time.) Perhaps it was because except for me, they were all dead. And I'll confess, that she wasn't shy about mentioning my tragedy when I was in the room. At one point I clearly heard her say, "I bought servants to walk my fields with guns immediately following the Corstair raid," to another guest named Henry Creighton.

The mention of servants and the casual way in which Elizabeth regarded them reminded me that this was the first time I had been inside the Bacon house since the days of their arrival. It was a softening thought. It caught me up in a reverie of a time when blackbirds and tendril weeds were the worst of our invaders, and the land was rich for anyone willing to work. Suddenly Helen appeared to me, wrapped in a bee-net bonnet of her own design, carrying a bucket of honey from her hives behind our acorns. Her pathway fused in a bright morning light, until I finally lost sight of her.

I shook myself awake to see Elizabeth take notice of my lengthy inward gazing. She gave me a sympathetic smile and then she was off greeting Byrd and Creighton. We were quickly escorted into a hall that must have held a dozen candles, all burning at once! And off the rear of the two front rooms, where there was yet another that gave one a sense of being in a wholly separate place. Surrounded by men, Elizabeth became more fetching, and fairly started glowing when Nathan at last entered in. He took over the duties as host, and placing a hand to our backs, led us down a hallway to a den.

"I imagine those men outside are in need of some provision," Elizabeth said, directing a quick and coy curtsy at me. What she meant by this I could not rightly say, but the thought of her pouring out a hundred cups of cider, alongside a buttered biscuit was in the realm of consideration.

We assembled in a withdrawing room of all things, where Byrd and Creighton went directly at Bacon's brandy. I took a seat at the polished cherry table, somewhat outside of the group. On Bacon's introduction I accepted William Byrd's hand as Henry Creighton stood ponderously by the fireplace filling up his pipe. I stayed to my corner, vowing to listen, and speak only if indeed I were called upon. The best way I thought to serve this lofty company was as intermediary, an established contact between them and the men camped outside.

"We mean to get our money back from the corrupt and decrepit governor," Byrd stated right off, "and resume our full rights to trade."

His rather refined features belied a powerful voice. I'd

heard that he and Bacon had set up a business in pelts, but how he hoped to manage it while spreading war upon the Indians escaped me. Still, I imagined that once the dust was settled, what he truly expected was part of the lucrative tribute money that tribes paid out to the governor.

"No doubt you've heard that Berkeley has claimed all dealing with the Indians practically unto himself," Byrd went on. "And the delusional man expects us to believe this is for our protection."

Creighton had begun pacing behind me and was becoming a distraction. He was by far the largest man present; actually fat in fact, which for me was fairly novel, living among the full time gaunt. He wafted back and forth about the room putting off a steady cloud of smoke, lighting and relighting his harsh smelling grade of tobacco. He presented a comical picture though, whenever he passed the diminutive Bacon, peering as he did so heavily down behind him, with jowls thick around his eyes. I half mused that Creighton could just up and eat him if he decided it was worth his while. But as far as I could tell, despite his oversized girth, he held his interests to himself. And though he filled the room with great agitation, he remained completely closed mouthed. Comparatively speaking I guess, and in trying to give him respects, I suppose that my concerns were very simple when standing next to his. As for myself and the men I rode with; we were only here to fight. Draw up your plans, and point us in the right direction. We'll see what happens when we survive.

"Governor Berkeley has taken possession of over fourteen hundred pounds of our pelts," Byrd continued, "a sum that must be repaid."

"How do you expect to convince him of that?" I asked, surprising myself by blurting. But Creighton's irritating tension had suddenly got on my nerves. I was also thinking about the upkeep for our so-called army. Small though it was, it would still need to be supplied for an open-ended march. If the men in this room were not prepared to pitch in their support, and make our mission clear, it would be doomed from the very start. I don't know what I expected for an answer, but in an exchange of quick glances, Creighton broke his pipe.

"Godammit!" he shouted, swatting at the embers on his vest. "Did you know that as we speak a band of Susquehanna is occupying the outer woods of my own land?" he demanded. I instantly fell quiet. "And the governor has his council asking us for reparations! A tax on us to aid the enemy!" He was moving about the room again, looking not unlike a state solicitor ready to pounce. I noticed too, that he had jabbed a broken piece of the pipe into his hand. "Reparations for Susquehanna land destroyed... in *Maryland*. Reparations for the murder of their most respected men! Berkeley has ordered his own investigation, but I want you to tell me yourself, Corstair. Do you know who killed those Indians?"

I was becoming confused. I looked around the room, and then to Bacon. Byrd appeared slightly perturbed, after all Creighton had wrested away his topic, but Bacon looked plainly bemused. Who was this boor? I thought, and I literally bristled in defense. Was he trying to make me his scapegoat? Someone vulnerable to extort?

"Rumor says," Creighton continued, "that the governor means for the guilty to be severely punished. But *we*, the clearly innocent, are already being punished aren't we? Hmm? Whether we are forced to pay the reparations or not, we still have to pay for his re-enforced garrisons on the border. And all on account of some half cocked action taken up in *Maryland*."

Here were the bits to the aristocracy that proved what little I knew. I waited for Bacon's explanation, but he was acting entirely uninterested, as if Creighton's problems were Creighton's alone. I decided then and there that I would ride out that very night, and take any of the men that followed. Damned if I'd play pawn for a fat hot head that couldn't find a seat to fit his ass.

"Mr. Corstair, would it interest you to know that I am now without a market? Quite right, sir. Ever since the bottom fell out of tobacco, my business has been guns. That's right, and I trade them to Indians. Only confirmed friendlies of course, but up 'til now hell-be-damned, we were all friendly! Friendly with fur. Friendly with guns. And friendly for the common business sense of being friendly! And now that they've turned against us, and it's against the law for me to trade my guns, what, I ask you, would *you* have me do? I mean to support a *living* family."

I made an effort to strike him, but my head was in a sudden swim. Were his guns available to the Indians in Piscataway? Were they finding their way to kill families up north? Or were they only in the hands of those that did their slaughter in the south? At the plantation of Corstairs? His imposing waist was planted right before me, and when I stood up the back of my chair got caught into the rug. The next thing that I knew I was sprawled out at his feet.

"And now that our trade has been destroyed," he continued, his purple face looming above me. "Most all the no-counts want to blame the governor. Well, I can place blame squarely where it belongs. On the shoulders of a drunken mob in Maryland."

"Then Henry," Bacon lightly broke in, "we'll just have to take a little trip down to Occaneechee Island and see if we can't get back your losses."

I pulled above the fallen chair, and Creighton straightened like a bear in a hurry for lunch. Both of us were looking at a worn leather map that Bacon rolled out on the table. The tension drained so fast from Creighton's body that he actually grew limp. And though I was still shaking, I watched him glide across the room like an oversized child being pulled on top a pond of ice by his loving parents. His eyes were so immediately fixed upon the map that the insidious facility he had only just expressed no longer held his interest. I stood and braced myself, without the smallest feeling for what might come next.

"I'm taking Mr. Corstair and his men along with me." Bacon said, pointing at the map now between us. "But I mean no slight to you, Henry. Not in the least. Why don't you come too? Understand however, that the provision for truffled pheasant may be somewhat limited. But with any luck we should find you enough snake to eat."

He gave me an easy wink, while Creighton stepped back, fairly filling up the fireplace. "You know the infirm condition of my heart just as well as I, Nathaniel," he softly replied.

"Then I suggest that you let Mr. Corstair here, solve our gut practicalities and you sit your excitable heart down," Bacon said. "In fact, why not soothe yourself with another glass of my brandy?"

This game, with which I was so clearly out of step, was one that Bacon was enjoying like a master. Viewed from where I stood the maze of motivations embodied by the rich, slid and baffled. In the fields and forests where I worked no one hid behind the smoke of contrived misunderstanding. There was no couched opinion on what was heard and what was said. And insult, out of ignorance or deliberate dishonor could get such a foolish man killed. I felt troubled and strangely inadequate in the company of these men, and then suddenly only bone tired. I glanced at Creighton, who having other things to stew, stood with his back to me at the fire. "My evening is done," I simply announced, and tried to rid him from my mind.

"Gentlemen, let *each* of us retire. We'll make a detailed plan at first light." Bacon was cheerful. "Mr. Corstair, you are most welcome to take your bed here, unless of course you wish to remain with your men." He extended his arms from the apparent endlessly scheming Creighton to the sullenness in myself. The reach of a bridge to a distant accord.

"I have made myself quite comfortable in the woods," I said, and nodded good night. William Byrd nodded in return, his face in a perfect blank.

Nathan quickly followed, walking me from the candle warmth of his house through the yard out towards the trees. The night was brisk but the distinct odor of spring teased at the senses. There were even a few brave crickets trying out their new love songs. Campfires dotted the woods to near distance, and the exotic smell of coffee lay like perfume on the late evening air. Bacon's servants had pleased my men at least tonight. Off to the left came a howling burst of laughter.

"Is this why you brought me here?" I asked testily.

"I thought it would be good for you to see what we are up against. And I respect you enough for you to see it first hand. You did very well."

I tried to act like I was indifferent, as if more important things occupied my mind.

"Make no count of Henry Creighton," Bacon went on. "He's overstuffed and fiercely loyal to the king, but exasperated enough to work for changes in Virginia. He's testing everyone right now. But the time will come when his influence will be needed."

"What will these men out here have to live on, if I can keep them together, I mean?' I asked him direct. "A promise is nothing to a hungry family man marching to fight. They must have hard compensation."

"They will stay together," Bacon replied evenly, "because *I* will pay them." The shadows fell across his face, so that I couldn't detect how serious he was. But then he took my hand firmly into his, in a gentlemen's agreement. "You have my word."

I watched him walk back towards his fancy-paned home, and stood where the smoke spiraled through the pines. I stared in the dark upon my open palm. The strength of his grip felt like a mark on my hand. A gentleman's agreement, I thought again, more befuddled than ever.

I awoke before dawn feeling pulled, as if magnetically into the surrounding fields. The servants had finished the milking and their kitchen-fires were radiating heat in the air already, unusually warm. The mixture of a cooking breakfast, and fresh turned soil filled my nose with such richness that I had a sudden longing for home. I knelt on the ground as if offering a grateful prayer, and broke some dirt between my fingers that I brought to my mouth. Without thinking, I began pulling at the weeds growing thick around the barrel path, gouging out giant clumps of clay. The green stain of stalks and sap on my hands made me blissful, feeling as though I had a part, and actually existed in time. Then, with the rising sun hard upon my back, I straightened up gasping, realizing that this much early heat would punish the coming planting.

Out of the pink haze, and marching towards me on the path, I saw the men that Elizabeth had hired to guard her fields. A half dozen appeared, looking serious as stone, and each one carrying a musket. The one bringing up the rear, a sunburnt harsh looking bloke, was brandishing a buck whip. They were escorting an assortment of Manahoac, Appomatoc and Rappahannock Indians, about twenty in all, to the next field over for hoeing. The Indians were bound at the ankles, and moving in a slow, uniform rhythm that was interesting to watch given the animosity that stood between their tribes. One of the guards gave me a curt, required nod, but the rest of them were lost in their general sort of foulness. Their branded wrists made the weapons that they carried illegal, and though appearing professional enough, there were any number of laws that they were breaking.

"Halt that looking!" yelled the foreman with the whip. He stepped to one side and sent a lash up the line.

The Indians responded by keeping their attention to the square foot of ground before them, except for one young brave that lingered midway in the file. He stared at me calmly, direct and defiant, as if wanting to ask me a question perhaps. But there was something unnerving about the searching, scorching look in his face.

"Move on!" the foreman snapped.

And so they did. But the troubled one in the middle held onto me with such a weighty gaze that he tripped up the hostage before him into faltering a step. Another lash from the whip snaked out a piece of his cheek. They were gone some fifty paces before I recognized, like an object becoming familiar in the dark, that he was my own Tomas and Laura's cousin, their father's sister's son. Tenakahwhe, he was called, for Floating Tree on Fire. I looked after him, but by then he was lost in the line, and the taste of pure revulsion struck my tongue. The encounter set me so far off balance that for a moment I felt truly altered, and didn't know who I was. The clods of dirt in my hands confusing me, the hollow ache that now reached down into my bones. It even hurt to breathe. I watched them disappear behind the next rise, while I grew increasingly numb. Then the dry ground crumbled beneath me, sliding me down in the hole I had dug.

Hoof beats startled, and I turned to see Bacon riding straight for me from down the lane. He had geed his horse into a gallop, appearing to be running me over, but then he broke, still fully sprinting, and vaulted the hedge to a field. It was curious. To feel the pain of my breathing, while taking part in a breathtaking thing to watch. As if I were suddenly outside of myself, whisked of my shadowy feelings, by the force of his power and grace. I may as well have been standing inside a promotional picture, *The Serf at New World Sunup, and the Virginia Gentleman Greets His Estate.* I looked at the dirt I had dangling in the roots and felt like an utter fool.

I made it back to the house with a head full of ambivalent clouds. A state of mind, I felt sure, that was infrequently known to Elizabeth Bacon. As I stood upon the steps of an enclosed back porch, I watched her bringing a heated plate of corncakes from the nearby kitchen. I began to imagine that she was attempting to feed the whole camp.

"These are for you," she smiled. "And I've a fresh supply of salted beef that I'm packing for the expedition."

As self-assured as ever, as if our *expedition* were something like a picnic to which she wasn't invited.

"My appreciation for your trouble," I replied. Where had Bacon ridden off to? Where was his strategy? "Forgive my asking," I said feebly, "but you seem somewhat more informed than me as to the details of your husband's plans."

"Do not worry too much, Philip," she led me into the dining room. "Nathaniel is sure to do the proper thing. Sit and have a breakfast."

The home had been greatly expanded since the days of my earlier visits. In the full light of day, the hallway and the number of rooms that it now included continued to impress. I sat alone at a large table covered with fresh linen, and admired the craft in a mahogany sideboard. Utensils of engraved silver, etched pitchers of crystalline glass. So this, I thought, is what the beaver brings.

Most intriguing though was the presence of an African that appeared from a small service pantry and prepared to pour my coffee. He never looked directly at my face, but I was so fascinated by the closeness of his proximity that I am sure he caught me staring. I had seen black men before of course, but rarely, and always at a distance. If I happened to be at the pier where a ship from the West Indies had docked, and was just as suddenly gone, or the few occasions, when out on the river, I spotted an African bent over a far off field. But it was most uncommon. Lately I'd heard that Virginia could expect to see a lot more Africans dwelling amongst us, just as any common, subject to the Crown, but I'd never seen one working as a servant, inside of someone's *house*.

We must have been close to the same age, but his nappy white hair and the collar of his starched white blouse gave him an air of distinction. In any case, after serving me a dish of egg and chipped ham gravy, he turned about very erect, and silently withdrew to the doorway. I was in fact, so taken by his presence that when Elizabeth returned I'd barely taken notice she'd been gone. I looked down at my plate and beside it was a letter she had placed on the table.

"I don't wish to trouble your appetite," she said sitting, as the black man quietly slid forth her chair. "But, you see? It's Nathan's request for a proper commission."

I attempted to concentrate on the document at hand, but the presence of the Negro staring overhead was too distracting. Elizabeth Bacon may have been perfectly at ease in the presence of such an exotic figure, but for me it downright got on my nerves. I had no wish to share privileged information with a stranger, and more than that, I had the uncontrollable urge to ask the fellow if he'd please just sit down. Join us in a blackberry scone. I pretended to read the letter though, and sipped my cup of coffee, twice, before it was refilled.

"It's just a copy, of course," Elizabeth continued, "he sent the original by courier to Jamestown late last night."

It looked properly official enough, but I had no notion that the governor would deign to sign it. "I saw a hostage in the field this morning," I said, forcing the issue to matters closer on my mind. "A distant relative in fact. His name is Tenakahwhe. He was a cousin to Tomas and Laura."

Elizabeth's face tightened like she had just bitten into a sour apple. She made a point of retrieving the letter, as if emphasize its greater importance. "Perhaps this is awkward for you. No, I'm certain of it," she replied after some time. "But we have been ordered to keep various suspects until their innocence is evident. In case you didn't know, the governor himself decreed it. All the local tribes must offer up some of their men ...until peace is again secure."

I looked at her incredulous. Is this what Nathan told her? Or was this a justification that she'd cooked up on her own? Even if Berkeley had sanctioned such an act, he certainly never intended it as an excuse to enjoin slaves. She then turned to me with a look that could make you believe in anything she might say. Her colorful array of expression receded within the bloom of skin so clear and fair that it conveyed an innocence most people aren't even born with. Her brilliant blue eyes delicately framed by the strands of her shiny black hair could, if she had wanted to, charm the very angels to move aside. I had to look away. Once again I found myself slipping; the comfortable surroundings, elegant in their bounty, could easily make one forget a day in the life of a slave.

"Anyway, the case of Tenakahwhe is practically sealed," she said before I could make further comment. "He was caught red-handed storing away kegs of powder and guns." The fine lines around her aristocratic lips threatened to break into a smile. But she quickly stifled her enjoyment in the pun, when she saw that I tried to ignore it. "This is what is vital now," she said tapping the letter again. "Your support and Nathan's triumph over this... evil. So that we may *all* enjoy a prosperous peace."

"Send word through out the camps! We must move at once!" Came a shout, distinctly Nathan's, that interrupted us, from outside on the lawn.

Elizabeth and I hurried from the table at once and into

the vestibule of the hallway. We met him headlong at the door as he bolted up the stairs.

"Berkeley is on his way with three hundred men," he smiled. "It seems he's gotten round to taking us seriously."

"So, he's accepted your commission?" Elizabeth asked. She made it sound more like a statement than a question."

"Afraid not, my dear. It seems that I'm to be arrested." He gave me one of his devil-may-care winks, but then he took Elizabeth's face in his hands and changed his tone quite quickly. "This is the contingency that we prepared for, dear heart."

I felt the thoughts behind his eyes moving swiftly in her, each one real with measured purpose.

"Go, and gather my things."

Elizabeth made no reply, but softly nodded, and then turned back into the house. "Mr. Gibbs!" she cried. The self-possessed African appeared as though emerged from a wall. "Mr. Bacon will be leaving directly, please see to his horse."

She betrayed no anxiety, a quality worth noting, given that she understood what could come from the governor's punishment very well. I observed her instructing the staff, dispensing a calm authority, starting them in on the procedure protecting her home. She commanded her domain with the single-minded goal of a mother bearcat, but I still could not help but be afraid for her. And even a little envious of her determined naivete.

"I'd better speak with the men." I said, stepping back outside.

"No need," Bacon replied. "I've set my courier to the task."

"You have my admiration Nathan. You prefer to have people think you are much more impetuous than you are."

"Keeping an ear in Jamestown is hardly clever," he said. "It is a matter of raw survival."

"Survival is surely what we're for now," I replied. And surveyed the grandeur of his estate for what I expected was the final time. For all of its imported finery, it still kept the feel of a home. "You realize that you've forced the governor to the point of no return."

He stopped for several minutes and tipped his head curiously, this way and that, like a dog hearing sounds indiscernible. "We do what we can," he finally smiled. But his eyes had lost some of their boyish luster, even a hint of melancholy edged into their frame. I watched him watch Mr. Gibbs water his horse, appearing all the while to be very far away.

"Where are we headed?" I asked to rouse him.

He reached into a saddlebag and withdrew his well-worn map. "I'll lead ahead, and ride alone," he said. "I cannot be encumbered by the men." Suddenly he turned meaningfully to me, almost taking my hand in a show of concern. "You know, Corstair," he paused to find the right words. "Please make the men understand. Precious little will be accomplished by my rotting in a Jamestown jail."

He then threw his gaze back upon the map, without lingering long enough for me to respond. "Come tomorrow we should rendezvous at this point on the southwest end of the swamp. Sir William will never chase us there. The old wheezer's too scared of fever."

He led his horse round the back of the house while I laid the map out on the ground. I did my best to match its primitive detail with the landscape that I carried in my head. When I looked up, Elizabeth had returned with several servants, carrying packs from the house and pouches of food. The bulkiest bag, which she dragged behind her in the dirt, appeared to be crammed with correspondence. It slowly dawned on me that this was the volume of letters that Nathan had written, his political recordings and notes that he did not post. Cinching the belt to his mount, he nodded without speaking, and Elizabeth placed each piece of parchment down the chute of a furnace for clay. On *any* given day, not just the one where the law was due any time to make an arrest, such a sight would cause a lettered man to gasp. For just that quickly the breeze was afloat in a litter of red-black ash. The cost for pulping that much linen into paper made the air into a year's worth of tobacco. A very good year, back when tobacco commanded a price.

Bacon's horse brought back a sense of urgency. Seeing Mr. Gibbs tie a musket to the saddle and a cartridge box with powder to his rump. Servants bustled about, storing and securing items inside trunks that they then placed in vaults beneath the house. Lamps were carefully tended, along with Elizabeth's collection of silver, and a gold framed painting of someone dressed in lace. The chaos moved with a surprising amount of order, until I realized that this departure had been carefully rehearsed. Suddenly, seeing the accumulated mess that Bacon was making of his social station gave me a sense of comfort, I don't know why.

I returned his map and he climbed atop his horse, posing for all he was worth like a rustic cavalier. And just like such, he leaned across his saddle to press Elizabeth up to him; her skirts hitched high upon her thigh. For a long moment she was so stretched, with her delicate parts on full display, but then the Bacons had always relished in this kind of tomfoolery. They turned and caught my face growing red, and laughed their careless play of affection away.

"Don't let Sir William burn the house down," he said to her when she was back on her feet. "Tomorrow then, Mr. Corstair." And touching his hand to his hat, with ridiculous panache, he was gone.

Elizabeth remained neither strained nor worried. Rather, she thought to remind me of the corncakes and dried beef. Across the way I saw a hundred or so men beginning to gather at the head of the southern trail. From this distance they amassed a much more ragged intensity than was seen in a view closer up. And this was the troubled group that Bacon hoped to stand with him against the governor, as apparently events had now led to such. Then, I looked upon Elizabeth, a busy blur of motion, and was renewed by the sheer abundance of her childlike faith. I believe that I even felt jealous. Jealous of what I remembered more than not. But jealous too, of youth, so passionately full of itself that it bloomed in a godless wilderness, in the face all that was moving in upon it, inexorably to see it stopped.

Nathan's courier rode in bringing up my horse and introduced himself as Timothy Gale. He said that we had met once at a hunt in Henricus, but I did not recall his name. I simply could not take my eyes from off Elizabeth. I walked back towards the house with a new appreciation for its grandness, and the sudden hope that the governor would leave it alone.

"We are going to win, Mr. Corstair," she said, handing me a hefty pack of rations. "Because we are right."

Unshakable, forgivable charm.

Atop my horse I could just make out the low-lying dust being kicked up by the hoeing in the far off field. At the very least, I thought, Berkeley will release the Indian's in bondage. Tenakahwhe will have his freedom, and we'll have another savage to kill.

*A*ll day and all night our meager army swayed with the terrain, drifting southwest from the river and the governor. When we hit the bog it forced the men to walk in a wide enough arc to keep from sinking in the steps of the man ahead. Then the air rose up so thick with insects that we had to make torches out of scrub beech bush. After we'd stopped and started like this, having smoked the bugs off, I observed the approach of a strange ilk of men that quietly slipped in to our ranks. The trailing ends of these groups came in so mysteriously that you'd swear they emerged from the mud.

As a breed they seemed so inured to their low condition that they barely had use of a language. At least from what I struggled to understand. They appeared singly or in twos and threes, and always wielding their bizarre, if ingenious homemade weapons. One man had coiled a jagged blade of ripsaw around the end of willow pole, which he released with a decapitating whip. So equipped, and with only the basest skills for living, it was almost as if they were turned into primitive creatures. If you looked them in the face they'd invariably drop their heads and glance for a place to hide, on the other hand though, by skulking on the edge of our flank they always found the most solid ground that led in a better direction. Once, when I got so turned around that I was sure we had only made a circle, I called out to one with a tangled mane of greasy hair.

"Meke do I," he said, and pushed ahead, indifferent of those who followed. He then marched us around ten miles of marsh where we might have been stuck for a day. All told, I was glad to accept their knowledge and their numbers, and by the time we reached our rendezvous with Bacon, we had a couple hundred men.

We had just made the trek through a blind of chest high field grass when we suddenly broke onto a stand of acacia trees. There he was in the grove ahead, bent at a makeshift table and working away with his quill. The picture he presented was so incongruently absurd that I could not keep from laughing. The men staggered through the glade behind me, so crazed by bugs that they were blasting them with birdshot, and here was Bacon, sitting in the shade of a mimosa tree, and scribbling upon his paper like a banker. I could not even guess how he'd managed to construct such a scene.

"Good afternoon, he said, refusing to look up. Whatever he was writing was obviously more important than a couple hundred men tearing up the landscape. "You're late," he went on, "and would you please tell those men to stop shooting? It's scaring off the game. And you may let them know that they will be called to account for unnecessary loss of ammunition. And… please send up Timothy Gale."

"Certainly," I replied, adding just a touch of mimic.

"Then bid everyone make themselves to home."

With a slight shift of his head he indicated the surrounding wood while holding up his page to dry. It took me a minute of squinting before I realized that this nondescript clump of wilderness was in fact, a fully developed camp. Bacon's office in the undergrowth wasn't near the half of it. A score of other spaces had been cleared, and in the absence of a running stream, there was a common barrel wood cistern. A separate area had even been dug to function for latrines, but what commanded the eye more than any other object were the casks of rum stacked neatly on the ground. The sight of such, as Bacon knew well would have every single man's devotion. I shook my head and made a big guffaw. I could not comprehend the madness that lay in store for men who were shooting at bugs.

"A gift from your friend, Henry Creighton," Bacon smiled. "Purely antiseptic. The water here is rather brackish, don't you think?"

And thus was I informed of just how long this operation had been in the works. I considered the simple logistics, the transport of this much supply, and recalled the bully taunting of Creighton. There must have been some carved out wagon trials, but how had I ever missed them? Baffled and hesitant, I surveyed the layout until I let myself grin. Grin like a basic full-blown idiot. The rich, was all that I could think of, and the peculiar lives that they led. Staring at the stash of whiskey, my frustration felt dispersed. In the end my only concern was that the drunks would keep their hardest fight for the Indians, instead of for themselves.

"How do you keep this place so well hidden?" I asked.

"The Indians are further to the south. They stick to the trade routes that lead to the Occaneechee village on the Roanoke. There is nothing of interest for them here."

This is, I thought, but it was something I withheld. The men tromped in from the weeds and let loose a big whoop when they got an eyeful up the bank. It was like a person waking up to a new golden morn after spending a night with the sweats. They formed in rough lines while Bacon, the quartermaster extraordinaire, divvied a share to any man that held out a cup. Along with every half pint, he offered them his heartfelt thanks, and they in return conferred congratulations. They called him "General Bacon" now, and he, without accepting the appointment directly, beamed in his silent approval. "With your difficult march endured," he pronounced. "You are due your soldier's reward."

The forced march, I supposed, was the cutting test of their loyalty, but no more revealing than watching him wear a politician's cloak. He'd sit for a spell with one group, then move easily to another, appearing just as much at home as with the gentlemen friends in his parlor. He indulged their woodsy quirks, and laughed at each raw joke, pretending in all, to be as comfortable here as in any spot on earth that he could think of. He listened intently, and kept steering their complaints towards anything that'd stick to Berkeley.

I sat for this awhile, before taking a chance to slip away and scan the papers he never grew tired of working on. Predictably, there were his reasons for taking control of a military command, but compiled in the pages beneath was an aggressive list of the grievance he bore against the governor. Whole paragraphs were devoted to Berkeley's reckless disregard for the lives of the frontier farmers, as well as detailed accounts of corruption, and finally, a list of the governor's cronies, that he named individually as thieves. Through the course of that late afternoon, I'd watched him, unsure of where he meant to take his expanding politics; was he intending to stop with the drawback of the Indians, or was he out for control of Jamestown itself? I had heard him before, many times of course, denouncing officials in the government 'til he drove himself quite hoarse, but it was quite a different matter to have those accused written down.

Still. Watching him even now, win his way into the heart of the crowd his natural way of leadership won me over again. One had to respect the trust that he gained from such strong-minded, and often, (if I'm honest) mean lot of men. He talked, he drank, and he never stopped listening. Compacted in those hours, he bled a man with fever, and held the hand of another while someone cut off the man's rotted toes. And before the day was out I got the sense that whatever had been set in motion, no matter what would come; I was in a run with history. He truly raised that much exhilarating noise.

The latter part of evening however, brought a belly scraping hunger that all the cheap whisky did was enhance. And after some no account fishing from a shallow mud pond, Bacon made the noble act of laying out Elizabeth's personal pack of his stores. It was a gesture that he knew would not go very far, but it played well in his one-for-all good purpose. I elected to try and sleep on my empty stomach, and take some rations at first light, but when I laid back I felt a familiar tingle, that flitted at the top of my gut. As if touched by a premonition, I took a walk about, and found a few walnut trees that had escaped my earlier notice. Reaching out in the dark, I scraped half an inch of dust from a stumpy branch, all withered with leaves. Aside from the rummy men drowsing by the fire, not another living sound was heard. I picked up a walnut, but before it even came off the ground it crumbled in my hand. This was no place to tarry, was what my gut had already told me, this was a place of blight. The Indian's lack of interest here was because of its lack of food. And unbeknownst to our gentleman general, the reason he could make this camp unfettered, was because there was nothing to hunt.

I decided to keep this observation to myself, (not that such a thing would be lost upon the men) and let Bacon give voice to his loftier discontents. Then, there was the arrival of Timothy Gale. He broke into camp very late, having herded the last of the stragglers, and proceeded to spend the rest of the night at a campfire by himself. He examined all of Bacon's paperwork, paragraph by page, as though he had to run it through a sieve. Only when the moon had finally dipped completely from our view did he give his eyes a rest. Then he got up, stuffed the whole works in his satchel, and mounted his horse to make the return trip.

"Hold off awhile, Mr. Gale," Bacon said smiling, "enjoy a bit of refreshment."

It was obvious that Gale wanted to leave at once, but he made himself available, attaching himself now to Bacon's side. He sipped a bit at Creighton's rum, acting more and more uncomfortable, as if forced to endure this distinctly ungentlemanly time. But fortunately for him, the men did not make him suffer their company for long. Soon after, when Bacon apparently deduced the liquor had gained its maximum momentum, he suddenly announced the formal naming of his officers. This was received by a new wave of toasts, but with much more brew-ha and honor well-met. The speechmaking was largely incoherent, going back and forth from the treachery of Indians to the fear of God. 'General' Bacon then proclaimed that the first duty of the officers, "to prove they were worthy of these brave men," was to sign their names to the list of crimes that he'd listed against the governor. Cheered on by the camp, and skewered with drink, they happily complied without so much as half reading it. They were, in fact so greatly lit that by the time they'd finished their scribbling, their signatures had all been joined in the shape of a circle. Todd Manley started it off, as if adding flair to his already tipsy pen, but everyone then followed on, continuing to curl his name round the page, and producing what they called, "a most clever touch." To me the result looked ominously like a target, but I was much more discomforted by their careless concern for such a dangerous document.

"See here,' Bacon smiled, holding the completed signatures up. "The official stamp of my *own* inner circle."

Observing them like this, that is from outside their *inner circle* I picked out who would tremble most when he finally sobered up. A chorus of Jamestown jeers then was started, and Bacon sealed the papers into Timothy Gale's pouch. In the next second he was gone. While we, so it seemed, were to sit and wait for the governor's response. I did not know Gale well. To be honest, I thought him a bit of a queer duck, but I must say that he was a far braver man than myself. A midnight ride through that black and impenetrable swamp required more faith than I could count on. And faith was something we would sorely need, if against the judgment in my gut, Bacon insisted on staying here.

Sure enough, after this night of celebration, we faced a full week of delay. A delay that meant young Gale had been arrested or else had not survived. In the face of this, in addition to my earnest most pleas, Bacon would not be moved. In his opinion the loss of Gale, and his all-important papers, meant just as much as losing our campaign. It was clear that Bacon would take no further step until Berkeley had the document, his "whole host of rebels" in his hands.

Pointless to say, hunger quickly followed and made its own all-demanding path. Small hunting parties were formed, but produced precious little in terms of sustenance. There was simply no game to be found. Piddling scores such as a rat, or possum, or even an occasional snake were eaten just as quick as they were caught, and the best ones at this, the strange group of swamp men, were loath to share their catch. I finally lost my patience the day that I headed out to go far afield as I must in order to bring back a turkey. Eight hours later I was sure that I had trapped a pair nearby their nest when a tag along boy scared them off by taking a shot at a parrot. As I gathered up a meager pair of eggs I laid him out good with a heated diatribe of curses. He started crying and told me that he'd wanted a plume for his hat.

Bacon meanwhile, retreated into a belligerent grimness. He kept apart from the men, saying that he had to concentrate on the copies required of his (copiously notated) grievance. His army grew more restless by the hour, until it forced me (some thirty men all together) at last to confront him. I told him that it was likely Gale was only being held by Berkeley as a ploy to see us disband or perish. That the governor had a strong history of successfully suppressing local militias, and that some of the populace were reported already to be turning against us. Bacon seemed too bothered to listen, then simply said that he understood, and kept on piling up his papers. Time dragged like this, unbearably so, until finally came the morning that Gale returned. The outlying camps, (meaning those closest to leaving) were stirred from their doldrums, but it was not because he had good news.

"Berkeley's occupied your house on the Curles," he said before dismounting. "He *claimed* to have detained me these days in order to finalize his answer. He says that you will surely hang. After a fair trial of course. His words, not mine. And that the rest of the men are free to go, if they peacefully return to their homes."

'Homes?' I thought. What homes? Is the governor so out of touch, or have his years now made him blind?

"And Elizabeth?" Bacon asked, as grave as I'd yet seen him.

"Elizabeth is fine," Gale said. "She's bolted herself inside of her rooms, and holds the governor accountable for any damage to your property. Have you anything to eat?" he interjected anxiously. "It's been a difficult week, and I've had a hard ride. Berkeley forbade my carrying provisions."

Bacon looked at him, as if he expected more.

Gale was clearly exhausted; the devotion he'd displayed was clear above all else he had to say. And Nathan responded, a glint returned to his eye, which seemed to free him of his recently acquired fears. He fetched Gale the remains of the jerky from his pack. "Berkeley kept you all this time to tell me this?"

"He was waiting on a further announcement from the Assembly, which he states has dominion over this affair." Gale ate the dried beef, in tentative bites as he surveyed the mess that we'd made of our camp. "He's also called for new elections."

"Publicity!" Bacon screamed. "This is what it is! Devious attempts to placate the public's fervor while he sits on his protected estates!"

Then he became still again, in the way that he could quickly detach. "All that is left us gentlemen," he mumbled after a bit, "is to win the people by our *actions*. Corstair, gather up the men. We are moving out at once!"

"There's more," Gale quickly interrupted. "The Queen of the Pawmunkeys has tortured an Englishman she took as a hostage. A man that Berkeley confirms was acting on his behalf. She says that if her demands are not met, the governor should expect indiscriminate war. She claims she has hundreds of mercenary warriors gathering at the borders. Savages from as far away as New York "

To this frightful and astonishing news, Bacon only smiled. "The Queen of the Pawmunkeys hasn't the power of an English garden snake," he replied. "And if Berkeley is using her to scare us, he is no more than a common liar. It is for us then to force the issue upon him! Make him reveal his allegiance! Gentlemen! We are for the Occaneechee!"

Our movement, kindled at last to a purpose, unified everyone at once. And Bacon, now returned to his full confidence, barked about the riches that lay ahead in store. But speaking for myself, and my ragged group of followers the motive of food was enough of a reward.

And then. It was extremely rough going from the start. The enthusiasm of the morning was beaten by the heat and frustration of clawing through walls of barbed undergrowth. Undergrowth, I might add, that grew clear above our heads. The breaks came in stretches full of fist-sized rocks that beat at your heels like a hammer. As vexing as it seemed, the Occaneechee had their center for trade deep inside an inaccessible country. At least as far as a couple hundred beleaguered English farmers could figure. Then, out of nowhere, directly due west of its supposed location, a trickle of trails converged from the woods into a veritable roadway.

Bacon ordered the men to remain in the forest while we took our skittish horses to scout ahead. Holding them back to a bit-chomping walk, we leaned into our saddles, studying the thicket. Ambush, I was sure, was imminent. My steady mare, a horse that already had forded the unknown depths of countless streams, resisted every fretful step. The air was thick and smelled metal-like, almost of blood, although I couldn't be made to swear. It clung upon the heat, and coated the inside of my nose, making me taste my own breath. I stood from the seat and searched the source of the smell, when a clamoring came up the road behind us. I pointed to Bacon and we scrambled up the bank to view from a cluster of trees. A score of unfamiliar Indians were following just below us, moving past the place that we had left. Out of the twenty, five were well armed, wearing a mix of tailored clothing, suggesting to me that they traded with the French. The others were all young women bound together in single file, piled with bulky packs upon their heads and backs. Strutting at their side, the warrior in charge, in a waistcoat and a military cap kept them moving rapidly in line. He was shouting in a nonstop cadence that I couldn't understand, until he suddenly broke off to beat a girl who'd spilled her cargo on the ground. The rest of the women took this chance to rest, while the girl, dodging the blows as best she could, scrambled to gather up the beaver skins.

The Indian brigadier (by the rank of the insignia on his European cap) was all in a rage, but he took care not to strike the girl upon the face, a purpose, no doubt designed for her to fetch her best price. A spot evaluation however, could see she wasn't worth half of what the carcass would bring that she'd dropped out on the ground. Then, with the offending girl corrected, and her load re-aligned in balance, he doubled the pace until all had disappeared. Bacon and I followed at a quiet cautious distance, growing more wary by the minute, as we watched the sky fill up with vultures, and a thickening cloud of flies. Everything that crawled or flew in this part of the world, so it seemed, was here to enjoy the fetid air.

Another half mile and the road dipped into a muddy riverbank, and we took cover in the scrub of an overlooking bluff. The warriors and the women were once more below us, being ferried by a number of pirogues that were lined along a ramp. The distance across hardly warranted such accommodation, the river was quite shallow in fact, but the island fortress on the other side, seemed to command this special attention.

It held three separate structures; the most formidable at the center, with the outlying two linked by lines of shabby huts. Some of the hovels extended out over the river, propped upon stilts that had sunk level with the water. The current population looked to be about two hundred, representing a broad spectrum of tribes. From our perch upon the hilltop, I counted as many as thirty separate fires, each with a stout English kettle, some nearly four feet wide. They were boiling en masse, stewing the fat off of beaver. The finished pelts were wrapped in what looked about one hundred pound bundles, held together by long strips of hide, and these were fit out with heavy poles that slid into handles at their sides. The bales were then rotated into specially constructed racks by a team of girls whose job looked to be constantly rolling them up and then back out. This process, I supposed, was to keep the fur from drying out too fast or brittle by catching the oil from the skins just above. Smaller children were employed to tend the fires, and to keep away the swarms of flies. Women clearly did the work. Fifty of them at least. Packed together at blood-drenched tables, with their knives in nonstop motion, and up to their shins in entrails.

The other occupation, in this remarkable hive, was gambling. A business that was strictly for men, at least the ones not down from drinking, anyway. There were lively games of dice, and pitch, and what looked to be a table made specifically for faro. Other groups, male and female alike, milled about the town center, gathering anyplace there was room enough to barter. The newly arrived slave girls, with their brigadier master, filled one of these vacant spots. He was met by a brave in a white tasseled blouse who started inspecting the grade of his pelts. Every single nook held European pots, or swords or anything shining and metal. On a place just off the main thoroughfare, and by far the most popular, was an impressive assortment of guns. Just beyond, in high walled sheds built rearmost to the fort, stood two columns of kegs one facing one another. Like a couple of gods, they towered over all, one stacked with whiskey, the other of powder.

From where we stood to the island itself was only a good stone's toss, but way of crossing was by a stream of sludge, that seemed to lick at the shore in filthy gulps. I reckoned the boats were there to keep you from having to pick through the solid mess, and maybe more to the point, stood as a barrier for defense. Hefting an unwieldy load of stolen fur through this shallow slime would discourage the most determined man from theft. The water, if it were so called, was nothing but a mass of discarded animal matter being slowly devoured by the earth. A fully congealed lid of decaying beaver pulp. Their skinless bodies left to rot where they were thrown, provided an endless harvest for every breed of buzzard. I was accustomed to humid fields, ripe with new manure, but the stench that this river produced was crippling.

"I'm going to burn this place," Bacon said, "and every beast that's in it." I turned to him and he was already up on his horse. "But first we have to eat. You best get down there, Mr. Corstair," he smiled. "And start talking up some of your good Injun will."

And then he was riding away, as if to head off further debate, while I stayed where I was, angry and perplexed. "I'll bring the men up," he said, and then left out of hearing. Behind and below me the shot of a musket rang out. I jerked round to see a downed horse trying to kick free of its wagon. Then more shots, two, three, puffs of burning powder spreading through the busy marketplace. Amazingly, someone started cursing in broken English. As the wail of a woman filled the air, I began to walk toward the putrid water. I did not see a single Susquehanna.

16

wnership, or perhaps the simple lure of attainment, be it for an honest necessity or a worthless trinket, is the key to one man's dominion of another. And it was precisely this condition, to my cautious surprise, that I saw in the grin of the sludge boat pilot who greedily eyed my horse. More than unfazed by my sudden appearance, he even acted familiar. I assumed that he assumed I had a cache of weapons or such to trade that were hidden nearby. In a hodge-podge of accents and exaggerated signals, he let me know that he was willing to convey me to the village for the deposit of my mare. Feigning a careless shrug, I accepted his terms, and sat behind his back on the short sewage crossing.

My appearance at the gate was accepted without stir, but gave me little comfort as I milled among the residents to gawk at the disruptive scene. The reason I could enter without attracting more attention was due to the gunfire I'd only just witnessed from my overlook view. An extremely large half-breed, in the full pleated coat of a gentleman had placed himself square in the middle. He wheeled this way and that, jabbing the combatants with a gold-embroidered cane that had a pistol installed as a handle. Clearly disgusted, he stood over the slaughtered horse, as if wanting to give it a kick, but then turned on the man who had started the shooting some moments before. He shouted out orders that I only half caught and then seized up the drunken shooter's gun. He grabbed a girl that stood by, (that looked like the guilty man's daughter,) and gave both her and the gun to the owner of the dead horse.

The girl did not resist, and even approached the wounded man by offering him her help. He pushed her aside, the better to examine his new weapon, as the half-breed swept his cane to disperse the crowd.

"Eenglissh!" he suddenly shouted, turning to face me. "Eenglissh!"

The afternoon's unpleasantness behind him, he threw open his arms from across the way with an enthusiasm that made me immediately embarrassed. Doubtless, he had observed me from the moment of my entrance, but as he drew close with none in the crowd to obstruct him, he presented the strangest figure I had ever seen. His head was completely shaved and he'd covered his face, temples to neck, in a veritable garden of flowery tattoos. In contrast, the peak of his head shone like an apricot polished in wax. It was his mass however, easily six feet and three hundred pounds, that was his most dramatic feature. His smile was broad, as though seeking to be benevolent, but then the rows of his teeth were filed to sharp points. He had his arms thrown wide apart in welcome, walking directly for me as though I was one of his long lost allies.

I had no clue how to respond. Should I mimic his bravura and pretend we shared a phantom history? Or should I exaggerate the army that even now was stalking up from back outside, and make a threat to his apparent hospitality? Suddenly, I felt the shock that I, a conservative planter, who'd always calculated his options, was standing in the middle of a deadly fortress without a forward thought. On reaching me, he stretched a giant hand atop my head as if to bestow his pagan blessing, a gesture so unexpected and disarming, that it served to take away my fright. A conflict of perception surged within me and I determined to be direct.

"I am with the army from Maryland," I said. "Undoubtedly you have heard what we have done to the Susquehanna. We are now twice as strong, and expect your full support."

So much for the good will approach. Three other braves, standing by as bodyguards shifted in place. The giant meanwhile, looked merely exasperated. He stared at the ground before me, a novel act in itself in my Indian rapport, and I expected with each passing second, to feel my head roll free of my shoulders. Instead, a long silence ensued that had me debating if I should keep pressing the offensive. I scanned the early evening sky, as if it could signal the chance for my survival. But all that came clear was the starving headache pounding that reinforced the need to bring back food. So I stood, holding onto nothing more than empty time, while the giant offered a smile mixed with a grimace.

"I think that it is best for you to speak with our chief, Persicles."

This suggestion, so calmly understated, came as a revelation in separate parts. First, that he was not the ranking chieftain, and that his command of English was this excellent. "I am called Man-haut-te," he continued. Then he glanced at me as if to check my understanding of the nuance in his name. In a round about kind of translation, Man-haut-te was Mother-in-Law Medicine.

"And you are?" he asked, solicitous.

"Corstair," I replied. "Philip Corstair, officer in Bacon's Army of Virginians."

I needed to quicken this exchange. I was near complete exhaustion, and far too hungry to keep this paltry charade.

"Well Philip Corstair, officer in Bacon's Army of Virginians," he stated loudly. "Consider yourself my guest. Please excuse my confusion, but I do not know what you seek, or what you have come to offer. But then," he smiled, rolling a lip above his shiny sharp teeth, "who knows what we both may learn?"

I walked beside him to a large enclosed platform near

the middle of a square that led us directly past the dead horse. The new owner of the girl was barking orders as she cut into its chest to find the heart. The scene was so vividly full of meat and fresh flesh, that my stomach churned in sickly roils. "Where did you learn your English?" I asked, hoping that no one but myself had heard it. "The pistol you carry is Spanish, is it not?"

The big man stopped and turned to me as if he had reached the limits of his tact. "El presente de mi padre Espanola con les ojos por les oro imaginar," he replied. "I am hoping, Officer Corstair, that you have not wasted the insights gained by the folly of such men."

He seemed to catch my eyes into his, drawing out the silence for several fragile minutes. And whether it was my sinking need of food, or some new inherent weakness I could not tell, but I lost hold of my surroundings, as though I had fallen into inky pools behind his eyelids. I felt that I was in the presence of a man completely devoid of fear. A spirit lived inside his enormous body, but barely, as if it had slipped beneath the human grip. Man-haut-te had within him, a blank. An entity so opaque and deep, that it reflected *nothing*. Except for a very strange second, the shared understanding that just this dark wisdom had paid a visit to us both. Suddenly I had to remember how to move my head. I took a step away and saw again the floral face, like the green in a garden at night. The feeling was so intensely uncomfortable, that I looked about for an object, any point of reference, any *thing* that I could fix on, to try and restore myself. And there was the forlorn man who'd done the shooting, childless now, and ignored, staggering out of the village, broken down and drunk. Man-haut-te drew back the door to his tent, and the smell of roasting meat hit my nose with the force of kicking mule.

"Please, sir," he said. "To enter. To sit."

On the floor before me a couple dozen warriors from

practically as many tribes lay about on cushions of bear and buffalo coats, amid extravagant piles of food. Servants moved among them, bowing to obscure their faces, while offering parts of this bounty on greasy wooden plates. Observing my shock, and for that matter, weak-kneed delirium Man-haut-te handed me a leg of lamb from off of the circling feast. We settled on a platform at the far end of the floor, where I tore into the food, with both my hands and teeth.

"Here," he said, reaching for some broth, which he carefully poured out for me. "Drink first. You are too hungry."

"My men need food." I blurted, finding it too difficult to restrain myself. Even the steam from the various juices had crept into my body with hypnotic effect.

"Food?" He looked absently at the buffet just beside him. "You came here for food?" He was incredulous, and did not conceal his distrust at my request. The other warriors, content with the drink and the women, paid no attention to our English talk. "I do many things, Mr. Corstair. I control the bribes at hostile borders. I open more beaver trails where it is plentiful out west. I keep a difficult peace. And believe me," he was now patting his bald shaven head. "In work such as mine, it is best to keep your hair on the inside of your skin."

I half listened, mesmerized by the display of wasteful excess. Half-gnawed turkey bones, carelessly strewn about. I wondered how I could go about hauling it back to the men. There must have been four different types of game and equal amounts of fowl. Millet cakes, fried corn in gravy, brook and river trout. I watched, amazed as in a dream, knowing that two hundred starving men were making a dismal camp in just a short distance. Knowing too, that if I confessed to that fact, our army could just as well have been slaughtered. Man-haut-te dabbed delicately at his food as if suddenly embarrassed by the riches. My thoughts became giddy. How much could I stuff inside my shirt before making a run for the gate?

"Let me explain, Mr. Corstair, that I wish to welcome you as a guest. But the men you have brought with you bring no joy to this place. And as it happens you have stumbled here at the changing time. The changing river feast."

Before he could speak any further a commotion moved his braves back to the entrance and sent out a flurry across the sated floor. People pressed together and formed a corridor where a tightly bound Cherokee was roughly ushered in. He was then pushed directly to Man-haut-te, who had remained seated beside me on the platform. Man-haut-te looked at me, taking the time to articulate his English, so that others without his skill at the language might also understand.

"My status also requires that I perform certain duties," he declared, drawing up to his full height, "distasteful, as they may be." I was getting up with him when the nearest bodyguard hacked off one of the Cherokee's ears. It was all that I could do to shield my plate from the blood.

"Did you know Mr. Corstair, that direct trading with whites is a violation of our domain? There is no viler way that I know of to show your disrespect." Man-haut-te went on. He had adopted a noticeably more casual tone in talking to me as he faced the prisoner.

The Cherokee before him trembled out his urine, nodding as if he understood. He looked like he was about to faint when another brave shoved some kind of oily astringent up his nose. This brought his bleeding head straight up, and then, with more jostling at the door, three more Cherokee were thrown inside the tent. They were forced to stand, just in time to witness an Occaneechee brave cleave off their leader's head. The brave then quickly swept the head up by its hair, and threw it to the prisoners at the rear. After a quick and fierce scramble to retrieve the sticky face, one of them achieved the grisly prize, and held it tight inside his arms. He then got up and ran in full panic, out the door. His fellow prisoners, along with everyone else, screamed in a howling pursuit. The surrounding rush pushed me outside, and into a waiting crowd that had gathered at the entrance. Women and children, gamblers and drunks, even the slave girls started jeering as the terrified Cherokees ran. Stride by stride they endured a barrage of stones, so heavy that by the time they reached the open square the runner with the head was pummeled to the ground. The one behind then quickly grabbed it up, and turned for a dash to the gate. The crowd took sport in the chase, enough anyway to let it run, but when the new leader slipped and fell he was most horribly set upon. At last, the surviving runner was then allowed to go free. Severely bruised and bleeding, but safely outside the wall, he shook the head of his dead leader, as if in triumph back at the fort. Then, with his gruesome message in hand, he limped through the mud in the dark.

"An important part of my function," Man-haut-te said standing behind me, "is finding efficient means to communicate."

He was staring at the long line of campfires strung out along the banks of the opposite shore. As if in aftershock, I swallowed back my indigestion, feeling some relief anyway, that the men had thought to spread the camps and exaggerate the look of our numbers. Then, as if staying true to his sense of protocol, Man-haut-te conducted me back to his inconvenienced celebration.

The most obvious result of the violence was the exuberance that it left upon the crowd. People swarmed excitedly about him, but wherever he stepped, they made sure to clear his way. He greeted every merchant, and shared a joke with a man from a tribe I did not know. He took council with apparent drifters, asking about what they'd seen, and on what trails. At one point he stopped to hear a stranger's story about his disobedient squaw. He then took the side of the beaten down woman who cowered in the shadows behind.

All that I could do was to wait for the right moment, for a moment of I knew not what, between the greasy mouthfuls and the groping of bodies, both of male and of female alike. And as the night wore on, all that I'd learned was that if my men didn't eat, the buzzards would still feast come light. The Cherokee criminals were thrown in the river with everything else that it was designed to rot.

"Why do you wish to threaten us, Mr. Corstair?" Man-haut-te suddenly asked. I was staring numbly at a couple below me that was slowly expanding the circle of their lust. "We only wish to be your friends. As you see we are a loving people."

Wary as I was, I looked in his face and judged he was sincere. His powerful arm made a graceful arc above the debauchery.

"I have more love to share than Jesus Christ," he said, "so long as you are my friend."

"If we are your friends, then we must have food!" I said, surprising myself with anger. If Bacon attacked right then, I thought, in the thick of this pagan orgy, we would surely prevail. Then, just as quickly, I returned to my only real hope, getting back to the men unharmed, where we might regroup. Man-haut-te looked as though he'd just read my mind.

"Sit and play," he said briskly, changing the subject.

There came a dread thought that he meant me to join the men and women, but then he made space for a faro board. No sooner had he taken his seat than we were surrounded by a group of young men, each with the same cocky smirk, stepping up for the chance to gamble. Man-haut-te beamed his approval, welcoming each one warmly to his place, but when the game commenced, the atmosphere turned comically serious. The casual comments ceased, as the secretive cards were viewed, and with a deadly fear of looking up lest their eyes betray their moves. There would be the slightest nod, or a shake of the wrist, to signal the acceptance or refusal of a bid. Man-haut-te on the other hand, carried on a nonstop banter, pinching a young man's cheek and having streams of cawing laughter, as I suppose, from the way that the game developed, he had every right to do. After only dealing a few fast hands, he had won a silver powder horn, a fine-point English rapier, and a necklace made of pearl and gold. These, he tossed in a cask behind him, that nearly overflowed with such, while the loss of their possessions in no way curbed the younger men's willing appetites. Indeed, the earnest way in which they lost was altogether intriguing. I could only gather that the value they placed on winning and losing was exactly the same. Anyway, it was the first I'd ever seen of such fluent gambling. Like determined ducks paddling to the falls of a river they swam, where once they'd foolishly washed over it, they gambled all the more. And then, at the height of his reverie, by acting the part of my sponsor I suppose, Man-haut-te snatched out a pearl for my stake. Suddenly there was no choice about my joining in the game.

"For my friend and his starving army," he spoke in his own language as the others looked placidly on.

I took a card, my mind working angles to win my way back to my men, but no sooner were the cards laid out than Man-haut-te swept them up before they could even be seen.

"I win again!" he proclaimed, throwing back his head in a mighty guffaw.

This singular view of his prickly upper teeth was just as arresting as he had intended it, while I and the other gamblers nodded, growing more nervous and quiet.

"I win again!" he said grabbing up the stake.

His one sided game went on for two more rounds, making his laughter rise higher, until it became as aggressive as a weapon, with no one in on the joke.

"Eat!" he demanded, tearing at a loin of ham. "You're

hungry, eat!'"

All eyes then looked at me, as his giant hands were clamped to mine tight to the slippery meat. The next thing I knew, he'd spilled his entire keg of jewels out upon the table. "What need of this?!" he demanded. "When is gold more important than bread?! Everybody wins!"

A few of the gamblers tentatively reached for the bounty, while others stayed still, more cautious of his mood. Then when they saw that the bolder ones were allowed to abscond with their riches, the others jumped in for what was left. "Shoo!" Man-haut-te shouted, pounding the platform once with his boot. Each brave pressed his hands to his shirt pouch crammed with jewels, and scurried away.

"I have English guns and English whiskey," he turned to me deliberately. "I do not own a single fall-to-pieces Indian trading musket. And I want to be your *friend*."

"Your friends need food."

It was the only thing that I could say.

"I will help you with your troubles," he sighed. "The Susquehanna that you seek are camped just five miles from here."

"Take us to them," I demanded.

Bluntly expressing his impatience and disgust, he took a position at the head of the floor. Then, slipping the pistol from the top of his cane, he fired it once in the air. "We raid the Susquehanna!" he yelled. The smoke from the blast clung to stunned and naked bodies locked into a writhing swarm. "This night!"

A growl seemed to emanate from beneath the woolen floor that became a high-pitched howl. The platform on which I stood shook me down to my knees. Men leapt up in animal hides, in claws and fur, screaming together, then at one another, possessed of an instant, animal violence. Torches were lit and thrown; the air to the ceiling popped and crackled, a dance begun, electric and alive. Fear choked with food in my throat brought up like molten iron.

"The Susquehanna," Man-haut-te said, "are a backward and selfish people." He leaned in above me, above the fire and the dancing silhouettes along the back wall. "Tell your General Bacon that they are finished. He can eat *them* if he wishes, with the new morning sun."

I was made to leave the village. Women were preparing the dark silver paint for war. The force had awakened the whole fort. I slogged through the riverbed trying to keep my sack of food from the stinking water; my mind was far too numb to think on anything else.

I was not then, nor am I now a superstitious man. But in that hour, and in the sickness that I felt in that swamp, I was as close as I could be to meeting Satan.

I waded back to camp unmolested until halted by a sentry that was visibly disturbed by the terror he surely saw in my face. Bacon however was unfazed. He greeted me as if I'd only been out to gather up some firewood, and then acted disappointed at the sack of food that I had brought.

"You will make certain, Mr. Gale, that every man receives a bite to eat," he told his loyal courier, Gale being the only man I knew that might actually accomplish this impossible task. Nathan took no food for himself, but led me to a spot where we might be undisturbed. I understood that this was no insignificant gesture. His pretended indifference to the danger I'd endured was the face of his public persona, a show of detaching himself from the prospect of failure, of forging ahead in the throes of the impossible. His attitude was passive intuitive and stretched in to an awkward silence that stood ready for me to fulfill his expectations. Indeed, he acted as if he had all day to get what he finally he needed in terms of my support. And strange that being back in his presence, I found myself thinking, despite what I'd only just seen, how I might cushion my report. I had hoped to see some doubt in him, but even in this private conference, he revealed nothing of the sort. With the aid of his spyglass I pointed to the line of Man-haut-te's warriors heading westward in the dark.

"They want to be our friends," I said, handing him the scope. "They are out to finish the Susquehanna. And they promise to bring us food."

"Good," was all he said, counting their numbers in the

dim and distant view. "And when they do we will kill them. Is that not good, Mr. Corstair?" he suddenly demanded. "Is that not good?"

This was new. I could not tell whether he was suddenly insecure, or issuing a challenge. Then it might have just been plain old hunger that had put a nervous frailty in his voice. "In all honesty Nathan, I do not think we can accomplish it," I replied. "They have a terrible and powerful leader, who stands at the head of the largest coalition I have ever seen."

"Nonsense, Corstair," he replied. "Because they are no more than savage beasts, while we on the other hand, are English. Serving the hand of God."

I now became afraid that he had been touched. Hunger without sleep, the constant exposure; conditions that were ripe for slipping from one's mind. "Tell me then," he went on, "how is that old wizard, Persicles?"

But as usual, he always had a surprise. "I was unable to meet with the great chief," I reported. "I wish I had known that you and him had commerce."

"No, no, not at all. He's Berkeley's man. Sole agent and proprietor of all..." he said sweeping a hand in the dark, "...that you see here." The light in his eyes was unnatural, a cold peculiar glow. "All that you see, you see?" he said, laughing softly.

"Listen to me, Nathan. We must try to negotiate. These people are strong and they are brutal. They have a chief with an iron fist that he uses over all these western territories. And if he will eliminate the Susquehanna for us..."

"Are you so blind as to think this is an isolated dispute with godless heathens?!" he suddenly screamed. "Have you thought about what will happen if I return empty handed? The very failure that our governor counts upon!?" By chill or by excitement his lips began shake. "Our mission is to open this frontier. It will be our land, and there will be justice! And the many English that follow will... become rich! Mark me, Mr. Corstair, this is a moment I will not let pass! This country," he waved his arms wide, "will change the rule of monarchy. Starting here!"

If madness *was* stalking him, I thought, then I must watch for anything I said that would provoke it, and send him irretrievably off. If we were to survive this fierce severity, I had to use precaution. Choose each deed and word with care. He then raised his arms and trotted in a circle like a turkey with a foot caught in the ground. Snapping his fingers, he moved like this, backwards and around, as if hearing a most erratic rhythm of a drum. Then he stayed in one place, swaying for a while, before strutting with his arms held wide, as if to embrace the dark and empty sky.

"There is a country for us to create," he raved. "And we will do so at the pleasure of *Virginian* men. Men just like yourself, Corstair. Men just like yourself!"

"Bes' save sum ah that strength for gittin us on up outa here Cap'n," came a voice behind us. "We ain't in no condition ta waste away on no damn siege."

I turned to see a throng of defeated faces coming up from the outer fringe of camp. Torchlight flickered among rows of peeling sores and rheumy eyes. One man had a tattered sleeve tied round his oozing forehead. A couple, two or three looked so sick that they'd turned a shade of green. The result of cooking something that they'd spooned out of the river, I supposed. They started to sit, each with a face more gaunt than the next, listening to what Bacon had to say.

"We're what ones at's being sieged on," the man continued.

"Well I'm jus' as likely ta do my own brand ah justice, if'n I don't git my promised pay," offered another.

"If you go back now," he said quietly, and suddenly just as calm. "You will be dead before you reach the James."

He approached the huddled figures directly, moving between them in the dark, as though to hand out pieces of his confidence physically, which could only be done if one could eat it, of course. "Down there is food aplenty," he stated. "Down there is justice *and* your pay."

"I'm certain that the Occaneechee's will provide for us," I interrupted. I decided to take advantage of his slipping hold. And I suddenly felt responsible for keeping these men alive.

"If we strike now!" Bacon shouted over me, mingling and grabbing an anonymous shoulder for support. "While the enemy is away, we double our goal! The restitution for our property *and* the Susquehanna destroyed."

I saw a few nod that cautiously approved of this plan.

"Damn tha Susquehanna, I got ta get me sum'n eat." One of them stood up, quickly followed by some others, and with a rattle of their weapons they were gone. Off on a pointless coon hunt, or maybe to march in the fort on their own, I did not know.

"What's it about an Injun that tells me it's a trap?" another man demanded. "You know dey lying bastards jus' holin' up, waitin' fer tha Susquehanna ta join up with 'em in the middle night."

"Give them the chance to return with the food stores," I repeated. I was hard-pressed not to lose more ground.

"You men are of the strongest salt," Bacon cut me off. "And you will enjoy the fruits of complete victory. This, I assure you. A victory that has been ordained to our hands by none other than the divinity of Christ our Lord."

"Amen," came a mumbled response.

I had become regrettably acquainted with his willingness to do this. He was anything but religious. But now that he saw the disadvantages that this held for killing Indians, he allowed himself the right to use the true believer's God.

As for me, having just survived the very seat of evil, I, more than anyone present, needed the comfort of belief. But I had to put my faith in the down to earth sense I could talk into these simple men.

"They promised to bring food by morning," I tried again. And I determined to go on saying it, if it kept an impending slaughter at bay. Bacon then turned his cold mad stare at me.

"We *men*," he said evenly, "you and I, and even, Mr. Corstair over there, are assembled on this hill to begin building a fine new home for freedom. Freedom from the hideous murder done to us by heathens, and freedom from our government that has shown it doesn't care. From this unlikely moment, and this unlikely place, a new government will be born. So be it. Let it be expressed in the power of each voice. If God wills us to take this evil place, then it will be spoken by the choice of your vote."

"I say yay, I'm too hungry ta sit out tha night." A man in the foreground spoke up.

"Well I ain't goin' til I see what fer ta shoot 'at," someone replied, resting his head back on a cartridge pack.

"I don' care whichever way ya'll decide. But I ain' leavin' without me take home one n'em little squaws," another man stated. "'An I'm willin' ta pay fair for her, too."

And so it went for more than a couple of hours. To and fro, with every separate interest brought into account. Until at last, the number of men who voted on waiting for us to get fed, had persuaded those who were too tired to care. I encouraged every quibble, pried open each debate, seeing that by their God given pettiness, they were surviving a horrible death. Finally, the outcome not to attack was made just as much by snoring as it was by anything else, and for a few salvaged hours anyway, we remained right where we were.

Bacon, on the other hand, was seething. He was fully

aware that all the men's bickering had eroded his command. I stifled a smile, watching his improbable and improvised democracy in action, while he sulked off down the slope a ways, fit to kick himself in the pants. I had the feeling that we would soon be schooled in what Bacon's idea of government properly meant, but for the moment the demand of rest was keeping us alive. The men bundled up where they lay, to await the arrival of day.

Then, when it seemed that I'd only shut my eyes, I felt a hard tapping on my shoulders.

"They're back," Bacon reported.

I groggily got to my feet, stomping the stiffness from my legs.

"By the way," he added casually. "Half the men that joined us on the southern leg deserted us last night. I think they failed to perceive the delicate negotiations required for such a straight ahead mission."

This news brought a quick and fearful chill, but the look that Bacon gave me was, I swear, one of reckless joy. He then gazed out at the marshy pit beyond the Occaneechee village. "What a field of rice could be planted here," he handed me the glass.

In the violet light I saw a silhouette of figures moving along the far bank. I made a mental count of Man-haut-te's warriors boxing themselves around what looked to be members of a Manakin tribe. They were marching them towards the fort like they were captives.

"Do you see our breakfast, Mr. Corstair?" Bacon innocently asked.

There was no sign of any spoils. Nothing so much as a scrawny chicken. Nor were there any Susquehanna. Apparently all that the victory had brought Man-haut-te was a desolate lot of Manakins.

"I'd say your faith's been a bit mislaid," Bacon

continued, "now that they're back in *full force*." He looked
at me so severely that it threw me into a quandary of doubt. I
suddenly felt confused and ashamed. "Well then," he said at
last. "There's nothing left to do but gather a few of my *loyal*
men, and pay a visit to the great Chief Persicles."

I peered back through the glass and spied one of the
Occaneechee warriors break from the file to cross the water
below us. "Hold on a moment," I said. "He's sending us a
message."

And suddenly I realized that another source of water
was moving the languid stream. An additional current that in
fact had sharply raised the river's level while I was asleep. I
pinched my dull eyes and surveyed both the shorelines again.
The new flow appeared to be coming from a western point
above us, moving towards the east at a new and impressive
rate. Man-haut-te's 'Time of the Changing River,' I thought.
He's flooding it to drain the disease and infested muck. I
watched the warrior below us with greater interest, checking
his progress against the current. Noting the difficult footholds,
and the way he had to dodge the floating debris.

"What's going on?" Bacon asked.

"They're flushing the river," I said. "The high water
will add to their defense."

"Does this present a problem for you, Mr. Corstair?" he
asked me sharply. "Do you wish to debate a further delay?"

Reading his peeved expression I could see he neither
sought nor expected an answer. Then, shifting his mood, he
took me by the shoulder. "Best get on down there and see what
the Indian wants."

By the time we reached the bottom, the messenger was
getting a good jostling by a group of men with enough damn-
all attitude to shoot him just to see what would happen next.
Bacon immediately ordered them to withdraw, but the warrior
showed his disgust by refusing to acknowledge him as our

leader.

"Okima-hka'n nahapi-stam," he said, directing his words at me. Then, pointing at Bacon, "awasite so'skwa-ce."

"He says that his chief wants a parley right away," I told him.

And before Bacon could give him an answer, the Indian had turned and slipped back into the river. A man beside me raised his gun, preparing to fire, before I forced him to lower his aim.

"Well, I'd say that was an insult, wouldn't you, Mr. Corstair?" Bacon asked. "A flaunting disrespect for a proper English gentleman is what I'd call it, wouldn't you?"

The men were not sure if he was serious, but I knew he meant it as another barb at me.

"Do you suppose that this the way they would treat Sir William Berkeley?"

And then, thinking of the governor and his dealings here, it was enough to set him off.

"I will tell you men what you have witnessed here this morning," he said. "And I will also tell you that these filthy mongrels only take their orders from the governor."

He then began to shout excitedly across the water, as if the Occaneechee swimmer could understand.

"Well, maybe I'm a no count to the *royalty* in Jamestown, but damned if I'll be mocked by someone barely human!"

And at this point *I* could not tell if he was serious. He dashed this way and that, splashing deeper in what only yesterday had been muck-strewn sand.

"Tell your impertinent chief that I will counsel him at *my* convenience! Officers!" he yelled to no one. "Repair with me at once!"

The men spread upon the narrow beach, looking out and talking with excited gestures. While I, unsure of what was going on, lagged alone somewhere between the men that he called officers, and a group of straggling recruits.

"Mr. Corstair," Bacon turned and glared. "Why don't you go find the savage that's stolen your horse?"

And thus dismissed, where my discourse no longer mattered, I watched him lead his *inner circle* to a place they could draw up a battle plan. I did not return to camp. Despite my sensible and overpowering need for rest, I spent the whole day on the sharp edge of a rock, in a rare and stupefied rage. I did not look for the ferrying Indian. My horse was long gone, of course. My only thought now was how I'd let myself get so caught in the schemes of a madman? A madman little more than half my age.

As the sun began its afternoon descent, I was still sitting by the rising water, contemplating just what lay across the way. I thought a great deal about wandering off. Somewhere to the west or further south, but then to move, to find *out there*, the same eventuality, just didn't seem worth the pain.

Later on, well in toward evening in fact, Bacon approached. He was surprisingly contrite. "I can assure you the compensation for your horse," he said. And then we simply sat together, staring across at the deceptive idleness inside the fort. "Are you strong enough for crossing the current?" he finally asked. "The filthy place is cleaner for it anyway."

"The ferry man has apparently abandoned his business just when it's needed the most," I offered.

"Nothing but another common thief," Bacon shot back.

"It is our presence here that has shut this place down," I said. "In no uncertain terms, Nathan, we are confronting the most savage congress of Indians that I have ever seen."

He sidled into the stream and was immediately drawn in shoulder high. He then found a step back to me, and extended one of his hands. I accepted it and got in behind him.

The water was numbingly cold. I asked him right off if he was going over in order to offer the Indians such a peaceful hand. He smiled. "We'll do what we can," he said.

eeping weapons and powder above our heads while slipping on the shifting bottom required such concentration that midway through the current we were surprised by two canoes. They suddenly appeared as if bobbed upon the surface, apparently from some hidden point upstream. My already troubled stomach formed into a hollow knot when I saw Man-haut-te paddling in the lead, his formidable weight pitching the launch level with the water.

"Our honored and most precious guests!" he called. "If you please. Let us to carry you across. You need not drown, and my boat needs the balance, yes?"

The late afternoon sun struck upon his sharp pointed smile, as if to emphasize its peril. Bacon and I froze, guns aloft, digging our toes into the bottom in order to withstand the stream. We were the perfect picture of surrender.

"When the river is flooded, it is difficult to cross, yes?" Man-haut-te added, unnecessarily. "Here then." And he extended Bacon one of his large open hands. "We help each other, yes?"

I kept my eyes on Bacon, not knowing if he would slash the smiling face with the butt of his musket, but he only bowed his head. We offered up our weapons and by an agile use of the rushing water, the Occaneechee took us aboard on the separate canoes. Soaked to the skin, I settled in a middle row as the paddlers turned round for the village. They slipped us into an ingeniously constructed mobile dock, (one that I could see was specially made for this occasion,) which was the only spot safe to disembark. I was further surprised to see Bacon sharing in a laugh with our giant host. It was a sight so thoroughly unexpected that it startled me into hope.

The next shock that awaited came after we had entered past the large swinging gate. A quiet emptiness prevailed upon the village workplace. Where there should have been the frenzied skinning, the rendering, and the traders hawking their wares, people were lined in a long civil corridor that extended from the square to the outer wall. Older men and younger, women, slaves and children had formed a promenade of welcome, two lines filled with attentive faces, that looked like a solemn greeting laid out for conquering heroes. Indeed, they were so transformed, so respectful and reverent, that I wondered if the whole town was under the spell of witchcraft. More than once I blinked in disbelief that I was walking the same bloody earth that I'd only just visited on the day before.

At the end of the passage was a dais draped in colorful silks with an odd orderly row of boots set out along its edge. In the middle of this stage, sitting atop a carpeted chair was the elder statesman, the great King Persicles himself, all feathers and fur, with armbands of gold that gleamed in the distance. A troubled awareness of the night before made me keen to capture all that I could of these impossibly new surroundings, but then I found I could not take my eyes from off him. He, in turn watched our approach, (evidently not so engaged, and even easily distracted. At one point he grabbed an errant child and pretended to give him a spanking. A gesture that endeared him to me at once, so opposite as it was from what I expected.)

"But how you go on, Mr. Corstair." Bacon said through his teeth, observing my fond fascination. "Obviously he's got wind of our great army and has come out in style to pay us tribute."

Bacon, employing his ever-ready sarcasm, was

expressing his doubts about my previously dire predictions. I
turned and saw a smile creep into his eyes. "But lest I forget,"
he said, continuing his fun. "It *is* the *Time of the New River*."

"It is also to our victory over the Susquehanna," Man-
haut-te stepped in. Even he seemed to defer to our strange new
status. "It is because you come, that we now have provided for
more labor."

He pointed to a filthy pen attached to the northernmost
wall that held the group of Manakins I'd seen him bring to
the fort that morning. Their dozy eyes followed us with
indifference as the pigs rooted about at their feet. But I did get
a jolt of alarm when I saw a group of children scuffling near
a pile of weapons. It was only a primitive collection, clubs
and shields, arrows and mace, but they were propped in such
a way as to cover the bore of a six-pound cannon. Its sudden
appearance brought a sobering dread, but I refused to believe
that anyone here had the skill required to aim and fire it. A
guard came round from the back of the pigpen to send the
children running off.

"What prisoners are those?" Bacon asked, as if
purposely not mentioning the cannon.

"The Susquehanna were holding them. Those Manakin
in there did most of our fighting," Man-haut-te replied, barking
out a laugh. "The King will decide their fate." Then he grew
serious. "He is ready to receive you now."

The great chief made no effort to stand, but addressed
us by way of a sweeping gesture over the array of goods that
filled up his pavilion. He seemed graceful and precise, quite
the opposite of Man-haut-te, who was standing just behind us,
prompting us to take what we liked. I gazed into a glare caused
by the last rays of the sun. They were illuminating such a trove
of booty it was difficult to focus on any one object at a time.

Randomly scattered in layered heaps on the floor
were fine woven rugs of every size and color. In between,

perched inside their cages, was a collection of exotic birds, the smaller ones trilling songs, as the larger preened at their rainbow feathers. There were pots and pans that shone like glass, holding several types of fruit I'd never seen before. The platform itself was ablaze with mirrors. Some ornately framed, others amusingly distorting, and each strategically placed to enhance the King's abundance. There was all manner of jewelry. Minutely beaded bracelets, and necklaces of ivory and quill. Intricately carved fangs from large cats, as well as boar and bear. A remarkable pyramid of pink and clear black pearls was held perfectly together as if by magic. There were several suits of armor packed into cherry wood chests, and two trunks of cedar exclusively for helmets. Elaborate models of ironwork, of Spanish, and English, and French, a Fleur-de-Lys chest brace, and a broadsword draped in mail. There were solid gold headbands, earrings and hairpins, all sparkling by the set of precious stones. But the most awe-inspiring object was a fancy Dutch-made clock that sat inside a cabinet, mounted in a crystal case. It held the high position, as though valued with the reverence to lord over all the rest. I could see that Bacon had been drawn to it as well, but much to my relief, he picked out some lacework to take as Persicles' gift.

The King however, took his greatest interest in a demonstration of his keys and locks. They ran the gamut from strongbox clasps to doors and dungeon bolts. He beckoned us to watch him lock, then open each in turn, and however much he repeated this act, he never failed to laugh. He was of average size, noticeably losing his yellow white hair, but his posture conveyed a tautly muscled man beneath his feathered robes. His arms or what I could see of them were covered in scars, the wounds of self inflicted rites, or long ago battles; there was a strength that resided in them still.

The banquet displayed a feast of like proportions to the one that I had seen the night before, but Persicles was eager to prove, in his off handed way, that he was the consummate host. He pointed proudly to the numerous pairs of boots that lined the edge of his platform while Man-haut-te related that they represented the King's friendly relations to whites. To travelers in general, he said, which were allowed to come and go, and freely use his lands. I restrained myself from questioning what this policy brought in practice, at least in as much as the Cherokee were concerned, and Persicles interrupted him to press his view on the matter. "Besides," he offered, not waiting for Man-haut-te's translation. "If anyone showed up in need of boots, well, there you are." Then he fixed upon the lackluster state of our shoes, and immediately jumped to the task of fitting us with replacements. Within the next few minutes, both Bacon and myself were snugly secure in a polished pair of dry boots. The only price, we were told, was for us to leave our old ones behind. Perhaps they might be repaired, Persicles quipped, although he doubted it.

It was during this unusual exchange, while I looked on with a whimsical eye, that Bacon started making me nervous. In response to Persicles' offer, which was clearly made to show that he was humbled, Bacon twiddled his toes in the kneeling man's face and examined each boot from the inside out. After all of which, he handed the old warrior a half-eaten drumstick. Little did I see it at the time, but this was to be the tone for the rest of that remarkable evening. In the hours ahead, and at every translatable juncture, Bacon aped the part of a village simple. That, and gorge on everything in his reach.

"He says that the English want the trade routes kept open, so we will keep them open. And whether you come with fifteen men, or fifteen hundred, you are our friends," Man-haut-te kept trying to maintain his role, in the face of Bacon's behavior.

Bacon grunted like a pig, more concerned with stuffing himself than in hearing peaceful proclamations.

"I am greatly loved by the whites," Man-haut-te continued speaking for his chief. "After all, the whites are here to stay. And the Susquehanna have been silenced from complaint."

This last bit, he laid on very heavily, but I and everyone else were too caught up in watching General Bacon.

"It is the Europeans who pay so well," he went on. "And there is so much for everyone, it is a loss to those who fail to understand."

Bacon hooted and ate for another hour, growing more intense, and never finishing one handful before grabbing at another. He showed no signs of slowing down. All that I could think to do was keep Man-haut-te distracted by letting him regale me with stories from the battle, and his particular praise for the bravery of the Manakins. He seemed able to ignore the fact that these were the very men now squatting inside of his pigpens, but then, we were both about the business of ignoring many things. I listened to the story about the sleeping Susquehanna, which he conveniently insisted on repeating over and again. Then he started in on a lengthy explanation of a complex system of dams and tunnels that actually pulled the water from underground in order to flood the river. The maintenance of which, he confessed, was so tedious that his status in the tribe rested entirely on his procurement of trainable slaves. I watched his hideous face bouncing in and out of the torchlight, with my demented English general just behind me at my right. I still could not fix this gentle giant's face with last night's brutal savagery, as indeed, all was growing more and more unreal.

At the same time Bacon's bizarre performance had become so popular that crowds from the various tribes started laughing from the shadows where they watched. The way he pondered each new particle of food by holding it tight against his eye, only to snatch it down or gyrate it in the air, doubtlessly had them thinking this was but an addition to our strange dinner prayer. He gave a tongue of lamb this treatment, before torching it to a glowing crisp and dousing it with water that he sprayed from out his nose. At the very least, I thought, the inanity of his antics prevented him from being sick. The amount that he consumed, after such protracted hunger would have had the best of any hearty man.

Man-haut-te, as if to provide a counter force, became the very model of diplomacy. He seemed determined to present himself as a man so removed from the cruelties I fully knew of, I could no more believe the role that he was playing than that of Bacon's fool. Nonetheless, he spoke in calm assurances of Persicles' protection and support, while looking away every chance he could, in order to avoid Bacon's insolence. I came to feel that I was sitting on a burning powder keg, due to explode at any second. Drenched in nervous sweat, I started to soak my freshly dried clothes, pretending myself to go on listening until I could escape this flimsy precipice. How was I expected to keep Bacon's leadership intact? Explain that he was starving? Sleeplessness? Emotional shock?

Outside our circle the laughter grew louder, while Man-haut-te and the King maintained a neutral concern. I found little comfort in the fact that this wasn't the first white man that they'd have seen in the wilderness go completely mad. But when the audience began spilling onto the platform, and bringing their children in tow, Man-haut-te stood up to address me. The show of respect that he'd made sure was provided, was turning his authority to ridicule.

"Perhaps, you had better see to your General Bacon," he said to me quietly. "Tell him that we will offer him the help that he wants. We will speak with him further, when he has had rest."

"What are you doing with the prisoners?" Bacon suddenly asked.

He was eyeing us through an empty piece of marrowbone he had just noisily slurped clean. He shifted his view to a group of braves herding the Manakins toward our platform in a sleepy line. He had calmed a bit, and I was glad that he remained silent, at least while the Manakins received judgment from the King.

"Kiwa mana tisihta-w, ki mana tisiht-ew," Persicles stated, brushing each of their arms with a feathered baton.

"Give them to me!" Bacon jumped up and demanded. "And all of their plunder!" He was standing upright, fast as a bobcat, furiously pacing in front of the startled King.

"These men have shown great bravery and they will go free." Man-haut-te said slowly, but his eyes were tense and keen.

Then, before anyone on the stunned pavilion could react, Bacon grabbed the closest prisoner by the crotch and sent him howling to the ground. In the immediate confusion, one of the Manakins seized a musket from a distracted guard. He then aimed and shot at Bacon, who jumped behind a flurry of bodies trying to get out of his way. From inside of this scramble in a twist of people trying to get free, there was a piercing scream, and just then I collapsed from the blow of a heavy war club striking the back of my knees. Only half-conscious, I could feel my face being ground into the dirt, and then beyond all power to explain it, the entire fortress began to explode.

Muzzle fire lit up the inner walls in a concussive barrage. The smoke of burning powder was suddenly so thick upon the village that it became a struggle to breathe. The very air seemed to erupt in balls of fire. Countless explosions from every side and angle came at such a deafening charge that I lost my sense of bearing. Amidst hysterics and senseless shouting, both from men and women, I heard babies howl in the exploding night. I was trapped in a full hurricane on fire. A shrieking wail cut a singular chill that forced me to look through the jumble in a panic, the bodies running, then thrashing, then jerking back hit, hanging for a moment suspended in mid-air. One mad group, growling like a pack of dogs, leapt directly into a solid wall of musket fire.

Then dreamlike, as if he were looking for me, I caught a glimpse of Man-haut-te, yelling and waving his cane. Just as suddenly, he was towering above, close enough for me to see his nostrils flare. Then his face just disappeared. It opened up in a bright burning hole the size of both my fists, with him walking around in a wide and crazy circle like his body disputing it no longer had a head. Then all at once he fell straight to the ground.

Another ball hit a brave in the chest, standing right beside him, and then it bounced harmless to his feet. I saw him pick it up, and do a whooping backward dance directly toward the wall of flame. A woman with a tattered leg appeared, pulling herself and a burning infant in her hands.

Something was pulling at me hard; I grabbed my knife and kicked back around, ready to thrust, and there was Bacon. His entire upper body, covered in blood and pieces of brain. In just that second, a huge blast pushed all the air from my lungs. Feeling like I was struck in the chest with an anvil, in spasms I was spitting black phlegm. The powder store on the far south wall made a skyward burst of flame. Then the pavilion behind me started to explode.

"This way!" Bacon shouted, yanking at my collar. We were both retching out an ashy mix of dinner, as he hauled me across the muck.

We gained the shelter of an upturned wagon and I struggled to my knees, stupidly staring, too shocked to think. I felt sucked into the vacuum of the magazine on fire. Shielding myself from the heat I stumbled over a softer solid weight that brought me back down to my feet. I was looking directly into the face of Persicles. The incision in his neck only bled a little, and had dried in the shape of the moon. His eyes were open, staring at a star that somehow shone through all the acrid layers of smoke. Everywhere was on fire.

"The fools had better not burn my pelts!" Bacon shouted. "Let's go!"

In a stupor, I followed, and found myself holding onto the bloody knife still stuck in his belt. The deranged and disgusting dinner guest had become like a killing machine.

Even through the intense heat, the ground was slick with blood. I lost my footing two more times, before finding a place where the wall had just begun to go up in flames. It was a hard choice. We had to charge the fire, or try to stay under cover until the men outside had finished their work. But the inferno in its raging screams could not match the deadly whirls of lead. There was nowhere to turn where the musket balls weren't filling the air. Suddenly, one of the serving girl slaves stepped from the shadows and made deliberately for us. The hatred in her eyes was as black as the smoke. Then, just as suddenly they erupted in two fountains, cascading blood before she fell. Bacon and I looked around once more. There was no finding shelter in here. And yelling with all of our might, we ran a heedless gallop into the flames.

Miraculously, we landed face up in a mud filled ditch, feeling like we'd been slung from a catapult. The billowing air had blown us within a foot of the river. Blistered and bruised we slipped into the water, and then, just realizing we'd survived, we started screaming like a couple of lunatics. We lay in mid-stream with water rushing round us, reverently staring at the spectacle of war.

The men surrounding the fort, indeed almost in it, were in the midst of a controlled killing fever. With every pause to reload, at every hole and gap, a gun was replaced, cleaned, and placed again loaded, in a method of nonstop fire. They had turned the very village into a blizzard of lead. Surely, I thought, this was more than simple hunger. Something else, unexplainable, made horror come alive in these men. There was not enough fury in a farm boy to kill with abandon like this. The shrieking and howling assaulted my ears as though I were being punished. It was a sound that had power to shatter the mind.

Bacon and I moved back from the flames in a crawling swim to the other side. A little ways out we ducked from the people running from their homes and outlying huts. We watched them push the children in canoes, while mothers raced as far as they could follow on the bank. How they expected to get past our men that were waiting downstream was not something that I worried about. Then, when our feet finally found a place to ford, we got across, staggering, wading, and then crawling out.

Bent with exhaustion, we watched the battle rage below us from the bluff. For some mysterious reason, a reason I had no desire to find out about, the men kept up the slaughter throughout the whole night. Then, near dawn Bacon decided to descend and see what he'd accomplished. I did not move. My body did not respond to any demand that I might put upon it. I knew that I was awake; there was simply nothing that I could think of that was worthwhile to do. But as the smoke drifted off with the new day's light, I think I saw Bacon walking below in the distance. I imagined him anyway, striding among the burning corpses, delivering praise to his blast shocked men. Later when the sun had been climbing for awhile, it revealed that over two hundred Indians, from a dozen different tribes were dead.

At last, Mr. Gale came to fetch me. He reported evenly, (though quite amazingly to me) that the casualties to our army amounted in total to three.

With victory came the return of the flies. It seemed the place was swimming in them, once I had entered the stifling ruin. They clustered about the men who were picking greedily through the stores of food, and those that scavenged the ash for melted jewels. They stubbornly fought for their place at picnics. They buzzed a severed Souian head that someone had set on his blanket like a centerpiece. And another that was either a chest of charred mutton or the torso of a child. At an unburned patch, where someone had brought in a split magnolia tree, Bacon sat like a land office clerk, carefully unfolding bolts of finished fur. He was taking the time to give his personal thanks to each and every man lined up, before handing him his fifty pounds of skins. A number of storage vaults had been discovered where the clever Occaneechee were preserving the precious coats, even underground.

I looked for, and happily did not find either one of the two great chiefs. I felt certain that when all was lost they'd been secreted away. No need for the white man to defile them. But I did get a shock when I discovered King Persicles' astonishing clock. It was buried inside a mound of damp and smoldering blankets amazingly intact. I wiped the grease from off its delicate case and pried the tiny latch. Tucked neatly in back of the inside mounting was a piece of rolled parchment. *To Alliance with the Great Chief Persicles on the Occasion of A Lasting Peace. Sir William Berkeley; His Majesties Royal Governor of Virginia; In the Year of Our Lord 1670.*

I carefully wrapped it back inside the blanket, and fit its cumbersome weight to the bottom of my sack.

Part Three
Jamestown

Over a week has passed and neither Mr. Lawrence nor myself have seen any trace of Seycondeh. Nor have we heard the surprisingly sure steps of Tintipon, our blind shaman friend, who will occasion our hidden cave door. The most unpleasant consequence of this development is that once again we have run out of food, and in the last few days I have been watching Mr. Lawrence slip further and further into full time sleep. I suffer greatly at this decline, given that we have survived this long. Long enough, anyway, to see the awakening of another spring.

Only this morning I noticed a cluster of wild crocus facing off a stubborn bank of snow. An indigo was picking through the patch for a proper twig to repair its winter-damaged nest. Mr. Lawrence did not show any interest. He has become fully occupied with his interior landscape of late, sensing I suppose, his only freedom, for it has become painfully clear that we are indeed, prisoners. Yesterday, I ventured out to find our Indian nurse and was met by three strange warriors from an unfamiliar tribe. I can only guess that they come from regions to the north and west. Time served inside this cavern hospice has taken such a toll on my powers of observation that I was not even aware of them until an arrow struck the tree above my head. There was no offer of any dialogue. Their leader, a tall sinewy man with skin dyed black and red, simply ordered me back to the cave.

But today my effort to keep Mr. Lawrence distracted from the emptiness in our stomachs has been rewarded. He's been actively recalling the events that led to our destruction of Jamestown. This recounting however takes a delicate balance and I must monitor his sometimes spirited output against the energy it requires. The passion he invokes is so committed that he often pounds it out in force; a force he clearly wishes could crush Sir William's head.

"The villain!" Mr. Lawrence shouts. "The treacherous villain! Did you know, Corstair, that if Bacon had not escaped, the vile governor would have had him hanged?! Even after giving him his public pardon! The old wretch could not bring himself to believe that we had gathered a force of thousands! Loud, and in the streets! All swarming against him! Ha! Couldn't believe it! Even as he spied them from the cloister of his chambers!"

Mr. Lawrence supports his bending weight by a flimsy root of pine sticking out at the entrance to our cave. He starts his railing out against the governor. Against the sky. Against God, I suppose. I can only hope that the savage strangers from the west do not use his bellowing madness as an excuse to kill him. Such thoughts have taken hold upon the tenuous security that we're afforded here, letting me know that I must plan for our escape.

* * * * *

After the annihilation of the Occaneechee, the mood of the country began to take unexpected turns. I accompanied Bacon back to his plantation at the Curles, fully expecting Berkeley to arrest us, but when discussing this likely outcome, Bacon asserted his full responsibility for criminal activity solely on himself. It was a nice speech, but everyone knew such sentiments were wholly at the whim of the governor. In assuming this posture however, Bacon was hoping to become the people's hero and have their numbers keep him safe. "You give me but a foothold," he stated, "and I will tread the grounds to meaningful reform."

As it turned out, the predictions he made about the public response came out half right. Passing through the three hut towns, half the people came out to cheer us, and half of those tagged along on our march. Dirt scrabble farm boys skirted and stumbled into the rutted paths, acting like they were one of the 'righteous avengers,' as we'd come to be called. Evidently, the other half of this population was too strapped with the job of sustaining their families to have enough time to care. But the fellows that decided to follow, enlisted on the spot, eyeing the riches in fur that we brought, as the means of escaping their debt.

Elizabeth appeared at the Curles every bit as clear as a bright October morning. It was remarkable to me that the shadow of the governor's occupation left no doubts on Mrs. Bacon's estate. First she threw herself upon her husband, (more shamelessly enthused than ever) and then proclaimed us no less than Virginia's rising stars. "In the hearts of *true* Virginians, you are heaven sent." No small praise for a hundred filthy men that were wearing human ashes. But the elections that Gale had previously reported was her proudest point. Nathan's new Assembly seat "voted on by a fair and vast majority," being "our most grand and victorious event." Meaning Nathan's of course, but the fact remained that this loud and popular outcry had forced the governor to withdraw.

Observing her make such a fuss and fanfare, I gathered that her ambitions for her husband stretched further than the Assembly. She began entertaining Nathan's officers in earnest, where she used her considerable charm to bolster their favor and support. Her manner, so gracious and self-assured, enlivened everyone, including a regular circle of powerful planters as well. It even became an item of status to be invited to these groups. I went to one once and ended up standing in a line, like an attendee at a royal reception. She took my hand, half like a stranger she wished to impress, (but she did offer me her personal thanks for keeping Nathan safe. Which amounted of course, to an irony like none she could have known of.) She then moved onto Geoffrey Gant, I think it was, conferring on him her hopes for a bright common future. She acted the part of the perfect first lady, asking after the back-at-home wives, and never missed out on showing special interest in a person she didn't know as well.

For awhile there, Elizabeth was all the talk there was in camp. "The most unique and plain spoke woman, that come from position that any had ever seen." It was as though she'd become Virginia's new *dame,* or the new Virginia's *dame,* depending on how you looked at it. Where else, I thought, could such a thing be possible? Where one could so flourish after having been rejected from using their family name?

The festivities were beset by all number of tributes and toasts. To the country that Nathan swore to reform. "And the open frontier where men will be unhindered." "To a place constrained only by the limits of one's toil." "To a place where one is free from another's inheritance, as ..." "As he is from his own past," someone laughed. But, "to a place…" is how it mostly went. Either that or, "If it's treason for Nathan to protect the poor and slay the savages, then I make treason to be a service."

Meanwhile, Sir William Berkeley, a seasoned man himself in the battle for public relations, simply set out to steal Bacon's platform. Just after Nathan was legally elected, Berkeley directed the sheriff at Henricus to pronounce his own slate of reforms. I attended the meeting and can say unconditionally, that the agenda the governor was proposing called for everything Nathan had proclaimed. But Nathan, quick to grasp the impact that this had upon his power made such a fire-storming shout that the sheriff could not even finish.

The crowd then vaulted to the rostrum and dragged the poor man away. I later heard that some in Bacon's rougher group nearly beat the man to death.

But then it was always chilling to see how a crowd could grow so fearless in his presence. (This was part of the unspoken code in having an aristocrat to speak for your side. A formula so potent it could magically absolve you from doing *any* wrong.) But I must also add here, as to the circumstance surrounding the sheriff, that he had already conducted a number of evictions, with a number of the dispossessed right there in the audience.

"Lock him up inside his own jail," Bacon pronounced. "Read him the list of *the People's* Reformations! And repeat them 'til he can recite them to the governor word for word!"

This was the way he finessed a violent mob. For all of his driving right up to the brink, he hated the thought of taking another Englishman's blood. God knows he would never condone the act of outright murder, and I know personally, how relieved he was when he learned that the sheriff would survive. He also knew that as for instructing the thugs that had beaten the man, the bit about teaching the People's Reformations would never get done. In the first place, none of them could read. But it was mostly the way he could *sing* a thing out, that had them feeding from his hands. Then too, in the middle or in front of the crowd was the place where he came truly alive. Indeed, later that day when he learned that Berkeley had placed his wife on a ship that was bound for safe harbor in England, gentleman Bacon led the rabble in a song.

"*Oh Boo Hoo, what'll I do-o?*" he chanted, "*Me little bit a breast has lef' me hard an' blue.*"

Oh, he could tickle the rude crowd up until it worshipped him. And he could present the risks that he took for them as if he was accepting their honored gift. Whether he did this tongue in cheek, or was making himself out as a paradoxical hero, I do not know. I never completely learned his workings way inside. I do know that he never accepted them as equals, though. Accepted their stubborn superstitions, their ignorance, and their shape as a victim in mass. Nathan was at bottom an enigma, too much his original self to be for anyone else. While for them, he was their highbred class betrayer, a notion of which they could never get enough.

For my part, I never liked the demonstrations, or his preachy politics and bluster. I had already seen too much of human cruelty, my own hands were deep in blood. So in an attempt to feel what remained in me of my simple, bygone past, I withdrew to enjoy what was left of a fleeting spring on the Bacon plantation. I took early walks through wild-flowered dales that stretched out before me in vivid gold and in red. My boots, the very pair fit by the noble Persicles, gathered up the blossoms filled with dew. But with each return as the sun climbed in the sky, I felt its force strike stronger day by day. Come summer, I knew, the fields that I now trod upon would parch. By early afternoon an unseasonable heat pressed down upon the land without a trace of cloud. Even the night held unnatural warmth. Uneasy, I stared at this same sun that had given me my years of abundance, and saw in it an angry auguring for change. Even as I took in greater amounts of water, I watched the land choke its trickling springs until they stopped. Then, the morning that my Persicles shoes gathered naught but dust, I decided to bury his clock.

I made a hardwood box, and wrapped the magic timepiece on the inside of its blanket. I dug a pit and covered it with stones. My years of learning Indian ways and all that I had known of death gave my movements deliberation. When the box was hidden, and looked as natural as the earth, I knelt and prayed for the spirits to guide the great and humble chief. I prayed for him to accept once again this weak man's offering, and asked if he might release his vengeance from out of the wrathful sun.

I was little qualified to make such a request I know, but when the world gets shifted beyond recognition you will try anything to see what catches hold. Anyway, it did no good and it did no harm. The disaffected sun ignored my presumption and continued to burn the grass, showing that drought was here to stay.

Throughout the following weeks a portent hung over our camp, empty as a picture frame, filled only with anticipation. We recognized that something of great moment was near, but were also unclear as to what it exactly was. At least, I suppose, until the date of the new Assembly. As for me in this meantime, there was nothing that held much attraction. Things that I felt called to do (such as putting in a plot of Elizabeth's early corn) slipped, like the useless seed it would become, into the sun's distracting rhythm. I seemed to have wandered upon the decision that the less willful I could feel, the more vulnerable I'd have to become, and maybe in this way be shown just how I could accept things. For me this was progress of a sort, and describes as accurately as anything else, how I became part of what people started calling Bacon's rebellion. Although, God knows, I was just someone too tired of living to walk away.

In this way, I took an idle interest in observing the man of the hour, which I found I could do by almost being invisible, as often as I was kept from the *important* things in his range. And the first one I had to give him credit for was how good he was at political games.

After having done his best to provoke him, Nathan must have been bewildered by the fact that the governor was refusing to make him a martyr. He certainly kept stoking the flames as if he were counting on such, and those that surrounded him spoke in terms of his 'untouchable aura.' Writing had become his new obsession; usurping even the time he spent on scheming up ways to rid the country of its Indians. He wrote list after list of grievance, discourse and manifestoes. He hammered out a dozen sermons that sounded pretty much the same. Each and every paper blared out against injustice, just as each and every paper blared forth the name of God. When he wasn't speaking to the Lord, he was speaking for Him, and made every opportunity to work the Divine in the need to kill savages.

In paving the way of reform, however, his methods seemed deliberately confused and inconsistent. Writing on the war that he had brought, he explained it as an unforeseen consequence and humbly beseeched the council for their pardon. When they then agreed, he denied that he'd made such request. Into this fiery missive, he also included an angry demand that the governor compensate him for freeing his Indian slaves.

Nor did he limit the reach of his hot quill to Virginia's shores. He pushed his complaints against the government all the way to the Palace. When he got word that Berkeley was preparing a case against him with a London law firm, Bacon made inquiries towards his own contacts at court. Then, as if the pace of these proceedings from an ocean away had only just occurred to him, he abruptly dropped the matter, as if these problems needn't bother the king. Basic apprehensions, like those of his maturity began to prickle at me once again. For though I'd seen him inspire the highest sense of morals, both in thought and deed, he could just as soon let loose with a tantrum that made him into an undisciplined child. Something wholly insignificant could set him off, then leave just as quick as it began. I once saw him whip a man for tying a thirsty dog outside a tavern where the poor fellow had fallen asleep. Nathan then went and killed the dog and set it out in the woods. (He said that he wanted to see how long it took for buzzards to find the carcass, a trick that he insisted would help him track

Indians.)

There's no doubt that I wasn't the only one to notice his extremes, but the hangers-on and otherwise displaced outside of his tight circle, tossed off his behavior as what befit the gentry, unwilling to question their upper-class gift. Until at last came the day when he stuffed his satchel with his eloquent ultimatums and a stack of his crude threats. (As well as another pouch that I later learned held petitions for the governor's mercy.) Assemblyman Bacon was ready to make his entrance into Jamestown.

But then. The frightened youth emerged from under the cover of his taunting veneer. On the morning he was to depart for the delegation, I watched him grow more rigid with fear. At the due upon hour, he had even made himself physically sick. He sat paralytic to his drawing room chair, mumbling incoherently about carrying the fight out further along the more rustic routes, using phrases like "the call of the wild," or "springing at a moment's notice from the shelter of the woods." I am sure I heard him make mention of a Virginian Robin Hood. And if my memory of this self-absorption be both harsh and loose, let me state clearly that although he had been chosen as a legal representative, Bacon was officially, still a wanted man. To put this in terms of how life was at this time in Virginia, by taking his lawful seat at the Assembly, Bacon could've just as easily been walking in the lion's den.

For me this scene in the drawing room was very upsetting, made more so by his cock-eyed bravery at the Occaneechee camp. Persuaded by Elizabeth, I kneeled at his side and told him that we must forge ahead, (probably unconvincingly, since I had no belief in this myself.) And that we were at the service of something bigger than ourselves, (and similar kinds of balderol that somehow came out of my mouth.) He looked at me like I was a stranger, and I kept babbling in words that had no meaning, until it occurred to me that things would go better if I pretended to be him. "We serve," I started off, "The principles on which we found all our ability to trust..." and such.

In the end though, despite my fancy effort, it was Elizabeth that talked him back to good sense. The good sense anyway of finding forty more men to stand guard with him on board his ship.

But once we were loaded, and had rowed a short way down river, the sloop came alive, if only by anxious cheer. The tension was produced in large part from the rumors that ran suddenly, and had us headed straight to town for a hanging. I continued to discount these reports, but Bacon, (appearing bold as ever in front of the men) gave them stock enough to stay snug to the southern shore. He stood nervously on deck, keeping calm as he could manage, as a handpicked detail of the more trusted men prepared to guard him. And though they considered this charge an honor, the work was not overly strained. He stood perfectly still and gritted his teeth, peering through his glass on the open river. Any of his normal attempts at bluster, he barely maintained. Then halfway into a widening bend of draping thickets, he ordered everyone to drop their unnecessary chatter. Silence, he insisted was the best method for detecting one of Berkeley's gunboats.

He started to pace between the crammed in weathered faces, as sets of eyes glinted back at the water light, dutifully following his steps go back and forth. Many were young, younger than he, but already showed the crook at the hips from long days spent hoeing someone else's land. There wasn't a gentleman in the lot.

"Will the governor expect the g-governed..." Bacon spoke softy, actually stuttering a bit, "...to accept the execution of their elected represent-ta-tives?"

Was this the same man that had engineered the destruction of the Occaneechee? I could not recall ever seeing him like this. I suddenly felt that I was in the presence of a penitent young child. He appeared as if he'd been caught in the midst of some mischief, and approaching his father head bowed, he awaited the lash from the stick. I was thankful that he just left off; barely finishing his sentence, and retreated to the outer rail to brood. Then when we were at last within the view of the Swan's Point fortifications, he simply ordered that the sail be wrapped, and refused to go any further. We drifted for a moment carefully fixed on the cannon that always gaped from the ramparts, that I myself had helped build, a mile or so from Jamestown. Bacon then ordered the men sitting aft to drop anchor. He held a quick conference with Timothy Gale, to which I was not a part, and which ended with Gale manning a skiff off alone to make for the opposite shore. Bacon then turned around to re-assure the rest of us he had merely sent Gale to obtain the governor's approval, and his instructions as to how we should proceed. "We will not," he said somewhat sadly, "enter Jamestown without Berkeley's sworn protection."

Timothy Gale never made it back. The governor's response to our riverboat diplomacy was a volley from the cannons that shredded the trees above our heads. The rain of trunks and limbs that this created threatened the forward keel.

Bacon reacted like he'd just been grabbed and shaken to his senses, and became a man of deliberate action. Standing firm amidst exploding shells that split the air above us, he called out orders in sharp commands. Everyone on deck was swept up in his authority. In short, he was transformed. He directed a tack back upstream by running back and forth across to steady each whip of the sails. He grabbed one petrified farm boy and slapped him until the youth stopped screaming, and then sat down beside him to row. And after what seemed like the longest few minutes, he had planted the anchor in a nook back upriver, while keeping us in view, outside of cannon range.

The novel relief of having been caught out so vulnerable, and having escaped the danger, passed excitedly into the men. Goose calling after every short and wayward shot quickly became the new sport. And more than this, the *General* that they, with all their affection appointed, had finally returned in full force. Each one of us felt something of a marvel, and I gave the grinning Nathan my own admiring nod. Perhaps he *was* touched by greatness, if greatness was indicated by clarity under stress. I had seen it before, seen enough to amaze me at the Occaneechee fort. It seemed that panic, which so easily grips a normal man, acted for him like a steady, guiding hand. Or even perhaps, the calm that overtook him in the midst of an unleashed storm was nature's way to balance out his overly active mind.

"I see that we have gained some insight into our governor's opinions," he said when the Swan Point cannons decided to quit. And without another word, he set himself a line and a hook and spent the rest of the afternoon fishing. "Something about the concussion over the river," he explained, as he hauled in a juicy fat bass, "makes the critters snap at anything."

This led to a discussion on the merits of the silver snail as bait for trout, and the advantage of nighttime fishing in general, to which he asked several men their opinions in a genuinely interested way. We napped and ate the fish that we smoked under a tent made of a sail. But exactly one hour after it came fully dark he beckoned me off to one side. "If I'm not back before dawn," he whispered, "I need you to make for the falls and wait for my orders. Try the best you can to keep the men together."

Then he slipped off the sloop into the river, and keeping to the most shadowed edge, he silently let himself float down towards Jamestown.

"**G**iven the circumstances..." Mr. Lawrence is saying. He's recounting the first and to hear him tell it, most important meeting that he had with Bacon. The emphasis with which he uses these words lets me know that his excitement is drawn not so much from its secret nature, but that the ideas behind the rebellion were yet being formed. Mr. Lawrence is an unabashed fool for potential.

"It was a highly pressured debate. Nathan was already jumpy from swimming past Berkeley's guards and slipping through the gate. But he finally settled down to hear an honest appraisal of our political strengths. Those who were with us, those against. And those we might pull from off the fence. Then, after all our careful plotting, Bacon turned round and threw the whole messy lot of it back in our face. 'Much too slow', is what he told us. 'The rebellion would be picked apart and crushed before it's even got started.' But..."

And Mr. Lawrence rises up to give me a whispery smile. "I have to hand it to him. No one had a greater gift for reaping reward from his willful and reckless acts."

This is the gentle Mr. Lawrence. A man that everyone but our vindictive governor regarded with respect. An Oxford scholar possessed of both prestige and wealth. And a man, I need hardly remind him that had the most to lose by aligning himself with rebels. I study him now, happy for the chance to listen. He is propped against the wall of his gravelly bed, and his eyes still seem to search the air for answers. His nose drips steadily. Wisps of hair jut from the sides of his overlarge head, a head that he's helplessly surrendered to bobbing. I cannot count the number of his scabs.

But whenever I listen, I try to detect his most hidden motivations. The ones he lets slip out beneath what he's willing to confess. The most puzzling one being, why Mr. Richard Lawrence, a man of class and means, would willingly give up the things that every peasant I know was only fighting to obtain.

"Mr. Drummond and I offered up everyone we had in the way of our royal contacts," he continues.

William Drummond. Yet another man of mystery. Mr. Lawrence's closest ally, and anti-Berkeley to the core. William Drummond was no less a figure than the governor of North Carolina at one time.

"When we reported our latest information on the situation in New England. The all-out war with the Pequots. Terrifying, simply terrifying. I told him, surely the slaughter in Massachusetts would win us the support of the king. He couldn't possibly sit by and let Virginia suffer this way."

Mr. Lawrence laughs. It is a sound that lacks commitment or mirth, but is strong enough to rattle up a fit of coughing.

"Perhaps, it would be best for you to lay quiet for awhile. " I say, knowing that he will not listen. If he lets himself, he can get so worked up on the subject of politics, that it will overwhelm him. He dribbles out a strand of slobber, which does nothing to relieve his chest congestion, and then he eyes me, as if wishing I were to blame me for his being so incapacitated. He makes a frivolous adjustment to his mat, carefully, like a prim old lady, and then brushes a few leaves in a pile on his blanket. I can see that he's concentrating hard to control his cough, but ends up giving me a petulant look. This is to let me know that he's perfectly free to die in the way that he wants.

"The king of course, was only concerned about his revenues," he picks up. "He wanted nothing to interfere with his hundred thousand pounds per annum. And who could blame him? After all, he had a whole new list of bribes to keep up in the new Parliament. All he wanted was to make certain Berkeley didn't renege on his payments. Complaints only meant a threat to his cash flow! Well, I'll tell you right now Mr. Corstair! The blood that the king washed his hands of, was the blood that we lost every day on our frontier!"

Then surprisingly he stops, and tilts his head as if trying to remember an important detail.

"Do you think the Indian maid will come today?" he asks.

The hope in his eyes is no less than that of a small child.

"I'm sure of it," I reply. "If not, I will go and find her."

My chief duty is in keeping hope alive. I do not tell him of my recent meeting with the red painted hostiles. He looks at me sad, but wistful, as if he were keeping the biggest secret to himself.

"Bacon understood everything," he says, continuing his way of explaining. "He *was* extremely quick, you know. No doubt that his sloop being fired upon had him hot in the head. And finally, after Drummond and I had presented our case, which only boiled down after all to the necessity of a political base, he jerked up and said he was going to concentrate solely on the *real* fight. 'The savages aren't playing parlor politics with Berkeley!' He shouted. He became so agitated that I expected Berkeley's marshals to break down the door. 'The savages are too busy with our slaughter!' He carried on. Well. What if you're successful? I asked him back. What if you find yourself with an army powerful enough to catch Berkeley by surprise? Eh? Are you then prepared to take his place? Become our new *military* governor? Oh, and how will you greet the king's redcoats, when they're certain to arrive? Well. This gave him pause, but only long enough to weigh the consequence in his favor. He was also thoroughly preposterous, you know. Possessed of a genius that was half lunatic at least. But even I was not prepared for his response. He calmed down, becoming deadly serious, and then proclaimed that in the end Charles would negotiate with him rather than waste so much in men and material for the paltry profits in so difficult and distant a place. Can you believe this, Corstair? This is from the mouth of a man just two years in the colony. Well. Drummond and I just sat, shaking our heads in our open hands. 'The colonists would be fighting in their wilderness home,' he then told us, 'and the king was up to his neck still fighting with the radicals in Parliament.' Well. Drummond and I stared back in horror, directly into his youthful face, wondering how we'd ever come to entertain this madman. It was obvious that Squire Bacon had been wandering among his backwoods friends for too long of his little time here. And so…" Mr. Lawrence now pauses, considers me, and then starts in again. "…I recommended that he give himself up."

"You wanted to turn him in!?"

This is the first I've heard of this, and I am shocked by his confession. Mr. Thomas Lawrence; the symbol of our legitimacy, who framed the justice of our cause! Who here and now, sitting ill inside some unknown mountain, simply stares back at me, calmly absorbing my being appalled.

"As a successful planter, Mr. Corstair, and unencumbered as you are by a classical education," he says after a time, "you must certainly be attuned with the forces of nature. Much more so, I assume, than would be our hotheaded friend. Now consider. With Bacon's arrest, Drummond and I could rally a thousand of his countrymen for an immediate march on Jamestown. A march that would expose the governor and his vapid indifference to their plight. We could force him to come to terms! The whole countryside was bubbling like a cauldron underneath! Ready to explode upon the surface. Unseen from Berkeley's view of course, but shifting with the strength of a volcano. True. I could not be sure that Berkeley wouldn't have Bacon hanged. Cannon fire makes for a very clear argument. But I will tell you Mr. Corstair that we drew up half a dozen papers of vital reforms that night. Documents that we agreed upon, and articles we discussed in depth. What we could demand, and what we could and couldn't get. A document that precluded the need for a military defeat. *And* tied the hands of the governor. I told Bacon plain; we needed a leader to expend himself for *this*. And frankly, he surprised me by seeming to understand. He looked at me and nodded, as if he accepted this fate. But in the end, you know, he ran."

I watch Mr. Lawrence's eyes sharpen to a piercing gleam, and I consider this, the second, of the day's mounting shocks. Who would have guessed that what Mr. Lawrence was willing to sacrifice was based upon mere *principle?*

"Nathaniel Bacon was far too much a romantic to be of political use," he says, with a dismissive shift of his seat. Then he stares off above the hills, and settles himself down more rueful.

* * * * *

One thing for certain, run, Bacon did.

Throughout my anxious-ridden night of waiting on the river, (while Bacon and Lawrence merely *debated*) with each new minute I expected to be caught in a crushing crossfire of Berkeley's patrolling ships. I stressed over what was left to do should Bacon not return. I pictured myself running mad through the woods, hounded for the rest of my days by vagrants pursuing me for reward. What, after all, had I in common with a boatload of similarly wanted men? Then, just before sunup, appearing like a watery resurrection, Bacon pulled himself aboard. Straight way he ordered that we turn about upriver while the night still afforded us the cover to escape. We heaved back on our oars, as fast as could be managed, when another fiery blast tore near our starboard bow. A faint light was breaking on the river, revealing a row of guns on a ship that stood on the opposite shore.

"This could be it then," Bacon calmly stated.

The next shot ripped through the hold, amazingly causing no bodily harm but the sloop released a heavy sigh, and slowly began to sink. Bacon walked the length of slanting deck, quietly self-conscious, as if this act of balance was a re-assuring sign. He gave strict orders about not returning fire, and then strung up a sheet to be used as a surrender flag. As we watched the gunship make its steady crossing, every man aboard cinched up in a knot of nerves. Nathan however only grew more listless. It seemed like he'd commanded his naturally combative spirit to leave his body, and replaced it with a haggard face overcome with fatigue. He looked perfectly alone. The men closed him into their circle, as if he were protected by their tension, but his eyes focused on an object, impossible for anyone else to see.

"Look to yourselves men," he said, as the gunship latched onto our side. "We are now political prisoners. I expect for you to conduct yourselves as such."

Assuming yet another role, here he was as commanding officer, showing his pluck in the face of defeat. Then just before we were boarded, he asked if I might look in on Elizabeth, in the probable event of his death. He placed himself at the head of the crew, insisting that we comport ourselves like gentlemen, insisting too, that he would bear all blame. Watching him perform like this, a model of grace for these bucktooth men, would make you think he was sacrificing himself for our freedom. But the truth be told, everyone on that boat expected nothing but the gallows.

I will say that the men held back the normal vileness that took hold of their tongues, meeting our captors in fact, by respectfully bowing their heads. But then, just after this strange exchange of courtliness, the arrest took another form. Berkeley's captain, a man named Gardner, was evidently so affected by Bacon's civility, that he forewent the use of shackles. Nathan was simply escorted to Gardner's cabin under the most accommodating terms. As for the rest of us incorrigibles, (some having family connections with the men in Gardner's patrol) we milled about the ship with them in idle chatter.

A stranger sense too, that awakened in my farming blood, was the gratitude for relief. Our arrest provided resolution, and stability of a sort I undoubtedly had been craving all along. Even if that stability came from the walls of a cell. So much so, that I began to view incarceration as a chance for renewal, a return to my natural rhythms, as a place I'd be forced to slow down. The simple fact is; I despised the random life. And becoming a prisoner, believe it or not, confirmed in me a sense of doing my duty. Society as structure, responsibility for actions, and all that; expectations one could count on. Besides, from the government's treatment, so far at least, I was beginning to believe that we were all but true Virginians at heart. We shared a bond being spoken on that prison boat that was made up by friends far more than by foes. We talked at length about the weather, and the many hard learned quirks and follies that accompany one trying to farm.

Aiding these impressions was the fact that our arrival into Jamestown was nothing of what we'd predicted. Surely it must have been evident the moment we docked that our ship was on some serious business. For one, Bacon was immediately transferred *with* ceremony by a tightly formed escort of guards. He descended the ramp and gave us a solemn nod, before Gardner's men could clear the reluctant streets enough for him to get by. It was most remarkable, this lack of public interest. We prisoners were certain that the captured core of Berkeley rebels would generate enough excitement to set the town ablaze. Crowds would be jammed in the streets, shoving each other's shoulders, jabbing elbows for a view. But the truth is that no one showed the slightest pause. Bartered deals and hard cash trades were kept at their feverish pace, (as I recall the speculation on a corn that popped was running very high) as indeed, commerce over any piddling thing, attracted more attention than us. The call for a New Assembly, which should have created a storm of debate, stirred no more interest than a month old rate insuring shipped lumber. The rebels stood on board, (some begrudgingly baffled) until we were finally herded off in different lots. (Those that owned land to the brand new jail, and a camp outside town for all others.)

"Who are they then?" I heard a feather merchant ask when we were passing.

I was happy though to find that a whole new sheriff's quarters had been built, housing a street level jail specifically for men of land holding status. Admittedly it was pretty tight quarters for the number of our group, but more comfortable by far than what was afforded our fellow prisoners kept beyond town. The food was regular, as was the changing of the pots, and making the most of the space that I could claim was mine, I eventually, mostly lost trace of time. I took my shift at dozing on the earthen stone floor, and whiled away whole hours playing finger games of chance. Not that we were made incautious. Whenever one of the sheriff's men ventured a question about the Occaneechee, it was batted amongst us until we made it a nonsense amusement, and once successfully diverted, it was ignored. And while my cellmates and I found it easy to avoid matters of importance, our guards proved quite willing to share their local talk. If any weight *was* given to a topic, it concerned The Royal African Trading Company and their cargo ships with their radical function of design. The entire make-up of a score of inner decks was no more than a series of strut like supports that fixed them into shallow layers. The space between the floor and ceiling was but to lie or crawl in. Their business was in hauling Negroes from West Africa, in unheard of numbers, to be sold outright and bound for *life*. The effect of this news, when heard by my fellow rebels, and each one still an active farmer, was a deafening silent crush. More than by weather, more than by Berkeley, more than by savages, or anything else, the specter of labor provided by lifetime bondage was going to put an end to the middling farms. And with it any chance for a freedman to have holdings, once his indenture was done. For all of that, those prisoners still waiting for their chance back in England had no way of knowing that their most cherished hope was gone. More than ever, the men that surrounded me bent themselves with chatter, but a silent growing dread was taking hold. It was the type of trick men use to bolster their denial, like the first waking moment the day after an early frost, and pretending it didn't kill every shoot and bud. But *I* saw it. It was the flash of ruin at work behind the ashen look in every eye. And each man there, in his own way, was silently counting how he could beat the odds. But no matter how fantastic he drew up the numbers, the inevitable picture loomed at them large. The truth, and everyone in that cell fully knew it, was that we could fight the savages back out west, but we couldn't compete with what was rolling in from the ocean. From as far away and as exotic a lands as we had ever heard of. And from the ports along the coast of the Caribbean, too.

We knew what the breeding of lifetime slaves would

do. The overwhelming vastness of African labor, an enterprise exclusive to the pockets of the rich, would force those inside this jail with me from off their plot of land. Within a generation was a fair enough prediction. Else, what would be left for one's children, but a debt-riddled hole in the ground?

But equally as cold as my grasp of these futile economics, was the fact that the fate of middling farms was no longer a problem for me. I had none such, and no family to return to. Everyday that I lived I moved deeper into *my* sense of loss. And this thought I saw slipping through and hovering in this buzz of inmate worry, was perversely freeing in its way.

Blam! The sound was close enough to shake the walls. It came at once, followed by a loud burst of shouting. Blam! Blam! The explosions jolted the brooding jail into a flurry, and knocked the abstractions from my head. I rose from my bed, watching my cellmates hoist the light boned Henry Simms to a slot in the wall that was too high to reach. A tiny vent cut at a joist in the ceiling provided a limited view. I kneeled back down, and pressed my ear to the wall that faced the street.

> *"Hey to Governor Berkeley!*
> *An' Mr. Bacon, too.*
> *Hey to the lads in tha militia,*
> *There's a meetin 'ta git to!"*

The yelling seemed to come from all directions, as did the bawling oxen, confused and in complaint. But then another sound, a pounding that beat upon the ground as if it were a drum. It made the floor beneath us tremble and it drowned the gasps of little Henry Simms. "Ah thousands people!" his dry throat cracked. "Thousands ah people in tha streets!"

* * * * *

"Haah! Haah!" Mr. Lawrence jeers like a half-wit. He sits up across from me, as if suddenly jolted to life. His eyes dance together like flames. "They came, Corstair, they came! The work of William Drummond and I to get them there," he says. "As soon was we learned that Bacon was arrested, we sent out the word. And they came! By the thousands! They came!"

I watch his abandon with a happy caution, and he begins to settle down.

"It was a such a reckoning that it had me believing, I'm not ashamed to tell you. Believing that we truly had a chance."

This from the man who's just shocked me by confessing that he had made plans for Nathan to turn himself in.

"Those fools looking out from their fancy town homes didn't know what had hit them. Drummond and I knew. Drummond and I, and Bacon, of course. But Berkeley? Utterly, and completely caught off guard."

Mr. Lawrence laughs. It's a deep and satisfying sound that echoes to the back of our cave. "Then, that fop of Bacon's cousin got him to speak that idiotic confession, and all bets were off. If Drummond and I could have prevented that, prevented that one secret meeting, we could have gotten Berkeley to sign on every demand. Including his resignation. Our rebellion would have ended then and there."

Now he is lamenting. But, truly so. His pale eyes look about our dank hole, so painfully symbolic of his fall. I wait him out for the moment. Whenever he is this strong to recall, his moods will often shift like this, reliving the damage like watermarks left by disaster. I try to steer him free from the snares that will surely take hold, but to little avail. The problem is that when he is steeped in such indulgence, I can become likewise engaged, until we grow silent, peering out like two old men, past forgiving our mistakes that we've made.

"I heard them, of course." I am prodding him now. "And then I saw the thousands. Inside our jail was all joy and celebration."

"Even to this day," Mr. Lawrence finally says, "I do not know the details of how Bacon let his cousin compromise him so. But the result, at least as far as I'm concerned was that it turned him into a coward."

I am mildly surprised that he has come to feel this way. He is seeing naught but the betrayal of his principles just now, while my experience with Bacon was certainly more fluent. Suffice it to say that if a man was ever at the mercy of his searing conceit, it was he, so I do not put limits on what he was capable of, but Mr. Lawrence should take pride in the number of men that responded to his call. *And*, I'm quick to remind him that had to leave their all-important planting, in the middle of the season no less. From a hard two-day ride, they came, with most arriving on foot.

* * * * *

My fellow rebels and I were but the width of a brick from two thousand armed and angry men, each one screaming out for blood, or for our freedom. But it sounded to us inside the walls, in a mix with the shouts from without, like one grand joyous noise. From our side, we each got a turn at the hoisted-up view, while our petrified guards barricaded themselves in their office. We had a little fun compounding their fear, (since they adamantly refused to venture out) by describing for them the deadly extent of the danger. From our pigeonhole view my eye beheld a street completely covered in a sweat-stained sea of homespun. I spotted a man in the crowd that I once knew by the name of Clinton Blaylock. He was shaking a reaping blade high above his head, and shouting profanities down the lane right toward the governor's house. There was in fact, a whole contingent of these wild sorts, making threats and thrusting pitchforks, menacing anyone foolish enough to get caught out in the street. Others began firing off their muskets, tracing smoke that left a whirling path over the statehouse. The law of Jamestown was in total; cowered. It was hiding from the shock of a mob that was still in the process of growing. In all, the degree of this rage in one place was approaching uncountable numbers. On the inside of our prison walls, we jumped up and down, feeling at once triumphant and astonished.

Where, I suddenly wondered, was the feather merchant now? The one that could barely be bothered by our passing.

* * * * *

"I wasn't allowed to meet with him before the opening of the council." Mr. Lawrence tells me.

I see this memory work upon him, quietly raising his hackles.

"And when I finally did, he wouldn't look at me directly."

He continues to bristle, until he finally shrugs it off, after letting me see how it's defeated him. Absurdly, I sense that he wishes to show me how far he has come in the realm of forgiveness. Even for what are unquestionably, the most grievous offences.

"What do you think of that, Corstair? Hmm? I bring him two thousand men. We occupy the very streets! And there was Bacon taking up his council seat as if he were finally accepting his birthright. Wouldn't so much as acknowledge me!"

"I think," I offer softly, "that he knew what he was doing."

I see that I have stirred him to a smile.

"Yes, of course, of course," Mr. Lawrence nods. "He

was ever the showman. *Everyone* was pretending! Except for that idiot cousin of his. I think he actually took Berkeley at his *word.*"

I keep my thoughts to myself. Bacon's elder cousin was the President of Berkeley's Council. It was an office that he used on Nathan's behalf, to temper the mighty wrath of Sir William Berkeley. From what I understood of the agreement, he had written a confession for Nathan to read before the council, and then, according to the governor's script, Sir William would bestow his public pardon. It was a deal that was struck however, before the shock of two thousand armed peasants came careening down the Jamestown streets. My own view was that Bacon's elder cousin acted in good faith. He was delusional, but he was a man from the old school of honor, simply trying to save his younger cousin's neck.

"You should have seen it, Corstair!" Mr. Lawrence suddenly wheezes out a laugh. "What theater! There was Bacon, performing the most grandiose bit of over-acting that I've ever seen. Sweeping himself to his knees, reciting the words prescribed for his contrition. I swear there was even laughter! Away from Berkeley of course, but definitely provoked from the delegates along the backbench. To which, to which…" Mr. Lawrence pulls himself into his famous Berkeley imitation, complete with his faintly fey voice. "God forgives you. *I* forgive you. But seriously, Corstair, *seriously.*"

He now releases a full-throated hoot. And I am happy to see him forget himself like this, if only for the moment.

"Now imagine," Mr. Lawrence recovers and continues. "Into this circus strides the Queen of the Pawmunkeys dressed up for an audience with the king. All fur and fringe stretched clear to the floor. A magnificent crown of pearls! And demanding, *demanding,* mind you, that Berkeley pay for the death of her husband when he fought with us at the skirmish of Bloody Run. Then, just when her feathers were sufficiently up in a high tangled ruffle, Chairman Davis calms her down, and asks how many *more* men she's willing to commit. 'We need your guides,' he says, 'for our *new* Indian war.' Oh you should have seen it, Corstair! It was a regular full fledged Indian fit that she threw, a royal stomping affair."

"I was not yet out of prison," I remind him, "but I remember how quiet the mob outside had grown when the queen had made her appearance."

"A pathetic, ignoble show," Mr. Lawrence runs on without having heard me. "Berkeley calling on the Indians to confirm their alliance, and then watching it blow up in his face. The only thing that he did to save himself that day was in stating his intent to retire. And the king's a fool for not accepting it! But, I guess even *Charles* knows that by now."

He starts to slip away from me again. Back to the melancholia that's ever ready to grab hold of him. The land of, "what could have been, and nearly was," as he would call it.

"Did Berkeley actually set us free?" I quickly ask. "Out loud and for the record?"

"After his official rebuke of me, of course." Mr. Lawrence says, responding to the offer of my lead. "Me and the good Mr. Drummond. We got our proper public condemnation, alright. But what with the city about to erupt, he was too afraid to do anymore. Frankly, I was amazed that he got through the day with having *that* much composure. He was an old, old man, you know."

I nod.

"And yes, he spoke your pardon aloud before the entire Assembly. Once he and God had forgiven Bacon, he forgave you all."

I see that Mr. Lawrence smiling again. There's enough irony in his face to catch a portrait painter's eye.

* * * * *

As for we lowly prisoners, when the sheriff got word of the governor's clemency, he was more than happy to let us out. He never knew but when the mad mob would break the cell doors open for him. It was good to stretch my floor-stiffened limbs in the bright morning sunshine, and where I could feel firsthand how tense the streets had grown. But. At the head of a crowd, Bacon stood on a rickety bench, admonishing the lingerers to join with those who were already dispersed. "Go home," he kept saying, "Return to the important work of your farms, and I will return to mine." And then he waved a hand in the air, pointing back to the doors of the Assembly.

"I have here in my hands the first of many reforms," he held aloft a ribboned stack of papers. "And the council is preparing to act upon our wishes. Not least of which, is the pledge for my commission! Now! Let me finish my legislative duty. And while you must raise a profit from your soil, I will have raised an army for your protection!"

Some backed away, and then turned to leave as if what waited at home was something they'd only just remembered. Others whistled and cheered, but it sounded confused, forced and half-hearted. Still others joined together in a boisterous surge, declaring the day to be theirs in "A clear and final victory!" All that I felt clearly was dismayed. I watched them depart, surely to more pressing tasks, (even if it was the work of someone else's land) while Bacon drew me aside, on his way back to the Statehouse.

"Stay in town with me," he said, without even breaking his stride. "See Mr. Lawrence about accommodation. I am in the midst of such business that I cannot speak just now." He indicated again, his handful of bills. "It is imperative that we strike while the winds are with us, but I need you to stand by." He then paused and faced me. "We have won a great deal, Corstair. Much that we have done we can be proud of."

And like a firebrand country preacher, he took a firm

hold of me, as if to acknowledge our deeply shared brotherhood. The second that the door shut behind him, I heard his shrill tones berating the Assembly.

* * * * *

"He knew just what to do," Mr. Lawrence says.

And I hear the sarcasm in his voice cut through the dust reflecting our cave light.

"He ordered those men... the men that *I* recruited! There fully armed and ready to fight! To... go... home! Do you know? Do you know Corstair, the deal he made with the devil? Sold us for his chance to finally have *legitimate* glory. His precious commission for a *military* command. Do you know!?

He explodes with the sudden fury of a rocket. I wait a minute for him to catch his breath. And for what I have come to learn always follows these demonstrations. His twisted wave of self-contempt.

"Of course, I was always too damn dull *to do* anything about it. Words," he laments, "are not worth the necessary spit."

There will be at least another pause before he recovers.

"Well. What's to come of banking all your faith upon a youthful shining star? Hmm? Our bold Nathaniel Bacon. And now with his legitimacy *officially* assigned, well. He developed a pretty quick taste for *political* power."

Whatever else he may express, I know that Mr. Lawrence's love for Nathaniel is beyond question. It's a devotion that Nathan stirred by bringing him in touch with human suffering, as odd as that may seem. The country at this time had whole families that were homeless, even precious children were being sold, while Lawrence only saw Jamestown as a den for legal thieves. It was Nathaniel Bacon that opened Mr. Lawrence's eyes. He showed him men that roamed in Indian woods, half naked and half alive.

"And he certainly had the knack," Mr. Lawrence continues. "Bacon played that Assembly like a cardinal in the Vatican. But my, he could make a personal harangue. And by the time he was finished, the council had signed on for universal suffrage, regular elections, and limited terms of office. He got published audits of every government agent with his hand in public funds. He had..." and here he pauses for a full effect, "Berkeley's cronies kicked right out on their ass."

And then shoots me an appreciative wink for letting him go with his course tongue.

"After tireless provocation of three very long days, he had so fatigued the old man that Berkeley had to leave for his plantation back at Green Spring. In short, Nathaniel Bacon ended by astounding us."

Now he turns dead still, and starts shaking his head, almost tenderly defiant.

"I told him. Right in the face of his enormous success, I told him. I feared too much was happening too easily. I told him that. Entirely too quick. I wanted Nathan to see things through. To be more careful. Then, of course, Berkeley disappeared without even signing his military commission....! Aach!"

Mr. Lawrence spits.

"Berkeley was scared to death of a coup! Had every right to be... until..."

And now he writhes with disgust.

"... He had his military! He sent those armed men home! With Berkeley run away to Green Spring! Even then! *Damn* the work of his cousin! Bargains for worthless pardons! Ordering *my* men to disperse!"

I see them now, these simple tenants, (men without the

right to vote didn't count for much in the Assembly,) returning to their fields, as if they hadn't just had their necks stretched out for pieces of paper they couldn't even read. All that they knew was that a gentleman named Bacon was speaking loud in Jamestown for their part. I can almost see them walking, with their implemental weapons, the leg and backs permanently bowed and bent. It is perfectly fitting how undistinguished they are, what with the hoeing, and the clearing, and furrowing to be done. I hear Mr. Lawrence muttering sounds of anguish, even as I watch the last of these simple heroes trickling out from the Jamestown gate.

Then with his peasant army vanished almost as suddenly as it appeared, a night or two later Bacon's war against corruption turned against him. Safe from his retreat at Green Spring, Berkeley issued a new warrant for his arrest. And this time, the governor's bootjacks had everyone assured, Bacon's execution would be swift. It was Nathan's bedeviled cousin (God bless the man for bungling things back right) who warned him about Sir William's change of intention, and got him word that he should flee.

"Not a moment too soon," Mr. Lawrence says, to me brightly. "The sheriff's men came to my Inn and slashed through every mattress! The fools! Can you imagine? A man like Nathaniel Bacon hiding himself in a pack of goose fleece?"

I do not say, that as a matter of fact, I could.

𝕴 must make arrangements with my dear Elizabeth. For what we have started, and have yet to do, we remain as one. Bacon.

These words, addressed to me, were on a torn piece of legislative parchment slipped in the toe of my Persicles boot. And so following his prior instruction, I struck out into the pitch of night for the western road. I kept low to the saddle, riding at a breathless walk, with my ears to the ground for the sound of the governor's men. All the next day I spent like this, with half of it hidden from sunlight, before I had made our point of rendezvous. Forty miles inland in a tucked expanse of hollow that the country folk called The Crandall Dip, I began to see isolated groups ranging in from backwoods and regions more remote. These people were not the usual down and out itinerants, or runaway indentures with time still left on their contract, these were frontier families, surprising in their number that were strung out on the borders north and south. The mystery of how they got news of this clandestine gathering was more than I could say, but here they were, stoically plodding the long hot march that was leading them to what, was not exactly clear.

Over the course of the following week our campground expanded to accommodate the new arrivals that were ever straggling in, with each man bearing any type of rumor to gain entry, and maybe even a dinner. The most interesting came to report that no one had joined Berkeley's militia, "To crush," as he said, "These bands of common vagrants prepared to do us harm." This was a story that I felt was worth repeating; that the Governor of Virginia could find no one willing to do his fight.

When something over a week was out, we were living in a makeshift village, with a population of about six hundred. Half were displaced or simply on the wrong side of the law, but the other half came to us as families, caring less about their civil rights than for their own protection. In any case, the one issue that all consented on was that the land be free of Indians.

The other condition that we all held in common was that the woods were extremely dry. Seven straight days of hot wind raked at the nerves already raw and fearful. Strange waves of heat would suddenly billow through the brush, at times even seeming to ignite it, pushing a flame in towards a tent, and causing inevitable conflict. The families always rallied to smother the blaze, but only with harsh words about tending to one's own campfires. The cool of late evenings offered the only rest. The fellows that were the "common vagrants" though, formed a highly responsive community that patrolled our woodsy perimeter both day and night. They helped out many a family that truly needed it, and always had a story about some poor butchered family that didn't "make it in." I kept to myself as much as I was able, walking the withered bush and wondering where was Bacon, collecting the endless rain of pine needles that fell into my hat.

But because of my dogged reputation for violence I suppose, I often found myself, quite against my wishes, at the center of an evening circle. The kind of questions that were put to me, constructed along the lines of God knows what these silly young men thought, pressed about me, turning me ambivalent and numb. What could I say? Should I tell them that I'd come more alive in Bacon's wake than anything I'd ever felt? And if I actually spoke to these fellows, I mean to somehow reach and convince them of what we were, and what we'd all become, it only left me feeling old.

There was Peter Cabot for instance; standing in the shadows, talking about the gall of the careless heathen. Such as the way they'd take to wandering through his house.

"Oncet after sittin' up half a night with the two of these stone silent bucks, I told 'em ta leave an' come back nex' mornin' if they had a mind to. They come back all right. With a few more of them besides. An' before they left, they ate up all the wife's potatoes, an' her cornbread, too. Nex' day she was too afraid ta even leave out an' fetch tha daily water."

"Celia Fairchild like ta lose her second born to tha migrant Maniock," Sam Carlisle put in. "She was spinning out some bunting in her front yard when a man and his wife come up with a dead baby in their hands. Claimed she'd killed their child with her white witchcraft an' demanded her daughter in return."

"There ain't no amount of reason gonna give them people learnin'," someone else confirmed.

I chose not to relate the story of Felicia Crenshaw. Among this crowd it would only have found a way to be twisted back around. But ten years before, Helen and I were called to mediate between Felicia's husband, Gilbert, and a Chickahominy brave named Taa-kri. Two summers before that, Felicia had wandered off to her blackberry patch and was never heard from again. Until that is, this meeting of Gilbert and Taa-kri. Felicia had finally reappeared at Syfert's Trading Camp where Gilbert had by chance bumped into her, and when she ran away he tracked her down to Taa-kri. Now that he knew where to find her, Gilbert gathered up a group of his friends and brought them along for support. He then accused the dumbfounded Taa-kri of abducting his wife. Now whether or not Taa-kri had actually taken Felicia was never completely understood, for when the charge was put to him, he answered in excited gestures that only added to the confusion. In any case, under an interrogation conducted by several of the settler's wives, Felicia firmly denied any such criminal act. She said that for her, the episode was an unfortunate case of ancient history, which was to say that she had no intention of leaving Taa-kri and returning to Gilbert as his wife. She went on to confess that her life as a Chikahominy Indian could not have been more pleasing; the state of which she shamelessly enforced by raising up her blouse to expose her swollen belly. "I am carrying," she said with a pride directed to us all, "Taa-kri's second child."

"Heeiy! Hiy! Hurrah!" Came a sudden shout from just outside the camp.

"Heeiy! Hooay! Heeiy!"

The voices shooting through the dark stilled the toads and crickets. The whoops were sent aloft in the clarity of the nighttime air and spread in circles all about us. "Hoot! Hoot! Hurrah!" The men a fireside over formed a narrow lane. A lone rider bowed his head beneath the skeletal trees, as wave after wave of dirt dry hands reached out to touch his cape. Apparently having waited for just this moonless pitch, Nathaniel Bacon had finally arrived. The lateness of the hour however did nothing to deter a massing crowd. Men came at him in a stream, some of them with guns, their women holding sleeping babes quickly followed behind them. As he strode his horse directly to our camp, someone handed him a torch. Then, after offering me an appreciative nod, he turned to face the crowd.

His hours with Elizabeth had served him well. I knew nothing of how they had arranged such stolen time, but he was obviously replenished. Sitting in a striking pose high above his ragged congregation, his eyes were focused, even gained I might say, a wiser strain of compassion. He removed his gloves to reach across a solid mass of shoulders, and briefly took the hands of his admirers. I watched him slowly scan each face, until the shouting was reduced to a tone of reverent confidence. It was nothing less than a phenomenon. The driving confluence of fearful passion that acted on these men seemed to have been lifted. The uncertain loyals and the irrational extremists seemed reconciled for no other reason than for being in his presence. This, I thought, was Elizabeth's handiwork. I heard her calm and steady voice, as when he was suddenly afraid to go to Jamestown, and making himself sick on their front room floor. Now, she'd managed to turn the anger he had for the betrayal of his elected office into a cohesive force. The importance of her role to him was something that could not have been known by the people in this wood, but their marriage, this rule-breaking coupling of the upper crust, was just what poor folk could love.

"Good and dear friends," he began. "My fellow sons of Virginia, and a family to which I most proudly belong." Once again the cheers broke apart the night air. "'Tis true, I was born a gentleman, but it is an association that I must deign deny. For what have the landed gentry of your hard won country rendered if not but greed and corruption? Indeed, it is your honest labor that plows beneath a yoke of their Royal debt!

The crowd exploded in expected angry noise.

"We are," he continued with the settling, "in the middle of this forest, in the middle of this night, truer to the people of Virginia than any assembled in Jamestown!"

"Hiyah! Hiyah! What need we of ANY government?!" Someone yelled.

"But please!" Bacon yelled. "Let no one say that our grievance is to our king. The crown resides in a far off country, and cannot know of the perils we face. Of our daily lives steeped in danger."

This was Elizabeth, certainly.

"But can the same be said for Jamestown? A government proven wholly impotent, but in its unrightful levy of tax? No, my friends. My fight and yours is with the self-imposed isolation of our decrepit governor, a man whose usefulness has passed him by. A man that keeps company with our enemies, and robs our land for his favorites in court! What does he know of the common man's struggle to survive?"

"Hiyah, here! Hiyah, for Nathaniel Bacon!" Leaves were shaken free of parched trees.

"I see Jeb Smithers here before me," he continued when they finally grew quiet again. "Tom Langford, too" he nodded, "Ben Stratton and his family. And many more I've come to know by name and honest reputation. Forced to live and work in a land made hostile by the deliberate neglect of our governor. Do your lives and the lives of your precious children no longer count?"

"Here, here!" came the response.

"But I am come to bring you hope! I have learned that the governor can form no army to oppose us. All the people of Jamestown have witnessed his deceit! They wait for us now! To rally their support!"

More yells and whistling burst forth, loud enough at last, to awaken an infant that began to scream.

"I beseech you now to return to your campsites," he said softly. "Take your little ones to their rest. Tomorrow we will march to renew *their* birthrights. And by our duty served, win back our land to bequeath to them."

Slowly, very slowly men began to split off, but still milled about to keep him in sight. Here at last was a rumor come to life. A gentleman unafraid to speak the truth, to take up their fight, and asking only for the exchange of their good faith. Of course they would linger. They had to confirm he was more than fancy man talk, and not suddenly cut and leave.

Who could blame their excitement preventing any chance for sleep? Perhaps they'd awaken, and just like the lies, which brought them across a violent ocean, everything promised would once again be gone. And anyway, as put by someone that I overheard, "Bacon's a bloke the dimmest in our lot could see was in need of protection."

I watched and I listened, half awed and half bemused, as he voiced his opinions for what remained of the night. His expertise, at least since last we spoke, had evidently expanded its range. He held forth on subjects diverse as the tripling of the borrowed rate, to a suspected epidemic of stillborn calves. One young man, closer in years to a boy, asked him what he thought about the idea of elopement. "If your Miss says yes," he rapidly replied, "then her father's better wishing her good-bye." Then when at last, the last had crept away, Bacon turned to me. I made sure that we were kept in supply of a surprisingly good mulled wine.

"Corstair," his face beamed, "have you heard the news? Berkeley could gather less than thirty men. And *they* gave up their heartless search barely fifteen miles from town. There will be no more deception. We will have new law and *I* will have my commission."

The spell that he wove was so seductive that he even had me believing in the life ahead, past the insatiable haunts of loss. But putting my preoccupations aside, I still could not grasp the total vision he unraveled, and spread through the wee hours that night. He spoke in terms of "an inevitable independent nation," and "a government of enterprise." He webbed philosophy and politics; "Let the common good *be* the profit of individual will." But as the gray of morning came slipping in first light, I found that I had questioned his notions, and his motivations less and less. Maybe, he just wore me down. (Not so difficult a prospect considering that my setting one foot down consistently ahead of another, was a day that

I counted a success. If I'm honest in fact, I spent a great part of his lecture, listening to the differing croaks in the dark. The yaw of tree limbs scraping in dry wind is also an interesting sound. Proving, for me anyway, that even Bacon's voice could merge with this much natural noise if you let it hard enough.)

He continued holding court like this well into the dawn, even as the outlined forms of men took shape, and grumbled about in the bush. He kept right on talking, through the standing and stretching, and the reaching high with hands, and the twisting back around to loosen stiffened necks, and even after these break of day motions all had been made he talked. While the men huffed about on the ground. The new sun hit his eyes and glowed back into mine, as wild as the look I've been told will visit saints. In any case he was certainly possessed of tongues. And at last when he had saddled up, and climbed on to his horse he never once stopped talking.

"And think on this," he said, sitting astride his four legged pulpit. "Opening our markets to the *whole* of Europe will *increase* the profits to the king. It might even prevent his expensive wars. If we convince Charles that we will be his partner, that we can act the part of *mediator,* we could even end his pesky problems with the Dutch."

He cantered ahead, leaving me the impression that the fight before us was but an inconvenience, a necessary stop in order to relieve oneself, along the road of his active imagination. He then picked up new banter with the men.

"William Fallon," he yelled, as if the toothless tenant was his long time friend. "How's it come that you could leave your fiery wife? She hasn't kicked you out again surely?"

And this was how we marched. His doling out compliments, and making bold endearments in good jest. He circled ahead and then walked his horse back to mingle among the scattered rows. I moved on, occasionally waiting up for him, while he distributed his cheerful disregard. In all it was a jolly method he applied for treading this dangerous path.

By the next mid-day however, a drudging pace had set in that was eerily weighted and solemn. The news of our approach seemed to have preceded us like the scent of some contagion. Houses and barns were completely shuttered up, and the few people that we spied upon the road scurried ahead, like frightened stray dogs. Everyone on the march became wary. Bacon called for random halts, and reconnaissance sent out, but it never discovered an ambush that was waiting for us in hiding. There were stretches when the air was so wrought with tension that I just about wished they had. Then, as if it were all a grand joke being played, we were suddenly at, and easily through the city gates. The next steps however, were measured with an anxious inspection of each and every lane that seemed to echo the pounding in every heart. Eyes were peeled wide to carefully survey each brick and corner for the chink that held a musket into place. And still, the streets lay out before us, empty as the day. Whether it was a row house, or a business, each was safely cleared after having been called out, and not a guard, or a resident or single merchant could be found. The whole of Jamestown looked abandoned, as if some secret picnic was being enforced.

With the mounting apprehension Bacon became agitated. He began to decry the governor's cowardice in a loud and reverberating voice. He stationed men at every crossing, and then picking up his pace, he made a reckless angry march upon the State House.

Apparently the town *was* truly spooked. Every home was empty, even the guard posts upon the outer wall, as well as every street and shop. It felt utterly deserted, as if lived in long ago, but still holding the impression of its people having left in a hurried state. There was no calling out the prices of goods crammed alongside of the dock, nor any pints being lifted, saluting deals concluded, inside the dark tavern walls.

The city's disquieting vacancy made the men jumpy, and even unwilling to explore. (Frankly, I was surprised that no one started in on the breaking and the looting of things behind locked doors.) And if, after all his threats to us, Berkeley had chosen to flee without a fight, then where were the citizens that had sworn us their support? Did the governor force a march and take them with him? Were they all arrested, and being held in mass?

Then, when we reached the lawn of the Assembly a clamor arose from the front of our lines. I saw our first row of men raising and aiming their weapons, and felt my heart leap immediately back in my throat. I pushed ahead to find out what was causing this reaction, and I saw a group of council members clustered in a second floor window, staring down at us in fright. Clearly terrified, they all bundled closer together, while whispering, and pulling at one another's sleeves. But I must say that after our progression up the streets, having been nothing but tension, along with the picture they now presented provoked some genuine laughter. With the powdery sweat that clumped in their wigs, and their lips just a smear of red paint, behind the glass, magnified as they were, they appeared like exotic fish. At the very front was the double-chinned William Boyd crying freely into his collar, and looking for all the world like he would faint. The man behind him that I did not know by name, held a trembling kerchief to his nose, undoubtedly filled with strong salts.

"Bacon! Bacon! Bacon!" Our ragged troops began to shout. Then, "The commission! We will have it!"

The men shook farm blades directly at the council, with several aiming guns toward the clownish faces. Those at the rear started throwing stones. The governor was nowhere to be seen, but Nathan, in no mood for further delay, called for me to form an escort and follow him into the Hall. I quickly pulled ten men that I knew, and forced an entrance through the heavy doorframe. The sudden spectacle of an armed group of men, (so much the worse for being beggarly servants) breaking down the door of justice so panicked the remaining council that they leapt up and jammed the far exit. As for me, the confusion that we caused made me simply stand and gawk.

I had never been in such a large room. (The cavernous space made suddenly larger by the hastily abandoned benches.) The surrounding balcony; buttressed with rows of dark stained pilasters, were each carved of oak over four feet thick. There were mahogany doors leading into paneled corridors that had an upward sweep in an intricate design that looked like giant seashells. There were separate stairs to private chambers that circled behind the chancel, which set off the walls, (white as snow) and lent the room an immediate freshness. There was a burnt wood molding framed into the ceiling joists and a dozen rafters arching at a height to accentuate the open spaces. The overall design stood, in its way, for the respect that was due an elder statesman, (if only to limit his access) but for me it was a symbol of much more. I saw it at once as a testament. To the time-consuming labor that only an indenture could know and fulfill. It was the undeniable fact of what made Virginia work.

It contained, quite literally, a most impressive air. Step a foot outside, and you would feel the stifling weight of Virginian humidity, but here, with *someone* having taken the pains to layer each coat of plastering, the air remained quite cool. It was exhilarating just standing in the hall.

Then, there he was, larger than life, emerging from the doorway just before us. The one time statuesque governor with his face frozen in a grimace and his shoulders bent with age, being shuffled along by a clique of his closest aides. The young man that had a hold of him moved haltingly, in sheltering steps, seemingly oblivious on the way to Berkeley's private rooms. My own men fumbled nervously about, and watched, with dry mouths agape, while Bacon without the slightest hesitation pounced on the entourage, by planting himself directly in their way. Sir William, looking up to find his passageway blocked, gave a long regal turn of his head, and after regarding each of us with a cold and studied glare, asked, "What do you want?"

The question, so direct and simply put, surprised us. But it was projected with such an undercurrent of venom towards Bacon, that he had what I can only describe as a moment of hysterics.

"I have come for my commission!" he shouted. "And 'ere I leave here, God damn my blood, I'll have it!"

The pitch of his voice produced an echo that bounced like a shot high upon the ceiling. The governor responded by merely turning away, and as if dismissing him thus, trundled deliberately back down the hallway. Bacon began running up and down the narrow passage, seemingly lost to his senses, and kicking his legs and feet out far from both his sides. His thought perhaps was impeding Berkeley's progress, but he looked as silly as a turkey with its head cut off. Then, as if the dance he was performing only further propelled his fury, he suddenly became completely transformed. He started making wild gestures with his hands, as a sort of counter motion to the active kick of his feet. He jabbed his fingers in the air, quite violently at times, and then to his hips, and then his head. For a while he looked like he had settled on this pattern, bringing his hands to his hips, then back to his head, then back to his hips once more, so that I thought he was in the throes of a convulsion. One of his hands grabbed the brim of his hat then it swooped to the hilt of his sword, and no sooner had it touched his sword than it flew to his hat again.

Exactly what was meant by this bewildering pantomime I could not say, but he continued these flapping gyrations, without uttering a sound for five minutes more, leaving everyone watching amazed. Having witnessed his antics, (in dire straits I should add) I need not have been so surprised, but the shock of a gentleman, acting like an ape man and careening about council halls, so frightened the governor's aides that they picked the old man up and forced him into a seat that they'd formed of their hands. He was then packed off to his rooms.

* * * * *

"Did you know of any insanity in Bacon's family?" I ask Mr. Lawrence. And I am sincere. "Back in England, I mean."

Mr. Lawrence is stirring. He's been moving about our cave, mumbling incoherently, nodding occasionally at the slate hole of sky. I want to gather his attention before he gets too restless. He could easily wander off when he talks to himself like this; and talk himself right into trouble.

"Oh, you mean that prancing business in front of the governor?" he finally responds. "That was Nathan giving us his ridiculous rendition of the conspiracy against Caesar. He was acting the part of the statesman Cato."

I cannot help but thinking that if one finds himself inside a hostile border, being held hostage in a savage's cave, he could do a lot worse than having a scholar for a fellow prisoner. There's no end to the bits that I've learned from the world of Mr. Richard Lawrence.

"And who was Cato then?" I naturally ask on cue.

But then he just looks at me. As if checking to make sure that I'm not just provoking him. My just seeing what he'll say by way of having fun with him. As if he suddenly needs to approve of the way that we're spending our time.

"For the indulgence of your generous care and concern for me, my dear Corstair..."

And then he prepares to give a lesson with that most

welcome of signs, the clearing of his throat. This is how he sputters to let me know that he's willing to engage me in a diversion, one that he knows that I hope will keep him from harm's way.

"...Cato was a stoic. A purist of the Old Republic within the Roman Senate. When he was called forth to explain his position on Ceaser's absolute supremacy, an episode that was really more of a trial, he kept touching his head, and then dropping his hand back down to his sword. It was a gesture we interpret whose meaning was twofold. First, to illustrate that the *idea* of Republic, the touch to the head, could not be stopped. Not even by the force of a vengeful throng. And second, the hand to the sword to show that he was prepared to drive it through his chest. As a matter of *proving* this point. Right there on the senate floor if need be, ... he was Latin, after all..."

He gives a slight pause, so that I should appreciate his famous dry conceit.

"Cato was elite. He was appalled by the base instincts of the masses. The natural diffusion, one might say, of a quality to spread *downward*. And Nathan, in his almighty confusion, was calling, like Cato, for the Assembly to come to its nobler sensibilities. All while he courted the mob that was outside. In short, he was acting like a complete buffoon..."

And I am glad to hear Mr. Lawrence set himself out on a veritable ramble. As for *my* opinion of Bacon's perplexing behavior, setting aside his oft-repeated curse for God to curse his blood, I never believed for a minute that he would kill himself. Not for his *beliefs*.

* * * * *

Nathan's response to this unforeseen development, (that is, scaring the governor and his council into hiding, and then refusing to come out) was to take his turkey dance down the outside steps and into the head of the crowd. But his flailing arms and jerking trot, even for its being more adept, dumbfounded the men no less than it had me.

"I'll have it!" He shouted at the door that he'd left gaping wide in its proper church-like façade. "God damn my blood, I'll have it!"

"The commission!" someone yelled, but sounded unsure, and confused.

"God may damn the council and the governor, too!" Bacon squawked. "But, I will have it!"

"Give us the commission!" the rest chimed in.

The afternoon had taken on the aspect of circus. Entirely too strange and untrue for what I'd seen of honest men, and innocent, now dead.

"God damn my blood!" Bacon shouted again.

Meanwhile the men kept waving their arsenal of weapons at the members of the council, who popped in and out of the windows, too frightened to take a long view.

"No more levies!" Rang a cry from the back of the lines. Then, "No more levies! No more levies!" became the new chant for a while.

The volume grew, in noise and in the number of curses, which made for more heated demands. "Give me a wife!" I heard someone yell.

Then the governor was suddenly standing in the doorway, sending everyone into shock. In complete defiance of his arthritic age, he bolted across the lawn and froze just an inch from Bacon's face.

'Shoot me!" he screamed. And with trembling hands, he tore apart his blouse, exposing a wrinkled, white haired chest. "Here! Fore God, a fair mark! Shoot!"

Then in a careful back step of retreat, never breaking his gaze from Nathan, he reached the distance of a duel. The men all ceased their shouting at once, struck as much by the turn of this event, as the sight of the old man's breast. Everyone seemed to take a cautious breath then began to jostle each other to the front. I knew these men, and I knew well how many would have liked to take Berkeley at his word. Settle this affair right there and then. Settle it by a trial made simple, and make God's intentions clear.

"Fore God, fair mark! Shoot!" Berkeley screamed again. And for all his palsied shaking, the challenge in his voice rang strong.

"Sir," Bacon responded calmly.

And then I saw his change. I could not be sure if it was sorrow, or awe, or what might pass for pity, or if it was compassion that struck this headstrong youth. Or if it was just plain fear. But I saw Nathan come suddenly aware, in some new way, of what was about to happen here. And the height of a heated posture made pure arrogance come revealed. But he could not hide his embarrassment. Before him, so obviously rattled, the fragile old man, exposing his heart. Sir William Berkeley, The King of England's Governor to Virginia, jeered by a common crowd.

"No. May it please your honor, I'll hurt not a hair of your head," Bacon said. The voice was benevolent, and unstrained. "Nor of any other man's. We are come for a commission to save our lives from the Indians, which you have so often promised. But we must have before we go."

Sir William kept his ground, staring quietly for a moment, almost sniffing the air for deception. He then made a noise, displaying his contempt, and wheeled to return to his chamber.

"God damn my blood!" Bacon seized immediately on his swearing once more. And then pulling his sword half free of its scabbard, he pranced forward, swinging his limbs in the same wild birdlike manner, trailing Berkeley's path to the door. "I'll kill Governor, Council, Assembly and all! Then sheathe my sword in my own heart's blood!"

Berkeley was gone, he'd slammed the inside bolt to the floor, so the last of these words Bacon shouted at the council in the window. The merciful moment, I knew in that instant, was done.

"Make ready, and present!" he commanded.

The men at the rear were shouting again as those in the front dropped to one knee. Time seemed to spin imperceptibly, and then seemed to hold quite still. I smelled the acrid powder, and heard the scrape of matchlocks, the unmistakable slish of ramrods sliding their cartridge home. Bacon gave the order to shoulder and take aim.

Even my young years seemed vapid and wasted now, rushing and crushing me all at once. The hard edges, the very thickness of my skin, and a lifetime of worthless accumulated thought. I saw myself, saw my whole body in fact, right there along with the most noxious of braggarts, unable to even give a name to my acts. And yet, I recall a sense of horror. An evil often seen in the faces of cowards.

Perhaps, I thought in some grand way, I was only playing the part of the collector. A functionary for the greater law. I was here to take a payment that was long overdue, in the shapes of these neglectful men. Comfortable men, some that I knew of, some that I actually knew, afraid even now, hiding back in staterooms, inside their perfumed closets. Men so vain that they rarely felt ashamed but found themselves in fear of facing me. The me of no account, like the men right here, the ones by whom I'd let myself become surrounded. I wondered too, what these ignorant souls would do when they suddenly became the government.

"We will have it! We will have it!" yelled the men from the middle of the pack.

As a boy I'd rolled barrels of flour up the street on

which I stood. From the receiving docks right to Madame Porters Inn. I'd hauled office bricks and fresh cut planks, wood that I'd lumbered myself. I heard my father's voice, a voice that I'd long lost the ear for, whispering through the haze of this nonsensical moment. "Was I aware," he said, "that I was holding the city I'd helped to build up, up in a siege of terror?"

"We will have it! We will have it!"

The men at the rear, surely mad with the drink started another assault of their cursing. Then Bacon called for silence. The next and only sound permitted was to be the roaring flame of guns. The full summer sun rippled in a glare upon the windows, temporarily blocking the targets from our view. I automatically girded my ears to the explosion, and shifted my weight to absorb the recoil. Then I caught a trembling shimmer, a frenzied movement, of shaking up and down inside the window. I looked across to Bacon, immediately relieved he'd seen it too. I pulled my aim away from the motion in glass, and there it was again, right above the barrel. A shaking pink fist fixed to a piece of white fabric.

"Halt!" Bacon cried, putting himself in front of the line of fire. I saw his face release, as if in a huge breath, a burden too dear for simple victory. He replaced his sword in his belt.

Slipping beneath the shadow of the eave, I could see William Boyd, shaking his lace of surrender, making circles in the pane, and then wiping back his tears.

"The commission. You shall have it! You shall have it!" he mouthed through the glass, over and over again.

"Whatever became of old Cato then?" I ask Mr. Lawrence. "Killed himself, true enough," he says.

He seems to want to drop the topic now, an indication perhaps that the story of the ancient statesman is beginning to look too much like his own. But then he surprises me by going on.

"An up-to-his neck casualty of political intrigue, and way too stubborn to play the game of compromise," he tells me. "While our Mr. Bacon was the excitable opposite. The very quality that held his virtues *and* his faults. Nathan was simply too full of himself to cut out his own heart. Do you want me to tell you what I *really* think?"

He doesn't pretend to stop for my answer.

"Nathaniel Bacon was an adventurer, simple as that. You know Corstair we are living at a time where many are disaffected of his class. It began of course when our little world began to break open, what with all the ocean navigation. Or maybe it's been a natural response to these damnable religious campaigns. So I believe that he felt genuine about the need to make reform. And God knows he was perfectly at home with much of the atheistic thought. His truest calling however was his need to *perform*. But even in this he was not so alone. Many of the young and disgruntled have found a voice in William Shakespeare's rude theater, for one. Both male and female. In Nathan's case, the search for his proper role just happened to coincide with the making of a new country, no? Anyway, the men clearly loved him for it. But he should never be compared to Cato. Not at all, no, no. Have we anything left to eat?" Mr. Lawrence suddenly interrupts himself to ask.

He stops to pull apart his tattered mound of blankets, inspecting the folds for an overlooked morsel or crumb. The day has progressed and the early morning cold has left us, so hunger can make its hovering presence more known. I bring him what is left of Seycondeh's flat cake, and think about how I can go about finding her. Without her help there is little chance for our escape, and I resolve myself to the risks I must take in order to see her.

"I thank you, Mr. Corstair." Mr. Lawrence says, carefully picking out the nuts. "Insane?" he discovers a pumpkinseed with delight. "The council certainly thought so. The way that Bacon ranted and raved at them. He demanded unconditional pardons for all of his men. He ordered the immediate removal of any of Berkeley's favorites that had a seat on the council. And this he demonstrated by physically assaulting the unsuspecting fool's himself. Then he appropriated seventy pounds for the damage that Captain Gardner had done to his ship. Oh, it was quite a show. But none of it was particularly meaningful in any way. When it came to real reform, he used his new powers to offend important people that could have been useful to our cause. In my view he was acting insane. He let loose on that Assembly like he was the devil's own dog."

"Was Berkeley sitting for all of this?"

"I doubt that he was sitting. Stomping up and down his chamber is more likely. He was so beside himself that he refused to make an appearance. But by the next day, his council had worn him down enough to sign off on the commission, which as you know put Bacon solely in charge of Virginia's militia. His prize-winning *role*, so to speak. He was sane enough to get what *he* most wanted. And what he most wanted was permission to go and kill Indians. As for new law, well that would have to wait."

Mr. Lawrence takes one of his regular moments to look befuddled into space.

"Maybe at bottom, Bacon was the 'comfortable rebel' after all," he continues. "That's what the council was calling him. But then he was sane enough to keep his motives to himself."

"If, in fact he knew what they were."

"Truly astute, Mr. Corstair," Mr. Lawrence chuckles, "Are you running for some office?" Then his face grows immediately taut, listening to his hollow laughter, bounce from the back of our cave. "My, that was some tasty bread," he quickly says.

I look hard at Mr. Lawrence to try and determine if he is being honest. His comment nags at my concern. If he's truly enjoyed the bit of bitter mold that I have given him, then he may be slipping further away than I think.

"Still, I should not presume to complain," he says, but awkwardly. He forces his backbone to stretch, stopping to take in shallow gulps of air. His eyes meet mine in a sudden surprise, and for a second I sense there is something he's concealing.

"Trust me, Bacon said." Mr. Lawrence re-gathers himself quickly. "More times than I care to remember. 'First comes control of the military, then of the Legislature.' So, I trusted him. What choice did I have? If... we... only had more time, and if..."

And now he goes sad.

"He had the love of the men to look after," I quickly add. "He needed to justify their reasons for joining him."

"True, true. He had the love of the men. And *he* had great love for the rabble." Mr. Lawrence yawns, as if he's come suddenly bored. I take it as a signal for his twice-a-day nap. "Look at that bird."

I look, but see no bird.

"An intoxicating thing," he muses, "rabble love. The rabble being nothing if not toxic. Can you hear it?" He cocks his head out towards the exit. "So pretty for this time of year."

* * * * *

Exactly one hour and a half past Bacon's showdown with the governor I was leaning against the wall of Lemuel Stone's New Virginia Tavern. *I* was a full-fledged member of the rabble that Mr. Lawrence speaks of, and what access this credential got me was an earful of sedition right from off the street. Rabble talk steamed from every greasy table, after Lemuel Stone reopened his place of business to us, of course. As it happened, while Bacon was attacking his colleagues in the Assembly, the company that I was with battered down the inn-keep's door. I finally persuaded one of *my* colleagues to go up and fetch him, and when Stone appeared, he was shaking so much that he slipped down the stairs.

"If you don't get up and start serving," the poor man was informed, "you'll have us measuring your pints on our own."

So began our proper rabble reception. Bottles to pitchers, each one presented with the tavern owner's smile. A service he said, that he was proud to make for free.

"I don' got no Injun problem down where I'm at," a planter at the next table confessed. "Hell, you'd never find a savage dumb enough to try that land. I'm fightin' for one reason, an' one reason only. An' that's ta clear my debt with that bleedin' credit broker Charlie Frawley. Once I take 'at blood sucking skunk's head off, I'll be back on even ground."

"The way I figure it, this little roust-about like tha one that we got comin' up is gonna free me from tha tribute pelts that I have to pay that double tongue Sey-Hatchity chief."

This last confession was offered by a trapper who smelled the part from every pore. A lynx cat gives off a fairly pungent musk when he's cut to the bone in a trap.

"Wher's that at?" another asked.

"West ta south fork Rappahannock. But it don' mind where all you operate. Governor's got his heathen Injuns out there ta collect from you."

It was intriguing for me to see farmers and trappers, so normally distrustful, sitting together to share their complaints.

"Govermaint runs all 'em skins out that part of the country."

It was a surprising sit down all the way round. There were runaways that talked of extorting their masters into an early settle out. There were small-lot free holders, cursing tobacco's free fall. And rented labor misfits, feeling as pleased as you could be drinking up a week's worth of wage for free. There were trappers planning new routes, and conniving up ways to trade with the French. There was even a fisherman named Joseph McKay that happened to put in that morning, sitting with Stan Jenks who had a limekiln way back from the river quite a ways. This, I finally came to realize was Bacon's army. And they kept trickling in, when word about the doings down in Jamestown got full out. Above all else that Bacon did, or could ever be accused of, he was receiving more allegiance than what real soldiers brought. Throughout the heated conversations of that long and steaming day, the constant drifters, the displaced searchers, and the planters with growing families to support had one thing clearly in common. Nathaniel Bacon was their binding source.

He emerged several times, throwing open the Assembly doors, to deliver reports about his progress, or to warn us of an unacceptable compromise. The men in response crowded in the passageway, hooting and hissing each item with glee.

(Most were bills that were already passed, but what with Jamestown being occupied, they had to be reviewed, *again*.) The loudest bullies had an easy time of voicing their feelings in regards to these new laws. They shouted down every one of them, save the right to go and kill Indians.

Nathan made a great sport of it. A chorus of drunken and vulgar obscenities flooded through the air to show when he'd had enough of political discourse. His very gesture towards the doors made them something of demonic devices. (At least if you had the floor of the Assembly at the time.) For whenever the debate reached its crucial or most contrary points, Bacon simply turned both the knobs and let in a hailstorm of profanity.

"WE don't need laws!" he bellowed in such an instance. "But the laws that WE deem necessary, at the time when WE SHOULD DEEM THEM!"

For the moment at least, he was fully aware that he was espousing nothing less than anarchy, but that is how it went with him before a crowd. I believe that he had come to draw from them, quite literally, something akin to animal excitement. I'm not precisely sure when this transformation took place; he had become by then so far from the man that I knew, but after a full night of being berated, Berkeley's Council and all of the Assembly finally gave him his due. With sunrise, and one eye closed from exhaustion, while the other stood open in fear, the delegates gave way to his every whim. And I must say that Mr. Lawrence is mistaken about some of the laws he had passed. When the session had finished, councilmen were no longer exempt from paying taxes, and debts could be paid with tobacco leaves. Freedmen were given full rights to vote right alongside of landowners. A decent price was upheld for the carcass of a wolf. In all it proved that the ruling body in Virginia, in the clout of collective wealth, was no match for one of their own that the mob had made vital. And in the end the only man that stood against him was the cloistered and humiliated governor, all alone.

It was getting on noon, and our army was snoring through their thick and aching heads, when the rattle of a horseman's reins startled us awake.

"Eight more murdered in the heart of York River!" A young man cried into the heavy air.

His voice was thin, and he was out of breath when he arrived but *his* were the words that finally wrenched the governor from his belligerence. The York River Settlement was only twenty-three miles from the squabbling occupation that currently governed the streets of Jamestown, and its proximity roused Berkeley to alarm. His bitter pride notwithstanding, he was shocked into taking emergency action, one part of which was signing for Bacon's commission. That coveted power, and his obsessive claim for legitimacy now put him in military command.

I stared down with curious disinterest at the slip of parchment Timothy Gale had put into my hand. There was not much to read. A space left open on a line for the date, the governors' stamp, and another blank spot provided above his impressive seal. Gale instructed me to fill in my name, and write out the rank of a Field Captain. When I looked up to ask him just what this meant, he had already moved off, handing out a stack of such, right through the center of town. I could not keep from scratching my head as I squinted at the official looking scribbles, but evidently I was now Captain Philip Corstair, whether I liked it or not.

I watched Gale weave through the crowd, picking out those of us similarly appointed, struck by the irony that I had just been made a crone to the anti-crone crusader. I smirked, a pointless half turned smile, and stuck the form in my shirt unsigned. Even more startling than the presumption that I was now an officer, was the fact that every *seasoned* colonel commissioned in the militia was to serve under Bacon as well. I remember seeing Mr. Lawrence especially excited by the occasion. He and I, and everyone else knew that 'General' Bacon had never commanded a single sanctioned force, nonetheless our ranks grew, both in officers and mere recruits, 'til the end of the day saw a thousand men swarmed at Jamestown's Gate.

In a twenty-four hour blistering course, Virginia was turned on its head. Our elder governor, utterly abandoned and amazed, did not even tarry to bolster his support. He reportedly drew up and sent the king his resignation, before slipping quietly from town to tend his beloved orchids at Green Spring.

General Bacon at the head of his newly formed *official* army, headed westward for the Falls.

A team of oxen strained to pull an overloaded wagon up the grade on which I stood. I knew what was coming next, but I didn't approach Bacon until the men behind the wagon came into view. A half dozen of these 'volunteers' had to follow the wagon in close to keep it from tipping over the endless ruts and stumps that lay in this so-called road.

"Is Gale operating under your orders?" I asked him.

He had taken a pause to mark our progress and was jawing with a few of his officers. I reined my horse in along his, and together we turned to watch the dazed and tethered men being marched behind the wagon. By my accounting the total of these recruits for the last thirty miles had come to near a hundred.

"It's his county we're protecting." He shot me a look, silent and severe, and geed his horse to move on.

I shook my head. So like Nathan, I thought. One step forward and two steps back. Just after he'd put the wary locals at ease with our presence, his plentiful corps of officers were riding through the country, pressing every man, gun and squealing pig into his service. And Timothy Gale, now prancing with a whip behind this latest batch of pitiful soldiering, was by far the worst.

But, there was no mistaking where the problem truly lay. I looked at Bacon, leaning from his saddle, cajoling and directing the traffic, knowing what little he would do to upset the loyalty of his friends. If this meant pandering to the selfish domains of his men, (with their personal sets of motives) it also meant that he had no traitors. But to my lights, his open-ended selection of officers was reaching the point where soon we'd be a whole army of such. The result of his handing out so many entitlements was undermining respect for his command. Nonetheless, he seemed ready to reward anyone that spoke of their commitment so long as the rugged oaf appeared to agree with him.

A few nights earlier, a woman came screaming into camp, the bottom half of her dress in tatters, and her legs all scraped and puckered with thorns. She demanded that we return her boy. More to the point; her boy, her flour and her sheep. I took the time to look for the lad; like so many of Gale's recruits, purposely spread out in the company, but when I finally found him he was too full of pride to return with her home. I saw that his mother got back equal value for her supplies, (I even threw in a goat for interest,) but needless to say, she was hardly satisfied.

"Who's protectin' tha people from tha people's army?" she hissed.

I thought of Bacon, and his distorted need for keeping the respect of his officers, and I had no answer.

Just the day before, I had words with Gale over my releasing two of his 'volunteers', one of whom was lucky to be alive. Gale had tied them up in an abandoned well while he made a tour of the outlying settlements and one of the poor men got snake bit. He was so convulsed by the time that I reached him I was barely able to bring him around. And only then because I spotted an anti-venom shown to me by a Manioc medicine man. I sent him home when I saw he was going to pull through, only to face the brunt of Gale's temper.

I did not count it for much as Gale had been asserting himself well beyond his station, but the incident represented the strife that was growing under Bacon's command. With so many of his staff wearing the feathers of a chief, disputes about the nature of our mission erupted at most any hour. Typically this was a trifling test of wills and the splitting of hairs for differences sake, but things could also get infused with sudden malice.

Carl and Matthew Nelson were uncle and nephew related, and between them they ran a hundred twenty acres back in Surry County. As an example of the arbitrary logic that Bacon gave to these affairs, he thus concluded that the two could share the command of a hundred and twenty men. The morning that I came upon them, they were refusing to direct their separated crews to the clearing of a forty-foot fallen oak. The tree was plenty thick and dug in at a difficult angle, but the two Nelsons would not agree on the best technique to keep the saw from binding. Later when I returned to the spot, the tree had been untouched, while nephew and uncle were pacing themselves off in a duel. The nephew had accused the uncle of making bad corn liquor, (evidently an egregious offence, at least within this family, although I was certain there was more to the story) and the uncle had demanded immediate satisfaction. Incidents such as these came and went with daily variance, (part of an undisciplined army) but it was the actions like those of Colonel Gale that would most come back to haunt us.

By the time we were finally drawn up at the border, contentiousness and self-interest were at each other's necks and raging in full bloom. One faction wanted us to turn around and take up raiding the wealthiest plantations. Another proposed that we keep moving west until we found a spot to start a country of our own. One contingent, smaller in number but certainly no less committed, said that they were going off to find the Northwest Passage, and those that wanted to get rich and stay rich had better come along.

This is not to say that the driving agenda for hunting down and killing Indians had grown less important, if anything, destroying the enemy wherever they were in this part of the woods was the one coherent theme. But having spent most of our time only engaged in fighting back a solid wall of forest, the immensity of our task was beginning to take shape. Fights and grievances abounded, fueled of course, by the lack of sighting any hostiles, and the inconsistent, gratuitous commands issued by Bacon's officers.

Searching for shadows immersed inside a vapor is not unlike the war we sought. A wisp of smoke through the leaves could be seen and confirmed, and then simply disappear. Excitement over a telling item, a broken arrow shaft, or a swatch of treated deerskin, ended like nothing but a long forgotten hint. Then too, we were in a state of constant false alarms. Word of new attacks, on farms that were now behind us, off a path that we'd only just passed. Deadly gossip that only seemed conspired to taunt us, then spread like a fire to show us up. It is the type of work that would put a strain on the hardest of troops in any sort of war, and so did not take long to unravel our best efforts to keep us moving forward. Well meaning men, sick of hacking at the sea of vegetation, and mindful of their neglected families, began drifting off for home. All the faith that Bacon had placed in his 'good fellow met' approach to his army was reaching a new and lowly ebb.

On an afternoon dense with the heat of July we had stopped to rest in a depression by a shallow tributary. We were still somewhere in Henricus I thought, but just as well could have not. I had just fallen into a hot and hazy doze inside the shade of an acacia tree when a pair of indentured runaways, new to the country had me back wide awake. How they had managed to find us was beyond what I could tell, but just the day before they had stumbled in, needing care while fearing for their arrest. I leaned upon my elbow, watching their heads bob in the willows as they sifted through the pyrite that would surface on most any bank. Pyrite was a folly that fresh immigrants were known to fall for, and could give scoundrels an easy way to cheat them out of their pants. I sat up to watch their lust come aflame in the presence of our New World gold.

"Bleszed Cow Bells! Look at this! Do you think? Really?" The young man's head swung forth on an extraordinary length of neck. Then he got quiet and nervous. I noticed his eyes beginning to shift.

"Could be, could well be," the other one soberly assessed. "But, how'd we clean enough of it ta make its weight in stone? But Gads, look at it!"

It took a full minute for him to absorb the magnitude of the glittering specks, but then his mouth was torn between an urgent need to gush forth, and the reasonable understanding that they should keep this to a hush.

"Naw, but look here!"

The first one was now so excited that his great difficulty was in holding himself still.

"If'n it's like this down here by the water, it must be filtering down from somewhere in there." He shot a quick hand to the thick stand of woods just behind them. "We'll find the big parts in the ground, I'll bet, in there."

He threw his finger up again, but his friend quickly caught it back down. They started to consult in agitated whispers, and backward furtive looks, and I wondered how long it would take before they figured it was safe enough for them to slip inside the trees unnoticed. But before they could complete their secret appointment with wealth, a loud commotion on the opposite side of the creek turned all attention towards Bacon.

"Safe man in!" Each sentry was yelling in turn up the line.

A sweat soaked runner broke into camp, who was immediately conducted to the 'general.' I could not make out the quick exchange of words, but Nathan snatched a note from out of the exhausted man's hand. As he absorbed the message's contents, I watched his face move from cautious introspection to haggard disbelief. Then, turning around and catching the sunlight speckling through the leaves, he seemed amused but with pity.

"The governor," he loudly announced, "has seen fit to challenge us again! While we have set on the hard road of hunting down Virginia's enemies, he has raised an army behind our backs. The good people of Gloucester have taken issue with the recruitment of their men, and have joined forces with Berkeley to defeat us."

He threw a direct glance at Gale, one that was surely not lost among the other men, and all that I could think of was how this report would drive us apart. If the men back in Gloucester had risen against us, then those from that county already pressed into our ranks, would have to endure an impossible task. Not only in a fight to kill their neighbors, but the shame they now faced from the rest of Bacon's men. To me the strongest mark of our army's legitimacy was in the fact that the boys who joined up came from every corner of Virginia.

"Well then, men!" Bacon shouted. This unlooked for and unhappy news suddenly appeared to have cheered and inspired him. "It seems that we must once more postpone our noble efforts, in order to fight a civil war! A war, let everyone know, that I have spent these long months in avoiding!"

There it was at last. The declaration that any thoughtful man most feared. And it slipped from off his tongue as if it were merely mischief. The destiny of this young country was pronounced on a steaming afternoon, on a dribble of a creek, amid the gyp and locust bush, somewhere in the wilderness of North Country. And everyone attending had not even heard it. Even the hardiest of the men with me were bugged to exhaustion and searching for an excuse to go back home.

"Well then," someone behind me mocked, "if we're through killin' Indians, I may as well go weed what's left'ah my corn."

This part of their answer however hardly came as a surprise. Weeks of beating a path to nowhere had wrung the freedom from their oppressive government, and the righteous call for justice right out of anyone's care.

"Let not a one of you stay, if you feel you must go." Bacon exclaimed, seizing the shift in their mood. "And we, your brother Virginians, will do what we must. We will bear all responsibilities, and gladly take this dear sacrifice for you."

He took a long pause, as if to allow the lingering dissenters the chance to consider the judgment that would now be placed upon them. To let it sink in.

"But to all of those who are true to us," he humbly continued. "And to those who remain our *friends*, let them now say so, by putting their name to this oath. Wherein we swear allegiance to our cause and to our king!"

From his saddlebag he produced a previously scripted paper. He then waved it aloft like some fakir at a fair, impressing me as always with his ubiquitous supply of inks and quills. He mounted this arrangement atop a rough-hewn limb that had served as a table for crude attempts at maps, and making sure that he was seen by every discontent, he recorded his name with a flourish. The royal rebel could not have been more perfect. His manipulative skills now played the gambit over every would-be deserter, and grouser playing homesick. Whoever omitted his mark was not only showing his disloyalty to the king, but just as important was forsaking his duty to their nobler Virginian brethren. I could finally appreciate his affection for making so many officers of them. Bacon was getting pretty good at this oath-taking game.

"HE-LP! HELP HERE!" The cries behind me startled the slow forming line away from its business with the paper. The immediacy of a savage attack suddenly made the grappling with politics very small indeed.

"HELP US!"

Bacon left his pledges behind, and running full speed vaulted the dry stream to our right. Each man turned in a stealthy rush, priming his weapon, doubtlessly hoping to score the first kill. We raced through the undergrowth, keen with alarm, breathing fast and shallow, moving in wide counter lengths to trap an apparent ambush. Then in a break between the scraggly branches of a myrtle bush, the flushed and panicked face of the long-necked gold digger suddenly appeared. It jarred me at once for being so unexpected and out of place. Spying him in through the yellowing clusters, his head was entirely disembodied, with his lips perfectly formed into a frozen 'O'.

"PLEASE GOD, HELP!"

I then saw his friend nearby, caught to his waist in a sinkhole, struggling fiercely, and slipping in further, desperate to get free. The long necked youth was up to his chin in dead middle, with his lips locked in the circle that no doubt helped him to breathe. They'd dug their way into quicksand at the spot that they'd determined leaked the gold, then when the bottom shifted beneath them, they were sucked in whole.

"Alright men, throw a line to that man there!" shouted Bacon, striding upon the bank. "And pull on my orders! You!"

he directed the one sunk to his waist, "Grab onto this limb!"

The shouting man quickly complied, and Bacon simply pulled with men in behind him to haul the poor sod out. But the one that was swallowed up deeper was going to be a trick. With his arms locked beneath the thickening mire he had no way to grab hold of the rope. Several tries produced no effect, and the man that was doing the tossing was now trying to hook it round the simpleton's neck.

"Stop that, you fool!" Bacon shouted at the rescuer. "We'll all be hanging shortly without your assistance! Colonel Gale, fetch me my horse!"

Gale was off through the wood and Bacon turned to the survivor, who heaved uncontrollably on his side, with his head to his knees like a fist. The man was so overcome that he starting shooting mud from his ass. "Why are you separated from your unit!?" Bacon demanded. "What in God's name do you think you're doing back in here!?"

"Sir…?" the poor man blubbered.

"Speak!" Nathan watched with impatience as the long necked dolt thrashed about sinking deeper still.

Perhaps the man at Bacon's feet had seen first hand his general's famous bouts of temper, or perhaps he was thinking that even now that he should guard his worthless horde, but since he was not to be forthcoming, I decided that I should step in. I reached down and scraped a sluice of pyrite from off the side of his face and smeared the shining specks out on the back of my hand.

"Gold!? You're looking for gold?!"

Bacon laughed. Derisive and amazed, but with such a burst of spontaneity that it seemed to fill the forest. He then jumped on top his frightened mare as Gale stood by, and holding her steady, he eased her backwards, step by step into the sinking drift. Steadily and ever deeper, she slipped back down, and with gentle tones and whisperings, her tail completely covered, Bacon calmed the growing terror fraught within her eyes. Then just as she was about to bolt, he caught up the boy by his hair, and everyone, myself included, became enraptured by a man so at one with a horse. It was the grandest bit of riding that we had ever seen, when turning, not yet out, he guided her back forward, and grabbed up the youth from beneath of his arms. A silence filled every space in the swamp.

"Behold, the lure of gold!" Bacon shouted.

The pitiful lad slid down the side, at last on solid ground.

"While *I've* a thing far more valuable to offer!" he paraded now, easing down his jumpy mare. "I have for you the gold that will forever keep giving! This rich Virginia soil!" He clenched a handful of it, and squeezed it through his fingers. "This promised land! This New World! But have you courage to take it!? Have you the courage now?!"

"Yes," the boy managed to wheeze. "Yes, thank-you, sir. Yes, thank-you...thank-you...yes... yes..." This he repeated, over and over, delirious, no doubt. I doubted that he knew he was still with us at all.

The entire army crowded in, surrounding him with laughter, until one of the larger men hoisted him up in the air. Others joined in passing the dazed boy along and over their heads. While he, looked about, no less astonished than a living sacrifice, having just been rejected by the gods. At last he was set down at Bacon's table, and then shown the oath that, of course, he could not read. But after no small amount of prompting he took up the pen and marked a slow shaky X upon the page.

Amidst the relief and joy that I and everyone felt for the boy, I couldn't help but wonder if the contract he'd just signed might be the work of the devil. I noticed too, that his Cornish accent was of rustic peasant stock. Surely he knew the way of bogs. Where but in the New World though, were bogs filled up with gold?

The route that Bacon chose to necessitate *this* particular return to Jamestown skirted the outer plantations and passed along the edges of thick woods. From these positions he sent out his more affluent officers, (or those that could actually converse with the local gentry) in order to determine their mood. But the homes, they discovered, were strangely empty. A barren wind, scented with fear seemed to blow, telling of places shuttered up, and the occupants gone into hiding. In all honesty I could not determine if it was the Indians that they feared, or if it was their fear of us.

The one obvious development that had occurred while we were traipsing through unknown parts of the forest was the removal of the cannon from Berkeley's expensive forts. This tactic was meant to make clear that he had returned to his true fighting grit, and put our troops in jitters. Especially those that were worth their salt. For we knew well, if but a small loyal force was mustered to Berkeley's guns that they could cut us down. We surveyed the approach round every hill, half expecting an explosion of mortars, but on reaching a distance west of Berkeley's Green Spring we still had encountered no resistance.

We did however spot Bacon's closest friend and ally, Mr. Giles Bland. He was riding at the head of several dozen of our soldiers with Sir Henry Chicheley following right behind. And there, behind him, grouped in scattered bunches, was Berkeley's Gloucester militia, apparently in the act of deserting. When I recognized the proud Colonel Chicheley, my first thought was that if he, the governor's most loyal defender, was coming to our aide, then this war just might be finished before it started.

"You will be tried and hanged, Mr. Bacon! Along with the filthy mongrels that follow you!" Chicheley shouted.

So went my hopeful observations, and then I noticed his manacled hands.

"That may well be, Colonel," Bacon answered him. "But traitors are determined at the *end* of difficult times. And if I'm to judge the actions of these Gloucester mongrels behind you, you might do well to withhold your ominous forecasts."

"Bacon! Bacon! Bacon!" The deserters started to cheer.

Sir Henry cringed, the clamoring of voices, no doubt an intolerable torture.

"They're leaving Berkeley in droves!" cried Giles Bland.

"True enough, General Bacon," one of the Gloucester men spoke up. "The governor said that he was leading us off to fight the Indians, which is our rightful cause and duty. But when we up and told him that we had no fight with you, the old man broke down in a veil of weeping. Fairly shook with the sobs. Then he fainted right away sir, right atop his horse sir, fainted right away. An unnerving sight it was sir, our governor so pale and gone with crying. Unnerving to me and all of the rest." He added a smile in the direction of his company.

"Where's he fled to then?" Bacon demanded, dismissing the image.

"Accomack," Bland replied.

The peninsula of Accomack was a long ferry ride clear across the Bay. Berkeley had chosen to stand with the friends he could count on in this isolated county.

"Where I am to meet him, and make an alliance against

you," Sir Henry boldly stated. "An alliance of those still loyal to the king!"

"Small wonder!" Bacon shouted over him. The news of Sir William's renewing his activities had clearly provoked his rage. "What does far off Accomack know of bloody murder from the savages!?"

I could not tell if he was angrier about the governor's escape, or the citizens of Accomack for offering him refuge, in any event it was a case of one frustration surely compounded by another. But I wondered, had Bacon actually anticipated taking the governor as his prisoner? Had these events ruined further chances to negotiate? This and other thoughts took off with me at a run until I began to see that what truly got Nathan's goat was near the same as his frustration with the Indians. The more that he was ready the more he could find no definitive fight.

"In any case, *General* Bacon," said Sir Henry. "Whether you keep me from my appointment or not, you will soon find these fields ablaze in civil war. The king's own troops are under sail."

Chicheley made a purposeful shift in his saddle to search our ranks for faces he might know. While I, and everyone else could see that his bluffing had gone purely sad. I knew he was lying, Bacon knew he was lying, and every mongrel in our brigade knew as well. With the two months that it took for an *easy* one-way trip overseas, there was no possible way that the king was already sending troops.

"If that is the case, Sir Henry, then you'll want to be somewhere out of the way," Bacon responded with strained aplomb. Doubtless he entertained the inevitability of Sir Henry's make believe. "Mr. Bland, conduct the hostage to a place of confinement where he can be made to feel safe. Good day, Sir Henry. Gentlemen!" he turned abruptly. "We have our own appointment to make! To the governor's!"

"*Gentlemen.*" Sir Henry repeated, as he was pushed aside. He spat the word from his mouth like a piece of rancid meat.

Giles Bland grabbed at his reins, nearly bumping him from his horse, while Bacon moved his growing army out the opposite way. The firing line of redcoats that was just freshly conjured inside those farm boys' heads was already replaced by the goods that they imagined inside of Berkeley's estate.

Then too, they were heartened by the fact that with each new mile in New Kent came more of Berkeley's deserters. The way they strolled in across the open fields could make you believe that they owned them. Some even arrived as whole units, having crossed a wide swathe of land and picking up their own recruits. (I will say that threatening to set a man's house and crops afire can go a long way as a tool for persuasion.) But Bacon had also gained something new since his encounter with Sir Henry. A quality that could appear subtle, then decidedly more grim and determined. I watched him grow colder after hearing about Berkeley's renewed defensive efforts, and I felt as though he'd been given a view of our final consequence. He harnessed his devil-may-care attitude with his version of military discipline. He made his yeas and nays sudden and final, regardless of how it pleased the men. He started to complain in front of the offending parties for second-guessing his commands. He began sending out patrols, led by his truest friends, to round up whomever he had called a government spy. (This now included anyone that refused to sign his loyalty oaths.) So it seemed to me, that his judgment took on a Pandora's box of fear. As we stood among the fancy plants inside the governor's gardens, two of Berkeley's purebred hounds charged us in attack. A trapper named Tillman took aim and killed both the dogs with one shot.

"Nice shooting." Bacon said, without turning around.

His melancholy laid hold of a firmer grip when we battered down the governor's doors. Although, and I'll be the first to admit it, it was a very eerie feeling to stand in that silent hallway. We walked on detailed carpets in dark and empty rooms, where walls once crowded with parties and golden-framed paintings, were now cast in dusty shadows, covered in linen, deathly still. On a table made exclusively for backgammon sat a candlestick holder and a pear that appeared to be melting but was actually made of wax. Cheesecloth shrouds hung over colorful pictures like that of hunting day, with the riders sporting thick red plumes above their velvet hats. There were portraits of the ancestral fathers that looked like stern faced judges, who wanted you to give an account of yourself. The tapestries and fabrics must have come from halfway round the world to cling about the windows shuttered from all light. A few of the chandeliers and full-length mirrors were carefully placed to protect their fragile glass, but others were propped in hasty piles meandering out on the floor. I found a toy horse with a string that pulled it along moving every separate joint.

But the strikingly abandoned lavishness only served to further darken Bacon's mood. He fell so far into himself that I began to suspect his rebellion had taken him to a turn he'd entirely overlooked. As if what had awaited him here at the governor's beloved Green Spring was suddenly a step too personal. He looked like a man who'd journeyed a hard road to reach a place where he didn't belong.

I, on the other hand, took the opportunity to soak for two straight hours in an upstairs porcelain bath.

Bacon restored his confidence in his usual way by bursting into action. He announced a congress of the country's remaining elite, (attendance being mandatory) and left a few of his staff to sort out the mess of Berkeley's estate. He then headed for the more hospitable quarters of his friend Captain

Otho Thorpe. Nathan had by now developed an impulse that he'd gotten from his brooding over Berkeley into an official imperative. The necessity for building up a navy. He was convinced that by invading the shores of Accomack, and recruiting the core of the governor's support, he could force the old man into abdication. An abdication, he additionally reasoned that the beleaguered Berkeley would be thankful for.

"After all Corstair," he told me as if to solicit my support. "He's wanted to resign, then we should accept it. It is not without precedent. There are precedents galore! For the benefit of the king, Corstair. To benefit the *king*."

It was when he used tones like this that his fear was so apparent. God knows his penchant for action had always been his strongest suit, even while it blinded him to what he left behind, but it was a quality that agitated his natural willfulness and revealed for me anyway, his most fatal flaw. Pretend as he might, but Bacon could never square his ruling class roots with those of the noxious crowd. He lit up like a child at Christmas over the image his gun ships would make, but his truest reason for leaving the governor's Green Spring was so he wouldn't have to see it sacked. On the road to Otho Thorpe's he spoke litanies of what he wanted from his congress, but the nonstop talk was to keep him from his army's greasy hands smeared on the governor's walls. Nor when we arrived did he even let up. The slightest excuse could bring a meeting of his officers at any hour of the day or night. He drafted new laws for a martial command, and made sure he was abreast of the important persons gone and which of them remained. His purposes were valid, but none so strong as forgetting the vandals on whom he fully depended, from fully embracing their parts. Carrying off banisters of carved red teak, roughly splitting shares of Lady Berkeley's wardrobe, or ripping them perhaps, in spite. On the afternoon that he sent me back to check in on the governor's place, I got so affected that I spent the whole day fiddling with the pieces of a broken china doll.

The only thing that slowed the pilfering was when two determined thieves locked hands on a mutual claim. At this point an officer would be called to intervene, and providing that he didn't assume protection of the disputed goods himself, he'd offer a draw of cards, so the official confiscation could proceed. On my one afternoon of inspection, I found a perfectly packed crystal tea service buried outside in a chamber pot. That, and a gold leaf lamp shoved into the timbers of a well.

And Berkeley's plantation was but one of the estates so nakedly plundered. More than a hundred homes of distinction were targeted by roving bands of servants, whose passion for vengeance had overcome their ingrained fears. Still others became disoriented by the abandoned homes, places in some cases where their masters had worked them half to death. I came upon a man and three women that experienced such a fury that they'd set the house and barns ablaze. But when I asked them about it, they fell into a despair of sobbing and wailing hysterics, so concerned were they for the lady that owned them. When I left they were painting their faces with the ashes as they watched the house burn down, "To protect us from the witches," they said. "The witches now abound."

Somehow, when I found Jamie Hardwell digging a pit in a wood far removed, I could not even fake surprise. I was scouting out a spot to build a powder house, and he was heaping dirt beside an artisan's walnut cupboard. The swans and flowers etched into the glass glinted out at me in the bright morning light. A few feet away, as if prepared for a formal evening, were two silver candelabras with their candles still intact.

"Jamie Hardwell," I called. He had worked for me a time before, and I had known him to be an honest man. "Well then, I just can't imagine what we have here."

"What we have here is some buried treasure," Hardwell replied. He stopped shoveling long enough to blow his nose. "An' when this bit of turmoil's over, I mean to come back for it. No matter which side wins."

"And how much do you think the thing'll be worth, stuck rotting in the ground?"

"Maybe, there'll be something left. Which is more than I can say than if I'd left it where it was found. The silver will make it for sure, if I'm ta have a dole of your discretion."

Lacking the will to stand against him, I turned my horse away. Unlike gentleman Bacon, I never felt the need to court their ragged love, but I wasn't going to preach them any moral code either. And as for our rabble leader, with reckless pen and parchment he returned to his more familiar work. That of making words that he was sure would draw attention.

The first was a document he called his People's Declaration, which essentially rejected Berkeley's right to levy taxes, and put Virginia's finances under the control of "common men," in order, he said, "to assure that revenues maintain an innate fairness." I thought it was a pretty nice piece of publicity considering that he was more concerned with drawing up his congressional guest list at the time. There was Beale, Scarsbrook, and Ballard to consider, and Swann, Bray, Jordon, and Smith. Along with a few selected others that had sat on the council with Berkeley. Of the men of means remaining on this side of the Chesapeake, every one of the governor's most trusted allies was summoned. They came in the protection of groups, "the carriage patrols," the common men called them. "And here comes another prime line of rooster" was heard whenever their servants appeared on the road. Some had even been turned around, when caught trying to make a last minute exit across the bay.

But losing one's property for failing to answer assured if nothing else, that Bacon's meeting would have broad appeal.

Thus, he claimed, "The convention was open and fair." By now of course, our general was hardly troubled by the law, and the simple truth was that these men were called to endorse his revolution. This was the purpose for his congress, and in very few words he let them know that things had developed beyond any other care.

When he presented his declaration to William Drummond he signed it right away, as did Mr. Lawrence, who sleeps beside me here. But Bacon saved his most outrageous moment for *after* he'd obtained his supporting signatures. As I stood watch from the hall outside, no one was more stunned than I, when he snatched up the page before the ink was even fixed. To articles that proclaimed his right to office, he scribbled an attachment that called for his right of arms against the governor. *And if need would have it, to defend against His Majesties troops*. I saw the flushed cheeks and furtive eyes of everyone in that room. The collective seizing up of breath, the booming silence behind their burning stares. The unmistakable certainty that they were dealing with a madman.

"But, now that it is over," as Mr. Lawrence himself has stated inside our forgotten cave. "I can say that Bacon was mad all right. The maddest and most popular tyrant the world would never know." And if anyone *did* know, it was our dear Mr. Lawrence. "At that particular meeting," he later told me, "he plucked and bagged the cream of the crop."

The men in that room had already seen Bacon's henchmen haul away different of their neighbors. Everyone had witnessed the night roads come alive with moving things. A floating set of upholstered chairs on the backs of stolen oxen. The moon reflected in a standing mirror atop an awkwardly loaded cart. Once I found a wide oak desk sitting in an open field entirely by itself. But if Nathan had no appetite for controlling his thieving army, he showed exceptional skill at manipulating the esteemed. Every one of the names that he'd tricked onto that document had just signed himself on to a hanging offence. And by now this rebellion had become a British war. I heard the sickened mutter, "there is little choice but in making it succeed." "Nathaniel Bacon was half a lunatic, set off in the wilderness, just like the original Baptist ... " and I am quoting Mr. Lawrence again. "... with just as strong a hankerin' to twist the world's balls."

As always, Bacon looked for action to dissuade encroaching fear, so when he learned that the governor's transport ships could be converted to good use in a war, he ordered Giles Bland and his friend Captain Carver to the Jamestown port to seize them. Seeing a chance to avoid his growing volatility, which is to say avoiding *him,* I volunteered to ride courier with the two that very night. But at this point, Bacon had become too erratic for nearly everyone to be around. Earlier that day, when he received a note that Berkeley had agreed to meet with him at the port of Accomack, Nathan bristled in a huff, and then returned the very same summons to the governor.

"Who does the old fool perceive is in power!?" he shouted in the general direction of the bay.

He gave the governor four days to make an appearance at the Thorpe plantation, to answer for the criminal charges that he continued to pile against him, then, as if to amuse himself while waiting for a meeting that he knew would never come, he took time to sit as judge for one of his tribunals.

A young man named Terrence Minlaw, one of the deserters that we picked up from Berkeley's failed militia, was brought before Bacon having been convicted of being a spy. Minlaw had moved into Lieutenant Fears' encampment along with a dozen other men seeking amnesty, but Minlaw it seemed was always moving about. One day he would be present, and the next he would be gone. No one seemed to know what he did or worse, even who he was. (A very strange condition for this close-knit group of farmers.) In due course, he drew enough attention to be followed, and was seen loading up a skiff of goods under cover of the night. The boat was immediately seized and its cargo unwrapped, but it revealed very little in the way of a conspiracy. I think Lieutenant Fears brought him up before Bacon more to win the general's favor than anything else. But Nathan fairly jumped at the chance to conduct his very first bush trial.

The items put into evidence included a whalebone brush, a comb, and a silver-framed hand mirror wrapped with a scarlet bow. The spy was also in the process of shipping an ornate copy of William Shakespeare's Sonnets, a half dozen bottles of port, and an oversized shaving mug. When I heard about it, I thought Minlaw was simply a bloke that'd been smitten by a stylish woman, possibly one that was married, but I also knew that whatever his reasons for engaging secret commerce, given the country's climate, things could hardly go well.

He confessed to being the nephew of one Abigail Waddleton, a well-to-do dowager who had taken her leave when Berkeley had abandoned the country. Meanwhile Minlaw, newly arrived from England, found the home that he was to stay in had been evacuated. He went on to say that he had no qualms with Bacon or with Berkeley, and had fallen in with the deserters out of ignorance and protection. Mrs. Waddleton had evidently gotten word to him that he should take the crossing over to Accomack as soon as he could slip away, and bring as many of her personal belongings as he could manage. The shaving mug, he said, was a special endearment to the memory of her late husband.

"That's a very good story," Bacon mused. " But certainly you do not expect us to let you run off to Berkeley, given the value to him that you possess. I will however offer, that if any man here will vouch for you..." and this he stated, while casting a searching glance at each of his distinguished guests, "...then I will stay your execution."

Not one of the distinguished guests spoke up.

It was an incident that illuminated, more than anything else, Bacon's way of shaping impressions. The land was rife with deadly threats, many more real than imagined, but Nathan's feinted show of mercy bolstered his popular appeal. Moreover, it set gossips to proclaim his only cause was fighting savages, and that he would never consider taking Christian blood. But I also knew that in this particular company, he very much counted on no one speaking for Terrence Minlaw, and was actually using the poor boy as a test for their allegiance. Just as poignant to this scene was the fact that each of these men was only glad to be leaving the Thorpe Convention, and thought most of hastening back across country, trying to secure his home. Having already been deceived into signing Bacon's treasonable papers, the most they could hope for now was in making the distance between him and themselves as much as was practically possible. From their point of view, these men of position and roosters every one, Bacon was running nothing more than a peasant reign of terror. And something that gave one to wonder, watching Minlaw's fly pocked body still swinging in the birch on the day that I returned.

But I did not come bearing happy news. The undisclosed and primary part of my mission was to verify that Berkeley had been put on a ship bound for England. Before Bland, Carver and I had gone, Nathan told us privately that he was through with the old man's confrontations, and just wanted him out of the way. He reasoned that by the time Sir William made his shameful appearance back in England, we would have made a brand new government, one that Bacon was convinced he could make more appealing to the crown. And to those of us living far outside the realities of court, it even began to make sense. For one, it was common knowledge how much the governor despised the king, a feeling that was mutually endured. But in any case, Bland was sent to facilitate the governor's removal, and I was to confirm it to the men.

The plan was for taking control of a British Captain Evelin's ship that was due to leave for England on an upcoming day that was near. In short, we were to keep it from sailing until we forced the governor to go with it. A ship carrying a handful of Bacon's emissaries, a Mr. Clay, a Mr. Robert Lancaster, and a Mr. Thomas Pindafors, each with valuable connections at court, would then follow on. Bacon was convinced that his volume of signed affidavits, among his many legal documents of grievance would provide the support he needed for forcing Berkeley to resign. Charles would then be free to acknowledge his newly established, "friendlier" Virginia.

At best it was a long chance, but fate turned against us before we'd even begun. By the time we reached the southern shore, Captain Evelin's ship was already underway, loaded, no doubt with inflaming reports of Bacon's insurrection. Giles Bland then seized another ship under a Captain Larrimore, but our best outcome was already underway on the open sea. The governor, we were defiantly told, remained in Accomack, alive and well and was gathering strong support by rallying his loyal friends.

Bacon hissed when I gave him this dispatch and moved swiftly to make up the damage. He ordered that Larrimore's ship to be fitted with the cannon from the Jamestown stockade, and for Bland to prepare for an all out assault. At the head of two hundred cannon and three hundred men, Giles Bland was sure to conquer Accomack.

Then, right in the midst of this tumult, came the assault along the Indian front that brought the fence sitting moneyed loyals down on our side. A large-scale Indian confederacy, said to include "a bloody cauldron" of tribes had attacked the York County settlement at Tindall Point.

"But how can this be?!" Bacon exclaimed, feigning dismay. "The governor has protected that town with a great armored fort! Are the people already so heavily taxed that they will risk death before having to replace Berkeley's expensive munitions?"

He was by then making up any words to fit his design. He and everyone else knew that Berkeley had removed the fort's cannon to defend himself against *us*. But Bacon grabbed every opportunity to make the record show what mortal danger and disregard that Berkeley would leave for the people of Virginia. So much so, that just then, just in the midst of a raging battle fever, I watched him take an unbelievable two hours to edit a script to the king.

"The right tone," he stated seriously, "will win us our most important victories." He sealed it in with yet another stack of evidence, to be shipped to London at once.

Then, winking like a pig in mud, he climbed aboard his horse to lead his war upon the Indians. He had Accomack and Berkeley's loyals nearly in his grasp, he had the heathens killing Christians where they could be hunted at last, and finally, the uproar from the wealthiest class to free them from these evils.

ust like every other Indian hunt that we started out on, this one began with spirits high and a pace that was brisk and hearty. At last our mission was clear. We were off to avenge the destruction caused by a new alliance of savages up the creek from Tindall Fort. But then, as we approached the spot, our confidence seeped right out in the ground. The site of the supposed slaughter was intact, and in function, and apart from a few of the outlying locals, (who took the warnings seriously enough to seek refuge in the fort) I saw no clue of an Indian raid. That being the case, or largely perhaps because of it, Nathan refused to stop for interviews by announcing that we had already wasted enough precious time. (The allowance for his correspondence was evidently delay enough.) We then hastened on to catch the "thieving murderers" before they could escape us past the falls. He pushed us now, at more deliberate speed sure that we could close the gap, but when we arrived at the place the enemy of course went missing.

This time however, Bacon stalked this familiar frustration by remaining remarkably composed. He stood out in relief from his normally vile temper, as if he'd practiced what calmer state could prove more effective for him. The most persuasive point being I think that another heated tromp through the forest had lost its fervent appeal. And too, he was by now so embroiled in his political intrigues that he grew fearful with his back turned on Jamestown for overly long. In any case, with no chance for an immediate victory to bolster his public support, he shifted his priorities decidedly.

The foot of James Falls, for all intents and purpose, became his political headquarters. First, he sent out a call for a broader based Assembly to convene in a short month's time, and then he concocted yet another oath of allegiance that every person of property had to sign. This formidable task (daunting in logistics alone) was assigned to Colonel Washington, whom Bacon perceived as working his loyalties on both sides of the fence. And though Nathan had a knack for exposing his weaker links, Washington I think, surprised him. He and his men traversed the great distances in record amounts of time presenting Bacon with a list of those that could be trusted. The names of those refusing to sign, he immediately had arrested.

Three weeks had passed with the men growing foul and restless, when Colonel Brent showed up with a large fighting force that he had himself recruited. "I have seen no Indians," he reported in disgust. "Not a single sign of them."

Brent's attitude was defiant to the point of accusation, and the strength of his impertinence raised questions on the truth of the recent attacks. But Bacon moved quickly to stifle any discord by striking up one of his fire breathing speeches, which ended with merging our armies into one, and driving a sharp course to the north. Into a place where we *knew* we'd find Indians. The home of the peaceful Pawmunkeys.

"Dare anyone think that the heathen is our friend?" Bacon demanded. "It is precisely because of his peaceful charade, where we have trusted close contact, that we are in the greatest danger! They know our habits and where we keep our stores. They do commerce with our forts and defenses! They even sit in the pews where we pray! Has anyone not seen their *advantage*?!"

No one had a mind to protest. With weeks of weakening purpose, and the gnat gnawing boredom in preparing for nothing, the men were desperate for a fight. The last thing on anyone's mind was pointing out the contradictions to Bacon's amended views. But simply translated, our general, the man in charge of Virginia's militia had made it official; it was now a countryman's duty to kill any Indian you encountered. Those you'd called your friends were hereby put on notice; their lives were worth the delusion of peace.

He then forced a march, slogging through the outer extremes of the York River plantations until we came literally stuck in the mud. The rains of spring that had been holding out all summer descended upon us with a vengeance. Day after dreary day the sky acted as though it was turning inside out, and the very earth on which we stood become liquid. We were enclosed in walls of air filled with water, falling in cold thick sheets. Time came and went completely devoid of sunshine, and the men sat about under dripping covers, peeling layers of skin from off their ruined feet. Some lay for hours on end, unmoved by muddy holes, thinking no doubt of the crops they'd left back home and the roots that were rotting inside their washed out fields. After a full week of this, never once ceasing, and with the end of our slim rations in sight, the men began to pack. They worked as if it were a mutiny in silence, but each was preparing for a long walk home.

Bacon responded by taking the offensive. He called an emergency meeting, and by gambling his reputation on their past devotion alone, he accosted them from under his dripping tarp. He condemned those in the act of deserting as heartless and unworthy cowards, and the selfish disservice they were dealing their fellow soldiers and friends. Eating a share of food, he said pointedly, amounted to stealing it from the mouths of true men. Finally, after an hour or so of soaking in this tirade, they returned to their allotted spots and re-pitched their pitiful tents. They still grumbled of course, but the force of his words, as he'd predicted, had them coming back, even if slouched in brooding silence. Only a conjurer like Bacon, I thought, could take an empty belly and make it a badge of honor.

"Anyone," he said, his voice cutting through the dripping gloom, "who thinks more about his hunger than protecting his neighbors, is someone that does not belong in this army."

And except for three determined holdouts, each with a wife and baby left alone at home, he had them all back in the fold. This successful result however provoked him to no sympathy. He promptly led the three away from camp, loudly calling them deserters, and after taking their guns he sent them off in the sludge without so much as a blanket.

Then, as if it were but a paring of the weak by another test withstood and suffered, the sun broke through the very next day into a warming welcome. Now, he got instantly crazed about wasting more time. We lit out early picking up the pieces of some paltry trails, which eventually widened and led us to encounter our first Indians. Ten men were sent ahead to scout, and quickly engaged in hostile fire, but by the time the army had come up behind, the Pawmunkeys had simply vanished. Every blind turn in the channels led to nothing but more silt and mud, with some of the streams in the heavy rains now clear above our heads. We soon found ourselves trapped in a maze of swamp, with no clear passage out, and no sign of where to follow. Inside the clinging forest we could hear warning yells and the isolated musket shot, but we ended each time by merely spinning round on our horses. Sure of an ambush, Bacon commanded squads of men out towards every shout, only to have them calling back with no clear sighting. After a mad and confusing hour, and a great many more false starts, the scouts began to gravitate from out of the woods and back in towards our center. Most remarkably, not one of the stragglers reported an encounter, and not a single seen Indian was substantially claimed. Finally, after sweating in the mud for yet another hour, a corporal named Kinston appeared, wading his way back to us, carrying the body of a squaw. Another man followed close behind him, prodding his musket barrel at the back of a captured girl. All that we accomplished could be safely summed up as; General Bacon was fit to be tied.

"Where is your Queen," he demanded that I ask her.

With a nervous thrust of her hand, she pointed to a cleverly hidden break in the brush. We rushed through the opening, and found an empty settlement not fifty feet from where we'd just stood. There the Pawmunkeys had left us a solid ration of salted meat, and a stash of potatoes and corn. The men attacked this unexpected bounty grunting like a band of wild pigs, while Bacon cast a cautious eye, not attempting to stop them.

"Pwe stama ke," the girl stuttered. "Nito te em, kitasamitin ohcitaw. Wa piski-wiya."

"She says that her people only want peace."

She was very young to be speaking for her tribe, but I know that her Queen would not chance one of her warriors. The little girl did her best to control her growing panic, all while tossing nervous glances towards the trees in the opposite growth.

"Where is your Queen?!" Bacon again demanded.

I questioned her once more.

"Kiwa pamikowa wak," she responded.

"They see us," she says. "They see us."

"What is she looking at?!" Bacon suddenly yelled, whisking the fearful child along on her knees. "Some kind of trap!?"

The men huddled at the food broke off and fell in behind him as he dragged the girl to the edge of the camp. She did not resist or try to run away, even as Bacon stopped to trample every piece of pottery in his path, and stomp through the bushes breaking them off in sharp points. Then, an older woman's scream pierced the air. Next there came a violent struggle, men shouting curses in the brush, but within a few seconds two of our militia emerged pulling an old woman by the hair. She bit wildly at their hands as they dragged her through the clearing, where they finally hurled her down at Bacon's feet. Nathan responded by jerking himself back and planting a boot hard into her stomach. I got in between just as quickly as I could to see what I could salvage.

"Where are your people hiding?" I asked. "Where is your Queen?"

At first she would not answer, preferring to lie on the ground and moan, but when one of the men threatened to crush her skull with a hatchet she brought herself back up.

"Maskihki wiskew!" she said. "O te kisiwa kiwiw siwe. Matokahp, wapiski-wiya. Mana tisihta no sisim!"

"She's the Queen's nurse," I reported. "She says she returned to find the camp abandoned. Everyone ran away. She also says that she will show us the hidden places if we will spare her grandchild."

"Very well." Bacon said, moving off at once. He turned to shout his orders, as the old woman was hauled to her feet. "Colonel Gale, head up a detail to store away this food. Everyone else, fall in. We move while the enemy is still about!" He then led the old woman to the head of the column, making sure to keep the petrified child well within her view. "If she lies, the girl dies," he instructed me to tell her.

For the rest of the day she led us southwest, quite opposite of the way we had come but I was convinced of the old woman's concern for the girl. "Kisiwa, kiwi wey." "It is near; they are near," she kept repeating, as we entered and then passed another empty campsite. "Kisiwa, kiwi wey," she said, "Kisiwa, kiwi."

In the face of our growing apprehension, she showed us fire pits that still smoldered, with half-plucked chickens and unfinished meals. Signs strong enough to keep us moving even when the sunlight ceased to be of help. Then when it simply got too dark, Bacon called a begrudging halt.

The evening never settled; it shook as though ready to explode. The air got so thick with the need for violence, that it finally found release in teasing the little girl. She was tied to a tree in plain sight of the old woman, and a rowdy line began to form. And then, while egging each other on, the men took blind and reckless swings with a heavy sword. The taunting dares, the deadly tries at tripping each other up, drove each man ever closer to the one whose lack of skill would leave her body crushed. Yet somehow the more frightening turns their performance took, the calmer the girl withstood it. To look in her eyes made it seem as though she wasn't there. In fact, she stood so completely steady, so at odds with their wild heaving hacks, that it was the first time that day she seemed to be free of her terror. She altered her far off gaze by dropping her eyes only once, when the blade was sunk in the tree a quarter inch from her head. The watching old woman restrained herself as well, but had she the power to induce it she would have burned holes into Bacon's chest. Finally, as if tired of the amusement he stopped the last fool when he sliced open the little girl's smock.

But there was no question that by noon the next day, the old woman's trail had turned cold. Gone were the freshly broken branches of locust bush, and the occasional stamp of moccasin prints in the mud. As the morning wore upon us and with our pursuit getting more desperate, we got tangled up in vines so dense we could hardly turn around. The final way she pointed was to a mosquito nest inside a dead end sump. "Kisiwa, kiwi we." "They are near," the old woman said. "Kisiwa, kiwi."

Bacon was trembling with rage. First he had to admit to the men she had only gotten us lost, and then he ordered me to turn the lead around. I was glad for the job, grabbing at the chance to get out of his way, then, no sooner had I started than I heard the chilling thwap that cut the brackish air. Turning round, I saw the old woman's head, lying on its side in the bushes, looking as lost as us in fact, staring up perplexed from the bloody mire.

For reasons that I could not answer, Bacon allowed the girl to live, but he made it very clear that he wanted nothing more to do with her. I brought her up front alongside of me, where I saw her grandmother's death taking a profound effect. A listlessness came over her, as though draining her frightened spirit from out its excited shell. What was especially unsettling was that I actually observed her lose her physical youth. The sheer madness of the forest (a state which I fully accept) seemed to take hold of her body, and at times put her grandmother's face in the place of her own. But in spite of this phenomenon I perceived, I had to use her fearful aspect if I stood a chance of getting us out free. I scanned the hanging roots that would just as soon smother us, and studied the signs in her remarkable face. I searched for her to hint at anything familiar, all while praying this ancient little girl wouldn't leave me cold.

Bacon trudged on in determined silence that seemed to embody the company's despair. We marked another day, ending without progress, where even the heat at night lay upon us like a blanket. This was I think, the worst of it. The nights haunted with confusion about where we were and what we were doing. Our supplies all run out, the water tasting filthy. And pressing Bacon just as much as this was the date's fast approaching Assembly. The occasion whereby he'd sworn his triumphant return.

Briefly, we became heartened by the appearance of a road on solid ground but which only brought another abandoned camp. Here, he paced in a restless circle, stopping now and then to pick off the mud drying at his heels, until he

summoned Colonel Brent into a conference. A weary looking
Brent came forth, slumping like a mere recruit, and in a
mumbled exchange, they finally decided it was best that they
should separate. Brent was to return to the towns, give news
of our struggle by playing up as best he could what little we'd
achieved, while we of Nathan's original corps continued in the
hunt. Bacon affirmed that we would follow once the mission
was accomplished; a victory he assured within a fortnight. The
only thing about the arrangement that struck me for sure, as
I watched Brent turn his men on the homebound trek back
eastward, was being filled with envy. And I was the man with
nowhere else to be.

Bacon responded to our anguish with a speech.

Whatever forces conspired to make a man like Bacon,
I could not hope to know. I only know that his grip upon some
zealot's faith, be it of the devil or a saint, was no trifling affair.
Looking hard into the faces of starvation and dismay, he stated
calmly that he would need to divide our army further in order
for the rest to survive. And then, as if to flaunt the hopelessness
of our condition, he asked for volunteers to leave. His own
remarkable words in fact, *volunteers. To leave.*

"Attend to your families," he beseeched us. "There
will be no more than quarter rations for those that stay." Then
he turned away as if the choice of life over death for us was
a mulling matter. "Of course, I'd rather my carcass decay in
these woods, and never see an Englishman's face in Virginia,"
he added, "than miss doing that service my country expects."

His finesse with the stab of guilt, in his hands, was
with understated ease.

The men were more than tired. Tired of swamp life,
tired of marching, tired of sitting in the mud. Tired of hunger,
tired of being eaten by the fungus and the bugs. Tired of
Bacon's speechifying too. But mostly they were tired of being
tired, and fighting through a truly fatal exhaustion every time

they had to move. And yet they were stirred.

It is a type of contagion perhaps, that makes one endure because of his neighbor. Because you know right down to your painful bony feet that his suffering is no less than yours. And because he'd just vowed in a dumb vacant stare that he would go on if you would. This is a moment when you might glance up along the rows of bloody boots, but you're actually just passing the challenge along. And this is how it goes. Up and down a muddy path, stiffening, man to man.

"I vowed to perform against these heathen," Bacon went on, his voice becoming soft with emotion. "My adversaries insult, saying that my defense of this country is but pretended and not real. That I have other designs. But all shall see how devoted I am to this great charge the country has fit for me, and the hopes and expectations that they have. You gentlemen that are left must resolve to undergo all the hardships this wild can offer. All its dangers and success. If need be, we'll eat acorns and horseflesh before we return. But this is the resolve that I have taken, and I desire none but those who freely stay. For the others, who will now return, we will separate our camp. So that those who will go on with me can stand apart, without judgment, for those who must be bound for home."

It did not take a seasoned pioneer to see that we should *all* turn back. But Bacon had just maneuvered us the opposite of what a blind man could see with his gut. And what is more, he accomplished this with a calm deliberation. He put forth his case in a mood that wasn't a whit of what he felt. Every weary ear could hear it underneath him though. His all-consuming rage. It was boiling in the taunts of an invisible enemy and when he walked away he seethed so much it hissed. Some of men were simply too afraid of him now to show him their weakness. Or else just plain too sick to leave.

Then, the next morning a determined contingent, larger than I would have thought, spread their whispered grumblings until they felt safe about separating off. I stayed, not just because I didn't know where I would go, but I also believed that we should abandon as a whole or not.

In any case, I resolved to make sure that Nathan understood my next priority would be to concentrate my hunting skills on fetching game instead of Indians. So I went to him at once and presumed to point out the obvious; that our food supply would not last out the week. His response was less than appreciative. (Standing in view of half his army eagerly heading home.) He took the same patronizing tone that he'd taken with me when I doubted him at Occaneechee.

"We do what we can, " he dully said.

I turned away to look for someone I could trust to go foraging, but he turned me back by my shoulder.

"Why don't you go look after the girl?"

He made it sound offhanded but I knew that he meant it as an order. More than this, he seemed to be issuing a challenge, as if daring to make an example of me if there was any further subversion to his plans. I shrugged and walked away, wondering how I could keep an eye on our little captive, and bag us some dinner at the same time.

I found the girl chained to a rock in a puddle of mud, hardly acting like a child lost in a void. In fact she was in the midst of such bizarre behavior, that it struck me to my steps and made me observe. She was completely caked in filth and surrounded by a cloud of mosquitoes. I watched in a terrible kind of awe, as she repeatedly skimmed the wet scum from off the surface where she sat, and raised the foul drippings to her lips. The bugs were so dense that they covered her face, which made her alternately delighted and serious. She then sucked the vile liquid into her mouth and blowing gently out, released, to my disbelieving eyes, a plume of the rancid insects into full flight. She accompanied this repulsive act with a shrill of such high pitch that it gave an imitation of their whine.

Then, she *repeated* the abhorrent process. I had seen enough. Stifling my confusion, I rushed her, freed her from the chain, and yanked the child up out of the mud. I shook her violently, shouting to restore her senses, but she barely took my notice. I slapped the sticky film from off her face, and she let me carry her off quite easily. I then doused her head with cold water from my canteen and rushed her to the nearest fire. Grabbing up the largest pot, I removed her filthy leathers, and set about the work of a thorough scrub.

There is no doubt that we presented a curious picture. Men I'd hardly seen, and never thought of speaking to, broke for our camp to offer up their comments. Others simply stood and leered.

"Waste a' time, Corstair. Might as well clean dirt."

"Ought ta let her grow some part a' teats first, dontcha think, Corstair?"

"The man's no fool. He know she ain't gonna live 'at long."

Soon enough though, while I fashioned her a tunic from a worn and discarded blanket, the men moved off to join the new day's march. Bacon said nothing about my preoccupations. He leveled a look in my direction then quickly wheeled his horse about and bounded off. But there was also the fact that he had very little choice in the matter. Mosquitoes had so infested the air about him that he had to keep swatting them back, even as they chased his galloping horse. I pulled the shawl over the little girl and strapped her to the back of my saddle, sensing once again that she was hardly there.

As the day unfolded however, it decided to bring us a turn of luck. Before noon, we surprised an occupied camp, a group of Pawmunkey families that panicked as soon as they saw us. I watched them scattering in every direction, some so confused that they came directly at us, and picked out a squaw that ran a clearly determined course. I signaled to Bacon that she was the one that would take us to our enemy, and without thinking or caring what the girl might decide to do next I tied her to a clump of flimsy reeds.

At the end of an hour, after we'd tracked the ones that had nearly escaped, the Pawmunkeys came out, hands held high in surrender. At last. The final operation was so unreasonably easy that after weeks of lost and futile tramping, the men more than ever felt cheated of a sporting fight. There were a few that I stopped from taking a pointless murdering shot. In the end we had corralled forty-five prisoners, and collected several weeks worth of provisions. Aside from potatoes and a dozen pigs, there were twenty bolts of English linen, and a load of bundled fur. After such a hard earned bitter victory, it took a little time for Bacon to regain his generous mood. "We may as well have been playing with children," he finally said, shaking his head.

That evening's meal was the first in longer than we could remember where enough to eat was guaranteed each man. A remarkable fact given that of the thousand we started out with, a ragged one hundred and thirty six remained. But then, with all the shouting jug dancing echoing through the woods, we must have sounded like a legion of May Day troubadours. Until that is, the appearance of Timothy Gale. He approached Bacon like an undertaker, draining the spirit from men right there on the spot. Sometimes beside him, and sometimes staggering behind, was an exhausted sentry that we'd stationed on an abandoned plantation some forty miles back. He'd made his way into the heart of this wilderness to let Bacon know that his best friends Bland and Carver had been captured while preparing their attack on Accomack. And sadly, there was more. Governor Berkeley was now in command of six hundred loyal troops from the Accomack peninsula that had retaken Jamestown. "And," the sentry went on, as if making an aside, "the governor has revoked General Bacon's commission by calling it extortion of the lowest form."

With his victory over the Pawmunkeys, Bacon's confidence was restored. He'd already planned the show he would put on before the ruling faithless in order to gain their support. But in that moment, in the face of the disasters heaped upon him in that anonymous swamp, (and it must be added before his true and loyal men that couldn't have cared less) Nathan threw a tantrum over the loss of his commission. He called the celebration to an immediate halt and dismissed the cavorting by cursing up a regular firestorm. Nor could Colonel Gale force him to pause. When he reminded Nathan of how Brent and Carver were at that moment sitting inside of Berkeley's prison, Bacon never left off with his screaming. When Gale then suggested that his attention should be drawn to the army that had taken over Jamestown, and the importance of the upcoming Assembly, "Where's his bloody right for rescinding my commission!?" Nathan yelled. "Extortion! *This* is what he has to tell the king?! Extortion!? Our *governor*," he kept repeating to the stricken sentry, "is a man that has completely forsaken *his* legitimacy!"

Everyone hearing the whole horrid list of these reports could think of no smaller item than the dispute over Nathan's title, but its sudden removal burned into him like an infesting claw. Men shifted anxiously about his tent, confused and shocked by the extent of his rage, and acted embarrassed by the revelers who continued to make yips out on the camp's southern fringe. And then came the shift. The softening of the angles in the face, the eyes peering down but really in, as if he suddenly saw the confrontation in some new light where he could end it. It was Bacon on the State House lawn facing off with Berkeley once again. The same confidence borne of compassion seemed to steer him now. But Governor Berkeley was a hundred miles away, with his army in position and Bacon's vital allies in his jail. Nonetheless, he made no attempt to share his revelation; it just came, straight out of the night, and he was once again content to be triumphant. But it was enough of a turn to have Timothy Gale watch with concern. His other close aides were also standing still. Watching them, watching him made me wonder if the wheels in his head had finally relaxed their grip on him for good. If the pressures that he made upon himself, and the circumstance he welcomed had defeated him at last, releasing all his proud obsessions.

I watched as he reached out his hand to everyone that surrounded him, offering each a warm embrace. He spoke only of gratitude now, and asked that God be with each one in a whispered prayerful wish. The hawing in the distant background bellowed loud, then soft laughter, and then it ceased. We would hear no more debate over the matters of state that night he said, but his silhouette could be seen very late, sitting upright in his tent.

I stopped back by the reeds to see if by some small chance the girl that I had left was still there. To my amazement there she stood, in the pitch of darkness, studying the structure of a miniature leaf that she held in her tiny bound hands.

"Have you ever seen a caterpillar fly?" she asked me.

It took time to absorb the full weight of my shock. It was not just that she had spoken to me, but that her English was so perfect, and quiet. Then she showed me an outer portion of the blanket that I had made for her to wear.

"Yes," I finally replied.

"They eat the white man's cloth," she said. "Not the skins we make of leather."

"Where is your Queen?" I asked.

She wrinkled her brow, as though reeling in a far off thought. "She told us not to shoot the English."

"Where is she?"

She turned to look out at the shapeless night. "She is alone," the little girl said. And again after thinking for a moment. "She is all alone."

s Mr. Lawrence and myself are so painfully dependent upon Seycondeh's visits, her protracted disappearance has become most deeply troubling. Finally, there is nothing more than I can make of it but the necessity for our escape. And though I have no plan, nor any thoughts of suggesting it to the weakened Mr. Lawrence, I have been thinking on little else. Then today, when I was just about to slip from out our cave in order to scout the best route, she suddenly returned, acting as if her absence had not even occurred.

It is rewarding for me to see Mr. Lawrence excited again. His health has so deteriorated that I watch Seycondeh hide her concern, and watch him too, following her every move with the eyes of a little boy. On the other hand she does not stand for his fawning. She bends to inspect the state of disrepair that has overtaken our abode with scornful clicks of her tongue. I immediately ask why she was away, hoping to learn of changes in our status, but I'm mostly interested in the hostile strangers that I encountered a few days ago.

"Men make decisions between themselves, and bray like a mule that's been hit in the head," she replies in her now familiar dialect. Then she reaches into her robe to hand us parcels of food.

I note the smaller size of the portions, and deliberate on its possible meaning. I believe that she has stolen this food, and although I do not mention it, it indicates a new danger. It also means that she's willing to help us on the sly. She demands that I stop staring and eat, and then, as if providing a cover for her visit, she collects the bat guano from its thickest patch on the floor.

Our cave has become a refuge for a small colony of bats. I am quite sure that this is only a seasonal situation, and they do no more harm than defecate beneath their ceiling space. Mr. Lawrence has grown especially fond of their company. They can sound like a rotunda of distressed lawyers when they get upset, but they mostly just squeak softly or else whistle when they snore. Mr. Lawrence has given his favorite ones names. There is Denis, The Duke of the Pilfered Toehold, and Nigel of the Noblesse Oblige. I have come to believe that he does this in order to keep me from skinning the little rascals for a morsel of dinner than for anything else.

I watch Seycondeh hesitate at the entrance as she prepares to take her exit. She gently touches Mr. Lawrence's brow before giving him the last of her dried meat. His gaze shifts from her ever so slightly, as he struggles with his denying the fact that he may never see her again.

"Meskanaw tapwe mahohte we," I whisper.

She glances past me towards the distant valley and winces in a way to indicate great difficulty. "Ayiman, niso tipiskaw." She mumbles, and is gone.

"What did she say?" Mr. Lawrence asks, but then pretends to be completely absorbed in his meal. I watch him chew slowly, taking his time to relish every bite. The bit of smoked fish, he leaves until last.

Over the course of the past weeks, Mr. Lawrence has become more and more like a child. Subjects that do not force themselves directly upon him, fly straight from his mind. He can even forget that he needs to make his toilet. The other side of this dementia is that he most certainly could not be happier than he appears right now. Chewing to examine each taste with no more cares about tomorrow than our backroom full of sleeping bats.

"She says she will return in two nights." I tell him half.

I watch her slipping down the pathway beneath our entrance, and suddenly wonder if she's been commanded to keep us weak on purpose, or otherwise too weary for escape. This thought lingers and vexes, until curiously, I see her pause to pick up and throw a stone down a line of trees that crowd a gully to the right. It angles sharply and lands in a dry creek bed concealed behind a thicket of fern. I carefully fix the location, as it flickers in the shadowy light, and no sooner have I turned back to find her, than she disappears. From out of the west, I see that a wall of clouds is rolling in, billowing into dense dark layers, high above the creek where Seycondeh's stone still lies. Soon it will storm enough to make a rushing stream.

"Drummond and I had to run," Mr. Lawrence suddenly says from behind me.

I shift back around and see him sitting on his knees in the attitude of Catholic confession. But the look in his eyes lets me know that his wits have returned his sense of outrage.

"The old man promised everyone a pardon except for me and William Drummond. And Drummond, he merely called a traitor. I, on the other hand was the very devil. He named no one else in the entire rebellion that he was going to hang. Besides our Mr. Bacon, of course. Berkeley was even ready to deal with Bland and Carver. The very bunglers that were sent to make his capture. No. What he wanted to show was that *mine* was the most unforgivable treason. And while Bacon was traipsing the woods on another silly Indian hunt, *there* was Berkeley. On the river with sixteen ships and six hundred men. The lack of warning, his sudden grip upon Jamestown threw everyone into confusion. Just like that it was all or nothing, with no one knowing which horse to back. Berkeley, the elder, the corrupted *fixture*, or the fiery young

Bacon who didn't know a turn gone wrong from right. Hell, the only thing that was certain was the noose that Berkeley dangled for both Drummond and me. Where were the town's rabble then!? Goddam them! Damn right we ran!"

I settle back, happy for the chance that he's giving me to listen. His apparent confession however sounds an awful lot like venting more of his phlegm.

"You never told me, " I interrupt, "how Berkeley came to hate you so."

There is nothing that can restore the spirit like a bowl of everyday food. I watch Mr. Lawrence reveal his slyest smile. It's an expression that I haven't seen for quite some time.

"Maybe the governor was buying all of the Indian's fur," he says almost in a whisper, "but I was buying all their land."

And thus, comes the confession at last. In direct defiance of Berkeley's strictest orders, Mr. Lawrence was in the business of buying up the Indian frontier.

"I treated them fairly," he goes on, "in as much as a savage can know of such things. It's the squatters that followed that caused all the trouble. But what choice did they have? The governor had a grip on Virginia with nowhere for freedmen to go."

"Then why stick your neck out for Bacon?" I asked. "If you held as much land as Berkeley, you could set the policies you want."

"I never held so much as Berkeley!" he starts with a shout and then catches himself up short, as if even now he might reveal too much. I simply sit and stare at him, sharing this dirt floor, in this end of the world place, amazed by the power that seeks to serve oneself.

"I did it to save Virginia," he continues, a bit more wary now. "I could not deal with Berkeley! I competed with him for Christ sake! So. I dealt my cards with Bacon. Do you understand? I was one of the final buffers, trying to take care of a system at its end. Indentures coming free would have nothing if it weren't for me. You know fully well what Berkeley's solution was. Resigning Virginia's future to the African slaves. He actually thought he could protect his friends the Indians by halting the indentures from coming. Importing black labor with no chance of being free."

I have spent many hard hours thinking on these things, but here and now I force the thought away. Knowing what I do of forced indentured labor, I have come to see what he says as the most hideous of unstable propositions. "How in the world could you have let Bacon run off, scavenging for Indian blood, while you were dealing with them behind his back?" At the same time the depth of my passion surprises me. I have never before made him such a verbal attack, but the knowledge of his business makes me feel that what we sacrificed was naught.

"Let him?!" Mr. Lawrence fires back. "I never let him do a damn thing. Nor was I operating behind his back. Nathaniel Bacon always did what *he* wanted, what he thought the backwoods wanted, even if didn't make a lick of sense. I had nothing to do with his murdering Indians. And I had nothing to do with the kind of land swappers who created more problems. Cheating the Indians, who, as you well know always came back to reclaim their land."

"And reform? New law? New government? These things that you spouted meant nothing? Are you a double life, Mr. Lawrence? Or has your memory become feeble as your health?"

I cannot explain the misery that's come over me. I am heated and in shock. And I'm also immediately sorry. He glares at me. And then I receive his patent, indulgent smile.

"I may *be* feeble. But I want you to know that I dealt benevolently with many a hapless freed man. But reform Corstair, is only worth the economy it's made of. The truth can be hard. When I watched Bacon in Jamestown, giving sway to his mob, forsaking *all law*, these things were never discussed. He was ensnared by his newfound power and position. By his shining hour. The only law that he was proposing was the law of the anarchist. And such, he showed himself just as he was. An unformed youth, mistaking the crowd's loyalty for what was common lust. Ask your vandals and looters. See if they won't bear me out."

I am disarmed by his quiet meaning, shamed and without speech. Mr. Lawrence, for the moment, looks away.

"Now, Mr. Corstair. That is all. You have tired me. Still." He looks back. "You are my savior and my friend. And for that I am eternally grateful, which as we both well know, will be visiting very soon." He takes a minute and bows his head; I can see he's authentically sorry. "But before I am sent to… where? …the everlasting? And knowing of your personal tragedies as I do, I promise there is more that I'll reveal to you. But for now I will simply bid you to your corner to leave me to some peace."

And just like an aging English regent, no longer able to suffer the fool, he brushes the air before him, and I bow off, almost in a slink. My stiffening joints lend weight to my anxious discomfort. The rain outside arrives in a torrent.

* * * * *

One thing that I mean to tell Mr. Lawrence, when he's willing to speak to me again, is that mob love and anarchy was something that Bacon dealt with harshly on our final Jamestown march. Straggling along the rustic paths, we ran near several bands of highwaymen demanding tolls for the use of 'their' roads, if such they could be called, but whenever Bacon heard of such, whether up ahead or far behind, he halted all progress until they were hunted down and dealt a defenseless justice.

In some cases this meant shooting them in their sleep. It was a heated response that placed yet another piece of the puzzling mix of the man as a whole. Was he turning on the backwoods families now? Was he laying down the hateful law? But sitting tall on his horse, and barking out these local rapid judgments, no one questioned that he was in command.

Then while consolidating the appeal of his success over the Indians, I also took notice of his changing impulse. He became more aware of actions he'd heretofore simply carried out by rote. As though suddenly weighing his picture of a more stable future against the *consequence* of what was being done. This was a way of working that I recognized as new. On one such occasion I saw him calculate trampling through someone's bean field (a clear cut shorter way) as though it were a large political question. And as for the staging of our victory march, he could not have done it better. Numbers of men, completely unsummoned, left off their planting to join us, making it seem like whole villages from Gloucester, Henricus to New Kent had turned out. People spat at our openly paraded Pawmunkeys, or jabbed them with sticks like long reaching prods. (If the savages' reactions got too aggressive they were put at once inside a cage.) Eventually though, the tiresome trudging made all of them appropriately sullen, and while none were spared of the rocks and slung mud, neither were they greatly harmed. Oh, we were quite the procession crossing through those rude shack towns, and got ourselves entirely caught up in the praising jeers of the crowd. "Behold our heroes, the demon killers," I heard someone yelling our way.

Having taken on a certain value I protected the little girl from assault. She trod diligently along, bravely bearing up to the anger of strangers, while keeping her eyes fixed on nothing as if trying to will herself dead. Nothing that I offered, neither food nor drink, nor encouraging words could distract her from her silence, until at the halfway point I became so alarmed that I strapped her back on top my saddle. From this new perspective the sight of so many English crowding in around her jolted her into asking what was going on.

"We're going to Jamestown." I told her.

"That is good," she immediately replied.

"What is this to you?" I quickly demanded.

She spoke not to me but gazed out at the numbers gathered round. "It is good for whites to kill whites."

I was set to scold her for her insolence, but Elizabeth Bacon, slowly descending the low sloping hill that lay before us abruptly stole all attention. She was fully dressed in white, riding to one side a chestnut pony, nodding regally beneath her wide brimmed hat. The sun gleamed bright on her polished deerskin boots, and the lilac bouquet she had set upon her reins. She might as well have popped from some enchanted place you heard of as a child. Then, marching directly behind her, like Cleopatra's slaves, came the Africans. The proper Mr. Gibbs; holding fast to a musket, and as grim as I last saw him, led a solid corps of sixty or more blacks. They'd armed themselves with hayforks, hatchets, pikes and swords, and many other assorted tools molded into weapons. Their expressive eyes looked out in anger, and befuddled distress, moving right beside the white indentures equipped with equal motives. (Meaning of course, land of their own and freedom.)

"Mr. Bacon!" A woman was heard above the jubilance. "Let me join your army!"

"Me, too!" shouted another.

Which in turn sparked a chorus of eager female soldiers, or at least the volunteering of such. Elizabeth could not have been more proud, and her eyes brimmed up as full as crystals. Nathan had always received her unqualified adoration, but having this affection so publicly shared made her fairly shake with joy. He took her into his arms, catching a layer of ash upon her perfect dress, as the crowd seemed to hold a collective breath. Cheering then erupted, which went on undiminished for fully twenty minutes or more. Everyone, myself included, was caught up in their embrace. Looking around, I saw the little girl, staring so wild and silent that the light from her eyes produced a sudden chill. I cuffed her hard upon the shoulder, and Bacon began to speak.

"Gentlemen, good friends and fellow soldiers," he began. "How I am transported to find you thus unanimous. Thus bold, and brave, and daring. You have brought us victory before we even fight. Conquest, before we have even done battle. Our enemies lie in places of refuge, afraid to appear in the field before you. But by your show of heart, you invite the whole country where we march."

The crowd took up a festive cheer and whistling, as he directed the prison wagons to the front. "The Indians that we bear with us…"

The heckling grew so fast that it threatened to make him stop, but then he calmed things down a bit by pointing a scolding finger at the chief offending bands.

"… The Indians that we bear with us… are the reasons we are here. They provide our relief from all that intend us harm. See for yourselves! The results of their hostile actions! They have no courage left to fight you!"

The caged Pawmunkeys were slouched in postures of defeat, looking neither up nor out, appearing in fact to be rather sleepy. But without knowing the exact meaning of the English words, they knew well enough the part they were to play. Bacon stood in his stirrups and took a moment to scan the field of his new volunteers.

"Each one of you knows, that you have the prayers and well wishes of all the people of Virginia!"

With the cheering and drumming recommenced, and the officers reforming lines, we made our preparations to push on. But such a large number of soldier-farmers takes its time to move away from families this devoted. The distraction became a tableau. Mothers with sons, young wives with husbands, sisters holding brothers, and a father's final words on the work they were leaving at home. Wagons of supplies, some that were offered and the obviously looted had to be steered into line. There were new folk to meet, trusts to be gauged, and alliances of distance that had to be remade. Until, when the army was truly moving forward again, our number had grown by six hundred. Elizabeth looked wistfully confident, watching us leave like all the rest, but being such an object of envy she was engulfed by adoring wives. I'm quite sure she felt the rapture of a hundred marriageable girls. Even of the mothers, well into their homebound years, and respecting the bravery of their husbands off to fight, knew none could be called so brave as *him*.

Just as much, if it's needed to be said, did this wellspring of love embolden our Mr. Bacon. Even through the constant march, the endless retracing of steps, he strutted about like a cock of the post, and sloughed anything off to do with bad news. When we learned that Berkeley had obtained his quickly formed army by promising them their fill of Jamestown plunder, Nathan did not even act surprised. "And the governor pretends that we are but ruffians and thieves," he replied. And this was his answer *in total*.

This reaction was an example of what he began calling, with no shortage of irony, "allowance for my moral superiors." It was a tact that he occasionally adopted when he felt that the events stacked against him were taking on a shift. The posture cloaked his innermost thinking to be sure, but over his hot dagger anger it was welcome relief. When he was told, for instance, that Berkeley had given the 'good people of Accomack' a twenty-one year deferral of their tax, he simply said, "We shall see what kind of tax they owe."

His close to home worries were the ones he couldn't hide. And the greatest of these were his good friends Carver and Bland. The humiliating defeat of their mission to send the governor back to England ate at his joy of renewal entirely. What's more, he knew how everyone questioned the mystery of their failure behind his back. (Gossip that centered on how such superior forces could be captured so easily.) Bacon even made his weakness transparent when he punished those hinting of betrayal and scandal.

"I understand their failure," Mr. Lawrence, at one time observed to me. "It was a loss of nerve, pure and simple."

The story was that Berkeley's commander, a Captain Larrimore, boarded their ship under some friendly pretense and simply took the two of them prisoner. An action he performed with merely a handful of men. As a maneuver, it was certainly audacious, but more troubling by far was the message that it sent to the men. Of what ingredient was the fidelity of the upper crust? Disposable, forsaken or simply ignored? But as I've said, Bacon tolerated no ill words spoken against Carver or Bland, and set his mind solely on winning their release. Looking back on it now, perhaps it was only Mr. Lawrence that clearly saw the truth in their defeat. "That was the turning point, Corstair," he has said to me before. "The turning point, before we'd even begun. That old fox Berkeley strolled back into the capitol and had everyone behaving like a child. Hoping not to be punished for their misbehaving while the master was away."

Still. By the time we had the rough-hewn walls of Jamestown again within sight, we had met with no resistance. I could see at once that we were in for a siege. And so set my mind as best I could for the inevitable stretching of provisions, and thinking up ways I could escape the summer sun. The woods surrounding Jamestown, as anyone could see, were home to little more than brackish voles and river rats, while we'd arrived with six hundred men to keep fed. I was weary of it already, before I'd even completed the thought. But resigned myself the best I could to the stalemate, by trying to pretend this farm boy army could forget about the crops that they'd left back home.

We formed along a spit of sand that stretched before the gate and to the river, and then ran back into the woods. Bacon anticipated that the cannon mounted atop the city walls would soon be at work against us, so he immediately set to walling up a system of defensive trench. He appointed officers as foremen, and organized the labor into teams. There were diggers, choppers, builders and haulers, with Bacon himself as the conducting engineer. The afternoon air was hot as an oven, and everyone was breathing bugs and sweating buckets, but you could not find a group of men so well acquainted with the work. Speaking for the crew that I was with, no one uttered a single complaint. None of them were soldiers, even in the broadest sense, but they saw well what their general was up to; and Bacon was for keeping them alive. He was happy to join in, providing water for the thirsty, rallying the exhausted, and letting each man know how much he valued his skills. He was ever the champion at this; taking the care to learn the names of each illiterate, and generally acting like some holy preacher sent out to build a mighty church. He took time off to counsel one man who fell into a panic over the family he said he had abandoned by his death. Nathan assured him, while his friends kept dunking him in the river, that we were there to see a peaceful surrender of the fort. And most agreeably, for the first day's worth of the confrontation at least, the governor seemed to be doing his part.

We worked nonstop throughout the day and night, and in the shadow of those deadly arms, not a shot was fired. More than this, Berkeley's ships, with fully loaded cannon on the river, drifted menacingly downstream behind us, only to be rowed passively back. But the darkness made us skittish and could bring our digging to a sudden shushing halt. There, beneath the night in deep dank ground we huddled in a terrible silence, listening for the hiss of powder overhead. But the fire never came. By the second morning we'd dug a network of these ditches, and were entrenched behind a thick wall of trees. Then we mortared each crevice with a mix of sand and clay, and by early afternoon we'd selected our slots and watched the residents of Jamestown venture on the parapets to look back at us. Could hear them in fact, offering differing opinions on the construction right alongside of the pilfering Accomacks. No question but that we made an impression, what with several hundred muskets sticking out from a hundred yard heap of earth and rocks.

Bacon went about testing the strength of his breastworks at once. Before the sap was cleaned from his new pine desk he dispatched six men to challenge any guard that dared to peer over the Jamestown wall. And from the safety of our cover, we were pleased to see it go so well. The men crawled forward, edging slowly up beneath their steel forged shields until they reached within range. There, they got off six quick rounds, and beat a quick retreat back into our trench. No harm was done; the feint being more of a pronouncement, but Bacon was hoping that there might just be an outside chance of surrender.

Berkeley responded by sending out a courier that we observed slipping from a small side door and waving a piece of white bunting. I could tell by his hands that his trade was not in labor, and with his eyes amazed at our earthen chambers, I presumed him some kind of clerk. He couldn't decide if he should gape or be nervous at what like-minded men could do, but doubtless in the way that he fiddled, this was his bravest hour too. He stated that it was not Sir Berkeley's will to fight, and that the governor was using him as an overture for dialogue. Bacon looked the young man over keenly, and told him first off that he would have to make his own decision as to whether he would return to the fort or not. Then, just when I'd begun to trust that he'd affected a bit more tolerance, Bacon shocked the clerk and everyone else by asserting that his idea for peace was seeing Sir Berkeley kneeling at his feet.

"What's your name son?" Bacon asked.

"Jayson Stone, sir." He was close to, if not Bacon's age.

"What's the state of the town?"

"Not well, sir."

Jayson Stone then reported that he was not from Accomack County himself, but confessed to being torn down the middle. He had three children inside and his father-in-law was a staunch Berkeley man. "There's been some loss to physical property," Jayson Stone said.

Nathan suddenly seemed moved by the man, who in spite of his obvious fear, was speaking with an untutored honesty. "God be merciful to you, Jayson Stone. For I will vouch for you no further, " Bacon said and dismissed him.

We then watched Stone make a confused walk back to the east wall door. Bacon's lips curled into a smile, and I could almost see his head cranking up momentum. He felt sure that Berkeley was having regrets, that the mercenary Accomacks were not worth the trouble the beleaguered governor had taken to please them.

He then ordered that the Indian prisoners be chained by the feet and moved to our front lines. This was accomplished, (with the requisite amount of brutality) and they were presented to the citizens of Jamestown as though Bacon were making them a gift. The most belligerent savages were stretched along an anxious row at the top of our barrier, in hopes, (Bacon's quaint terms) that they might suddenly turn wild.

I hardly shared this view. I was thinking that even if the petrified Indians did not fully comprehend this war between the whites, the one thing that they'd always counted on was William Berkeley being their friend. They knew that they were only being used to provoke the people inside to give the governor up. I was certain they'd do nothing to encourage this. The show that they would put on, might even end by the reverse of Bacon's designs, and at best be chillingly pathetic. So they were prodded back and forth by the jabbing of swords into feet and flanks, and in being forced to move like this, performed a precarious kind of dance. More than once one fell from the ledge entirely, and pulled several others down behind. And when they finally managed a uniform motion with their leg irons in a narrow shuffling step, they started in on their high-pitched death songs.

"Good!" Bacon gleefully screamed. "Sing!"

It is fair to assume what the governor thought of this lurid exhibition. Of all the accumulated insults that Bacon had heaped upon him, this one was calculated to cut him the deepest. Berkeley had spent many painstaking years to enjoin the Pawmunkeys and their nation to him, and the alliance was one he was sworn to protect. In earlier times, the fathers of these very prisoners had sacrificed themselves in order for Berkeley to triumph over the remaining hostile tribes. They had in fact, been the first to accept and live on a system of his land reserves with absolute assurance that they would not be disturbed. Seeing them now, so broken in the hands of our colonial conflict, must surely have torn at his ancient heart. Bacon, meanwhile, never stopped his gloating. He egged the Indian's on, mixing in a variety of his own nonsensical sounds.

"We are not your enemies!" he shouted when he'd had enough of their chanting. "We are here to protect you from the scourge of savages like these! Your enemy is behind your city walls, residing there among you! Good people of Jamestown, see for yourselves! Behold these heathen murderers that your governor protects!"

Then, inexplicably as any other notion by which he was suddenly moved, he was finished with the Indians. (Before any real harm could come to his property, I suspect.) He charged me to conduct them back to their cages, "in the safety of the woods and out of my way."

The rest of the day was spent in one meaningless exchange of musket fire after another; exchanges I believe that were initiated by some of the more anxious Accomack guards. But as harmless an exchange as it was, the damage was irreparable for what it implied. The governor was now shooting at His Majesties subjects, and His Majesties subjects were returning the same. The battle for Jamestown, in its terribly twisted and slippery way had officially begun. I bade my respects for the moment by allowing my thoughts to drift free on the water, watching the captains walk along their decks, and noticing a stance at mid-ship was done with individual style. I tried to take a nap tucked safely inside my sweatbox of a bunker, but could only see a thousand redcoats landing in the lids of my eyes. I idly wondered if on the day when they finally came ashore, the color in the setting sun would be the same. It was a vivid purple streaked with pink that night, foretelling an almanacs promise of wind. And then, when the last bit of violet had surrendered to black, the sky turned ablaze with fire.

There is no doubt that this should have been a horrendous affair. But having had no experience with a barrage of heavy cannon, I cannot accurately compare. I *can* say that from the perspective of those around me, also including mine, that Berkeley's barrage was little more than a passing inconvenience. Make no mistake, bowels were moved at the first whine of metal ripping through the air, but once we knew that our underground fortress could withstand it, the sound of the shells eventually became tame. Bacon's demanding brilliance and his facility for inspiring men to accomplish much more than they could have on their own, measured out in such great concern for our safety that he surpassed his previous status as merely a hero. But by not putting too much of a point on it, let me also say that the fire falling down on us came hesitant at best. Our close proximity to the city gate coupled with the unsure art of nighttime precision scared the ships on the river into limiting their display. Nonetheless I surprised myself with how calm I remained. I looked to the occasional thump in the outside dirt for massaging my back while sitting against the cooler wall on the riverside of the trench.

Some of the men even ate their dinner through the cannon blasts. And if an explosion slammed the cushioned of earth particularly close, a feigned salute was formed, with everyone standing up for what they called 'a Bacon tip of the hat.'

"Where had he learned such maneuvering," someone asked, "I thought he was a lawyer." Another man compared him to the French peasant girl that took back the town Orleans, to which someone then demanded an immediate apology for " insulting our general with a dead Catholic spook." Which in turn prompted another to observe that, "It was indeed possible Bacon had some involvement with tha said mystical powers," which then sparked a debate over "Tha goddam greedy Catholics. In gen'ral." I slipped down the dark passage, terrifically impressed by the fact that the men could engage in such a fight, right in the midst of the governor's bombardment.

In any case, if the men deciding his divinity had caught a glimpse of him while in the midst of their discussion the question might have ended there and then. Frustrated to distraction by the governor's show of force, I found him banging his head like a clabber in a bell off both sides of the trench. Every time some dirt fell free he cursed and fiercely kicked it. He kept pacing to a chamber where we'd hauled a pair of the six-pound cannon, (the additional prize from the Occaneechee) and I saw that the pretended hold he had on his temper had completely slipped off from its moors. His demons were returned in full, and I corrected myself of the notion that he ever had the patience for a siege.

"What is still valuable to him?!" he screamed at me, at everyone. "Now that he's willing to kill his precious Indians?!"

Another dead thud shook the ground just below us and so he began cursing at the sound. Then a gleam in his eye, no larger than a splinter grew into a grin that soon over his whole face. "Does he wish to dance?"

A captain from an Accomack ship seemed to give him an answer by sending in another shell.

Bacon planted one hand up to the low ceiling, and began a drunken spin. He churned his right foot sharply in the ground, then hopped on his left in tight circles. "If he wishes to dance, Corstair, then we shall dance!" He shouted like an imbecile, his voice becoming big enough to bounce within the cave. "Come here, Corstair!"

There came a short screech and then another throbbing.

"It's time to fetch the ladies!"

"I'm afraid... I must insist that you wear this one." I pulled out the whitest dress that I could find in Madame Bray's wardrobe, doing my best to conceal my supreme humiliation. She was a striking woman, a good ten years younger than myself with a raven head of hair spilling from out a sensible bun. Standing beside me were Miles Crawford and Peyton Dodd, two of the cruder sort that Bacon had purposely given me on this trip. They stood as a gawking duo in the presence of Mrs. Bray, who in turn was filling the room with silent contempt.

We had surprised her in the flower garden, bent to the ground instructing one of her servants on the placement of her rhododendrons. The immediate problem was her clothes, in that the working frock she was wearing did not meet with Bacon's explicit instructions. "Each of the wives that you collect must be dressed as though prepared for a formal evening." He was very insistent about this, so much so that he repeated it several times, and my thoughts of the other officers being in equally awkward positions gave me as much comfort as the current chill in Mrs. Bray's glare. Positions that could only be described as occupying strange hallways while enduring the scathing aspects of the other ladies that refused to cooperate. In this case, Mrs. Bray was physically barring her bedroom door.

Finally, there was nothing to be done but have the woman held aside so I could pick out a dress myself. It was however, only when I'd threatened to tear it into shreds, and use it to set a fire on her bedroom floor, that she agreed to put it on.

"Who *are* you?" she demanded, *again*.

"Philip Corstair, ma'am. Rebel." I adjusted my manner to the performance of my duty, which is to say, rude.

"Yes, I see," she said, examining me more closely. "I want you to know that I had an argument with my husband about you people, but he is absolutely right. You have no legitimacy, no part even, of civilized decency. You are nothing but a pack of degenerate wolves."

She grabbed the dress from out of my filthy hands and strode with a kind of pounding grace back into her bedroom. She then turned and leveled her gaze at the grinning Crawford and Dodd. "Would one of you *gentlemen* be kind enough to fetch my girl?" Crawford and Dodd fairly bolted down the stairs.

I was impressed with her self-control when we rode up. The first thing she did was to grab and scold her gardener, who was fidgeting from foot to foot in fright. But I can see now that her behavior was also a performance. How, I wanted to ask her out loud, had her husband, a man who even then was engaged in defending Jamestown, left her so high and dry and mighty? Were the two of them so removed that they did not look upon our war as serious? It was hard to fix the life among these riverfront plantations, cloistered behind their gardens and their walls of wrought iron fence and stone. And still, percussive echoes could be heard in the distance, where the gunboats on the river had begun their bombardment again.

Meanwhile, as I was working my mind through these and other useless questions, Mrs. Bray appeared before me again in the startling glow of her fancy white gown. With her hatred fully gathered, I walked her to her wagon, (a truly first rate carriage that I was proud to confiscate) wherein she surprised me at the small ladder step by offering me one of her hands. After picking up the end of her dress with the other, she paused long enough to stare a hole through her hapless kitchen help, who each kept his head down while moving. They were in a busy line, one up top and three down below, transferring some much needed supplies from their wheel-barrows into the back of the wagon. When the loading was accomplished, we formed a train of four wagons, coupled together in pairs, and finally got underway. Mrs. Bray emitted a kind of stifled yelp when I made the announcement that all of her servants were now free.

The order came out more or less as an afterthought, but it provoked some resentment from Corporal Dodd. He started in on me, insisting that the terrified lot of them be pressed into our service, but I settled the debate with a sharp snap of the reins. We left them loitering, confused and aimless on Mrs. Bray's crafted front grounds. Any common fool could see what more harm they'd be than good.

It took two full days for the wives to be collected, but once together and safe inside the trench, the picture they presented was beyond compare. They slipped and teetered in a righteously embarrassed group, with the mud up to their ankles making its way into their highly fashionable shoes. In the dank cavern light, each one clearly put her mark on the art of appearing distinguished. Mrs. Crandall-Smith proceeded at once to faint, but then seemed to think better of it when she noticed the spot where she'd land. Bacon's cousin's wife struck an especially remarkable pose. The powder that she wore to protect her from the sun sent little puffs from her face whenever she turned or spoke. She soon began to look as if she were floating about like a ghost.

I stood to one side avoiding the glances of women I only knew by reputation, women, you might say, that accorded some stripe. Names like Page and Ballard and Christie, and Henry Bedford's grande dame of a wife. The unfortunate Mrs.

Crandall-Smith let out a fair squall when a leech suddenly dropped down the back of her neck, but Bacon quickly clapped his hands for order and announced that he wanted to assure each of the ladies got the utmost in respect.

"Why *are* we here?!" Madame Bray demanded. "If you mean to hold us hostage must we suffer this filth as well?"

"What kind of man are you? If you insist on calling yourself such." This was Thomas Ballard's wife, the very man that had sold his plantation to Bacon back upon the Curles. She was glaring at his cousin's wife, as if distant relations were accountable in his guilt.

"God shall see you to hell, Nathaniel Bacon." The older lady offered. They may have shared the same name, but as far as her allegiances went, she was not about to quibble.

"You may be right, cousin," he cordially replied, "and there we can instruct each other to better learn His ways." He smiled back at her, like an admiring benefactor.

It was a well-known fact that Bacon stewed in his vindictive desires towards his extended Virginian family. He laid his public shame at the Assembly, and his having to plead for the governor's mercy, entirely at his cousin's feet. Where Berkeley meanwhile had rewarded the elder Bacon by appointing him President of the Council. And now, in order to make his suffering for this insult most clear, Nathan ordered a long line of wagons brimming with her goods to follow her into our camp. I'd watched them come in, as did the scavengers who pounced from the bushes whenever something spilled from an overloaded cart. Bacon's truest motive for targeting her for this cruelty was in order to make an example. Let it be known, "Anyone caught aiding their loyal relations can expect a treatment far worse."

"Now then, first," he began. A piercing silence shot between the cousins, an impossibly strained truce. "Colonel Corstair, here..."

I cringed. Just like that I had become a colonel. I really hated this business.

"… will escort one of you to the gate, where this very night you shall rest in the bosom of your husband's security. I *suggest* however, that for whichever of you this may be, you take the opportunity to alert your faithful allies as to the conditions being suffered by your *friends*."

No doubt about it, he was the Devil's apprentice when it came to twisting minds.

"Now then,' he exclaimed, clapping his hands again. "Who to send, who to send?"

At this moment some unaware dolt wandered in from outside, making noisy use of a latrine that we'd dug in a corridor at the rear. Nathan made no attempt to disguise his delight. It was the perfect type of intrusion to rub in the face, so to speak, of noble desperation. Mrs. Crandall-Smith made another overture to swoon, but again stopped herself up short, and Madame Page bit her lip so hard that I thought it would surely start bleeding. Nathan watched and waited, and waited, and smiled.

"Would you like to have a go at straws?" he offered, and broke off some roots that protruded from the clay.

"Stop this nonsense at once," Madame Bray declared. "I shall make your report."

"That suits me fine," Bacon replied. "And you, ladies?"

No one said anything, but none of them would look at her either.

"Colonel Corstair," he motioned to me, "if you will."

I guided Mrs. Bray through the dark tunnel to the front, where I set to studying the distance to the gate. The silence from the ships, having viewed this new predicament, was particularly poignant. I paced the short open stretch in my mind, going through each move I'd have to make as it lay out before me. However brief a walk that this was going to be, it was still a dangerous piece of ground. I had as well, the obvious question for my return. The upper wall was empty, presenting an ominous open space, but when I turned for Bacon's observations he was dragging up the cannons with a couple of the men. Suddenly I made the connection, as though offered a glimpse into his devious head. Between the big guns on the water, and the crossfire from the wall, I finally saw his purpose for the ladies.

"I don't expect that it'll come to any shooting," he said, catching his breath and showing me one of his sarcastic winks. "But I would keep her close all the same."

Mrs. Bray was fiercely mute. I don't know if this was to keep out the sour smells of our earthworks, or to keep back her tongue from lashing out at Bacon. She looked grimly determined to keep her chance at freedom.

"We wouldn't want to lose anyone," he said as if to reassure her.

"And who is to cover my return?" I asked.

"Oh, we won't worry so much about that," he smiled. "Mrs. Bray, I return you in the expectation that you will convey the truth to your husband. That we have just cause, and are no mere ruffians."

Just the opposite of course, to what he was really counting on. More than anything he wanted her to fuel a husband's torrid fears, and then let those fears do their worst. And as for his thoughts concerning my returning safely, he was no less calm and just as cock sure. So with this final bit of instruction he bid us God's speed and protection, along with his "own faith in my sound judgment," and sent us out through our hole in the earth.

I got instantly off my guard by the sudden blast of sunlight and had to cling to Mrs. Bray acting as though I had to keep her from running, but it was just as much for my support. She was stiff as a board and seemed to be having difficulty moving, but then we collected ourselves and began a shimmy-skirting walk, shadowing each other's steps. I was carrying a barrel pistol but I forgot to hold it at her neck, (as I was supposed to) and I whispered somewhere near midway I think, how very sorry I was. The back of her great white dress, covered in soot, shook in a sobbing reply.

Time seemed to stand still until the creaking of the gate, or at the very moment when we finally we stood before it. The hinges, needing grease, I thought preposterously enough, rotated at a tiny angle as I slipped to one side of the opening. I pressed my back in a rough joint of the wall, and released Mrs. Bray, where, without a glancing word, she entered and was immediately shut inside. I was about to take a quick scan along the top for any sign of a weapon, but in the brightness that marked the presence of high noon, my attention was grabbed as if by a very strong hand. Staring back from the glare on our entrenchments, along the very same ridge that the Pawmunkeys had paraded, stumbled a line of Virginia's foremost ladies all in a jagged row. It seemed to me like a pageant of angels had only just descended from another world. Their fine dresses rippled lightly in the breeze and then got snagged in the muddy branches that jabbed from below.

Two of the women began to cry and were held in an attempt at comfort by two more, while another three appeared to be angry and tried to distance themselves from this group. They stepped gingerly through the rocks and jutting limbs, then by climbing or slipping down to a determined crawl they reached the top as if they thought that this would set them free. One of them, when looking back at the others took a hard bruising fall, then, when no one offered to come down and help her she belligerently sat in a heap where she was. A slow sequence followed that seemed strangely orchestrated, where each of the women made a turn of her head to send a murderous glare at the Jamestown wall.

Looking back on this moment now, I think that I shall never behold a more compelling sight. Not if I lived through a hundred years of war and peace, or worked in a traveling circus. The life of an average man, I know, affords very few times where he must muster all his senses simply to believe in what is placed before him, but that is exactly the state in which I found myself then.

But my attention wasn't permitted to marvel very long. It was quickly diverted by the distinctly squeaking sounds of rolling wheels, where I looked to the ends of our bulwark and there in separate teams the men were at work setting our cannons in perfect firing range. With nothing but digging spades to protect them they had the big guns in position, and then like a gang of jeering children, taunted the guards on the wall to go ahead and take a shot. I looked back towards the ladies, still not convinced that what I saw was real, and they were escorted back inside the trench.

"Good work, Colonel Corstair." Bacon said when I reached him.

He was surprisingly grave. So somber in fact that he provoked me into poking fun at his gallant sense of warfare. He pretended to ignore me, presenting himself as always, the devil to figure out. With Berkeley revealing his reluctance to fight, one would have thought that what had transpired that day should have made him happy, but he only started grousing about the heat and complained of how long we might have to stay where we were.

"Take two of the emptied wagons and drive the pampered lot of them home," he said.

Now that the ladies had performed their duty he wasn't about to endure their further insults or listen to the threats of their promised revenge. I led them out the back road, with the exception of his embittered cousin, whom Bacon himself had placed aboard an old sad mule. The actual job of transporting them was one I turned over to Crawford and Dodd.

Another stifling hour then passed with no more hostile exchanges, but the air growing heavier with tension. Neither man, it seemed was willing to commit to a battle and each sat waiting for the other's loss of nerve. Working under the inspiration of Bacon's preposterous flaunting, the men took to shouting up at the rough wooden wall. Especially when a helmeted guard would appear. Mostly they called for the Accomack soldiers to abandon 'old man Berkeley' and come on over, but an occasional reference to one's manhood might also be heard. Then, just when the sun hit its afternoon peak, the gates swung apart, and out marched the Accomack army in as strict a formation as I'd ever seen. They were corralled by a uniformed horseman who barked in his saddle like a sergeant in His Majesty's Marines.

"Right! Halt! Left Column left! Forward! Right! Right! Right!"

Even more amazing was the effort that the Accomack militia put in trying to please him. We all watched, derisive but impressed as they paired off into perfect flanking lines and quadrupled down the middle. We stayed hidden in the cover of our natural fortress, half in awe and half perplexed, taking in what was not so bad a show. There were some that missed a cue or otherwise struggled to keep up, but in the words of George Miller, who was leaning in behind me, "Was this the way they'd spent all their time? Rehearsing?"

"Hold your fire men, hold fire!" Bacon shouted sternly, nervously trotting through our line. There was no mistaking that he was plenty afraid. "There he is! The old fool."

He was standing right beside me, pointing at the swaying figure of the governor looking down at us from up above. Sir William was holding a scope to one eye, which he only seemed to need to better observe the lines being made by his troops.

"The old bat is trying to kill those people!" Bacon exclaimed.

He looked out wildly, on each fine set of rows, with every man among them such an easy target that in order not to hit them we'd deliberately have to miss. We took our aim, divvying up between us which of the anxious recruits that we'd be shooting at, all while being terribly revolted by the idea of actually doing it.

"Hold fire, men! Hold fire!" Bacon yelled. "Wait for my order and shoot overhead!"

God bless him for that. No matter what hatred that he had for the governor, he was not about to slaughter these poor fools. We then watched, trembling and fearful, with nerves as tight as fiddles, as the lines before us moved.

"Stuhp, quarter left! Stuhp! Stuhp!" The Accomack officer bellowed from his horse. "Stuhp, quarter right! Stuhp! Stuhp!"

There came a snap of a drum, and then they stopped. Thank God too, that none of our wilder boys had opened up their fire. But I could not breathe for feeling that with each passing second someone surely would.

"Hold on men! Hold on!" Bacon shouted again.

Another minute passed, then another thirty seconds. Bacon leaned forward, twisting this way and that trying to get a look at what the governor meant to do. Another silent minute, the sun beating down, unobstructed and intense, the Sergeant ceased from shouting, and the men from Accomack simply standing still. They were nearly within spitting distance, sitting up neater than a perfect row of bowling pins. I spotted Jayson Stone halfway down the center, appearing frozen with his face all drenched in sweat, unwilling even to lift a hand against the mayfly that plowed happily through his nose.

"Hold men, hold!" Bacon repeated. As we watched

the governor point his spyglass again. "What is the old fool doing!?" Bacon cried. He actually seemed close to despair.

"I think," I finally replied, "that he is waiting for you to start."

Oh, bloody Jesus," Bacon sighed, and raised his pistol in the air. "Over their heads, men! Over their heads!" The second that his shot tore into the far wooden wall, the entire side of our bulwark opened fire. "Over their heads!"

The roar of several hundred muskets in a simultaneous volley can easily damage your ears, but the sound sent the tightly packed Accomacks into a reeling panic. Screaming uncontrollably, the entire corps threw up their arms at once, confused as to whether they should run or surrender. The soldiers that were neatly lined up behind the first rows were knocked to the ground as the men before them wheeled blindly for the gate. By then the clouds of burnt powder made it difficult to see, but I spotted one that was bleeding that we'd surely struck down. In the midst of the confusion I pointed him out to Bacon the best that I could, and wincing forward in the acrid air, he came back up straight, waving his sword at the line of our fire.

"Hold fire men!" he shouted. "Hold fire!"

With the final scattering of shots, we waited with our hearts pumping in our throats. At last the smoke diffused and lifted across the empty yard. Not counting the time that the enemy took for going through their drills the battle took less than two minutes. In the clearing haze we watched the movement of the massive gate being trembled shut, and with it the governor's army from Accomack safely back inside.

"Recover that man!" Bacon shouted. He was pointing at the soldier that they'd left out on the ground.

Under the shield of small cover fire, a detail gathered him up and brought him back to our trenches. When his head was cleaned, I found a single neat hole, set in behind his right ear. Ricochet, I thought, feeling somewhat relieved. None of our boys would commit to cold murder. That said however, they immediately demanded that they storm the front wall.

"We got 'em in a hell of confusion, Gen'ral!"

"Bring on the cannon! Let's have at 'em while they're still knocked numb!"

Bacon shot his hand straight at the face of the loudest. "Attention! Here!" he shouted, thoroughly disgusted. "This man here died for nothing! For Nothing!" He was in a full screaming rage. "I will not stand for such a useless sacrifice! Return to your posts and see that he is properly buried!"

Even the most zealous among them squirreled back into silence, suddenly more afraid of Bacon than of anything else. Then each began to saunter off, to reflect perhaps on the shame he supposed from his bloodlust. But later, with the poor man buried, and the late afternoon sun settled down upon us again, Bacon turned to me, both secretive and mild.

"Jesus, Corstair," he smiled, "what on earth did you say to Mrs. Bray? She's driven those poor men *insane*."

By nightfall the men had replaced their awe for Bacon's genius with a general irritability that mostly second-guessed his refusal to attack. I passed several hours in the company of these malcontents, nearly all of whom were half-gone to drink, which was their only qualification to hold forth on their military expertise. But even the quiet consensus could see that Berkeley had no one with him who was willing to fight. I acted in Bacon's staid, trying to keep a lid on the mounting frustration and found surprising support in Mr. Gibbs' corps of Africans. Bacon's household servant was counseling his fellow blacks in the virtues of what the land with new law would bring to their lives.

"One thing for sure," his native accent added a distinct bearing to his proper English. "We must win this war, and defend the rights of servitude against the interest of lifelong bondage. If we allow the African system to take control, it will replace all of immigrant labor. Trust me when I say that General Bacon fights with this in mind."

"That may be well enough for you," spoke up one of his men. "Since Bacon done grant you sixty acres a' more when this here ting is finished."

Chuckles emerged from the crowd of black faces, flashing smiles of white into a background of night. As for myself, I sorely doubted that Bacon cared a whit about the consequence of lifetime bondage, but I kept the thought to myself.

"Hardly matters on the outcome," said another, "ceptin' we lose our heads, of course. Lifetime bondage is here and more coming. I jus' hope to get mine afore tha rich folk gobble up it all up."

I was impressed. The last man speaking handed me the bottle and I took the chance to look in his eyes. His face bore the scars of some tribal ritual performed in a place far across the ocean and from an altogether different life. "How long do you have?" I asked him.

"I *had* six months," he replied. "Now," he smiled. "It's all or nothing."

With only six months left of his service, he certainly *was* taking a chance. But then this fire flung time had stripped away all sense of choice.

"Three years and three months," offered another. "And if I can't afford no land protected from the savages, then I plan on gettin' me one a' them lifetime slaves an' head out past the safety zones. Me and one bought man whats good for watchin' my back. We'll square out our own."

"Where you get money for that? A healthy man's goin' for more'n six hundred."

"Maybe, maybe not. Not if we're talkin' 'bout winning this thing."

"Win or lose, what slaving Captain's gonna sell you a man for cheap?"

"Expect he'll have to, once we get the freehold vote to fix the price."

"Gentlemen!" Mr. Gibbs interrupted. "Do you forget why we are fighting? Listen to yourselves. We cannot compete with… we cannot allow lifetime bondage!"

A severe and sobering tinge descended on the idle chatter.

"I had me six months, oncet."

One of the few other Englishmen at the fire broke in. In

the low flame I could still see that his arms were fully branded up and down. Still worse was his face. His lips and tongue were so gnarled and scarred, (the punishment for running away) that he looked just like a monster. If you didn't listen hard you'd miss what he had to say, his speech was so difficult to follow.

"N'en, I run," he chortled. "One day old master Owens beat me so hard that I run agin'. Annat' came at a time, when my time was almos' up."

He stuck his beard out right above the flame so everyone could see him point to his deformities. The sum of his face was an ugly testament to the times he had run and got caught.

"Ne'n. I run agin, an' agin, an' agin..." he continued, until he had everyone shaking their heads or plain out disgustedly laughing. "What startit' out as a five year service wound up fifteen, and I ain' half as old as I look. Don't pay it no mind, though. I'm still pretty underneath."

"What's your name, friend?" I asked. "Do you have some kind of trade?"

"Will Jennings, tha last one I took. An' dodgin' tha sheriff bounty man's what I do best."

"Yeah, you looks it," one of the Africans observed, setting off another peal of laughter.

"Well, Will Jennings," I said, "before this thing here is over, you may just have to use some of that talent for running."

Will Jennings was the type of man more to the mold of our army. If anyone had the *least* to lose, it was the amazingly good-humored, lately called Will Jennings.

I took my leave and strolled back from the outer trenches and walked the dark woods to check on the Pawmunkey prisoners. I wanted to talk to the girl I had to lock inside a cage. Actually I wanted to try and help her if I could see she'd grown more compliant since I left her last. After shaking the sleeping guards awake I stepped through the hedges and noticed the place was unnaturally quiet. No crickets; not even a toad, only the swish of pines being released from my grip. Then I heard a low crying, mixed with the child's singing voice. I moved quickly past the other prisoners, crammed inside of their tiny cells, some with their legs bound in slats of greenwood that tightened each time it was soaked and dried. Others were pinned hands to feet, hooked to the floor with irons. They were all too exhausted and defeated to make sounds.

She had somehow gotten out of the cage where I had locked her and had both her slim arms slipped between the bars of another cell. The man inside was contorted on the floor and shivering uncontrollably with fever. When she finally turned her head back towards me she ceased her singing but kept daubing a pack of mud to his throat. He was delirious and not looking like he would live for very long, but his moans became more of a cooing under her touch. Without quitting her attentions she glared at me at once. "Kill us now, kill everyone, and you'll have done us a favor." Or at least I thought this is what she said, but her whispered fervor mixed with the sick man groaning made some of her words unclear. Anyway I ignored her and looked at the man as he trembled. My main concern now was if his contagion had spread.

"Can you make him well?' I asked.

She gave me a careless shrug, and gingerly lifted a porcupine quill from the outside edge of the cage. "It should have worked quickly," she said, "but I think he grew afraid."

I held the thing to my nose, catching its rich copper smell, and immediately flung it in the brush. The sharpened point contained a particularly strong toxin that I knew was extracted from hemlock. She was hoping the mud would draw it out of the miserable man's neck.

"If you want to die so badly then why do you save his

life?" I replied curtly in a sudden wave of disgust. But just as quickly I had no sense of her answer, or even what I meant of the question.

I was assaulted as if by a thousand emotions. A sinking gave way within me that seemed to stretch from my stomach below my legs even beneath the ground. Just as unaccountably came a gush of weeping, a rushing up and out like my body was but a broken dike at an unknown channeled stream. A face appeared; *my* face that melted before me like a burden I had carried for too long. It flowed down and away below some point where I could not find my feet. It was as though every hidden fiber of my will now lay exposed for me to see. I felt vaporous and light, free of guilt and of care, free as though I didn't even matter. But vibrant and shaking, striking the air with the clarity of a giant church bell. A sudden picture that every single moment I had lived before, and living still was nothing but a trick made vast. Tricked by who or what, I could not say, unless it was only myself, but that I was a part of this terrible and senseless plight from which I could not leave, indeed could not be anywhere else but here mistook and alone. I became in that moment, naked as my birth, lying limp in a blubbering heap, as if my own ancient spirit had at last been freed from thinking, but for its own inexorable reason needed to hover and keep watching me still. What I must have looked like, to the girl or to anyone else was equally beyond my control and devoid of meaning.

I looked up and recognized her staring down at me curious and alarmed, and I was suddenly overwhelmed by the fact that she would also leave me. A fear that so crushed and terrified I reached out for her, catching her hair, and clung her to me quite close. She struck back with her tiny fists, adding to my vision with her face becoming the face of many, peering at me in a vivid likeness. The drunken shaman, Ta-ye-naw that spilled into the river, Kotaka sipping water from a spring. Tecatomac, Tekanepet, and numbers of those I didn't recognize but knew that I had killed. Some were even laughing. Laughing at me who was losing his mind, and laughing too, at my pretended family. I held her even tighter, wanting to feel her hands and arms strike hard, as hard as she could possibly strike. Hoping to absorb her wild strength, to let it pull me back, restore my pain and make me something more solid. I kept to her like this, for quite an unknown while, until her struggle had quietly forced me from the precipice. Then we each dropped away, exhausted by our touch.

We spent a silent moment, confused now more than afraid, sharing this new understanding as though a strange couple caught together for all time as part of the same catastrophe. Then when I could stand, I walked shakily away. I filled my lungs with the damp forest air and reached the shadow of an old massive pine. And when I heard her sing again I turned to see her small silhouette swaying back and forth in an altogether different rhythm. I felt the dark grow deep across my face and I welcomed my mind returning its familiar form. What on earth did we think we could bring to these people? I thought about the man that she'd been nursing and wondered how the afterlife would look upon his suicide. What could be made of a self-mutilated spirit? Was it condemned, as my vision had so clearly spoke of me, to roam alone forever? What for all of that, was to come of this *place*? Possessing the untold measure of troubled spirits on this land.

On my way back to our outer line I listened to her voice fading in the forest, and wished with all my heart that she would run.

This remarkable encounter, be it a gift or some new mental plague I couldn't say, was not the end of the cautions I received that night. Nearly to the trench and my much-needed bed, I heard a commotion down upon the river that I didn't have the strength to investigate. I was so overwrought that I fell into a sleep, and my dreams into a torrent. Then I was awakened with a start by bitter accusations and voices pitched so angry that the words came spitting out. I soon learned that the late hour sound, which I had left unchallenged, was Berkeley and his so-called Accomack army escaping in the night.

I could not have felt more of self-disgust.

Bacon responded in a fury, naturally enough. "Where is our victory?!" He yelled back and forth. "What a conquest for an army of drunks! Where are our sentries?! Where!? They and their officers will be hanged as spies for failing to report at once!"

I honestly don't know if I was prepared to confess that the governor was aided by the fault of my exhaustion since before it could come to that Bacon's voice was lost in a new storm of confusion. Once word had gotten loose that Jamestown was abandoned, it would have taken Caesar's ghost to hold the excited men back. They scrambled over walls, bashed through side entrances and threw open the massive doors before Bacon's viable threats could stop them. There was no chance of their officers bringing them under control. Nathan, seeing his whole army in revolt, simply stepped aside and then put himself at the head of the nearest bolting group. He was prudent enough to leave off with his hard fist approach until the men were all gathered inside. A scattering too, of Accomack mercenaries began to creep up, popping out from hidden cellars or separately found under storage bin lids. But all ended by holding their hands out to us like we were their most welcome friends. Bacon sat atop his horse, taking in the motley scene, trampling through the square, demanding in a loud enough voice to get order.

"It is clearer by far that Berkeley is our common enemy!" he shouted, setting a more political tone to work. He was thinking that he couldn't simply imprison these

Accomacks; he wanted their connections to the peninsula, to have them *join* with him. "And that you good men were sadly exploited out of your sense of duty! You are hereby absolved of all guilt!"

The outburst of approval that came from both the armies showed me anyway, the fluid nature of our stewardship.

But then we found out that the 'good' men of Accomack had been deserting Berkeley from the start. Had in fact, already removed everything that Jamestown had of value. At this point I had to wonder if the governor controlled *any* part of his subject population, or where a man was in Virginia that wasn't working exclusively for himself. But putting the opportunistic plundering of our new brethren aside, we embraced these hapless fellows as friends. One, who was transferred to me and possessed a particularly eager attitude, asked right away when we'd be off on our next raiding party. "They's a lot ta be said for ta Gen'ral's good will," he winked. And while I watched General Bacon making the new assignments, I couldn't have even told you which of the two sides had won.

A partial answer came in perfect Bacon fashion, when he brought down the law after they'd sworn their support. Standing in his saddle, he growled. "Now!" The dispersed festivities came to a stop. "Any man that does not produce every item of his illicit gains will immediately be shot!"

The Accomack members of our new militia started milling about in an anxious kind of shuffle, and soon enough had replaced their idle talk with an exchange of sharp words. They stalled, denied and accused one another in an effort I supposed, to figure out what they might just be able to hide. In any case not a single one reported anything he'd stolen. Moreover they persisted in professing how *they* had been abused. "Gads truth! Had to give up everything I own to the cowards that done the running out! All's I got about me are the tattered clothes you see on my back." They went on in common suit, talking about the scores that they would settle, on Berkeley and his band of thieves, "once we've gotten our beloved Accomack back."

Any evasions that they offered, however, came but to meanness given the paltry size of the take. For when all was flushed out by a team of Bacon's jackboots, it amounted to little more than a couple crates half filled with broken plates and several dozen pieces of silver. There were twenty more torn and shriveled bolts of linen, a fermenting vat, a tanner's rake, and a collection of tools nearly worthless.

Investigation went on to find out that first act Berkeley had performed in the cause of Jamestown's defense was to secret away every precious item it contained. (The primary reason for the high rate of desertion in his army.) Then the men, who'd gotten hold of the best that they could hope for, simply ran away.

Nonetheless in spite of all this, an assortment of items still trickled in through the rest of the day. The piles, slowly built, were made odd by their additions. A gentleman's corset, a miniature harp, a warped and rusted pen for breeding rabbits. Hesitant offerings for all their slim worth, but slowly and steadily placed in a mound outside the Assembly doors. Bacon meanwhile, had locked himself and his advisors inside the stately building to deliberate an end to this growing nightmare. The heap of goods grew all day in open view, providing as it were a test of will for those who covet, or even perhaps an unspoken dare. But however it was understood, once an object was placed on top it remained there undisturbed.

As an honest gauge of discipline though, everyone knew that it stank of double-deals. At that very moment, indeed throughout the weeks of the war, the counties were crawling with far ranging bandits stealing what they could of what the loyalists left behind. Each of these packs had their own a 'rebel' leader, who worked under the authority of General Bacon, of course, but here, in legitimately conquered Jamestown, this sudden accounting for spoils was a policy entirely new. No matter that the victory brought little more than a barnyard full of junk. There was *principle* involved. And the whisperings that have their roots in back sniping had it that Nathan was losing his common touch.

Anyway, the sight of the stuff sure gave the highly self satisfied Timothy Gale a reason to pause. He rode hard up to the Assembly door, dismounted and stared curiously at the trash, then at the surrounding throng as if to compare their two values. Then with air of humor, (that most would call contempt) he closed himself inside the hall. It was precisely this type of tight-lipped restraint, so antithetical to what Bacon was loved for, that had the newly discontent flaring up with rumors. Conclaves were in themselves a means for dealing unfairly. "This," they said, "is where we break up the blood."

And yet. Throughout the long day, and without a hint about the goings on, I marked how the men *outside* had put away their petty arguing. Then, just when the last embers of sun were snuffed into a rich black night, the interior of the hall lit up with the shadowy motion of torches. The double doors were thrown open and apart, (a gesture only Bacon would employ) and he emerged with William Drummond and our dear Richard Lawrence. Each of them held a flame out from his face, a contrast of the moving light, and with a solemn nod like commencement, Drummond and Lawrence set off.

The crowd surrounded Bacon at once and then retreated as one in a step. They looked on in confusion and open face horror as he struck the pile of their goods with fire. The first to catch was a bundle of flaxen; the second ignited an old cabinet for bees. Just down the lane another fire flared, then everyone jumped excitedly at once. Someone yelled for a rescue, grabbed up a bucket and even formed men into a pail pitching line. Others lunged ahead, rolling out barrels to be filled, clearing up a corridor to and from the well. Then all seized up, as if frozen to the spot of their last step, to behold what everyone called an outright act of madness. There was the esteemed and scholarly Richard Lawrence setting his lodging and boarder rooms alight, right along with the sweep of his torch, the side and front of his house. Then there was the fire in the hands of William Drummond. He threw his torch in an arc upon the walls of his home, which roared back an agreeable flame. Both looked struck as if by lightening. Seeing these two blazes were set and climbing, Bacon then heaved his torch in the dark Assembly Hall. The flames struck through the rows of carefully crafted benches, then up to the balcony, in a blaze of solid fire. The stately artisan structure, with its vistas of open ceiling space, simply went up like a fuse.

* * * * *

"I shall remain here, Corstair, despite what means you gain for escape."

For the past hour, Mr. Lawrence has been sitting at the maw of our cave, staring glumly out at the pounding rain. I know that he's been stewing in the pros and cons of coming clean with me, to confess whatever he has to say. I've already asked him directly, while tucking him up in his only dry blanket, but he's chosen to ignore me 'til now. On the other hand, I have shared nothing about a plan to get away, not that this could keep him from reading it in my thoughts. The hidden creek he's determined not to look upon has built into a powerful stream.

"I am too feeble," he continues, "to run anymore, and will only slow you down. Nor do I wish to have the last of my energies wasted in arguing about it."

I determine not to mention the subject until the time comes when we must act.

"I have my friends," he says, pointing at the squeaking bats. "They will watch over me. Or, if I'm to believe the savages, perhaps my soul will become one of them. Then I can go about some *worthwhile* business. Like eating up these bugs that torment us so."

Hearing him talk like this makes me anxious to get on. And then, watching his near liquid eyes reflect the extreme amount of rain, I wonder unexplainably, if he knows what it's like to lose one's whole family. Like living inside of someone else's dream. Somehow I believe that he does. He turns to me again. The day outside has grown so dark that the bats are getting restive. I wonder too, if they think it's night.

"What was it like to burn your own house?" I abruptly ask.

I am glad that the question surprises him. It gives me a chance to take my focus from myself.

"Twasn't much," he replies carelessly. "There was nothing left in it anyway."

"Stop being such a martyr," I play along. "You were beside yourself. Rage *and* glee. If I hadn't known better, I'd have said you were drunk. Mr. Richard Lawrence; statesman. Torching the Jamestown streets like a regular firebrand. Inciting the mob with the cleansing fire, and all that."

"How you go on, Corstair. *If I hadn't known better.*" He takes a moment to look at me, the first in a very long time. "Perhaps your empty belly has addled *your* mind."

He pauses again, and I see he's becoming more comfortable in remembering.

"Whatever it's worth, burning Jamestown was a perfectly rational act. And all the enthusiasm I applied to the task was only meant to see it done."

"Was it your decision, or Bacon's? After all, he had no property in town."

"When Timothy Gale informed us that Colonel Brent

had become a turncoat and was marching toward us at the head of a thousand men, we weren't going to sit by and be set upon the same way he'd laid siege on Berkeley. But beyond all denial, Brent's treachery was very disheartening news. Plus the fact that we had good intelligence that a thousand of His Majesties troops were then under sail. Added up, Jamestown was a liability. And don't forget that all Bacon really wanted was more Indians to kill."

"As did a lot of us," I remind him.

"In any case," Mr. Lawrence says peevishly, "it was what *the General* had decided. So I asked him how he proposed to chase Indians, and defend the capitol at the same time. Finally, it was Drummond's decision to give Brent's traitors nothing to fight for. Cleansing fire, indeed. The destruction of my property was a matter of necessity. It had nothing to do with *ideals*. A bush war, Corstair, make no mistake, that's what we were in for. And it meant leaving nothing behind. We'd become just like Bacon's hated savages, God help us! The tactics of terror were the only ones available now!"

Mr. Lawrence suddenly starts howling with laughter. He sounds so dangerously ill, that I'm indeed unsure of what to do.

* * * * *

"Burn it, men! Burn it all to hell!" Bacon screamed, throwing fragments of the fire in every direction. Igniting too, the fever pitch minds of men that were now beyond his control. Like an ocean storm I once saw on my long past Atlantic journey, the chaos fed on itself, becoming another beast all its own. And appalled as I was at the wanton destruction, it was impossible not to get caught in its hold. The men scattered like a nest of unearthed insects, made mad by the fire and the cavernous roar. They grabbed and fought for anything that burned. Wagon spokes, leather belts, and splintered table legs, any flaming thing to be thrown. They shattered the windows of every hut and shop. And everywhere was screaming. Men made brave by their own hysterics ran through flaming walls and doors. Officers shrieked, making imbecile sounds right along side the wild farm boys. The howling and yips reached particular peaks when a councilman's house fell apart. And the inhuman sounds could almost turn reverent when the fire leapt over a rooftop. Wall upon wall of the heaving inferno fused and then exploded, the very streets turned red in a flood of burning dust. Heavy timbers, fortress timbers went up all at once, windows melted, or shot fiery splinters of glass. An especially joyous scream rang out when the smoke engulfed the Revenue House.

It was difficult to stand; Jamestown had become a huge heaving furnace. I watched, strangely afraid of my own elation as the flames took hold of Morehouse and Sons. And again, the same bitter mix at the Assay Office of John Staunt. In a crouch I followed a channel of air in time to see the Building for Deeds & Titles collapse, just as the astonishing William Drummond emerged. He swatted at the ashes covering his body, and the bundle of scorched documents in the crook of his arm. These, he handed to Timothy Gale, who just as incredibly was calmly standing by. Drummond had to throw himself down and roll in the dirt to douse out the flames on his pants. Bacon then appeared, and carefully placed the smoke damaged pages into a metal strongbox.

The entire sequence was outstanding to me for it being so meaningless and profound. William Drummond had just risked his neck to save the records of a government we had treasonably destroyed. Did he yet foster hope that we could somehow turn back?

Yet stranger to me still, was the ghostly pall that reflected off of Bacon's face. I cut directly through the

melee to quickly grab him, and see what was the matter.
Just as quickly he pushed me away. I held on, trapping us
for a moment inside a fiery alley, and felt his body shivering
against me cold as ice. He looked at me once, his eyes
deep in panic, and then he broke off at a run. I trailed him,
watching him reel from side to side, trying to dodge the
flames and the flying debris, until he seized up altogether,
in the midst of an oily black cloud. In a single motion he
doubled up and spewed in a violent stream. The entrance to
the alley shattered just above us, and then he was driving
on. Directing groups of men in a rush, pushing this one
or another out this way or that, and all while soaking in a
feverish sweat. Unwilling to believe, I kept him closer still,
moving with him then stopping sharp, then watching him
cramp and start shouting in fits. His aides scurried about us
suddenly trying to stay clear as if this were just another of his
tempers. I followed on; growing more alarmed, seeing how
he clenched his jaws, and ground his fist into his chest. He
moved like this, forward at a pace only to suddenly spin back
as if being thrown in all directions. Then in a secluded place,
he halted altogether and dropped into a tight binding knot.
There, his shaking began in earnest. I approached him in the
light of an oncoming blaze and saw the streaks of yellow in
his eyes.

"You are sick." I leaned in, whispering with force.
Next would come the fainting spells, the breathing weakness,
and the bloody onslaught in his bowels.

"Silence!" he hissed back, throwing out his arm.

I gathered him in and helped him to his feet, wishing
I could absorb some of his pain.

"No one is to know," he coughed back, twisting
upright. "No one!" He forced himself around, full on his feet
again. "The church, men! To the God Almighty church!"

He marched with this bent determined gait through

the corridor of flames straight up the steps of the tower. Lifting his torch at the top of the stair, he crossed its bright painted doors with fire. A minute later the church was a burning monument, throwing its light into the wilderness, where even the shadows of flame struck deep in the woods.

"Finish it, men! Finish the damned place!" Bacon screamed. And his disciples dispersed, as if to rid the world of Jamestown's unburned pieces.

"I must rest," he wheezed upon me. "Find an empty plantation."

I shuffled him into the only dark spot I could find. I looked back once when the church tower toppled, crushed by the weight of its bell. Bacon leaned up to try and see it as well, but he could only grimace. He did see some of the flames roaring their way through the pews, which surely to him was no less a fire than was consuming himself.

I moved like a cat, lurching between the walls of flame, while at once taking care to hide Bacon from the men. I packed him in a patchwork of livestock wraps that I'd soaked in a trough and then set out to find his horse.

"… at the tree line and… the creek," he mumbled, and then he fell back into cursing.

That he was still able to blaspheme gave me the confidence to leave him covered up inside a drainage ditch. I reasoned that if he was strong enough to pray in curses then he might just survive this trip. I came upon an old oxcart miraculously intact, but Bacon's horse when I found her was tethered to a fishing grate and about in a panic from having to stare at the fire. It took precious minutes for me to calm her to trust and by the time we'd picked our way back through the confusion Bacon had slipped out of consciousness. His presence however had a steadying effect on the mare, which once blindfolded I steered through the smoke to an old logging trail. My only thought now was to get past the sudden belligerent patrols. Too weak to utter more commands, too weak to even curse, Bacon was reduced to barking out a grunt each time we hit a rut.

His condition deteriorated so quickly that I knew he was beyond my cures, and as we struggled through the briar whip branches I went through my chances and limited choice. No matter which way I worked to avoid it, I kept returning to my only thread of hope. I kept my hand upon the bridle to comfort the horse and turned for the camp of Pawmunkey prisoners.

Neither the Indians nor any evidence of their cages were there. I had a surge of confusion and felt strangely abandoned by the little girl. I stared up through the outline of surrounding pine and of fir that shifted in the waves of rushing heat. The fire was still booming from behind me but all that I could hear were Bacon's moans. The wind took a change of direction coming in from the southeast so that the air was fast becoming thick and hard to breathe. To my right I saw a patch of clear night sky and there was nothing to do but press on.

I thought that the shell left of the governor's house might be a safe spot, and if we walked without being stopped we could make it by first light. There was no more fitting a place to make a miracle. I put the remnants of my faith into the mare and peered through the night for the least traveled trail. Then, just like a trick of the eyes the girl was sitting and then getting up, walking towards me. My first impression was that she had become a ghost. She looked entirely swallowed up by a lady's starch white dress, which she dragged the satin fringes of behind her. When I heard her speak in her peculiar elderly voice, I felt that I was being transported.

"I smelled the *general*," she told me cold and matter of fact. "He's very sick. What are you going to do?"

"We are going to the governor's house," I said, gathering my senses. Then I put her on top of the horse. "And you are going to help us."

The wind above pushed off some of the smoke from Jamestown and opened up a patch of bright stars. She stared down at me, seemingly devoid of judgment, offering nothing about her clothes. She looked like a grownup, altogether morbid.

"Where did you get that dress?" I asked.

"From a white lady that you know. She told me that

she believed it had power, but that she was afraid of it. But I think she was only crazy and wanted to take it off."

The puzzle of how she'd managed contact with a rich planter's wife would have to wait for now. My only interest in power was how it applied to her healing.

"The warrior you were treating," I asked, "did he survive?"

"I do not know," she said. "I ran off when he was taken away with the others."

"Can you help the general?"

She turned around to look inside the cart. Bacon's face was shining, pale and sweat drenched in the dark.

"Yes," she replied.

The governor's gardens, from his outlying corn to his hand carved hedges were blanketed by vines and weeds. And though it was a menacing emptiness, the absence of smoke from the kitchen, or from the house itself was encouraging. The windows were wide open and broken out, the shutters and sashes undone, and the doors split in pieces swung a jagged edge. This was Green Spring, the governor's beloved retreat. In the drab gray of dawn, a ravaged tomb. I approached with a ready weapon, having little choice but in trusting the little girl, but I was far more fearful of surprising a pack of renegades than of her part to do us ill. I quietly passed through the front doorframe, jutting its hinges and nails, and into the dim downstairs hall. Once inside, I poked through several of the first floor rooms until I could be convinced that they had indeed been forsaken. The empty chamber walls were stripped of their fine silk paper and the portraits of the family scattered in shreds on the floor. The only sound to be heard was the picture glass crunched beneath my boots. There was not a single stool or chair.

"Hallo! I am with General Bacon! Make yourself known!"

Daniel Watkins

A bird chirped nervously before taking flight from a room up the stairs. Climbing swiftly I entered and found a burnt mattress, its stuffing being scavenged by the bird for her nest. I noticed a watermark on the floor, a reminder of the luxurious tub and a prize so exotic that doubtless it was the first thing out the door. I re-stuffed the mattress and set out to find some water. If luck stayed with me for just a little while it would lead me to an uncorrupted well. I leapt down the stairs trying to make some noise.

Once outside, I found my patient where I'd left him at death's door but the girl had taken off with the horse. Gagging myself on his ripening stench, I carried him to the upstairs room. He was delirious with cursing, but taking the care that I could, I removed his soaked and filthy clothing. I had to hold his head up steady (not an easy job when untying the strings of someone else's drawers), it burned hot as fire and swung in erratic circles.

"Burn it! Goddam my blood! Burn it!" he cried, but was far too weak to make or shake a fist.

"God has certainly answered that unfortunate prayer," I said out loud and took his clothes back down into the yard. At this point it was all that I could do to stifle *my* own damnable despair. But I gathered my thoughts; cursing *myself* for the trust I had placed in the girl, and grabbed up containers for water. When I reached the first well, the sun was high enough for me to see that someone had dropped in a dead goat, but the spring a little further on was untouched. I doused myself, soaking in the cooling water as much as I possibly could, and then filled up the bladders and kegs. When I returned to the house, the horse was tied again out front, stirring to one side in its confusion. I filled her a bucket and bolted back to Bacon's room. The girl was wiping his naked buttocks, cleaning the delicate places where he'd soiled himself. Without a word between us, I took hold of his head. In trickles and tiny patient gasps, the two of us tried giving him the water.

"We m-must arrange a p-p-prisoner exchange," he said, coming to again. But his lips quivered so that he was hard to understand. "Return Berkeley's men for Bland and Captain Carver."

"Shhhh," I answered, making other soothing sounds.

From his forehead to his backside he was hopelessly drenched. And he still was discharging a red and black flecked mucous. I gave the girl a silent look, but impossible is what I was thinking. He was well past the point of retaining any fluids.

"Hell!" he suddenly exploded. "Muster oaths of allegiance! Carolina, Maryland! Damn the King! And... Aaa, AAGH! Goddam my blo-ood...! ... the French, the Dutch..."

"Shhhh." I said, "shhh."

And then he was out again.

I could see that the girl had taken the horse to make a quick collection of her herbals. She crumbled some bark scrapings into a broken cup of water, and gave me the job of trying to get it inside him. She then tore long pieces from her white dress until it was nothing but shreds. Pairing up the widest of these strips, she enfolded them around another mixture. Then, when she looked and saw what small progress I was making, she sent me outside to boil water.

It was all I could do to keep the most desperate thoughts from my mind. I simply took each step of my task and filled it with a maximum attention. The methodical building of a cooking fire, one that would last the whole day, the gathering of twigs and stems, the timbers that I wrenched right out of the house's basement. The retrieval of a pot that had been splattered through with buckshot and then cradling the water into its deepest part. And thus, by not counting time, I found myself back upstairs, interrupting the girl in her singing. She soaked two of her compresses in the hot water and strapped them to his front and his back. I could see it was a practiced technique, one that belied her young age, but even as she performed it, Bacon jerked up in a rage. He screamed out at Brent the turncoat, and commanded the men to form an ambush and lie in wait. The little girl stared into him, waving a smoky smelling herb into his chest until he was quiet again, or half awake in distress. She then wet a thin strand of fabric with a liquid more like a cream that she made into an enema. I watched, with nothing more to do but trust, as a strange evacuation emerged, black as pitch and dry as dust. With this, her eyes flashed in quick alarm and she sent me out for more hot water. I let this mindless feat take me fully into its possession, a couple of dozen times at least, until I finally gave in to exhaustion.

When I awakened, a few fitful hours later, she pointed to the scraps of her fouled dress and told me I should burn them. Bacon's rapid breathing, I quickly noticed, had subsided and he almost appeared to be sleeping. I studied the girl, even as I carried out her instructions. Watched how she barely voiced her prayers but gave herself full to the singing. Watched the smooth brown skin on the palms of her busy hands, on her arms and on her shoulders. Watched the mystery of her startling weathered face, and the way that she could shield herself with the movements of her fingers.

"My grandmother had the power to do it," she said at last, "but she never killed anyone. When you came she said it was up to me to break the vision with the Healer. And then when she knew she had to die, she told me that I must kill this man."

She was speaking all at once, almost as if hoping the stream of strange English words might chase away her questions. Then she suddenly stopped to look slowly at Bacon. His eyes in a glaze, his mouth so dry it was peeling.

"I tried," she said strangely.

And then she made a strange gesture with her hand to her lips by blowing on her fingers as though to make them fly. And suddenly I saw her, just as she was back in the swamp sitting in the mud, covered in mosquitoes. With a flick of her eye, she saw that I remembered.

"But I can not."

She looked like she might collapse. As if the weight of some vast unknowable conflict, at last apparent, was preparing to crush her to the ground.

"Can you save him?" I quickly asked. I needed to break her from this spell, or whatever this was, that was so far beyond my comprehension. I only knew that if I did not stop it, or find some way to help her, that death would surely come next. More than anything else, I needed her to stay here with me. I had never felt so strange and alone, and desperate.

"I will try," she said very slowly. And then she looked at Bacon again, as if she had forgotten him. "Do you have another shirt?"

I wanted to reach out for her then, but I grew afraid, afraid of what I saw in this new fragile creature. I forced myself out of the room and down the stairs. Forced myself into thinking only on the task that she'd assigned. I took my tattered pack from off the wagon and walked the mare to where it could graze. I unrolled my old clothes and scrubbed each part in a shallow bowl of hot water. I washed my one extra pair of trousers and my shirt, paying particular attention to the threadbare nap. I was glad for having to do the mundane, to leave the great questions upstairs. And after doing my best with the wash, I quickly assembled a drying rack and set it before the fire. I turned the trousers over and kept fixing the rack to catch the shifting sun. The only thing I did know that I *could* comprehend was that my last set of clothes would soon get ruined.

The girl came down just before they were dry, reeking

of Nathan's smell. She noticed me holding back my breath whenever she came in close, and noticed too, how the outside of the house had become my place of refuge. But she simply said that she needed the hot water. I handed her the clothes, and set the fire to do more boiling. When she went back in, I felt free to give up hope.

When I finally returned up the stairs, his discharge had turned a frothy yellow, "a good sign," she affirmed sitting beside him while singing softly to the floor. I tried getting her potion past his tongue, which was black and completely swollen, but he retched it back out in a long stringy film. The most I could do was to keep him in cooling cloth baths, and as the day wore into night with him slipping in and out of spasms (sometimes twisting himself up in knots) he gradually advanced to a state that was calmer. She sang her songs, and dealt her concoctions. I carried the water and dealt with the stains.

Then, with the dawn, Bacon sat up, demanding to know where he was.

"We are at Green Spring," I replied.

"We must leave at once," he proclaimed. "Where are the men? What of Brent and his turncoats?"

He started up, but his pain-racked body immediately struck him back down. I looked for her help and just as suddenly realized that the girl was not around. "Stay still," I said, "you are not strong enough to travel yet."

"This place will kill me," he gritted, fighting back. "Where are the men that I posted here?"

"Gone," I replied, "along with everything else. Now calm yourself and try to drink a little water. You are very sick."

As I held the cup to his lips, the girl returned with another heated compress. Bacon stared like a madman when she kneeled down beside him; the sunlight was up enough to illuminate the remnants of her tattered formal dress.

"Get rid of her!" he screamed, trying to kick her away. His violent movement thrust him into searing pain. "Aaaa! Aaa! Goddam my blood! Get the heathen witch away!" He crumbled back in a twisting agony, wailing loud enough to shake up the wall.

I jumped straight at him, forcing him to open his wincing eyes. There was nothing more important to me than making him look at his shit-encrusted angel that had only just saved his life. But when I squeezed and saw that his eyes were still just the yellow of pus, all that I could think of was "dead man." I even said it out loud. With another grimace he threw off my hand, and then curled himself up in a tight grunting ball. I stared at the stains on the floor just beside him.

"He must keep drinking this," the girl said at last, handing me the medicine. And without another look or word she turned and walked out the door.

Not knowing what else to do, I followed. I made no attempt to restrain her, even full knowing that she was taking with her the last of what hope remained for his life. But I could think no further. All that I had in me was silent respect, and knowledge of something that I could not even express.

"The hot mouth has his journey now," she spoke ahead of me, facing toward the ground. She never turned back. There was no more room for words. Not even deeds. There was only the barest breeze in the distance tugging at the fragments of an English Lady's dress.

When, at last I walked back up to Bacon, he was bent over, putting on my extra set of clothes.

"This place has cursed me," he said.

I nodded. He formed a diaper of dress rags into the seat.

"I will recuperate... and fully..." he strained, "at the home of Thomas Pate. Take me there at once."

I harnessed the horse and returned to help him down the stairs. I had no thought of making the inevitable worse. All the same I noticed that he had taken the last of her medicine.

"You must gather the men to meet the traitor Brent," he began again, more labored this time. "It is important that before we fight, there be new oaths of allegiance. All must commit to an ongoing war with the British. Anyone refusing will be thrown into jail. We are only Virginians now."

I must confess that to his credit, once we were past the governor's estate, he did seem to get some relief. Indeed, throughout the trip up country and back across the York he fought against all physical complaint. He shuffled down into the wagon, as if he could will himself cured. But as for myself, driving in a daze and viewing the effects of our ruined revolution, I was crippled. I didn't have one ounce of his new resolve. I passed the burned and the looted plantations, places where the air stank with greasy smoke. Carcasses of animals lying carelessly half-butchered to rot in the middle of the road. This was what our noble cause had wrought. It was twice more monstrous than what the savages had threatened. And I was glad for what my Helen was spared. I looked out at nothing; all that remained in me was shame. And I thanked God for that shame, there's no question that it kept me from running amuck. As the oxcart stalled, and Bacon cursed behind me, the land seemed to shrivel further in decay. Our blighted tribute to Virginia, the New World.

29

Incredibly, he held on for yet another month. It was an agonizing duration. Eventualities were set, bound beyond the scope of what could be done by his recovery, or even by his death. He did get a brief reprieve. It came at the time we learned Brent's men had now turned on the turncoat, Brent himself, (and in effect creating another faction that had to be dealt with.) But it was a story that satisfied Nathan to hear. Then too, a sudden visit of good health just before the end was common to the disease of bloody flux. The army, or what we controlled of it was then like a deck full of fish, flipping desperately in search of substance. But viewed in this light anyway, Bacon's scheme for total destruction had worked. With Jamestown in ashes and scattered to the winds, Brent's men simply decided there was nothing left to fight for. They dispersed to burn what remained of the plantations or plunder what they found in the unguarded homes.

Not once in the trial of those final days did Bacon allow a visit from Elizabeth. This, he insisted, was to keep her safe and off the roads, but in truth it was because of his vanity. The most that he wouldn't allow was for her to see him so weak and emaciated.

What I saw at the very end, and what I believe dragged him under, was his flirt with devil of chaos. He spent long hours cursing the crimes that his very own actions had inspired. (Cursing having always been his hopeless way of confessing that he'd lost all control.) He sent the remaining core of his support out to enforce martial law, but then they had to break up patrols to cover the distance. The order of command could not be held at the center, and soon enough they got so distrustful that they started shooting one another. Just as sad was the fact that those of us who stayed on with him at the home of Thomas Pate adopted a practice of humoring his rage.

He spent the time between fevers by constructing more elaborate loyalty oaths, but by now even the few faithful left in the field destroyed them as soon as they were read. He sent a warning to the people of Accomack that demanded the freedom of his close friends Carver and Bland. (Along with an impassioned plea and a promise of a generous reward if they turned the governor over.) No one let him know that he was being thoroughly disregarded. And far from the walls of his stifling bedchamber came the news of each new crisis. They poured in a ceaseless stream, in the approach of a courier's hoof beats. Lawlessness and hunger prevailed; people were living naked in the woods; the weight of his holding onto 'victory' came crashing in upon him like the waves of his many convulsions. I once saw his head thrown back so hard that I was sure that it had killed him. In what were clearly his final days, I could not bring myself to tell him that Berkeley had Captain Carver hanged and his best friend Giles Bland had made a deal for his own pardon.

The worst of these scenes came with the arrival of Elizabeth. I watched her struggling up the road in a wagon with an axle bent on one side. Alarmingly, she was unescorted. I went out to meet her, thinking that her driver had deserted, but her eyes interrupted me and spoke of things far more grievous. I had no courage to impart my darkest knowledge.

"I have brought fresh clothes for Nathan," she stuttered.

I would never have believed that she could be so stripped of her natural confidence.

"I had to hide them beneath my skirts. The distance

from here to the Curles is a bloody terror. Highwaymen patrol every road and vie amongst themselves for our possessions."

In a fit of nerves, she grabbed out the clothes from within her petticoats and began folding them in a stack.

"I had to take a shot at one of them myself," she cried. "I know the ruffian must've recognized me, but he wouldn't let me pass. I sent him bleeding after he figured I would miss. Where is... N-Nathan? How is he...? P-p-please, Mr. Corstair. Please take me to him. Please tell me, you will b-be kind."

It was worse than I'd imagined. Me standing, holding onto Bacon's clothes, she, addressing me as Mr. Corstair.

"Nathaniel is gone." I stated awkwardly. "His suffering ended just before daylight. This morning."

She released a small whip-like cry, and quickly turned away. Then she suddenly brought her head back around and held me in an accusatory gaze. All about me appeared a sudden procession of mourners, Joseph Ingram, James Crewes, Thomas Hall. They stood stiffly apart, acting lost, facing in separate directions. Then Elizabeth brought her head up, as if her fear had been magically transported, but still she fixed me with a look, deathly cold and harsh. I could not help but feel that I was something small and rootless, as though some great weakness in me was exposed. But then I saw more clearly that I simply no longer served her a purpose. I was helpless to the needs that she must now address. The others turned from me as well. As if caught up in the sudden realization that I was the only man they knew who had managed to lose his entire family. *I* was surely the harbinger of horror, a soul so cursed it could only hunger for more. In that field and in one stare, I felt as though Elizabeth Bacon had laid the loss of her husband, perhaps the whole lost revolution, entirely in my hands.

How could I deny it? Nathan had given himself into my care from his first fevered throes on the burning streets of Jamestown to the last of his dry hacking coughs. And

I had crouched before the whim of a witchy savage girl. I crouched even now, trailing behind the young general's wife as she marched ahead up to the dead man's room. I followed like a simple dolt, with a stack of his freshly arrived funeral clothes.

Then when she reached the upstairs door she shuddered with a violent gasp. At the end he was nothing but a skeleton, his desiccated skin had fully turned black. He seemed to me like a shell, like an empty vessel that burned itself cleanly out. And that the life that it had used, had used it full, used up every want and passion. What lay under Thomas Pate's funeral shroud was not even an ember to the actual man, not a telltale thread. Elizabeth tried, as best she could to gently cradle his head, but it was drier than parchment, scribbled through with brittle veins. The others in the room looked at floor, and we heard her mumble something to his shoulder. One at a time, we slipped out the door.

Down the stairs outside, Mr. Drummond was waiting to greet us.

A handful of leaders were gathering in to hear the grim news. Heated arguments erupted regarding the meaning of Bacon's death, and a case was being made for hiding it from the men. I listened to their bluster, knowing what useless folly it was. For one, the ferryman that brought us across to Pates' place knew full well what he was looking at. And more, he'd obviously spread the word. Then went the final wisp of any faith I held when Drummond gave Ingram the charge of the army. I watched him sign his name with a slight gush of misplaced pride, while I never knew what it was before to feel so foolish for someone else. Either that or just plain insubstantial.

This business accomplished, the reports flooded in like a torture. Redcoats were expected to make landfall at any time, British trading ships were already making reconnaissance up the York. Berkeley had regrouped the fickle folk of Accomack and was making attacks on our garrisons to the south. Middle of the road planters that had stood with us, were now all turned against us, and demanding the governor's protection from the riot and unrest.

Thus the anxious council convened, stricken beneath the shadow of Bacon's death, straining for a way to respond to the impossible list. I breathed the open air of Pates' elaborate yard, no longer caring, generally wondering at what the dead man upstairs had wrought. Elizabeth opened the front door and the dissembling hushed. Someone shouting out some declaration dropped it in a mid-sentence halt.

"Gentlemen," she stated, shaking slightly, doing her best to keep her control. "I would like… I demand a memorial. One that is suited to so great a man. I want history to know why he fought, and the cause for which he… died. …The very least… no one… forget."

"Yes, yes of course," Ingram bowed.

I exchanged a pointed look with Drummond, and moved quickly to her side. She turned to me like I was a stranger, but when I took her by the arm she came easily along. For a second it seemed as though having someone escort her was all that she was looking for. Together we walked a ways off to one side.

"Elizabeth," I began. "In the past, before we knew what would happen, we knew each other well, did we not?"

"Of course," she said.

I was not sure that she remembered. She was almost as cold. Just as absent.

"I only ask that you will hear me."

"Of course," she repeated.

"Nathaniel will never be forgotten, no matter what comes. His story will be told for generations. On every farm. Wherever the frontier expands."

She was watching me then, not so proud, seeming

suddenly to sag beneath the weight of my words. There was no sign of her defiance, no trace of her impulsive desires. I looked away for a moment, wondering what to say next, and when I turned to her again, she was sucking on a lock of his hair. I grabbed her by the shoulders and gave her a violent shake.

"If Nathan is buried, even in private, they will hound you 'til they know where his body lies. They will spike his head to a public post! Is this what you want?! Tell me! Tell me now!"

She drew back in a fury, freeing her arm as if to strike, then twirled around and crumpled to the ground. I felt the release of her body hit the hard earth from several feet away. I stood by. Frozen. Watching. "Of course, sir," she said, when she finally sat back up. "Of course." I offered her my hand. "I must go home," she ignored it and continued. "To England." She spoke without feeling. And then we were both just staring at the wilderness further out. The trees were rippling softly in a greeting, swaying back and forth.

She allowed me to help her up and return her to the house. There, Mr. Lawrence stood waiting. He walked a few paces from the conference and seeing her afflicted state, openly broke out into tears. Elizabeth, seemingly moved by his affection approached him as if to comfort his distress.

"My dear Mr. Lawrence," she said. "How good of you to come. Would you be so kind as to dispose of my husband's body? It was you, wasn't it? That got him into this?" She then removed a handkerchief from her breast and started patting it at his face.

The rest of the men looked down, or slowly moved off doing their best at pretending not to be there. When Mr. Lawrence finally spoke it was delicate.

"Elizabeth, let Mr. Corstair here, see you home."

"It's north, I think." She smiled at me, slipping back to my side. "Those ships. When they return?"

* * * * *

I am watching Mr. Lawrence's tears come welling. This part of the remembering has made him quietly weep. The water that pours outside our cave on the other hand is here in sheets and torrents. I'm beginning to fear that mudslides will impede our escape.

"When you left," he says, "I took his body and burned it in a field beyond the Pate's. A ritual that I performed entirely by myself." He gasps back a couple of breaths that stick inside of his throat. "I loved him in my way, Corstan. I wish for you to know that. He was like a son whose time had run before his father's grace."

I wish I could take the time to encourage this rare moment of his openness, but I am pressed to our cave's entrance, looking for Seycondeh's help.

"The water was cold, wading out in the York. But I liked the idea of his ashes carrying on," he flaps his hand through the air. "To fertilize new growth. This damn country," Mr. Lawrence wheezes, pulling his blanket in from the damp. "Makes you believe that you can land anywhere and plant."

"I had no idea you were so poetic, Mr. Lawrence." I try humoring him, to push his spirits outward and up, to the necessity of our trip.

"Did you know that Robert Beverley, a man that turned to Berkeley, *after* Bacon had recruited him, surprised one of our rebel compounds in Surry? He caught our own Colonel Hansford in a confiscated bed on a confiscated plantation making confiscated love to one of the servant girls. How's that for a revolution? Could even inspire the French."

He's taken the bait. Now I need to work him toward a readiness to leave. Seycondeh is our only chance, where is Seycondeh? Mr. Lawrence will follow her instructions, I am certain of it. He'll grumble in the pouring rain, but the storm is flooding the stream that she said the rains would bring. He mumbles on about Ingram's incompetence, but I can no longer wait. I must make one more desperate attempt to find her. I'm praying crazily enough to imagine that she's hiding a canoe.

I slip out and down the soggy path while Mr. Lawrence recites his mournful list of friends. The 'honorable' men that our governor has hanged. The evening hour is coming fast, but with a sky that's been in continual clouds, it is difficult to keep specific time. If my skills have not abandoned me altogether, I can use the gray of day for decent cover. I creep inside the village, seeing no one; not even the dogs. But there is something in the soaking air that gives me a sense of departure, of some great movement that is underway. I smell the smoke and hear the noise within the long hut, and see the big chiefs are gathered in a meeting there. I crawl close enough to peer through a crack in the floor, where a tribal council is taking place. The mud covers me enough to conceal my position, unless the braves should suddenly depart.

The floorboards an inch above my face shake beneath the pounding feet of the grand chief, a man I know who's been Mr. Lawrence's and my protector. He is fully dressed in claws and feathers, and appears to be performing a dance of coup. His warriors keep to their side of the room, and are singing along in a measured beat, but are unnaturally stiff, seeming uncomfortable. The red and black dyed foreign chief laughs and points at the old man's face. The older chief maintains his rhythm, moving more aggressively, appearing undeterred by the lack of respect hurled from across the room. He works closer and closer to them over the floor, beating his wrinkled chest like a drum, filling the space directly in front of the painted tribe's faces. He shouts and touches the chief's red arm in three swift punches, but the painted chief laughs harder each time. The old chief walks swiftly back to his warriors, sitting heavily, heavily breathing to one side.

"Ite-kispaka!" The painted chief across from him shouts and now stands. "Nipiw-we!"

He commands the attention of the entire council. As I try following his words, he yells about the Indian's useless ways of making war against the whites. "See him!" He shouts and points an accusing finger at the exhausted old chief. "The old man still acts like he does not know how the whites care nothing of honor!" He spits. "The whites fight only to kill! The women, the children, everyone must die!"

The house erupts into shouting making it hard for me to understand. The painted men from the west complain about tribes from the east taking up all of their hunting grounds. Then yell at their hosts for preparing to make another such move. One of our hosts answers that they would be gone already, but can reach no decision about what to do with the English in the cave.

The room calms a bit. The same man states that his only wish is for no more whites to follow, but he is afraid that more whites will come for the two English criminals.

"If we kill them," he says, "we will surely be hunted."

The room breaks into cacophony again. And there are many accusations about trading with the whites.

"You destroy your people," an opposing brave shouts above the rest. "All for an English coat!"

"We will take care of the white men for you!" the red and black chief suddenly states.

This announcement fires up the debate once more, but I have seen enough. I quickly scour the grounds for anything I can take. Where is Seycondeh? I only find some leather stripping and a runner from a broken sled.

When I return, I tell Mr. Lawrence to prepare to leave at once, but he has decided that now is the time to make his confession. He also reminds me that he's completely indifferent to escape.

"But it is something commendable for you, Corstair. To have survived an escape from one enemy, and then to escape that enemy's enemy. All in one lifetime? Hmmm?"

I ignore his posturing, and pull together anything I can find to make a paltry pack. I stare into watery air for Seycondeh.

"Drummond hanged. Thomas Hall hanged, along with good Mr. Crewes. Ingram; surrendered. An entire unit of Africans, with armaments to spare tricked into captivity. Hansford hanged, Wilford hanged, Pygott hanged... Rookins, Cheesman... Well..." he sighs. "It's been the privilege of my life, Mr. Corstair, to have ridden this far on your rescue..."

"Will you stop prattling!" I yell, bursting with anger. Anger at the weather. Anger at Seycondeh's abandonment. It does nothing but give me a dizzy spell. "Get your boots on."

He pays me no mind, and acts more interested in a line of rats that have decided to straggle in along the left wall. They shovel beneath the jutting rocks looking for a space to dry themselves out.

"Methinks those mice wore feathers," Mr. Lawrence says in a frivolous tone. And then looks at me strangely.

At another time I would think that he was mad, but too much has passed between us. He knows that he has grabbed my attention. For he has just confessed to something that he could not possibly know. *Mice that wear feathers* was the farmer's code along the border. Any damage done to crops, any loss of grain, from pests or natural occurrence was to be blamed on thieving Indians. It was a call to arms. A poor man's grab for a stretch of fertile land. A silent frontier policy, far from the meddling of Jamestown.

"Raped, is what I heard." Mr. Lawrence says to me quietly. "*All* of the Corstair women molested. I am truly sorry about that, Philip, I truly am, but does that seem like the work of savages to you?"

All of a sudden I am thrown inside a thunderbolt of thought and image. Doors that I'd successfully willed shut stand shocked, and wide apart. I feel slapped in the face by my every cruelty, every one of my assorted sins. This soft urbane *white man* has pointed out what I refused to comprehend. No brave I knew of, of *any* tribe would sexually assault a white woman. Such a disgraceful act, and its loss of face, would surely mean banishment. In the codes of the Indian warrior, nothing could be more demeaning.

"Who?" My voice is a scratchy whisper.

"I'd look to Henry Creighton," he responds quietly.

I also sense that his general sadness has been lifted. I can almost feel it floating right out from his chest.

"Henry Creighton is dead," I reply. No matter what the danger, I resolve that I will not move until he tells me more.

"Would you say that Creighton was a man who protested too much?"

I think back, all the way back, to my early run-in with the man, and our first night's meeting at the Bacon estate.

"But," Mr. Lawrence continues, renewing his contempt. "We are all just a pile of scavenging rats. Looking for our moment to seize upon new land. The Africans were here. You knew that, with more and more slave ships coming. What did you expect?"

"Shut it!" I am standing over him now, muscles shaking, hard enough to strike.

"Creighton clearly saw the conflict. The inevitable. And he saw his chance. First thing to do was start a full fledged Indian war, and for that he needed full fledged... incidents."

"And you... knew this?!"

"Not at first, not at first I didn't. I believed in... something... But soon enough, soon enough I saw the game for what it was. And by then, of course, I was in it up to my neck."

Something deep inside my skull, beneath the rage that's vaulted there, releases. And then hovers, just powerful enough to crush me back down. I stare at Mr. Lawrence. His drizzling face, floating in and out of focus, and see that blood is pouring from out of his blanket.

"Leave me now," he says softly, and shows me the gash that he's made of his wrists. "Just like good old Cato. Good luck to you, Mr. Philip Corstair." He smiles at me, paler than a ghost.

I do not hesitate. I jolt forward, and am sliding fast. A sliding run, and a roll, and I am pulled down again. I stumble, drenched and blinded by mud, not letting myself think. Think on Mr. Lawrence. What he's said. His bleeding. Even so I can hear his shallow breathing, and see his life so clearly draining out. I need only to think of Creighton. Of Creighton and his murdering men. And then I hear the stormy stream ahead.

I think how Creighton died just before the governor could hang him. Died of his own weakness and disease. But there must be others, the ones that carried out his orders. Others I can find and kill.

I am outside the reach of fear, indeed without heed of my enemies, whether they are white, or with red and black painted skin. Whether they watch me from under fallen trees, or stand straight before me, it is all the same. Maybe I am dreaming. A pathway to my right opens up a clearing that I know I must avoid. And then I see some movement up ahead. Distinct, an animal I do not know. Shaped by darkness and the rain and the ripping of leaves. A figure hunched between the dripping ferns, and moving much too slow. It emerges heavily forth, and then in sudden jerks. I wait and watch with a heavy stone in hand, fixed for an angle to attack. Suddenly it turns. The head of a wolf falls open, and I look straight into the pulp of skin and sealed up eyes of Tintipon, the long gone sorcerer, his baffling return.

"Corstair?" he says, "Philip Corstair?" I did not know that he even knew my name. "Miywa sin Seycondeh, maskihkiy." I hardly hear the words, but am anxious to accept what he brings. He is dragging a short dugout canoe that he shoves into the mud and toward the water. "Seycondeh is good to me," he says. "You go away now, you go away from here."

I drag the canoe, and follow him. The forest is as dark as night but it hardly matters. Tintipon stalks before me, sure of his pace and we reach the water just below some massive rocks. I grab the boat in tightly, it slaps violently in the stream.

"You must watch for the boulders," he says. "After that, you will see your best way. Take this," he says, and shocks me by producing a powder horn and musket.

I take them up greedily, fixing the powder under my shirt. "Why are you helping me?" I ask, half crazy.

He wraps his hand to the boat with the strips of leather, and I balance inside with the broken sled run. "Where is Lawrence?" he asks, as if answering my question. When he sees that I ignore him, he gives me a toothless smile. "It is good for whites to kill whites."

He pushes me out, and disappears at once back inside the pines. I am pulled into the current, maneuvering in the dark, with only the sound of the water as a guide. Then separate churning streams suddenly converge, throwing me out of control. They split in two, gather force and converge again, sending me into a nest of fallen trees. I break away hitting the sides of jagged rocks that tear in the dark at my shoulders. All of my tension, all of my rage, seems to echo in the roar of the stream. And each time I'm crushed into a stone it takes my ability to breathe. I fight off black and unseen blows as they come pounding in at me, but each time I push away too late. Mr. Lawrence would drown in this most certainly. He chose his moment; spoke his awful truth, so as not to be a hindrance, making sure I would leave him behind.

The boulders described by Tintipon loom dark above me now, and I hear smoother water running east. There is nothing I can do. I am far too fast to make the last turn and my pole simply shatters in my hand. I am smashed like a gnat into a wall of granite. Spinning backwards, I fall whirling from pool to pool, fighting hard to stay conscious. And then I am flung with a fury down the falls.

If I survive this unforgiving water, it will take me farther West.

Apologies and Consequence

This book is a work of fiction that has followed the historical record such as it is, through the chronology of these important events. I have made a sincere effort to follow the general tone of the time, but admittedly it is far short of literal accuracy. The accents, for one, would be English and the written word, such as a journal would be nearly incomprehensible. At least by the standards of modern syntax. These are but two of many artistic choices that I have made in this writing. First because I wanted to create a story that was approachable, and second because I wanted it to sound American at heart.

As to the history itself, the actual records of the time are slim, and much of it is still disputed. History as we all know is not a science, and hindsight through the eyes of current politics is always subject to change. Thomas Jefferson for instance, wanted Nathaniel Bacon to be known as an important forerunner in the fight for American Independence. Robert Beverley, who first recorded the history, disagreed.

The prominent individuals of the day that are depicted here actually existed, while those we might call less important, (meaning they didn't merit being written about) were invented. The story's narrator, Philip Corstair, I made up. Other incidents involving Bacon's eccentric behavior, such as his dancing confrontation with Governor Berkeley and his tactics, such as displaying the gentlemen's wives at the barricade are well documented. The story of the Doeg Indian boy's baptism on George Mason's estate is also part of the historical archive. But certain motivations that I've attributed in this book, although making perfect sense to me, are fiction. I wanted to present a living story in a living place from the ground up so to speak, for the purpose of sharing a pivotal moment in our early history that has been largely overlooked.

With Bacon's untimely death, and the aid of British Captain Thomas Grantham, Berkeley soon overcame the scattered pockets of resistance. He allowed the common rebels that had homes to return to, to simply put down their arms and do so. The governor then faced the problem of accommodating a thousand of His Majesties redcoats, (a force that he claimed he never requested in the first place,) and who, by the time they made landing, were surely not needed. The ravaged countryside was hard pressed to support such an influx, and over time many of the soldiers turned into the rovers and frontiersmen they were sent to suppress.

The aftermath of the war was marked with a flood of suits and counter-suits, pitting well-placed families against one another, and resulting in the confiscation of large estates. The families of the obvious rebels, including those that Berkeley hanged, were forced to pay. Colonel John Washington (George's great grandfather) weathered the storm relatively unscathed.

Mr. Richard Lawrence, a principle in the revolt, was one of a precious few that was never punished. At war's end, he made a successful escape and was never heard from again. Nathaniel Bacon's body was never found.

A royal commission was quickly established, and after investigating leveled a hard judgment against Berkeley and his handling of the disastrous affair. Especially in regards to his liberal use of the hangman. The political scene in London had passed the old governor by, and Sir William spent his remaining years in England, trying in vain to repair his reputation. He was replaced by Herbert Jeffreys, (the man in charge of the king's commission) who pardoned most all of the rebels, except Bacon who was dead, and Richard Lawrence who had disappeared.

Elizabeth Bacon remained in Virginia and married two

more times. She tried to regain her share of her family's estate in England up to the last of her days.

Nathaniel was called *Squire Bacon* by the small tribes of Indians that had escaped his policy of total war. The Nansemond, the Weyonoke, and Nottaway were virtually extinguished as a result of this flight. There were no more troubles with any more tribes until the English started settling beyond the Blue Ridge.

Within the next century when tobacco had so depleted Virginia's soil, one of its most profitable enterprises became the cultivation of African slaves.

The fictional Philip Corstair ended up on the far side of the Blue Ridge making the wilderness his home.

Daniel Watkins
August 2005